Sheikh's
DEFIANT WIFE

Sheikh's
COLLECTION

May 2017

June 2017

July 2017

August 2017

September 2017

October 2017

Sheikh's
DEFIANT WIFE

Sharon
KENDRICK

Caitlin
CREWS

Maisey
YATES

MILLS &
BOON

Published in Great Britain 2017
By Mills & Boon, an imprint of HarperCollins*Publishers*
1 London Bridge Street, London, SE1 9GF

SHEIKH'S DEFIANT WIFE © 2017 Harlequin Books S.A.

Defiant in the Desert © 2013 Sharon Kendrick
In Defiance of Duty © 2012 Caitlin Crews
To Defy a Sheikh © 2014 Maisey Yates

ISBN: 978-0-263-93107-5

09-0617

Our policy is to use papers that are natural, renewable and recyclable products and made from wood grown in sustainable forests.
The logging and manufacturing processes conform to the legal environmental regulations of the country of origin.

Printed and bound in Spain
by CPI, Barcelona

DEFIANT IN THE DESERT

SHARON KENDRICK

Sharon Kendrick once won a national writing competition by describing her ideal date: being flown to an exotic island by a gorgeous and powerful man. Little did she realise that she'd just wandered into her dream job! Today she writes for Mills & Boon, featuring often stubborn but always to die for heroes and the women who bring them to their knees. She believes that the best books are those you never want to end. Just like life…

CHAPTER ONE

'THERE'S A MAN downstairs in Reception who says he wants to see you.'

'Who is it?' questioned Sara, not bothering to lift her head from the drawing which was currently engrossing her.

'He wouldn't say.'

At this Sara did look up to find Alice, the office runner, staring at her with an odd sort of expression. Alice was young and very enthusiastic, but right now she looked almost *transported*. Her face was tight with excitement and disbelief—as if Santa Claus himself had arrived early with a full contingent of reindeer.

'It's Christmas Eve afternoon,' said Sara, glancing out of the window at the dark grey sky and wincing. No snow, unfortunately. Only a few heavy raindrops spattering against the glass. Pity. Snow might have helped boost her mood—to help shift off the inevitable feeling of *not quite fitting in* which always descended on her at this time of year. She never found it easy to enjoy Christmas—which was one of the main reasons why she tended to ignore the festival until it had gone away.

She pushed a smile to the corners of her mouth, trying to pick up on Alice's happy pre-holiday mood. 'And very soon I'm going to be packing up and going home. If it's a salesman, I'm not interested and if it's anyone else, then tell them to go away and make an appointment to see me in the new year.'

'He says he's not going anywhere,' said Alice and then paused dramatically. 'Until he's seen you.'

Sara put her purple felt-tip pen down with fingers which had annoyingly started to tremble, telling herself not to be so stupid. Telling herself that she was perfectly safe here, in this bright, open-plan office of the highly successful advertising agency where she worked. That there was no reason for this dark feeling of foreboding which had started whispering over her skin.

But of course, there was…

'What do you mean—he's not going anywhere?' she demanded, trying to keep her voice from rising with panic. 'What exactly did he say?'

'That he wants to see you,' repeated Alice and now she made another face which Sara had never seen before. 'And that he craves just a few minutes of your time.'

Craves.

It was a word which jarred like an ice cream eaten on a winter day. No modern Englishman would ever have used a word like that. Sara felt the cold clamp of fear tightening around her heart, like an iron band.

'What…what does he look like?' she asked, her voice a croaky-sounding husk.

Alice played with the pendant which was dangling from her neck in an unconscious display of sexual awareness. 'He's...well, he's pretty unbelievable, if you must know. Not just because of the way he's built—though he must work out practically non-stop to get a body like *that*—but more...more...' Her voice tailed off. 'Well, it's his eyes really.'

'What about his eyes?' barked Sara, feeling her pulse begin to rocket.

'They were like...black. But like, *really* black. Like the sky when there's no moon or stars. Like—'

'Alice,' cut in Sara, desperately trying to inject a note of normality into the girl's uncharacteristically gushing description. Because at that stage she was still trying to fool herself into thinking that it wasn't happening. That it might all be some terrible mistake. A simple mix-up. Anything, but the one thing she most feared. 'Tell him—'

'Why don't you tell me yourself, Sara?'

A cold, accented voice cut through her words and Sara whirled round to see a man standing in the doorway of the office. Shock, pain and desire washed over her in rapid succession. She hadn't seen him for five long years and for a moment she almost didn't recognise him. He had always been dark and utterly gorgeous, gifted with a face and a mind which had captured her heart so completely. But now...

Now...

Her heart pounded.

Something about him had changed.

His dark head was bare and he wore a custom-made

suit instead of his usual robes. The charcoal jacket defined his honed torso just as well as any folds of flowing silk and the immaculately cut trousers emphasised the endless length of his powerful thighs. He had always carried the cachet which came from being the Sultan of Qurhah's closest advisor, but now his natural air of authority seemed to be underpinned with a steely layer Sara had never seen before. And suddenly she recognised it for what it was.

Power.

It seemed to crackle from every pore of his body. To pervade the serene office environment like high-voltage electricity. It made her wary—warier than she felt already, with her heart beating so fast it felt as if it might burst right out of her chest.

'Suleiman,' she said, her voice unsteady and a little unsure. 'What are you doing here?'

He smiled, but it was the coldest smile she had ever seen. Even colder than the one which he had iced into her the last time they'd been together. When he had torn himself away from her passionate embrace and looked down at her as if she was the lowest of the low.

'I think you can probably work that one out for yourself, can't you, Sara?'

He stepped into the office, his clever black eyes narrowing.

'You are an intelligent woman, if a somewhat misguided one,' he continued. 'You have been ignoring repeated requests from the Sultan to return to Qurhah to become his wife. Haven't you?'

'And if I have?'

He looked at her, but there was nothing but indifference in his eyes and, stupidly, that hurt.

'If you have, then you have been behaving like a fool.'

His phrase was coated with an implicit threat which made her skin turn to ice and Sara heard Alice gasp. She turned her head slightly, expecting to see horror on the face of the trendy office runner, with her pink-streaked hair and bottom-hugging skirt. Because it wasn't cool for men to talk that way, was it? But she saw nothing like horror there. Instead, the bohemian youngster was staring at Suleiman with a look of rapt adoration.

Sara swallowed. Cool obviously flew straight out of the window when you had a towering black-haired male standing in your office just oozing testosterone. Why wouldn't Alice acknowledge the presence of a man unlike any other she had probably met? Despite all the attractive hunks who worked in Gabe Steel's advertising empire—didn't Suleiman Abd al-Aziz stand out like a spot of black oil on a white linen dress? Didn't he redefine the very concept of masculinity and make it a hundred times more meaningful?

For her, he had always had the ability to make every other man fade into insignificance—even royal princes and sultans—but now something about him had changed. There was an indefinable quality about him. Something *dangerous*.

Gone was the affection with which he always used to regard her. The man who had drifted in and out of her childhood and taught her to ride seemed to have been replaced by someone else. The black eyes were flat and cold; his lips unsmiling. It wasn't exactly *hatred* she could see on his face—for his expression implied that she wasn't worthy of an emotion as strong as hate. It was more as if she was a *hindrance.* As if he was here under sufferance, in the very last place he wanted to be.

And she had only herself to blame. She knew that. If she hadn't flung herself at him. If she hadn't allowed him to kiss her and then silently invited him to do so much more than that. To...

She tried a smile, though she wasn't sure how convincing a smile it was. She had done everything in her power to forget about Suleiman and the way he'd made her feel, but wasn't it funny how just one glimpse of him could stir up all those familiar emotions? Suddenly her heart was turning over with that painful clench of feeling she'd once thought was love. She could feel the sink of her stomach as she was reminded that he could never be hers.

Well, he would never know that. He wouldn't ever guess that he could still make her feel this way. She wasn't going to give him the chance to humiliate her and reject her. Not again.

'Nice of you to drop in so unexpectedly, Suleiman,' she said, her voice as airy as she could manage. 'But I'm afraid I'm pretty busy at the moment. It *is* Christmas Eve, you know.'

'But you don't celebrate Christmas, Sara. Or at least, I wasn't aware that you did. Have you really changed so much that you have adopted, wholesale, the values of the West?'

He was looking around the large, open-plan office with an expression of distaste curving his carved lips which he didn't bother to hide. His flat black eyes were registering the garish tinsel which was looped over posters depicting some of the company's many successful advertising campaigns. His gaze rested briefly on the old-fashioned fir tree, complete with flashing lights and a glittering star at the top, which had been erected as a kind of passé tribute to Christmases past. His expression darkened.

Sara put her fingers in her lap, horribly aware that they were trembling, and it suddenly became terribly important that he shouldn't see that, either. She didn't want him to think she was scared, even if that moment she was feeling something very close to scared. And she couldn't quite work out what she was afraid of—her, or him.

'Look, I really am *very* busy,' she said. 'And Alice doesn't want to hear—'

'Alice doesn't have to hear anything because she is about to leave us alone to continue this conversation in private,' he said instantly. Turning towards the office junior, he produced a slow smile, like a magician producing a rabbit from a hat. 'Aren't you, Alice?'

Sara watched, unwillingly fascinated as Alice almost melted under the impact of his smile. She even— and Sara had never witnessed this happen before—she even *blushed*. In a single moment, the streetwise girl from London had been transformed into a gushing stereotype from another age. Any minute now and she might actually *swoon*.

'Of course.' Alice fluttered her eyelashes in a way which was also new. 'Though I could get you a cup of coffee first if you like?'

'I am not in the mood for coffee,' said Suleiman and Sara wondered how he managed to make his refusal sound like he was talking about sex. Or was that just her projecting yet more stupid fantasies about him?

He was smiling at the runner and she was smiling right back. 'Even though I imagine that yours would be excellent coffee,' he purred.

'Oh, for heaven's sake! Alice buys coffee from the deli next door,' snapped Sara. 'She wasn't planning on travelling to Brazil and bringing back the beans herself!'

'Then that is Brazil's loss,' murmured Suleiman.

Sara could have screamed at the cheesy line which had the office runner beaming from ear to ear. 'That will be all, thanks, Alice,' she said sharply. 'You can go home now. And have…have a happy Christmas.'

'Thanks,' said Alice, clearly reluctant to leave. 'I'll see you in the new year. Happy Christmas!'

There was complete silence for a moment while they watched the girl gather up her oversized bag, which was crammed with one of the large and expensive presents which had been handed out earlier by Gabe Steel, their boss. Or rather, by his office manager. But it was only after her footsteps had echoed down the corridor towards the lift that Suleiman turned to Sara, his black eyes hard and mocking.

'Quite the little executive these days, aren't you, Sara?'

Sara swallowed. She hated the way he said her name. Or rather, she hated the effect it had on her. The way it made her want to expel a long and shuddering breath and to snake her tongue over lips which had suddenly grown dry. It reminded her too much of the time he had kissed her. When he had overstepped the mark and done the one thing which had been forbidden to him. And to her.

The memory came back as vivid and as real as if it had happened only yesterday. It had been on the night of her brother's coronation—when Haroun had been crowned King of Dhi'ban, a day which many had thought would never come because of the volatile relations between the desert states. All the dignitaries from the neighbouring countries had attended the ceremony—including the infamous Sultan of nearby Qurhah, along with his chief emissary, Suleiman.

Sara remembered being cool and almost noncommittal towards the Sultan, to whom she was betrothed. But who could blame her? Her hand in marriage had been the price paid for a financial bail-out for her country. In essence, she had been sold by her father like a piece of human merchandise!

That night she had barely made eye contact with the powerful Sultan who had seemed so forbidding, but her careless attitude seemed to amuse rather than to irritate the potentate. And anyway, he had spent most of the time locked away in meetings with all the other sultans and sheikhs.

But Sara had been eager to be reunited with the Sultan's emissary. She had been filled with pleasure at the thought of seeing Suleiman again, after six long years away at an English boarding school. Suleiman, who had taught her to ride and made her laugh during those two long summers when the Sultan had been negotiating with her father about a financial bail-out. Two summers which had occupied a special place in her heart ever since, even though on that final summer—her marital fate had been sealed.

During the coronation fireworks, she had somehow managed to manoeuvre herself into a position to watch them with Suleiman by her side. The crowds had been so huge that nobody had noticed them standing together and Sara was thrilled just to be in his company again.

The night was soft and warm, but in between the explosions and the roar of the onlookers the conversation between them was as easy as it had always been, even if initially Suleiman had seemed startled by the dramatic change that six years had wrought on her appearance.

'How old are you now?' he'd questioned, after he'd looked her up and down for a distractingly long moment.

'I'm eighteen.' She had smiled straight into his eyes, successfully hiding the hurt that he hadn't even remembered her age. 'And all grown up.'

'All grown up,' he had repeated slowly, as if she'd just said something which had never occurred to him before.

The conversation had moved on to other topics, though she had still been conscious of the curious expression in his eyes. He had asked her about her life at boarding school and she'd told him that she was planning to go to art school.

'In England?'

'Of course in England. There is no equivalent here in Dhi'ban.'

'But Dhi'ban isn't the same without you here, Sara.'

It was a strangely emotional thing for Suleiman to say and maybe the unexpectedness of that was what made her reach up to touch her fingertips to his cheek. 'Is that in a good way, or a bad way?' she teased.

A look passed between them and she felt him stiffen.

The fireworks seemed to stop—or maybe that was because the crashing of her heart was as deafening as any man-made explosion in the sky.

He caught hold of her hand and moved it away from his face, and suddenly Sara could feel a terrible yearning as he looked down at her. The normally authoritative Suleiman seemed frozen with indecision and he shook his head, as if he was trying to deny something. And then, almost in slow motion—he lowered his head to brush his lips over hers in a kiss.

It was just like all the books said it should be.

Her world splintered into something magical as their lips met. Suddenly there were rainbows and starlight and a deep, wild hunger. And the realisation that this was her darling, darling Suleiman and he was *kissing* her. Her lips opened beneath his and he circled her waist with his hands as he pulled her closer. She clung to him as her breasts pressed against his broad chest. She heard him groan. She felt the growing tension in his body as his hands moved down to cup her buttocks.

'Oh, Suleiman,' she whispered against his mouth—and the words must have broken the spell, for suddenly he tore himself away from her and held her at arm's length.

For a long moment he just stared at her, his breathing hard and laboured—looking as if he had just been shaken by something profound. Something which made a wild little flicker of hope flare in her heart. But then the look disappeared and was replaced with an expression of self-contempt. It seemed to take a moment or two before he could speak.

'Is this how you behave when you are in England?' he demanded, his voice as deadly as snake poison. 'Offering yourself as freely as a whore when you are promised to the Sultan? What kind of woman are you, Sara?'

It was a question she couldn't answer because she didn't know. Right then, she didn't seem to know anything because her whole belief system seemed to have been shattered. She hadn't been expecting to kiss him, nor to respond to him like that. She hadn't been expecting to want him to touch her in a way she'd never been touched before—yet now he was looking at her as if she'd done something unspeakable.

Filled with shame, she had turned on her heel and fled—her eyes so blurred with tears that she could barely see. And it wasn't until the next day that she heard indulgent tales of the princess weeping with joy for her newly crowned brother.

The memory cleared and Sara found herself in the uncomfortable present, looking into Suleiman's mocking eyes and realising that he was waiting for some sort of answer to his question. Struggling to remember what he'd asked, she shrugged—as if she could shrug off those feelings of humiliation and rejection she had suffered at his hands.

'I hardly describe being a "creative" in an advertising agency as being an executive,' she said.

'You are *creative* in many fields,' he observed. 'Particularly with your choice of clothes. Such revealing, western clothes, I cannot help but notice.'

Sara felt herself stiffen as he began to study her. *Don't look at me that way,* she wanted to scream. Because it was making her body ache as his gaze swept over the sweater dress which came halfway down her thighs, and the high boots whose soft leather curved over her knees.

'I'm glad you like them,' she said flippantly.

'I didn't say I liked them,' he growled. 'In fact, I wholeheartedly disapprove of them, as no doubt would the Sultan. Your dress is ridiculously short, though I suppose that is deliberate.'

'But everyone wears short skirts round here, Suleiman. It's the fashion. And the thick tights and boots almost cancel out the length of the dress, don't you think?'

His eyes were implacable as they met hers. 'I have not come here to discuss the length of your clothes and the way you seem to flaunt your body like the whore we both know you are!'

'No? Then why are you here?'

There was a pause and now his eyes were deadly as they iced into her.

'I think you know the answer to that. But since you seem to have trouble facing up to your responsibilities, maybe I'd better spell it out for you so that there can be no more confusion. You can no longer ignore your destiny, for the time has come.'

'It's not my destiny!' she flared.

'I have come to take you to Qurhah to be married,' he said coldly. 'To fulfil the promise which was made many moons ago by your father. You were sold to the Sultan and the Sultan wants you. And what is more, he is beginning to grow impatient—for this long-awaited alliance between your two countries to go ahead and bring lasting peace in the region.'

Sara froze. The hands which were still concealed in her lap now clenched into two tight fists. She felt beads of sweat break out on her brow and for a moment she thought she might pass out. Because hadn't she thought that if she just ignored the dark cloud which hung over her future for long enough, one day it might just fade away?

'You can't mean that,' she said, hating her voice for sounding so croaky. *So get some strength back. Find the resources within you to stand up to this ridiculous regime which buys women as if they were simply objects of desire lined up on a market stall.* She drew in a deep breath. 'But even if you do mean it, I'm not coming back with you, Suleiman. No way. I live in England now and I regard myself as an English citizen, with all the corresponding freedom that brings. And nothing in the world you can do or say will induce me to go to Qurhah. I don't want to marry the Sultan, and I won't do it. And what is more, you can't make me.'

'I am hoping to do this without a fight, Sara.'

His voice was smooth. As smooth as treacle—and just as dark. But nobody could have mistaken the steely intent which ran through his words. She looked into the flatness of his eyes. She looked at the hard, compromising lines of his lips and she felt another whisper of foreboding shivering its way down her spine. 'You think I'm just going to docilely agree to your plans? That I'm going to nod my head and accompany you to Qurhah?'

'I'm hoping you will, since that would be the most sensible outcome for all concerned.'

'In your dreams, Suleiman.'

There was silence for a moment as Suleiman met the belligerent glitter of her eyes, and the slow rage which had been simmering all day now threatened to boil over. Had he thought that this would be easy?

No, of course he hadn't.

Inside he had known that this would be the most difficult assignment of his life—even though he had experienced battle and torture and real hardship. He had tried to turn the job down—for all kinds of reasons. He'd told the Sultan that he was busy with his new life—and that much was true. But loyalty and affection for his erstwhile employer had proved too persuasive. And who else possessed the right amount of determination to bring the feisty Sara Williams back to marry the royal ruler? His mouth hardened and he felt the twist of something like regret. Who else knew her the way that he did?

'You speak with such insolence that I can only assume you have been influenced by the louche values of the West,' he snapped.

'Embracing freedom, you mean?'

'Embracing disrespect would be a more accurate description.' He drew in a deep breath and forced his lips into something resembling a smile. 'Look, Sara— I understand that you needed to...what is it that you women say? Ah yes, to *find yourself.*' He gave a low laugh. 'Fortunately, the male of the species rarely loses himself in the first place and so such recovery is seldom deemed necessary.'

'Why, you arrogant piece of—'

'Now we can do this one of two ways.' His words cut through her insult like a honed Qurhahian knife. 'The easy way, or the hard way.'

'You mean we do it your way, rather than mine?'

'Bravo—that is exactly what I mean. If you behave reasonably—like a woman who wishes to bring no shame onto her own royal house, or the one you will embrace after your marriage to the Sultan—then everyone is happy.'

'Happy?' she echoed. 'Are you out of your mind?'

'There is no need for hysteria,' he said repressively. 'Our journey to Qurhah may not be an expedition which either of us would choose, but I don't see why we can't conduct ourselves in a relatively civilised manner if we put our minds to it.'

'Civilised?' Sara stood up and pushed herself away from the desk so violently that a whole pile of coloured felt-tips fell clattering to the ground. But she barely registered the noise or the mess. She certainly didn't bend down to pick them up and not just because her skirt was so short. She felt a flare of rage and *impotence*—that Suleiman could just march in here as if he owned the place. Start flexing his muscles and telling her—*telling* her—that she must go back and marry a man she barely knew, didn't particularly like and certainly didn't *love*.

'You think it's civilised to hold a woman to a promise of marriage made when she was little more than a child? A forced marriage in which she had no say?'

'Your father himself agreed to this marriage,' said Suleiman implacably. 'You know that.'

'My father had no choice!' she flared. 'He was almost bankrupt by that point!'

'I'm afraid that your father's weakness and profligacy put him in that position. And let us not forget that it was the Sultan's father who saved him from certain bankruptcy!'

'By demanding my hand for his only son, in return?' she demanded. 'What kind of a man could do that, Suleiman?'

She saw that her heartfelt appeal had momentarily stilled him. That his flat black eyes had narrowed and were now partially obscured by the thick ebony lashes which had shuttered down to veil them. Had she been able to make him see the sheer lunacy of his proposal in this day and age? Couldn't he see that it was barbaric for a woman of twenty-three to be taken back to a desert kingdom—no matter how fabled—and to be married against her will?

Once Suleiman had regarded her fondly—she knew that. If he allowed himself to forget that stupid kiss—that single lapse which should never have happened—then surely there still existed in his heart some of that same fondness. Surely he wasn't happy for her to enter into such a barbaric union.

'These dynastic marriages have always taken place,' he said slowly. 'It will not be as bad as you envisage, Sara—'

'Really? How do you work that out?'

'It is a great honour to marry such a man as the Sultan,' he said, but he seemed to be having to force some kind of conviction into his words. He gave a heavy sigh. 'Do you have any idea of the number of women who would long to become his Sultana—'

'A sultana is something I put on my muesli every morning!' she spat back.

'You will be prized above all women,' he continued. 'And given the honour of bearing His Imperial Majesty's sons and heirs. What woman could ask for more?'

For a moment Sara didn't speak, she was so angry. The idea of such a marriage sounded completely abhorrent to her now, but, as Suleiman had just said, she had grown up in a world where such a barter was considered normal. She had been living in England for so long that it was easy to forget that she was herself a royal princess. That her English mother had married a desert king and produced a son and a much younger daughter.

If her mother had been alive she would have stopped this ludicrous marriage from happening, Sara was sure of that. But her mother had been dead for a long time— her father, too. And now the Sultan wanted to claim what was rightfully his.

She thought of the man who awaited her and she shivered. She knew that a lot of women thought of him as a swarthy sex-god, but she wasn't among them. During their three, heavily chaperoned meetings—she had felt nothing for him. Nada.

But mightn't that have had something to do with the fact that Suleiman had been present all those times? Suleiman with his glittering black eyes and his hard, honed body who had distracted her so badly that she couldn't think straight.

She glared at him. 'Doesn't it strike at your conscience to take a woman back to Qurhah *against her will*? Do you always do whatever the Sultan asks you, without questioning it? His tame puppet!'

A nerve flickered at his temple. 'I no longer work for the Sultan.'

For a moment she stared at him in disbelief. 'What… what are you talking about? The Sultan values you above all other men. Everyone knows that. You are his prized emissary and the man on whom he relies.'

He shook his head. 'Not any longer. I have returned to my own land, where I have built a different kind of life for myself.'

She wanted to ask him what kind of life that was, but

she reminded herself that what Suleiman did was none
of her business. *He doesn't want you. He doesn't even
seem to like you any more.* 'Then why are you here?'

'As a favour to Murat. He thought that you might
prove too much of a challenge for most of his staff.'

'But not for you, I suppose?'

'Not for me,' he agreed.

She wanted to tell him to wipe that smug smile
off his face and get out of her office and if he didn't,
then she would call security and get them to remove
him. But was that such a good idea? Her eyes flickered doubtfully over his powerful body and immovable stance. Was she seriously suggesting that *anyone*
could budge him if he didn't want to go?

She thought about her boss. Wouldn't Gabe Steel
have Suleiman evicted from the building if she asked
him? Though when she stopped to think about it—did
she really want to go bleating to her boss for help? She
had no desire to blight her perfect working record by
bringing her private life into the workplace. Because
wouldn't Gabe—and all her colleagues—be amazed to
discover that she wasn't just someone called Sara Williams, but a half-blood desert princess from the desert
country of Dhi'ban? That she had capitalised on her
mother's English looks and used her mother's English
surname to blend in since she'd been working here in
London. And blend in, she had—adopting the fash-
ions and the attitudes of other English women her age.

No, this was not a time for opposition—or at
least, not a time for *open* opposition. She didn't want
Suleiman's suspicions alerted. She needed to lull him.

To let him think that he had won. That she would go with him—not *too* meekly or he would suspect that something was amiss, but that she *would* go with him.

She shrugged her shoulders as if she were reluctantly conceding victory and backed it up with a resigned sigh. 'I suppose there's no point in me trying to change your mind?'

His smile was cold. 'Do you really think you could?'

'No, I suppose not,' she said, as if his indifference didn't matter. As if she didn't care what he thought of her.

But she felt as if somebody had just taken her dreams and trampled on them. He was the only man she had ever wanted. The only man she'd ever loved. Yet Suleiman thought so little of her that he could just hand her over to another man, as if she were a parcel he was delivering.

'Don't look like that, Sara.' His black eyes narrowed and she saw that little muscle flicker at his temple once more. 'If you open your mind a little—you might find that you can actually enjoy your new life. That you can be a good wife. You will have strong sons and beautiful daughters and this will make the people of Qurhah very happy.'

For a moment, Sara thought she heard the hint of uncertainty in his voice. As if he was trotting out the official line without really believing it. Was he? Or was it true what they said—that something in his own upbringing had hardened his heart so that it was made of stone? So that he didn't care about other people's feelings—because he didn't have any of his own.

Well, Suleiman's feelings were none of her business. She didn't care about them because she couldn't afford to. She needed to know what his plans were—and how to react to them accordingly.

'So what happens now?' she asked casually. 'Do I give a month's notice here and then fly out to Qurhah towards the end of January?'

His mouth twisted, as if she had just said something uniquely funny. 'You think that you are free to continue to make the Sultan wait for your presence?' he questioned. 'I'm afraid that those days are over. You will fly out to Qurhah tonight. And you are leaving this building with me, right now.'

Panic—pure and simple—overwhelmed her. She could feel the doors of the prison clanging to a close. Suleiman's dark features blurred for a second, before clicking back into sharp focus, and she tried to pull herself together.

'I'll…I'll need to pack first,' she said.

'Of course.' He inclined his dark head but not before she could see the sudden glint of fire in his eyes. 'Though I doubt whether your mini-skirt will cut it in your new role as Sultana. A far more suitable wardrobe will be provided for you, so why bother?'

'I'm not talking about my clothes!' she flared back. 'Surely you won't deny me my trinkets and keepsakes? The jewellery my mother left me and the book my father published after her death?'

For a moment she wondered if she had imagined the faint look of disquiet which briefly flickered in his eyes. But it was gone as quickly as it had appeared and she told herself to stop attributing thoughts and feelings to him, just because she wanted him to have them. Because he didn't.

'Very well,' he said. 'That can be arranged. Now let's go—I have a car waiting downstairs.'

Sara's heart missed a beat. Of course he had a car waiting. Probably with a couple of heavies inside. That feeling of being trapped closed in on her again and suddenly she knew that she wasn't going to take this lying down. She would not go meekly with Suleiman Abd al-Aziz—she would slip through his hands like an eel plucked from an icy river.

'I have to finish up in here,' she said. 'I can't just walk out for ever without putting my work in some kind of order.'

His face was unreadable. 'How long will it take?'

Sara felt her mouth dry as she wondered realistically how much time she could plead to play with. 'A few hours?'

'Don't test my patience, Sara. Two hours will be more than adequate for what you need to do. I will be waiting with my men at your apartment.' He walked over to the door and paused. 'And don't be late,' he said softly.

With one final warning flickering from his black eyes, he was gone. She waited until she heard the ping of the lift in the corridor and the sound of the elevator doors closing—but she was still paranoid enough to poke her head outside the office to check that he really *had* gone. That he wasn't standing in the shadows spying on her and waiting to see what she would do next.

She shut the office door and walked over to one of the giant windows which overlooked the dark glitter of the river, feeling a stab of pain in her heart. She had loved working here. She had loved the freedom and the creativity of being part of Gabe Steel's enormous organisation.

But now it was all coming to an end, whether she wanted it to or not.

Like hell it was.

An idea began to form in her mind. A plan so audacious that for a moment she wondered if she dared go ahead with it. Yet what choice did she have? To go with Suleiman, like a sheep to the slaughter? To be forced to share a bed with the hawk-faced Sultan—a man for whom she had felt not one whisper of chemistry?

She picked up the office phone instead of her own mobile phone. Because if they'd had bodyguards watching her all this time—who was to say they hadn't bugged her phone?

It didn't take her long to get the information she wanted from the Business Development Director, who was in charge of the company's public relations. Judging by the noise in the background, he was clearly at some sort of Christmas party and gave her a list of journalists without asking any questions.

Her fingers were trembling as she dialled the first number and listened to the ring tone. Maybe nobody would pick up. Maybe they'd all set off home for Christmas—all going to some storybook destination with a wreath on the door and a roaring log fire, with the smell of chestnuts and pine scenting the air.

They wouldn't be spending their Christmas Eve like her—with a car full of cold-faced men sitting outside the building, waiting to take her away to an unknown and unwanted future.

'Hello?'

She took a deep breath. 'Look, I know this is going to sound crazy—but I've got a story you might be interested in.' Her fingers dug into the phone as she listened. 'Details? Sure I can give you details. How about the proposed kidnap of a woman, who is being taken against her will to the desert country of Qurhah to marry a man she doesn't want to marry? You like that? I rather thought you might—and it's all yours. An exclusive. But we haven't got long. I need to leave London before six o' clock.'

CHAPTER TWO

SULEIMAN BROUGHT THE car to a halt so that it was hidden beneath the shadows of the trees, but still within sight of the cottage. The other cars all waited in darkness at various intervals down the country lane, as he had instructed them to do.

He turned off the lights. Rain spattered relentlessly across the windscreen, running in thick rivulets down the glass. For a moment he sat watching the lighted windows of the house. He saw Sara's unmistakable silhouette going around, pulling the drapes tightly shut, and he felt a potent combination of anger and satisfaction. But alongside his triumph at having tracked her down, a deep disquiet ran through his veins like slow poison.

He should have refused this job.

He should have told Murat that his schedule did not allow him time to travel to England and deal with the princess.

But the Sultan did not ask favours of many men and the bonds of loyalty and gratitude ran deeper than Suleiman had anticipated. And although he would have given anything to have avoided this particular task, somehow he had found himself accepting it. Yet just one sight of her today had reinforced what a fool he had been. Better to have thrown himself to the mercy of a starving lion, than to have willingly closeted himself with the temptress Sara.

He remembered the honeyed taste of her lips and her intoxicating perfume of jasmine mixed with patchouli. He remembered the pert thrust of her breast beneath his questing fingers and the way his body had ached for her afterwards. The frustrated lust which seemed to have gone on for months.

His hands tightened around the steering wheel. Women like her were born to create trouble. To make men want them and then to use their sexual power to destroy them. Hadn't her own mother—a fabled beauty in her time—brought down the king who had spent his life in slavish devotion to her? A husband who had spent so much time enthralled by her that he had barely noticed his country slipping into bankruptcy.

He drew in a deep, meditative breath, forcing all the frustrating thoughts from his mind. He must go and do what he needed to do and then leave and never see her again.

With a stealth nurtured by years of undercover work, he waited until he was certain the coast was clear before he got out of the car and silently pulled the door shut behind him. He saw one of the limousines parked further down the lane flash its lights at him.

Avoiding the crunch of the gravel path, he felt his shoes sink into the sodden mud of the lawn which ran alongside it. But the night was fearsome and the weather atrocious and he was soaked within seconds, despite his long-legged stride towards the front door.

He was half tempted to break in by one of the back windows and then to walk in and confront her to show just how vulnerable she really was. But that would be cruel and he had no desire to be cruel to her.

Did he?

His mouth hardened as he lifted one rain-soaked hand to the door handle and knocked.

If she was sensible, she wouldn't answer. Instead, she would phone the local police station and tell them she had an intruder banging on the door of this isolated cottage on Christmas Eve.

But clearly she wasn't being sensible because he could hear the sound of her approaching footsteps and his body tensed as adrenalin flooded through him.

She pulled open the door, her violet eyes widening as she registered his identity. For a split second she reacted quickly, trying desperately to shut the door again—but her reactions were not as fast as his. Few people's were. He placed the flat of his hand on the weathered knocker and blocked her move until she had the sense to step back as he entered the hallway, pushing the door shut behind him.

For a moment there was silence in that small hallway, other than the soft drip of rainwater onto the stone tiles. He could see that she was too stunned to speak—and so was he, but for very different reasons. She might be regarding him with horror but no such feelings were dominating his own mind right then.

She had changed from the provocative dress she'd been wearing in her office earlier. Her hair was loose and her jeans and pink sweater were not particularly clingy, yet still they managed to showcase the magnificence of her body.

He knew it was wrong but he couldn't stop himself from drinking her in, like a man lost in the desert who had just been handed a jug of cool water. Was she aware of her beauty? Of the fact that she looked like a goddess? A goddess in blue jeans.

'Suleiman!' Her voice sounded startled and her violet eyes were dark.

'Surprised?' he questioned.

'You could say that! And horrified.' She glared at him. 'What do you think you're doing—pushing your way in here like some sort of heavy?'

'I thought we had an appointment to meet at six, but since it is now almost eight, you appear to have broken it. Shockingly bad manners, Sara. Especially for a future queen of the desert.'

'Tough!' she retorted. 'And I'm not going to be a queen of the desert. I already told you that I have no intention of getting married. Not to Murat and not to anyone! So why waste everybody's time by turning up? Can't you just go back to the Sultan and tell him to forget the whole idea?'

Suleiman heard the determination in her voice and felt an unwilling flare of admiration for her unashamed—and very stupid—defiance. Such open insubordination was unheard of from a woman from the desert lands and it was rather magnificent to observe her spirited rebellion. But he didn't let it show. Instead, he injected a note of disapproval into his voice. 'I am waiting for an explanation about why you failed to show.'

'Do you realise you sound exactly like a schoolteacher? I don't really think you'd need to be a detective to work out my no-show. I don't like having my arm twisted.'

'Clearly you hadn't thought things through properly, if you imagined it was going to be that easy to shake me off,' he said. 'But you're here now.'

She eyed him speculatively 'I could knock you over the back of the head and make a run for it.'

His mouth quirked at the corners, despite all his best efforts not to smile. 'And if you did, you would run straight into the men I have positioned all the way down the lane. Don't even think about it, Sara. And please don't imagine that I haven't thought of every eventuality, because I have.'

He pulled off his dripping coat and hung it on a peg.

She glared at him. 'I don't remember asking you to take your coat off!'

'I don't require your permission.'

'You are impossible!' she hissed.

'I have never denied that.'

'Oh,' she said, her voice frustrated as she turned round and marched towards a room where he could see a fire blazing.

He followed her into a room which had none of the ornaments the English were so fond of cramming into their country homes. There were no china dogs or hangings made of brass. No jumbled oil paintings of ships which hinted at a naval past. Instead, the walls were pale and contrasted with the weathered beams of wood in the ceiling. The furniture was quirky but looked comfortable and the few contemporary paintings worked well, though in theory they shouldn't have done. Whoever owned this had taste, as well as money.

'Whose cottage is this?' he questioned.

'My lover's.'

He took a step forward, so that his shadow fell over her defiant features. 'Please don't jest with me, Sara. I'm not in the mood for it.'

'How do you know I'm jesting?'

'I hope you are. Because if I thought for a moment that you had been intimate with another man—then I would seek him out and tear him from limb to limb.'

As she heard his venomous but undoubtedly truthful words Sara swallowed, reminding herself that it wasn't a question of Suleiman being jealous. He had only uttered the threat out of loyalty to the Sultan.

She wished he hadn't turned up and yet if she'd stopped to think about it for more than a second—she must have known he would follow her. If Suleiman took on a task, then Suleiman would see it through. No matter what obstacles were put before him, he would conquer them. *That* was why the Sultan had asked him—and why he was so respected and feared within the desert nations.

She had driven here without really thinking about the consequences of her action, only about her urgent need to get away. Not just from the dark certainty of her future, but from this man. The man who had rejected her, yet could still make her heart race with desire and longing.

But his face was as cold as a stone mask. His body language was tense and forbidding. Suleiman's feelings towards her had clearly not changed since the night he'd kissed her and then thrust her away from him. She swallowed. How could she bear to spend hours travelling with him, towards a dark fate which seemed unendurable?

'It's my boss, Gabe Steel's cottage,' she said. 'And how did you find me?'

'It wasn't difficult,' he said. 'You forget that I have tracked down quarry far more elusive than a stubborn princess. Actually, it was your sudden unexpected consent to my plan which alerted my suspicions. It is not like you to be so *acquiescent,* Sara. I suspected that you would try to give my men the slip so I hid outside the side entrance to your office block and followed you to the car park.'

'You *hid*? Outside my office block?'

'You find that so bizarre?'

'Of course I do!' Her heart was hammering in her chest. 'I live in England now and I live an English life, Suleiman. One where men don't usually lurk in shadows, following women who don't want to be followed. Why, you could have been arrested for trespass—especially if my boss had any idea that you were *stalking* me.'

'Unlikely—for I am never seen if I do not wish to be seen,' he said arrogantly. 'You must have known it was a futile attempt to try to escape, so why do it, Sara? Did you really think you could get away with it?'

'Go to hell!'

'I'm not going anywhere and certainly not without you.'

She hated the ruthless tone of his voice. She hated the unresponsive look on his hard face. Suddenly she wanted to shake him. To provoke him. To get some sort of reaction which would make her feel as if she was dealing with a real person, instead of a cold block of stone. 'I was waiting here,' she said deliberately. 'For my lover.'

'I don't think so.'

'And why not?' she demanded. 'Am I so repulsive that you can't imagine that a man might actually want to take me to bed?'

For a moment Suleiman stilled, telling himself that he wouldn't fall into the trap she was so obviously laying for him. She was trying to rile him. Trying to get him to admit to something he was not prepared to admit. Even to himself. Concentrate on the facts, he told himself fiercely—and not on her blonde-haired beauty, or her soft curves which nature must have invented with the intention of sending any man crazy with longing.

'I think you know the answer to that question—and I'm not going to flatter your ego by answering it. Your desirability has never been in question, but you seem to imply that your virtue is.'

'What if it is?' she challenged, her voice growing reckless. 'But I don't have to explain myself to you and

I'm certainly not going to take orders from you. Do you want to know why?'

'Not really,' he said, in a bored tone.

'I think you might.' She licked her lips in a cat-got-the-cream expression and then smiled. 'It might interest you to know that in between your invasion of my office and following me here, I have spoken to a journalist.'

There was a pause. Suleiman's eyes narrowed. 'I hope that's a joke.'

'It's not.'

There was another moment of silence before he could bring himself to speak. 'And what did you tell the journalist?'

She scraped her fingers back through her blonde hair and smirked. 'I told him the truth. No need to look so scared, Suleiman. I mean, who in their right mind could possibly object to the truth?'

'Let's get one thing straight,' he said, biting the words out from between gritted teeth. 'I am not scared—of anyone or anything. I think you may be in danger of mistaking my anger for fear, though perhaps you would do well to feel fear yourself. Because if the Sultan finds out that you have spoken to the western press, then things are going to get very tricky. So I shall ask you again and this time I want a straight answer—what exactly did you tell the journalist?'

Sara stared into the spitting blackness of his eyes and some of her bravado wavered, until she told herself that she wasn't going to be intimidated. She had worked too hard and too long to forge a new life to allow these powerful men to control her. These desert men who would crush your very spirit if you allowed them to do so. So she wouldn't let them.

Even her own mother—who had married a desert king and had loved him—had felt imprisoned by ancient royal rules which hadn't changed for centuries and probably never would. Sara had witnessed for herself that sometimes love just wasn't enough. So what chance would a marriage have if there was no love at all?

Her mother's unhappiness had been the cause of her father's ruination—and had ultimately governed Sara's own fate. She hadn't known that Papa was so obsessed by his English wife that he hadn't paid proper attention to governing his country. Sara remembered that all too vividly. The Queen had been his possession and nothing else had really existed for him, apart from that.

He had taken his eye off the ball. Poor investments and a border war which went on too long meant that his country was left bankrupt. The late Sultan of Qurhah had come up with a deal for a bail-out plan and the price had been Sara's hand in marriage.

When Sara's mother had died and she had been allowed to go off to boarding school—hadn't she thought that her father's debt would just be allowed to fade with time? Hadn't she been naïve and hopeful enough to think that the Sultan might just forget all about marrying her, as his own father had decreed he should?

Blinking back the sudden threat of tears, Sara tried to ignore the fierce expression on Suleiman's face. She was *not* going to be made to feel guilty—when all she was doing was trying to save her own skin. And ultimately she would be doing the Sultan a favour—for surely it would damage the ego of such a powerful man if she was forced kicking and screaming to the altar.

'I am waiting,' he said, with silky venom, 'for you to enlighten me. What did you tell the journalist, Sara?'

She met the accusation in his eyes. 'I told him everything.'

'Everything?'

'Yes! I thought it would make a good story,' she said. 'At a time of year when newspapers are traditionally very light on news and—'

'What did you tell him?' he raged.

'I told him the truth! That I was a half-blood princess—half English and half Dhi'banese. You know the papers—they just love any kind of royal connection!' She forced a mocking smile, knowing that it would irritate him and wondering if irritating him was only a feeble attempt to suppress her desire for him. Because if it was, it wasn't working. 'I told him that my mother travelled as an artist to Dhi'ban, to paint the beautiful desert landscape—and that my father, the king, had fallen in love with her.'

'Why did you feel it necessary to parade your private family history to a complete stranger?'

'I'm just providing the backstory, Suleiman,' she said. 'Everyone knows you need a good backstory if you want an entertaining read. Anyway, it's all there on record.'

'You are severely testing my patience,' he said. 'You had no right to divulge these things!'

'Surely the Sultan wouldn't mind me discussing it?' she questioned innocently. 'This is a marriage we're talking about, Suleiman—and marriages are supposed to be happy occasions. I say *supposed* to be, but that's quite a difficult concept to pull off when the bride is being kidnapped! I have to say that the journalist seemed quite surprised when I told him that I had no say in this marriage. No, when I come to think of it— surprise is the wrong word. I'd say that astonished covered it better. And deeply shocked, of course.'

'Shocked?'

'Mmm. He seemed to find it odd—abhorrent, even—that the Sultan of Qurhah should want to marry a woman who had been bought for him by his own father!'

She saw his fists clench.

'That is the way of the world you were brought into,' he said unequivocally. 'None of us can change the circumstances of our birth.'

'No, we can't. But that doesn't mean we have to be made prisoners by it. We can use everything in our power to change our destinies! Can't you see that, Suleiman?'

'No!'

'Yes,' she argued passionately. 'Yes and a thousand times yes!' Her heart began to race as she saw something written on his carved features which made her stomach turn to jelly. Was it anger? Was it?

But anger would not have made him shake his head, as if he was trying to shake off thoughts of madness. Nor to make that little nerve flicker so violently at his olive-skinned temple. He took a step towards her and, for one heart-stopping moment, she thought he was about to pull her into his arms, the way he'd done on the night of her brother's coronation.

And didn't she want that? Wasn't she longing for him to do just that, only this time not stop? This time they were alone and he could lie her down in front of that log fire and loosen her clothes and...

But he didn't touch her. He stood a tantalisingly close distance away while his eyes sparked dark fire at her. She could see him swallowing, as if he had something bitter lodged in his throat.

'You must accept your destiny,' he said. 'As I have accepted mine.'

'Have you? Did "accepting your destiny" include kissing me on the night my brother was crowned, even though you knew I was promised to another?'

'Don't say that!'

The strangled words sounded almost *powerless* and Sara realised she'd never heard Suleiman sound like that before. Not even after he'd returned from his undercover duties in the Qurhah army, when he'd been thirty pounds lighter with a scar zigzagging down his neck. People said he'd been tortured, but if he had he never spoke of it—well, never to her. She remembered being profoundly shocked by his appearance and she felt a similar kind of shock washing over her now.

For it was not like looking at Suleiman she knew of old. It was like looking at a stranger. A repressed and forbidding stranger. His features had closed up and his eyes were hooded. Had she really thought he was about to kiss her? Why, kissing looked like the furthest thing on his mind.

'We will not speak of that night again,' he said.

'But it's true, isn't it?' she questioned. 'You weren't so moralistic when you touched me like that.'

'Because most men would have died rather than resist you that night,' he admitted bitterly. 'And I chose not to die. I hadn't seen you for six long years and then I saw you, with your big painted eyes and your silver gown, shining like the moon.'

Briefly, Suleiman closed his eyes, because that kiss had been like no other, no matter how much he had tried to deny it. It hadn't just been about sex or lust. It had been much more powerful than that, and infinitely more dangerous. It had been about feeding a hunger as fundamental as the need to eat or drink. It had felt as necessary as breathing. And yet it had angered him, because it had seemed outside his control. Up until that moment he had regarded the young princess with nothing more than indulgent friendship. What had happened that night had taken him completely by surprise. He swallowed. Perhaps that was why it had been the most unforgettable kiss of his life.

'Didn't you realise how much I wanted you that night, Sara, even though you were promised to the Sultan? Were you not aware of your own power?'

'So it was all my fault?'

'No. It is not your "fault" that you looked beautiful enough to test the appetites of a saint. I blame no one but myself for my unforgivable weakness. But it is a weakness which will never be repeated,' he ground out. 'And yes, I blame you if you have now given an interview which will bring shame on the reputation of the Sultan and his royal house.'

'Then ask him to set me free,' she said simply. 'To let me go. Please, Suleiman.'

Suleiman met the appeal in her big violet eyes and for a moment he almost wavered. For wasn't it a terrible crime to see the beautiful and spirited Sara forced to marry a man she did not love? Could he really imagine her lying in the marital bed and submitting to the embraces of a man she claimed not to want? And then he told himself that Murat was a legendary lover. And even though it made him feel sick to acknowledge it—it was unlikely that Sara would lie unresponsive in Murat's bed for too long.

'I can't do that,' he said, but the words felt like stone as he let them fall from his lips. 'I can't allow you to reject the Sultan; I would be failing in my duty if I did. It is a question of pride.'

'Pride!' Angrily, she shook her head. 'What price pride? What if I refuse to allow him to consummate the marriage?' she challenged. 'What then? Won't he skulk away to his harem and take his pleasure elsewhere?'

He flinched as if she had hit him. 'This discussion has become completely inappropriate,' he bit out angrily. 'But you would be wise to consider the effect of your actions on your brother, the King—even though I know you never bother to visit him. There are some in your country who wonder whether the King still has a sister, so rarely does she set foot in her homeland.'

'My relationship with my brother is none of your business—and neither are my trips home!'

'Maybe not. But you would do well to remember that Qurhah continues to shoulder some of your country's national debt. How would your brother feel if the Sultan were to withdraw his financial support because of your behaviour?'

'You *bastard*,' she hissed, but she might as well have been whispering on the wind, for all the notice he took.

'My skin is thick enough to withstand your barbed comments, princess. I am delivering you to the Sultan and nothing will prevent that. But first, I want the name of the journalist you've been dealing with.'

She made one last stab at rebellion. 'And if I won't tell you?'

'Then I will find out for myself,' he said, in a tone which made a shiver trickle down her spine. 'Why not save me the time and yourself my anger?'

'You're a brute,' she breathed. 'An egocentric brute.'

'No, Sara, I just want the story spiked.'

Frustration washed over her as she recognised that he meant business. And that she was fighting a useless battle here.

'His name is Jason Cresswell,' she said sulkily. 'He works for the *Daily View.'*

'Good. Perhaps you are finally beginning to see sense. You might learn that co-operation is infinitely more preferable to rebellion. Now leave me while I speak with him in private.' He glanced at her as he pulled his mobile phone from his pocket.

'Go and get your coat on. Because after I've finished with the journalist we're heading for the airfield,
where the plane is waiting to take you to your new life
in Qurhah.'

CHAPTER THREE

THE FLIGHT WAS smooth and the aircraft supremely comfortable but Suleiman couldn't sleep. For the past seven hours during the journey to Qurhah, he had been kept awake by the tormenting thoughts of what he was doing.

He felt his heart clench. What *was* he doing?

Taking a woman to a man she did not love.

A woman he wanted for himself.

Restlessly, he moved noiselessly around the craft, wishing that there were somewhere to look other than at the sleeping Sara. But although he could have joined the two pilots in the cockpit or tried to rest in the sealed-off section at the far end of the plane, neither option appealed. He couldn't seem to tear his eyes away from her.

He wondered if the silent female servants who were sitting sentry had noticed the irresistible direction of his gaze. Or the fact that he had not left the side of the sleeping princess. But he didn't care—for who would dare challenge him?

He had fulfilled the first part of his task by getting

Sara on board the plane. He just wished he could shake off this damned feeling of *guilt*.

Their late exit from the cottage into the driving rain had left her soaking wet for she had stubbornly refused to use the umbrella he'd opened for her. And as she had sat shivering beside him in the car he'd fought the powerful urge to pull her into his arms and to rub at her cold flesh until she was warm again. But he had vowed that he would not touch her again.

He could never touch her again.

He let his eyes drift over her.

Stretched out in the wide aircraft seat in her crumpled jeans and sweater, she should have looked unremarkable but that was the very last thing she looked. He felt his gut tighten. The sculpted angles of her bone structure hinted at her aristocratic lineage and her eyelashes were naturally dark. Even her blonde hair, which had dried into tousled strands, looked like layered starlight.

She was beautiful.

The most beautiful woman he'd ever seen.

His heart clenched as he turned away, but his troubled thoughts continued to plague him.

He knew the Sultan's reputation. He knew that he was a charismatic man where women were concerned and that most of his former lovers still yearned for him. But Murat the Mighty was a desert man and he believed in destiny. He would marry the princess who had been chosen for him, for to do otherwise would be to renege on an ancient pact. He would marry and take his new bride back to the Qurhahian palace. He would think nothing of it.

Suleiman winced as he tried to imagine Sara being closed off for ever in the Sultan's gilded world and felt a terrible darkness enter his heart.

He heard the small sound she made as she stirred, blinking open her eyes to look at him so that he found himself staring into dark pools of violet ink.

Sitting up, she pushed her tousled hair away from her face. Was she aware that he had been watching her while she slept, and that it had felt unbelievably intimate to do so? Would she be shocked to know that he had imagined moving aside the cashmere blanket and climbing in beside her?

She lifted her arms above her head to yawn and in that moment she looked so *free* that another wave of guilt washed over him.

What would she be like when she'd had her wings clipped by the pressures and the demands of her new position as Sultana? Did she realise that never again would she wear her faded blue jeans or move around anonymously as she had done in London? Did she realize—as he now did—that this trip was the last time he would ever be permitted to be alone with her?

'You're awake,' he said.

'Top marks for observation,' she said, raking her fingers back through her hair to subdue it. 'Gosh, the Sultan must miss having you around if you come out with inspirational gems like that, Suleiman.'

'Are you going to be impertinent for the rest of the journey?'

'I might. If I feel like it.'

'Would a little tea lighten your mood, princess?'

Sara shrugged, wondering whether anything could lighten her mood at that precise moment. Because this was fast becoming like her worst nightmare. She had been bundled onto the plane, with the Sultan's staff bowing and curtseying to her as soon as she had set foot on the private jet. These days she wasn't used to being treated like a princess and it made her feel uncomfortable. She had seen the surreptitious glances which had come shooting her way. Were they thinking: *Here's the princess who ran away?* Or were they thinking what an unworthy wife she would make for their beloved Sultan?

But the most troubling aspect was not that she was being taken somewhere against her will, to marry a man she didn't love. It was the stupid yearning feeling she got whenever she looked at Suleiman's shuttered features and found herself wishing that he would lose the uptight look and just kiss her. She found herself longing for the closeness of yesteryear, instead of this strange new tenseness which surrounded him.

She could guess *why* he was behaving so coolly towards her, but that didn't seem to alleviate this terrible *aching* which was gnawing away at her heart, despite all her anger and confusion.

'So. How did your "chat" with the journalist go?' she asked. 'Did he agree to kill the story?'

'He did.' He slanted her a triumphant look. 'I managed to convince him that your words were simply a heightened version of the normal nerves of a bride-to-be.'

'So you bribed him, I suppose? Offered him riches beyond his wildest dreams not to publish?'

Suleiman smiled. 'I'm afraid so.'

Frustratedly, Sara sank back against the cushions and watched Suleiman raise his hand in command, instantly bringing one of the servants scurrying over to take his order for tea. He was so *easy* with power, she thought. He acted as if he'd been born to it—which as far as she knew, he hadn't. She knew that he'd been schooled alongside the Sultan, but that was all she *did* know—because he was notoriously cagy about his past. He'd once told her that the strongest men were those who kept their past locked away from prying eyes—and while she could see the logic in that, it had always maddened her that she hadn't known more about what made him tick.

She took a sip of the fragrant camomile brew she was handed before putting her cup down to study him. 'You say you're no longer working for the Sultan?'

'That's right.'

'So what are you doing instead? Doesn't your new boss mind you flitting off to England like this?'

'I don't have a boss. I don't answer to anyone, Sara. I work for myself.'

'Doing what—providing bespoke kidnap services for reluctant brides?'

'I thought we'd agreed to lose the hysteria.'

'Doing what?' she persisted.

Suleiman cracked the knuckles of his fists and

stared down at the whitened bones because that was a far less distracting sight than confronting the spark of interest in those beautiful violet eyes. 'I own an oil refinery and several very lucrative wells.'

'You own an oil refinery?' she repeated in disbelief. 'A baby one?'

'Quite a big one, actually.'

'How on earth can you afford to do that?'

He lifted his head and met the confusion in her gaze. He thought how inevitably skewed her idea of the world was—a world where kingdoms were lost and bought and bartered. His investigations into her London life had assured him that her job for Gabe Steel was bona fide, but he knew that she'd inherited her luxury apartment from her mother. Sara was a princess, he reminded himself grimly. She'd never wanted for anything.

'I played the stock market,' he said.

'Oh, come on—Suleiman. It can't be as simple as that. Loads of people play the stock market, but they don't all end up with oil refineries.'

He leaned back against the silken pile of cushions, an ill-thought-out move, since it put his eye-line on a level with her breasts. Instead, he fixed his gaze on her violet eyes.

'Even as a boy, I was always good with numbers,' he said. 'And later on, I found it almost *creative* to watch the movement of the markets and predict what was going to happen next. It was, if you like, a hobby—a consuming as well as a very profitable one. Over the years I managed to accrue a considerable amount of wealth, which I invested. I bought shares along the way which flourished. Some property here and there.'

'Where?'

'Some in Samahan and some in the Caribbean. But I was looking for something more challenging. On the hunch of a geologist I met on a plane to San Francisco, I began drilling in an area of my homeland which, up until that moment, everyone had thought was barren land. It provided one of the richest oil wells in Middle Eastern history.' He shrugged. 'I was lucky.'

Sara blinked at him, as if there was a fundamental part of the story missing. 'So you had all this money in the bank, yet you continued to work for the Sultan?'

'Why not? There is nothing to match the buzz of being in politics and I'd always enjoyed my role as his envoy.'

'So you did,' she agreed slowly. 'Until one day, something made you leave and start up on your own.'

'If you hadn't been a princess, you could have been a detective,' he said sardonically.

'So what was it, Suleiman? Why the big lifestyle change?'

'Isn't it right and natural that a man should have ambition?' he questioned, taking a sip of his own tea. 'That he should wish to be his own master?'

'What was it, Suleiman?' she repeated quietly.

Suleiman felt his body tense. Should he tell her? Would the truth weaken him in her eyes, or would it make her realise why this damned attraction which still sizzled between them could never be acted upon?

'It was you,' he said. 'You were the catalyst.'

'Me?'

'Yes, you. And why the innocent look of surprise? Haven't you yet learned that every action has a consequence, Sara? Think about it. The night you offered yourself to me—'

'It was a kiss, for heavens sake!' she croaked.

'It was more than a kiss and we both know it,' he continued remorselessly. 'Or are you saying that, if I had pushed you against the shadowed palace wall for yet more intimacy, you would have stopped me?'

'Suleiman!'

'Are you saying that?' he repeated, but he found her blush deeply satisfying—for it spoke of an innocence he had begun to question. And wouldn't it be better to air all his bitterness and frustration so that he could let it out and move on, as he needed to move on? As they both did.

'No,' she said, the word a flat, small admission. 'How can I deny it?'

'I felt shame,' he continued. 'Not so much for what I had done, but for what I wanted to do. I had betrayed the Sultan in the worst way imaginable and I could no longer count myself as his most loyal aide.'

She was looking at him in disbelief. 'So one kiss made you resign?'

He nearly told her the rest, but he stopped himself in time. If he admitted that he couldn't bear to think of her in another man's arms and that he found it intolerable to contemplate her being married to the Sultan and being forced to look on from the sidelines. If he explained that the thought of another man thrusting deep inside her body made him feel sick—then wouldn't that reveal more than it was safe to reveal? Wouldn't it make temptation creep out from behind the shadows?

'It would have been impossible for me to work alongside your new husband with you as his wife,' he said.

'I see.'

And she did see. Or rather, she saw some of it. Sara stared at the black-haired man sitting before her, because now the pieces of the puzzle were beginning to form a more coherent shape. Suleiman had *wanted* her. Really wanted her. And now she was beginning to suspect that he still did. Behind the rigid pose he presented and the wall of disapproval, there still burned *something*. He had all but admitted it just now.

Didn't that explain the way his body tensed whenever she grew close? Why his dark eyes had grown stormy and opaque when he'd studied her short skirt that day in the office. It was not indifference towards her as she had first thought.

It was Suleiman trying to hide the fact that he still wanted her.

She licked her dry lips and saw his eyes follow the movement of her tongue, as if he was being compelled to do something against his will. Was he remembering—as she was—when his own tongue had entered her mouth and made her moan with pleasure?

Her head was spinning; her thoughts were confused but as they began to clear she saw a possible solution to her dilemma. What if she used Suleiman's desire for her to her own advantage? What if she tempted him beyond endurance and *seduced* him, what then? If they finished off what they had started all those years ago, wasn't that a way out for her? He was a single-minded man, yes, and a determined one, but there was no way he could present her to Murat if he had been intimate with her himself.

Could she do it? Could she? She was certainly no seductress, but how difficult could it be to beguile the only man she had ever really wanted?

She rose to her feet. 'Where's the bathroom?' she asked.

'Through there,' he said—pointing towards the door at the far end of the cabin.

She reached up towards the rack to retrieve the bag she'd brought with her and Suleiman moved forward to help, but she shook her head with a sudden fierce show of independence. She might want him, but she didn't need him. She didn't need any man. Wasn't that the whole point of her carefree life in London? That she didn't have to be tied down and trapped. 'I'm perfectly capable of doing it myself.'

She disappeared into the bathroom, emerging a short while later with her blonde hair brushed and woven into a neat chignon. She had changed from her jeans and sweater and replaced them with clothes more suited to the desert climate of Qurhah.

Her slim-fitting linen trousers and long-sleeved silk shirt now covered most of her flesh, but, despite the concealing outfit, she felt curiously *exposed* as she walked back towards him. Her legs were unsteady and her stomach was tying itself up in knots as she sat down. For a moment she couldn't quite bring herself to meet Suleiman's eyes, terrified that he might discover the subversive nature of her thoughts.

'So what happens when we arrive?' she questioned. 'Will an armed guard be taking over from you? Will I be handcuffed, perhaps?'

'We are landing at one of the military airbases,' he said. 'That way, your arrival won't be marred by the curiosity of onlookers at Qurhah's international airport.'

'In case I make a break for freedom, you mean?'

'I thought we'd discounted this rather hysterical approach of yours?' he said. 'And since the threat of desert storms has been brewing for days, it is considered unsafe for us to use a helicopter to get you to the Sultan's summer residence. So it might interest you to know that we will be travelling there by traditional means.'

At this, Sara's head jerked up in surprise. 'You don't mean an old-fashioned camel caravan?'

Suleiman smiled. 'Indeed I do. A little-used means of desert travel nowadays, but many of the nomadic people still claim it is the most efficient.'

'And who's to say they aren't right? Gosh, I haven't been on one since I was a child.' Sara looked at him, her violet eyes shining with excitement. 'And of course, this means that there will be horses, too.'

Suleiman felt his throat tighten. Was it wrong that he found the look on her face utterly captivating? That her smile would have warmed a tent on the coldest desert night. 'I had forgotten how much you enjoyed riding,' he said.

'Well, you shouldn't—because it's thanks to you that I ride so well.'

'You were an exemplary pupil,' he said gruffly.

She inclined her head, as if she was acknowledging the sudden cessation in hostilities between them. 'Thank you. But your lessons were what gave me my confidence and my ability.'

'Do you still ride?'

She shook her head. 'There aren't too many stables in the middle of London.' She looked at him. 'But I miss it.'

Something about the vulnerable pout of her lips made him ask the indulgent question, despite his own silent protestations that their conversation was becoming much too intimate. 'And what do you miss about it?'

She wriggled her shoulders. 'It's the time when I feel most free, I guess.'

Their eyes met and Suleiman saw a sudden shadow cross her face. It was almost as if she'd just remembered something—something which made her face take on a new and determined expression.

He watched as she smoothed down the silk of her blouse, her fingers whispering over the delicate material which covered her ribcage. Why did she insist on doing that, he wondered furiously—when all it was doing was making him focus on her body? And he must *stop* thinking of her body. And her violet eyes. He must think of her only as the woman who would soon be married to the Sultan—the man for whom he would lay down his life.

'We're nearly there,' he said, his sudden lust tempered by relief as the powerful jet began its descent.

Their arrival at the airbase had been kept deliberately low-key, since all celebrations had been put on hold until the wedding. Suleiman watched the natural grace with which Sara walked down the aircraft steps and then moved along the small line of officials who were assembled to meet her. She had lowered her lashes to a demure level, in order to conceal the brilliant gleam of her eyes, and her lips were curved into a serene and highly appropriate little smile. She could easily become an exemplary Sultana, he thought, despising himself for the dull ache of disappointment which followed this thought.

Afterwards, he watched her look around her, as if she was reacquainting herself with the vastness and beauty of the desert. He saw the admiration in her eyes as she gazed up at the mighty herd of camels standing at the edge of the airstrip, where the land was always waiting to encroach. And wasn't she only reflecting his own feelings about this particular form of transport?

A camel caravan could consist of a hundred and fifty animals, but since this endeavour was mainly ceremonial there were no more than eighteen beasts. Some were topped with lavishly fringed tents while others carried necessary provisions for the journey. Men on horseback moved up and down the line, riding some of the finest Akhal-Teke horses in the world, their distinctive coats gleaming metallic in the bright sun.

'It's pretty spectacular, isn't it?' he observed.

'It's more than that. I think it's one of the most beautiful sights in the world,' she said softly.

He turned to her and suddenly he didn't care if he was breaking protocol in the eyes of the onlookers. Wasn't this his opportunity to make amends for having let his lust override his duty to the Sultan, on the night of her brother's coronation? Couldn't he say the *right* thing to her now? The thing she needed to hear, rather than the impure thoughts which were still making him hard whenever he was near her.

'That is genuine passion I hear in your voice, Sara,' he said. 'Can't you piece together the many things you love about the desert? Then you could flick through them as you would a precious photo album—and be grateful for the many beauties of the life which will be yours when you marry.'

'But they won't be mine, will they?' she demanded. 'Everything will belong to my husband—including me! Because we both know that, by law, women in Qurhah are not allowed ownership of anything. I'll just be there, some bored figurehead, sitting robed and trapped. Free only to communicate with my husband and my female servants—apart from at official functions, and even then the guests to whom I will be introduced will be highly vetted. I don't know how the Sultan's sister stands it.'

'The Princess Leila is deeply contented in her royal role,' said Suleiman.

Sara closed her lips together. That wasn't what she'd heard. Apparently, at the famous Qurhah Gold Cup races,

Leila had been seen looking glum—but it was hardly her place to drop the princess in it.

'I'll probably have to fight to be able to ride a horse,' she continued. 'And only when any stray man has been cleared away from the scene in case he dares *look* at me. *And* I'll probably be forced to ride side-saddle.'

'You do not have to be bored,' he argued. 'Boredom is simply a question of attitude. You could use your good fortune and good health to make Qurhah a better place. You could do important work for charity.'

'That goes without saying,' she said. 'I'm more than happy to do that. But am I to be consigned to a loveless marriage, simply because my country got itself into debt?'

Suleiman felt a terrible conflict raging within him. The conflict of believing what was right and knowing what was wrong. The conflict of duty versus desire. He wanted nothing more than to rescue her from her fate. To tell her that she need not marry a man she did not love. And then to drag her off to some dark corner and slide those silken robes from her lush young body. He wanted to rub the nub of his thumb between her legs, to feel the moist flowering of her sex as her body prepared itself for his entry. He wanted to bite at her breasts. To leave the dark indentation of his teeth behind. His mark. So that no other man would be able to touch her…

With an effort he closed his mind to the torture of his erotic thoughts—for that way lay madness. He could do nothing other than what he had promised to do. He would deliver Sara to the Sultan and he would forget her, just as he had forgotten every woman he had ever lain with.

'This is your destiny,' he breathed. 'And you cannot escape it.'

'No?'

He watched, fascinated and appalled as the rosy tip of her tongue emerged from her lips and began to trace a featherlight path around their cupid's bow. And suddenly all he could think about was the exquisite gleam of those lips.

'You can't think of any alternative solution to my dilemma?' she questioned softly.

For a moment he thought of entering eagerly into the madness which was nudging at the edges of his mind. Of telling her that the two of them would fly away and he would spend the rest of his life protecting her and making love to her. That they would create a future together with children of their own. And they would build the kind of home that neither of them had ever known.

He shook his head, as if emerging from an unexpected dream.

'The solution to your *dilemma*,' he said coldly, 'is to shake off your feelings of self-pity—and start counting your blessings instead. Be grateful that you will soon be the wife of His Imperial Majesty. And now, let us join the caravan and begin our journey—for the Sultan grows impatient. You will take the second camel in the train.'

'I will not,' she said.

'I beg your pardon?'

'You heard—and glaring at me like that won't make any difference, Suleiman,' she said. 'I want to ride one of those beautiful horses.'

'You will not be riding anywhere.'

'Oh, but I will,' she argued stubbornly. 'Because either you let me have my own mount, or I'll refuse to get on one of the camels—and I'd like to see any of you trying to get a woman on top of a camel if she doesn't want to go. Apart from the glaring problem of propriety—I have a very healthy pair of lungs and I doubt whether screaming is considered appropriate behaviour for a princess. You know how much the servants gossip.'

Suleiman could feel a growing frustration as he acknowledged the fierce look on her face. 'Are you calling my bluff?' he demanded.

'No. I'm just telling you that I don't intend to spend the next three days sitting on a camel. I get travel-sick on camels—you know that!'

'You have been allocated the strongest and yet most docile beast in the caravan,' he defended.

'I don't care if he's fluent in seven languages—I'm not getting on him. Please, Suleiman,' she coaxed. 'Let me ride. I've got my eye on that sweet-looking palomino over there.'

'But you told me you haven't been on a horse for years,' he growled.

'I know. And that's precisely why I need the practice. So either you let me ride there, or I shall refuse to come.'

He met her obstinate expression, knowing she had him beat. Imagine the dishonour to her reputation if he tried to force her onto the back of a camel. 'If I agree—*if* I agree…you will stay close beside me at all times!' he ordered.

'If you insist.'

'I do. And you will not do anything reckless. Is that understood?'

'Perfectly,' she said.

Frustratedly, he shook his head—wondering how the Sultan was going to be able to cope with such a *headstrong* woman.

But a far more pressing problem was how he was going to get through the next couple of days without succumbing to the temptation of making love to her.

CHAPTER FOUR

SARA GAVE A small sigh of satisfaction as she submitted
to the ministrations of the female attendant. Luxuri-
ously, she wriggled her toes and rested her head against
the back of the small bath tub. It was strange being
waited on like this again after so long. On the plane she
had decided she didn't like being treated like a princess, but that wasn't quite true. Because nobody could
deny that it felt wonderful to have your body washed
in cool water, especially when you had been on horseback all day beneath the baking heat of the desert sun.

They had spent hours travelling across the Mekatha-
sinian Sands towards the Sultan's summer palace and
until a few moments ago she had been hot and tired.
But according to Suleiman they had made good progress—and hadn't it felt wonderful to be back in the
saddle again after so long?

She had stubbornly ignored his suggestion that she
ride side-saddle. Instead, she had lightly swung up onto
her beautiful Akhal-Teke mount with its distinctive metallic golden coat, before going for a gentle trot with
the black-eyed emissary close by. When she'd been

going for a couple of hours, he had grudgingly agreed to let her canter. She suspected that he was testing her competence in the saddle and she must have passed the test—for it had taken very little persuasion for him to agree to a short gallop with her across the desert plain.

And that bit. That bit had been bliss…

She closed her eyes as the cool water washed away the sand which still clung to her skin. Today had been one of the best days she could remember—and how crazy was that? Shouldn't pleasure be the last thing which a woman in her position should be feeling?

Yet the freedom of riding with Suleiman beneath the hot desert sun had been powerful enough to make her forget that she was getting ever closer to a destiny which filled her with horror.

It had felt fantastic to be back on a horse again. She had eagerly agreed to his offer of a race, although at one point she'd been lagging behind him as they were galloping towards the sand dune. Suleiman had turned to look at her and had slowed his horse to match her pace.

'Are you okay, Sara? Not feeling too tired?'

'Oh, I'm okay.' Without warning, she had dug her knees into the horse and had surged ahead. And of course she reached the dune first—laughing at the frustration and admiration which were warring in his dark eyes.

'You little cheat,' he murmured.

'It's called tactics, Suleiman.' Her answer had been insouciant, but she had been unable to hide her instinctive glee at having beaten him. 'Just plain old tactics.'

It was only now, with the relaxation which followed hours of physical exertion, that her thoughts were slowing down enough to let her dwell on the inevitable.

One day down and time was ticking away. Soon she would never be alone with him again.

The thought of that was hard to bear. Within a few short hours, all those feelings she'd repressed for so long had come flooding back with all the force of a burst dam. He was the only man she'd ever felt anything for and he still was. She couldn't believe how badly she had underestimated the impact of being in his company again.

She had been planning to use him as her means of escape, yes. What she hadn't been planning was to fall deeper under his spell. To imagine herself still in love with him, as she'd been all those years ago. Had she forgotten the power of the heart to yearn for the impossible? Or had she just forgotten that Suleiman was her fantasy man, who had now come to vibrant life before her eyes?

On horseback, he looked like a dream. He had changed into his desert clothes and the result had been breathtaking. Sara had forgotten how good a man could look in flowing robes and had spent most of the day trying not to stare at him, with varying degrees of success. The fluid fabric had clung to his body and moulded the powerful thrust of his thighs as they'd gripped the flanks of his stallion. His headdress had streamed behind him like a pale banner in the warm air. His rugged profile had been dark and commanding—his lips firmly closed against the clouds of fine sand which billowed up around him.

She lay back as the servant continued to wash her with a mixture of rose water, infused with jasmine blossom. Next, her ears would be anointed with oil of sandalwood, a process which would be repeated on her toes. After that, her hair would be woven with fragrant leaves which had been brought from the gardens of the Sultan's palace and the intention was for her to be completely perfumed by the time she was presented to him at court.

Sara shuddered as she imagined the swarthy potentate stripping her of her bridal finery, before lowering his powerful body on hers.

She could not go through with it.

She would not go through with it.

For the Sultan's sake and for all their sakes—she could not become his wife.

And deep down she knew that the only way to ensure her freedom was with the seduction of Suleiman.

Yet the nagging question remained about how she was going to accomplish that. How could such a scenario be possible when silent servants hovered within the shadows of the camels and the tents? When the eyes of the bodyguards were so sharp it was said they could see a snake move from a hundred yards away.

The light was fading by the time she emerged from the tasselled tent for the evening meal. Against the clear, cobalt sky the giant desert sun looked like a fiery giant beach-ball as it sank slowly into the horizon. She found herself remembering the week she'd spent in

Ibiza last year—when, bikini-clad, she'd frolicked in the waves with two girlfriends from the office, enjoying the kind of freedom she'd only ever dreamed of. Would she ever do something like that again? Would she ever be able to wander down to the deli near Gabe's offices and buy herself a cappuccino, with an extra shot?

Her silken robes fluttered in the gentle breeze and tiny silver bells adorned the jewellery she wore. They jangled at her wrists and her ankles as she moved—and apart from their decorative qualities, that was the whole point of wearing them—to warn others that the Sultan's fiancée was in the vicinity. As soon as the sound was heard the servants would bow their heads and the male members of the group would quickly avert their eyes.

All except Suleiman.

He had been standing talking to one of the bodyguards but he must have heard her for he glanced up, his eyes narrowing. It was impossible to know what was on his mind but she knew she hadn't imagined the sudden tension which had stiffened his body. She saw his mouth harden and the skin stretching tautly over his cheekbones—as if he was mentally preparing himself for some sort of endurance test.

The bodyguards had melted away into the shadows and even though the temporary camp was humming with the unseen life of servants, it felt as if it were just her and him, alone beneath the vast canopy of the darkening sky, which would soon give way to starry night.

He, too, had changed for dinner. Soft robes of dark crimson silk made him look as if he were part of the setting sun himself. His ebony hair was covered with a headdress which was held in place by a woven circlet of silver cord. There was no aristocratic blood in his veins—that much she knew about a childhood of which he rarely spoke—but at that moment he looked as proud and patrician as any king.

He bowed his head as she approached, but not quickly enough to hide the sudden flash of hunger in his eyes.

'You look like a true desert princess tonight,' he said.

'I can't make up my mind whether or not that's a compliment.'

'It is,' he said, looking for all the world as if he now regretted his choice of words. 'It signals that you are accepting your fate—outwardly, at least. Are you hungry?'

She nodded. The sight of Suleiman was enough to make food seem inconsequential, but she could smell cooking. The familiar concoction of sweet herbs and spices drifting towards her was making her mouth water and it was a long time since she had eaten a feast in the desert. 'Starving.'

He laughed. 'Don't they say that a hungry woman is a dangerous woman?'

'And don't they also say that some women remain dangerous even when their bellies are full?'

'Is that a threat or a promise?'

She looked into his eyes. So black, she thought. So very black. 'Which would you like it to be, Suleiman?'

There was a split second of a pause, when she

thought he might respond in a similar, teasing style. But then something about his countenance changed and his face darkened. She could see him swallow—as if something jagged had lodged itself in his throat. And was it a terrible thing to admit that she found herself almost *enjoying* his obvious discomfort?

Well, it might be terrible, but it was also human nature—and right now, nothing else seemed to matter. She was achingly aware that beneath their supposedly polite banter thrummed the unmistakable tremor of sexual desire. She wanted to break down the walls that he had built around himself—to claw away at the bricks with her bare hands. She wanted to seduce him to guarantee her freedom, yes—but it was more than that. Because she wanted him.

She had never stopped wanting him.

But this could never be anything more than sex. She knew that. If she seduced Suleiman, then she needed to have the strength to walk away. Because no happy ending was possible. She knew that, too.

'It's dinner time,' he said abruptly, glancing at the sun, which she knew he could read as accurately as any clock.

Sara said nothing as they walked over to the campfire, where a special dining area had been laid out for the two of them. She saw the fleeting disquiet which had darkened Suleiman's face and realised that this faux-intimacy was probably the last thing he wanted. But protocol being what it was—there was really no alternative. Of course she would be expected to eat with him, rather than alone—while the servants ate their own rations out of sight.

It was a long time since she had enjoyed a meal in the desert and, inevitably, the experience had a story-book feel to it. The giant bulk of the camels was sil-houetted against the darkening sky, where the first stars were beginning to glimmer. The crackling flames glowed golden and the smell of the traditional Qurhah stew was rich with the scent of oranges and cinnamon.

Sara sank down onto a pile of brocade cushions while Suleiman adopted a position on the opposite side of the low table, on which thick, creamy candles burned. It was as if an outdoor dining room had been erected in the middle of the sands and it looked spec-tacular. She'd forgotten how much could be loaded onto the backs of the camels and how it was a Qurhah custom to make every desert trip feel like a home-from-home.

She accepted a beaker of pomegranate juice and smiled her thanks at the servant who ladled out a por-tion of the stew onto each of the silver platters, before leaving the two of them alone.

The food was delicious and Sara ate several mouth-fuls but her hunger soon began to ebb away. It was too distracting to think about eating when Suleiman was sitting opposite her, his face growing shadowed in the dying light. She noticed he was watching her closely—his intelligent eyes narrowed and gleaming—and she knew that she must approach this very carefully. He could not be played with and toyed with. If she went about her proposed seduction in a crass and obvious manner, then mightn't he see through it?

So try to get underneath his skin—without him realising what you're doing.

'You do realise that I've known you for years and yet you're still something of a mystery to me,' she said conversationally.

'Good. That's the way I like it.'

'I mean, I know practically nothing about your past,' she continued, as if he hadn't made that terse interruption.

'How many times have I told you, Sara? My past is irrelevant.'

'I don't agree. Surely our past is what defines us. It makes us what we are today. And you've never told me how you first got to know the Sultan—or to be regarded so highly by him. When I was a child you said I wouldn't understand—and when I became an adult, well...' She shrugged, not wanting to spell it out. Not needing to say that once sexual attraction had reared its powerful head, any kind of intimacy had seemed too dangerous. She put her fork down and looked at him.

'It isn't relevant,' he said.

'Well, what else are we going to talk about? And if I am to be the Sultan's wife...' She hesitated as she noticed him flinch. 'Then surely it must be relevant. Am I to know nothing about the background of the man who was my future husband's aide for so long? You must admit that it is highly unusual for such a powerful man as the Sultan to entrust so much to someone who has no aristocratic blood of their own.'

'I had no idea that you were such a snob, Sara,' he mocked.

'I'm not a snob,' she corrected. 'Just someone seeking the facts. That's one of the side effects of having had a western education. I was taught to question things, rather than just to accept what I was told or be fobbed off with some bland reply designed to put me in my place.'

'Then maybe your western education has not served you well,' he said, before suddenly stilling. He shook his head. 'What am I saying?' he said, almost to himself. 'How unforgivable of me to try to damn your education and in so doing—to damn knowledge itself. Forget that I ever said that.'

'Does that mean you'll answer my question?'

'That is not what I meant at all.'

'Please, Suleiman.'

He gave an exasperated sigh as he looked at her. But she thought she saw affection in his eyes too as he lowered his voice and began to speak in English, even though Sara was certain that none of the servants or bodyguards were within earshot.

'You know that I was born into poverty?' he said. 'Real and abject poverty?'

'I heard the rumours,' Sara answered. 'Though you'd never guess that from your general bearing and manner.'

'I learn very quickly. Adaption is the first lesson of survival,' he said drily. 'And believe me, it's easier to absorb the behaviour of the rich, than it is the other way round.'

'So how did you—a boy from the wrong side of the tracks—ever come into contact with someone as important as the Sultan?'

There was silence for a moment. Sara thought she saw a sudden darkness cross his face. And there was bitterness, too.

'I grew up in a place called Tymahan, a small area of Samahan, where the land is at its most desolate and people eke out what living they can. To be honest, there was never much of a living to be made—even before the last war, when much blood was shed. But you, of course—in your pampered palace in Dhi'ban—would have known nothing of those hardships.'

'You cannot blame me for the way I was protected as a princess,' she protested. 'Would you sooner I had cut off my hair and pretended to be a boy, in order to do battle?'

'No.' He shook his head. 'Of course not.'

'Carry on with your story,' she urged, leaning forward a little.

He seemed to draw in a quick breath as she grew closer.

'The Sultan's father was touring the region,' he said. 'He wanted to witness the aftermath of the wars and to see whether any insurrection remained.'

Sara watched as he took a sip from his beaker and then put the drink back down on the low table.

'My mother had been ill—and grieving,' he continued. 'My father had been killed in the uprisings and as a consequence she was vulnerable—struck down by a scourge known to many at that time.' His mouth twisted with pain and bitterness. 'A scourge known as starvation.'

Sara flinched as guilt suddenly washed over her. Earlier, he had accused her of self-pity and didn't he have a point? She had moaned about her position as a princess—yet despite the many unsatisfactory areas of her life, she had certainly never experienced anything as fundamental as a lack of food. She'd never had to face a problem as pressing as basic *survival*. She looked into his black eyes, which were now clouded with pain, and her heart went out to him.

'Oh, Suleiman,' she said softly.

His mouth hardened, as if her sympathy was unwelcome. 'The Sultan was being entertained by a group of local dignitaries and there was enough food groaning on those tables to feed our village for a month,' he said, his voice growing harsh. 'I was lurking in the shadows, for that was my particular skill—to see and yet not be seen. And on this night I saw a pomegranate— as big as a man's fist and as golden as the midday sun. My mother had always loved pomegranates and I...'

'You stole it?' she guessed as his words faded away.

He gave her a tight smile. 'If I had been old enough to articulate my thoughts I would have called it a fair distribution of goods, but my motives were irrelevant since I was caught, red-handed. I may have been good at hiding in the shadows, but I was no match for the Sultan's elite bodyguards.'

Sara shivered, recognising the magnitude of such a crime and wondering how he was still alive to tell the tale.

'And they let you off?'

He gave a short laugh. 'The Sultan's guards are not in the habit of granting clemency to common thieves and I was moments away from losing my head to one of their scimitars, when I saw a young boy about the same age as me running from within one of the royal tents and shouting at them to stop. It was the Sultan's son, Murat.' He paused. 'Your future husband.'

Sara flinched, for she knew that his heavy reminder had been deliberate. 'And what did he do?'

'He saved my life.'

She stared at him in bewilderment. 'How?'

'It was simple. Murat was protected and pampered— but lonely and bored. He wanted a playmate—and a boy hungry enough to steal from the royal table was deemed a charitable cause to rescue. My mother was offered a large sum of money—'

'She took it?'

'She had no choice other than to take it!' he snapped. 'I was to be washed and dressed in fine clothes. To be removed from my own country and taken back to the royal palace of Qurhah, where I was to be educated alongside the young Sultan. In most things, we two boys would be as equals.'

There was silence while she digested this. She could see how completely Suleiman's life would have been transformed. Why sometimes he unconsciously acted with the arrogance known to all royals, though his was tempered by a certain *edge*. But his mother had *sold* him. And there was something he had omitted to mention. 'Your…mother? What happened to her?'

This time the twist of pain on his face was so raw that she could hardly bear to observe it.

'She was given the best food and the best medicines,' he said. 'And a new dwelling place was built for her and my two younger brothers. I was taken away to the palace, intending to return to Samahan to see my family in the summer. But her illness had taken an irreversible toll and my mother died that springtime. I never…I never saw her again.'

'Oh, Suleiman,' she said, her heart going out to him. His mother's sacrifice had been phenomenal and yet she had died without seeing her eldest son. How terrible for them both. She wanted to go to him and take him in her arms, but the unseen presence of the servants and the expression on his face warned her not to try. Only words could convey her empathy and her sorrow and she picked the simplest and most heartfelt of all. 'I'm sorry,' she said. 'So very sorry.'

'It happened a long time ago,' he said harshly. 'It's all in the past. And that's where it should stay. Like I said, the past is irrelevant. Now perhaps you will understand why I prefer not to talk of it?'

She looked at him. All these years she'd known him—or, rather, had thought she'd known him. But she had only seen the bits he had allowed her to see. He had kept this vital part of himself locked away, until now—when it had poured from his lips and made him seem strangely vulnerable. It made her understand a little more about why he was the kind of man he was. Why he kept his feelings bottled away and sometimes seemed so stubborn and inflexible. It explained why he had always been so unquestioningly loyal to the Sultan who had saved his life. He was so driven by duty—because duty was all he knew.

Suddenly she realised why he had rejected her on the night of her brother's coronation. Again, because it was his *duty*. Because she had been betrothed to the Sultan.

Yet the price of duty had been to never see his mother again. No wonder he had always seemed so proud and so alone. Because essentially he was.

And suddenly Sara knew that she could not seduce him as some cynical game-plan of her own. She could not use Suleiman Abd al-Aziz to help her escape from this particular prison. She could not place him in any position of danger, because if the Sultan were ever to discover that his bride-to-be had slept with the man he most trusted in all the world—then all hell would be let loose.

No. She lifted her hand to brush a strand of hair away from her cheek and she saw his eyes narrow as the bells on her silver bangles tinkled. She was going to have to be strong and take responsibility for herself.

She could not use sex as an instrument of barter, not when she cared about Suleiman so much. If she wanted to get out of here, then she was going to have to use more traditional means. But she was resourceful, wasn't she? There was nothing stopping her.

She needed to make her bid for freedom without implicating Suleiman. Even if he was blamed for her departure, he should not be party to it. Somehow she needed to escape without him knowing—and escape she would. She would return to the military airfield

and *demand* to be put on a plane back to England—
promising them a sure-fire international outcry if they
failed to comply with her wishes. They kept wanting
to remind her that she was a princess—well, maybe it
was time she started behaving like one!

She rose to her feet but Suleiman was shadowing her
every move and was by her side in an instant.

'I must turn in for the night,' she said, giving a huge
yawn and wondering if it looked as staged as it felt.
'The effects of the desert heat are very wearying and
I'm no longer used to it.'

He inclined his head. 'Very well. Then I accompany
you to your tent.'

'There's no need for you to do that.'

'There is every need, Sara—for we both know that
snakes and scorpions can lurk within the shadows.'

She wanted to tell him that she knew the terrain as
well as he did. That she had been taught to understand
and respect its mysteries and its dangers, because he
had taught them to her. But perhaps now was not a
good time to remind him that at heart she was a child
of the desert—for mightn't that alert him to all the possibilities which still lay beneath her fingertips?

The beauty of the night seemed to mock her. The
sky was a vast dark dome, pinpricked by the brightest
stars a person was ever likely to see. The moon bright-
ened the indigo depths like a giant silver dish which
had been superimposed there—the shadows on its face
disturbingly clear. For a moment she wished that she
had supernatural powers—that she could leap into the

air and fly to the moon, like the most famous of all the Dhi'banese fables she had heard as a child.

But her sandaled feet were firmly on the ground as she walked through the soft sand, her eyes taking in her surroundings. She looked at the layout of the camp as she walked. She saw where the horses were tethered and where the bodyguards had been stationed. Obviously they were close enough to keep her from harm, but far enough away for propriety to be observed.

They reached the tasselled entrance of her tent and she wanted to reach up and touch Suleiman's face, aware that the sands of time were running out for them. If she could have just one wish, it would be to run her fingers through the thick ebony of his hair and then to kiss him. But nothing more. She'd changed her mind about that. She suspected that to have sex with him would rob her of all the strength she possessed, and leave her yearning for him for the rest of her life. Perhaps it was best all round that making love was an option which was no longer open to her. But oh, to be able to kiss him…

Would it be so very wrong to bid him goodnight, as she had done to male friends in England countless times before?

On impulse, she rose on tiptoe and brushed her lips over first one of his cheeks, and then the other. It could not have been misinterpreted by anyone. Even the Sultan—if he had been standing there—would have recognised it as a very unthreatening form of western greeting, or farewell. He might not have liked it, but he would have understood it.

Except that this time, that quick brush of her lips was threatening her very sanity. She could feel the hammering of her heart and the hot flush of colour to her face. She could feel the whisper of her breath on his cheeks as she kissed each one in turn. And she could hear, too, the startled intake of breath he took in response. It should have been innocent and yet it felt light years from innocence. How could that be? How could one innocuous touch feel so powerful that it seemed to have rocked her to the core of her being?

Their eyes met and clashed in the indigo light as silent messages of desire and need passed between them. Her skin screamed out for him to touch it. The thrum of sexual tension was now so loud that it almost deafened her.

Slowly, his gaze travelled from her face, all the way down her lavishly embroidered gown, until it lingered at last on the swell of her bodice. The sensation of him looking so openly at her breasts was so *exciting*. It was making her nipples prickle with hunger and frustration. She sucked in an unsteady breath which made her chest rise and fall, and she heard him utter a soft groan.

For a moment he seemed about to move towards her and she prayed that he would. Kiss me, she prayed silently. Just kiss me one more time and I will never ask again.

But the suggestion of movement was arrested as quickly as it had begun for suddenly he stiffened, his face hardening into a granite-like mask. His eyes dead-

ened into dull ebony and when he spoke, his voice was
ragged and tinged with self-disgust.

'Get to bed, Sara,' he bit out harshly. 'For God's
sake, just get to bed.'

CHAPTER FIVE

SARA AWOKE EARLY. Before even the early light they called the 'false dawn' had begun to brighten the arid desert landscape outside her tent. She lay there in the silence for a moment or two, collecting her thoughts and wondering whether she had the nerve to go through with her plan. But then she thought about reality. About needing to get away from Suleiman just as badly as she needed to get away from her forced marriage to the Sultan.

She had no choice.

She *had* to escape.

Silently, she slipped from beneath the covers of her bedding, still wearing the clothes she had slept in all night. Just before dismissing the servant last evening, she had asked one of them to bring her a large water-bottle as well as a tray of mint tea and a bowl of sugar cubes. The girl had looked a little surprised but had done as requested—no doubt putting Sara's odd request down to the vagaries of being a princess.

Now she wrapped a soft, silken veil around her head before peeping out from behind the flaps of the tent, and her heart lifted with relief. All was quiet. Not a soul around. She glanced upwards at the sky. It looked clear enough. Soon it would be properly light and with light came danger. The animals would grow restless and all the bodyguards would waken. She cocked her head as she heard a faint but unmistakable noise. Did that mean one of the guards was already awake? Her heart began to pound. She must be off, with not a second more to be wasted.

Stealthily, she moved across the sand to where the horses were tethered. The Akhal-Teke palomino she had been riding earlier greeted her with a soft whinny and she shushed him by feeding him a sugar cube, which he crunched eagerly with his big teeth. Her heart was thumping as she mounted him and then urged him forward on a walk going with the direction of the wind, not giving him his head and letting him gallop until they were well out of earshot of the campsite.

Her first feelings were of exhilaration and delight that she had got away without being seen. That she had escaped the dark-eyed scrutiny of Suleiman and had not implicated him in her flight. The pale sky was becoming bluer by the second and the sand was a pleasing shade of deep gold. Suddenly, this felt like an adventure and her life in London seemed a long way away.

She made good progress before the sun grew too high, when she stopped beside a rock to relieve herself and then to drink sparingly from her water bottle. When she remounted her horse it was noticeably hotter and she was glad of the veil which shielded her head from the increasingly strong rays. And at least the camel trail was easy enough to follow back towards the airbase. The tread of the heavy beasts was deep and there had been none of the threatened sandstorms overnight to sweep away the evidence of their route.

Did she stop paying attention?

Did her ever-present thoughts of Suleiman distract her for long enough to make her stray from the deep line of animal footprints she'd been following so intently?

Was that why one minute she seemed so secure in her direction, while the next...?

Blinking, Sara looked around like someone who had just awoken from a dream, telling herself that the trail was still there if she looked for it and she had probably just wandered a little way from it.

It took only a couple of minutes for her to realise that her self-reassurance was about as real as a mirage.

Because there was nothing. Nothing to be seen.

She blinked again. No indentations. No little telltale heaps where a frisky camel might have kicked out at the sand.

Panic rose in her throat like bile but she fought to keep it at bay. Because panicking would not help. Most emphatically it would not. It would make her start to lose her nerve and she couldn't afford to lose anything else—losing her way was bad enough.

She didn't even have a compass with her.

She dismounted from her horse, trying to remember the laws of survival as she took a thirsty gulp of water from her bottle. She should retrace her steps. That was what she should do. Find where she'd lost the path and then pick up the camel trail again. Bending, she lifted a small pebble out of the sand. Sucking it would remind her to keep her mouth closed and prevent it from drying out.

She patted the horse before swinging lightly into the saddle again. It was going to be all right, she told herself. Of course it was going to be all right. It had only been a couple of minutes since she'd missed the path and she couldn't possibly be lost.

It took her about an hour of fruitless riding to accept that she was.

'What do you mean, she's not there?'

His voice distorted with anger, Suleiman stared at the bent head of the female servant who stood trembling before him.

'Tell me!' he raged.

The girl began to babble. They had thought that the princess was sleeping late, so they did not wish to disturb her.

'So you left the princess's tent until now?'

'Y-yes, sir.'

Suleiman forced himself to suck in a deep breath, only just managing to keep his hot rage from erupting as he surveyed the bodyguards who were milling around nervously. 'And not one of you thought to wonder why one of the horses was missing?' he demanded.

But their shamefaced excuses were quelled with a furious wave of his hand as Suleiman marched over to the horses, with the most senior bodyguard close behind him. Because deep down he knew that he was not really in any position to criticise—not when he was as culpable as they.

Why hadn't *he* been watching her?

His mouth hardened as he swung himself up onto the biggest and most powerful stallion.

Because he was a coward, that was why.

Despite his supposedly exemplary military record and all the awards which had been heaped upon him— he had selected a tent as far away from hers as possible. Too unsure of his reaction to her proximity, he had not dared risk being close. Not trusting himself—and not trusting her either.

He hadn't imagined the white-hot feeling of lust which had flared between them last night and he was too experienced a lover to mistake the look of sexual yearning which had darkened her violet eyes. When she was standing in front of him in her embroidered robes—her hair woven with fragrant leaves—he had never wanted her quite so much.

Hadn't he wondered whether her western sensibilities might make her take the initiative? Hadn't he wondered whether she might boldly arrive naked at his tent under cover of darkness and slip into his bed without invitation, as so many women had done before?

He stared down at the senior bodyguard. 'You have checked her trail?'

'Yes, boss. She has headed due north—taking the same path by which we came, back towards the airbase.'

Suleiman nodded. It was as he had thought. She was trying to get back to England on her own—oh, most stubborn and impetuous of women! 'Very well,' he said. 'I will follow her trail. And you will assign three men to take up the other three points of the compass and to set off immediately. But no more than three. I don't want the desert paths disturbed any more than they need be. I don't want any clues churned up by the damned horses.'

'Yes, boss.'

'You will also send someone to find a high enough vantage point to try to get a mobile phone signal. I want the military base informed and I want every damned plane at their disposal out looking for her. Understand?'

The bodyguard nodded. 'Understood.'

'And believe me when I tell you that you have not heard the last of this!'

With his final, angry words ringing Suleiman galloped off at a furious pace, the warm wind streaming against his face as he followed the mixed track of the camels and the newer footprints of Sara's horse.

He had already realised that there would be repercussions. By involving the military, word would inevitably get back to the Sultan that the princess was missing. But he didn't care what criticism or punishment came his way for having lost the future Sultana of Qurhah. They could exile him or imprison him and he wouldn't care.

He didn't care about anything other than finding her safe and well.

He had never known such raw fear as he travelled beneath the heat of a sun which was growing ever more blistering. Even though she was out of practice, he knew that she was a sound horsewoman—a fact which had always been a source of pride since he had been the one to tutor her, but which now gave him only comfort. And he found himself clinging to that one small comfort. Please let her ride safely, he prayed. Please not let something have frightened the horse so that Sara might be lying there buckled and broken on the sand. Alone and scared while the sun beat down on her and the vultures waited to peck out her beautiful violet eyes...

He sucked in a breath of hot air which felt raw as it travelled down his throat. He should not think the worst. He would not think the worst. Think positive, he told himself. At least no snake or brown scorpion could touch her when she was high up on her horse.

But knowing that did not help him locate her, did it? Where was she? Where *was* she?

His eyes trained unblinkingly on the ground before him—he saw the exact point where her path had veered off from the main route. Had something distracted the horse? Distracted her?

He pushed forward now, letting the powerful stallion stream across the sands until Suleiman urged it to a halt and then opened his mouth to call across the desolate landscape.

'Sara! Sa-ra!'

But the ensuing response was nothing but an empty silence and his heart gave a painful lurch.

He forced himself to take a drink from one of the water-bottles he carried, for dehydration would be good for neither of them if he found her.

When he found her.

He had to find her.

The position of the sun and his wristwatch told him that he had been searching for her for over four hours. He could feel his heart pumping painfully in his chest. The heat of the midday sun was a tough enough combatant but darkness was a whole different ball-game.

He thought of the nocturnal creatures which came out in the cold of the desert night—dangerous animals which populated this inhospitable terrain.

'Sara!' he called again and then the horse's ears pricked up and Suleiman strained to hear a sound that was almost lost in the distance. He listened again.

It *was* a sound. The smallest sound in the world. The sound of a voice. If it had been anyone else's voice, he might not have recognised it—but Suleiman had heard Sara's voice in many guises. He'd heard it as a child. He'd heard its hesitancy in puberty and its breathlessness in passion. But he had never heard it sound quite so broken nor so lost as it did right now.

'Sara!' he yelled, the word spilling from his lips as if it had been ripped from the very base of his lungs.

And then the shout again. Due east a little. He pressed his thighs against the flanks of the horse and urged it forward in a gallop in the direction of the sound. He heard nothing more and as the silence grew, so too did his fear that he had simply imagined it. An aural version of a desert mirage…

Until he saw the shape of a rock up ahead. A dark red rock which soared up revealing a dark cool cave underneath against which gleamed the metallic golden sheen of an Akhal-Teke palomino. He narrowed his eyes, for the horse carried no rider, and he galloped forward to see Sara leaning back against the rock. Its shadow consumed her with its terracotta light but he could see that her face was white with fear and her eyes looked like two deep pools of violet ink.

Grabbing a water-bottle, he jumped from the horse's back and was beside her in a moment. He held the vessel to her lips and she sucked on it greedily, like a small animal being bottle-fed. He put the bottle down and as he watched the colour and the strength return to her all his own fear and anger bubbled up inside him.

'What the hell did you think you were doing?' he demanded, levering her up against him so that her face was inches away from his.

'Isn't it obvious?' Her voice sounded weak. 'I was trying to get away.'

'You could have died!'

'I'm not…I'm not that easy to get rid of,' she said, her lips trying for a smile but he noticed she didn't quite achieve it—though nothing could disguise the flash of relief which flared briefly in her eyes.

'Where were you headed for?' he demanded, watching as he saw her face assume a look of sudden wariness.

She looked at him from the shuttered forest of her lashes. 'Where do you think? Back to the airport.'

'To the military base?'

'Yes, to the military base. To demand to be taken back to England. I…I came to my senses, Suleiman. I realised that I couldn't go through with it after all—

no matter what you or the Sultan threatened me with, I don't care. I don't care about political dynasties or forging an alliance between my country and his. My brother will have to find someone else to offer up as a human sacrifice.'

Furiously, he stood up and pulled out his mobile phone and started barking into it in Qurhahian. Sara could hear him telling the military that the search should be called off. That the princess had been found and she was safely in his charge.

But when he terminated the call the look on his face didn't make Sara feel in the least bit safe. In fact, it made her feel the opposite of safe. His black eyes were filled with fury as he slowly advanced towards her again.

'So let me get this straight,' he said, and she could tell that he was only just holding onto his temper. 'You took off on your own into one of the most hostile territories in the world—even though you have not ridden for years and have been living a pampered life in London—is that right?'

Her gaze was defiant as she met the accusation in his eyes.

'Yes,' she said fiercely. 'That's exactly right.'

The absurdity of her quest infuriated him. He thought about the danger she'd put herself in and he felt the clench of anger—and fear too, at the thought of what could have happened to her. He intended to give her a piece of his mind. To tell her that he felt like putting her across his knee and smacking her. At least, that was what he thought he intended. But somehow it didn't work out like that.

Maybe it was the sight of all that tousled blonde hair, or the violet glitter of her beautiful eyes. Maybe it was because he'd always wanted her and had never stopped wanting her. His desire for her had been like an endless hunger which had eaten him up from the inside out and suddenly there was no controlling it any longer.

He made one last attempt to fight it but his resistance was gone. He'd never felt so powerless in his life as he stared down into her beautiful face and caught hold of her by the shoulders again. Only this time he was pulling her towards him.

'Damn you, Sara,' he whispered. 'Just *damn you.*'

And that was when he started to kiss her.

CHAPTER SIX

SARA GASPED AS Suleiman's mouth drove down on hers. She told herself that this was crazy. That it was only going to lead to heartbreak and tears. She told herself that if she tore herself out of his embrace, then he would let her go. But her body was refusing to listen.

Her body was on fire.

His mouth explored hers and it felt like a dream. Or some hot, X-rated mirage. It surpassed every hope she'd nurtured during these desperate last few hours. Long, grim hours, as she'd realised the full extent of her plight—that she was hopelessly lost in the unforgiving desert. Until the stern-faced emissary had appeared on the empty horizon, astride a gleaming black stallion like her greatest fantasy come true.

And then he had taken the fantasy and given it a sexy embellishment, by pulling her into his arms and giving her this hard and seeking kiss.

Yet this was dangerous, wasn't it? Dangerous for her heart. Dangerous for her soul. She couldn't afford to love this man, no matter how much she wanted him.

She meant to push him away but he pulled her

closer, so that she could smell his raw, male smell. He smelt of sandalwood and salt. The hard sinews of his body were pressed against hers and the proximity of his tight, taut flesh made her want to melt into him. His lips were hard and soft in turn as they kissed her. One minute they were cajoling, the next they were masterfully stating their intent to make love to her.

'Suleiman.' It didn't come out like the protest she intended it to be—it sounded more like a plea.

'Sara,' he said, drawing his mouth away from hers and cupping her face with both his hands. 'Foolish, beautiful, hot-headed Sara.' His gaze raked over her with a mixture of exasperation and lust. 'Why the hell did you take off like that? Why take such a risk?'

'You know why,' she whispered, moving her head fractionally as she sought out another kiss. 'Because I wanted to escape.'

He brushed his lips over hers. Back and forth in a teasing graze. 'Do you still want to escape?'

She nodded her head. 'Yes.'

'Do you?'

She closed her eyes. 'Stop it.'

'I'm waiting for an answer to my question.'

She shook her head. 'N-not any more. At least, not right now. Not if you keep on kissing me like that.'

'That sounds very much like an invitation.' He gave another groan as their mouths meshed together and his breath was warm in her mouth. 'I should put you straight back on that horse and ride you back into camp.'

'Then why are you unbuttoning my tunic?'

'Because I want to taste your nipples.'

'*Oh.*'

She tipped her head back as his lips trailed a fiery path over her neck, closing her eyes as sensation washed over her. His fingers felt hard and calloused against her delicate flesh. She could feel the slick, wet heat of her sex overwhelming her as he lowered his mouth to trail his tongue over one hardened nipple.

Her mouth grew dry as her lashes fluttered open to watch him. He kissed each breast in turn and then turned his attention to her tunic, peeling it off entirely—along with her slim-fitting trousers. He freed her aching body so that at last her skin was bared to the warm desert air. And to his eyes.

She heard him suck in a ragged breath as he looked down at her and she was glad she was wearing the provocative underwear she'd brought from England. The balcony bra in electric-blue lace and matching thong were both pretty racy, but she'd discovered a while back that she liked wearing expensive lingerie. It had been another aspect of the freedom she'd relished—that she could go into any department store and stock up on X-rated undies and nobody was going to tell her she couldn't.

He said something she couldn't quite make out and the expression in his slitted eyes was suddenly forbidding.

'Is something wrong?' she questioned tentatively.

'Who buys your lingerie for you?' His voice was dark with some unnamed emotion.

'I do.'

'But you buy it for you? Or do you buy it for the men who will enjoy watching you wearing it?' he persisted, slithering his finger inside her thong where she was so wet and so sensitive that she bucked beneath his touch and gave a little cry. His finger stilled. 'Do you?'

Sara nodded, so strung out with pleasure that she barely knew what she was agreeing to. But men liked women to indulge in fantasy, didn't they? She'd read enough erotic literature to know that. Men liked you to pretend to *be* things and to do things. She read that normality was the killer in the bedroom.

Not that they were anywhere near a bedroom, of course—but who cared about that? Why not feed into his fantasies—and her own? Why shouldn't she make love with Suleiman in the wild desert which had spawned her, on this shaded patch of sand? She might not like all the restrictions of life here, but she was sensitive enough to appreciate its beauty. And if Suleiman wanted her to play the femme fatale, then play it she would.

'I'm enjoying wearing it for you,' she answered coyly, her finger moving to trace the curving satin trim of her bra. 'Do you like it?'

He made a sound mid-way between hunger and anger as he pulled off his crimson robes with impatient disregard, until he was also naked. She let her gaze drift over him, her eyes widening as her gaze locked onto the most intimate part of his aroused body—and suddenly she was a little daunted by what she saw.

'Suleiman…' she whispered, but her words faded because he was back in her arms and was touching her again. Moving his hand intimately against her sex and stroking her with pinpoint accuracy. She could smell the scent of her arousal on the air. She could feel the warm rush of blood flooding through her veins. And shouldn't she be touching *him*? She reached down to whisper her fingertips against his silken length, but he stilled her movement by the abrupt clamp of his hand around her wrist.

'No,' he said.

She looked into his eyes, confused. 'Why not?'

'Because I'm too close to coming, that's why. And I want to come when I'm inside you. I want to watch your face as I enter and hear the sounds you make when I move inside you.'

It was the most erotic thing she'd ever heard. Sara swallowed. Suleiman deep inside the one place where she had always longed for him to be. She could feel her skin burning as he spread his robes down on the shaded sand, like a silken blanket for them to lie on. His face was dark and taut as he peeled off her electric-blue underwear, until she lay before him like a naked sacrifice.

She could see the hardness of his erection and the dark whorls of hair from which it sprang. His olive skin gleamed softly in the terracotta light and his dark eyes were as black as tar as he reached for her, bending his lips to hers. The kiss which followed made her gasp with pleasure. It seemed to unlock something deep within her, but when he lifted his head she could see that his eyes were dark with pain.

'My greatest fantasy and my greatest sin,' he said, his voice shaking. 'And it is wrong. We both know that.'

Suddenly Sara was terrified he was going to stop. That she would never know what it was like to have Suleiman Abd al-Aziz make love to her. And she couldn't bear it. She thought she could pretty much bear anything else, but not that. Not now.

Her hand reached up to touch the blackness of his hair, letting her fingers slide beneath the silken strands. 'How can it possibly be wrong, when it feels so right?'

'Don't ask disingenuous questions, Sara. And don't look at me with those big violet eyes, a colour which I've never seen on any woman other than you. Just stop me from doing this. Stop me before it goes any further because I don't have the strength to stop myself.'

'I *can't*,' she whispered. 'Because I…' She nearly said *I love you*, but just in time she bit back the words. 'Because I've wanted this for so long. We both want it. You know that. Please, Suleiman. Make love to me.'

He tilted up her chin and gazed down at her. 'Oh, Sara,' he said, saying her name like an unwilling surrender.

He entered her slowly. So slowly that she thought she would die with the pleasure. She cried out as he made that first thrust—a cry which was disbelieving and exultant.

Suleiman was inside her.

Suleiman was filling her.

Suleiman was…

He groaned as he found his rhythm, moving deeper with each stroke. And Sara suddenly felt as if she had been born for this moment. She wrapped her legs around his back as he splayed his hands over her bare buttocks to drive even deeper. Her breath was coming in shuddered little gasps as he moved inside her. She'd had sex before, but never like this. *Never like this.* It was like everyone said it should be. It was...

And then she stopped thinking. Stopped everything except listening to the demands of her body and letting the pleasure pile on, layer by sensual layer.

She felt it build—desperately sweet, yet tantalisingly elusive. She felt the warmth flood through her as Suleiman's movements became more urgent and she was so locked into his passionate kiss that the first spasms of her orgasm took her almost by surprise. Like a feather which had been lifted by a storm and then tossed around by it, she just went with the flow. She cried out his name as his own body suddenly tensed, and he shuddered violently as he came.

But it was over all too quickly. Abruptly, he pulled out of her—so that all she was aware of was a warmth spurting over her belly. He had *withdrawn* from her! It took a couple of disconcerting moments before she felt together enough to open her eyes and to look at him and when she did she felt almost *embarrassed.* As if the sudden ending had wiped out the magic of what had gone before.

'Why...why did you do that?'

His voice was flat. 'I realised that in our haste to consummate our lust, we hadn't even discussed contraception.'

Sara did her best not to flinch, but it seemed a particularly emotionless thing to say in view of what had just happened. Consummate their *lust*? Was that it? 'I suppose we didn't.'

'Are you on the pill?'

She shook her head. 'No.'

'So we add a baby into the equation and make the situation a million times worse than it already is,' he said bitterly. 'Is that what you wanted?'

She flushed, knowing he was right—and wasn't it the most appalling thing that she found herself wishing that he *had* made her pregnant? How weird was it that some primitive part of her was wishing that Suleiman had planted his seed inside her belly. So that now there would be a baby growing beneath her heart. *His* baby. 'No, of course it wasn't what I wanted.' She met his eyes. 'Why are you being like this?'

'Like what?'

'So...*cold*.'

'Why do you think? Because I've just betrayed the man who saved my life. Because I've behaved like the worst kind of friend.' His gaze swept over her and somehow she knew what he was going to say, almost before the words had left his lips. 'And you weren't even a virgin.'

It was the 'even' which made it worse. As if she'd been nothing but a poor consolation prize. 'Were you expecting me to be?'

'Yes,' he bit out. 'Of course I was!'

'I'm twenty-three years old, Suleiman. I've been living an independent life in London. What did you expect?'

'But you were brought up as a desert princess! To respect your body and cherish your maidenhood. To save your purity for your bridegroom. Your royal bridegroom.' He shook his head. 'Oh, I know you spoke freely of sex and that beneath your clothes you were wearing the kind of lingerie which only a truly liberated woman would wear. But even though I had my suspicions, deep down I thought you remained untouched!'

'Even though you had your suspicions?' she repeated, in disbelief. 'What are you now—some sort of detective?'

'You are destined to be a royal bride,' he flared back. 'And your virginity was an essential part of that agreement. Or at least, that's what I thought.'

'No, Suleiman, that's where you're wrong.' Sitting up, she angrily brushed a heavy spill of hair away from her flushed face. 'You don't think—you just *react*. You don't see me as an individual with my own unique history. You didn't stop to think that I might have desires and needs of my own, just as you do—and presumably just as Murat does. You simply see me as a stereotype. You see what I am *supposed* to be and what I am *supposed* to stand for. The virgin princess who has been bought for the Sultan. Only I am not that person and I will never be!'

'And didn't it occur to you to have made some attempt to communicate your thoughts with the Sultan, *before* he was forced to take matters into his own hand?' Suleiman demanded. 'Didn't it occur to you that running away just wasn't the answer? But you've spent your whole life running away, haven't you, Sara?'

'And you've spent your whole life denying your feelings!'

'I have never denied that!' he flared back. 'It's a pity that more people don't stop neurotically asking themselves whether or not they are "happy"—and just get out there and *do* something instead!'

'Like you've just done, you mean?' she challenged. 'What, did you think to yourself? "Now, how can I punish the princess for running off? I know—I'll seduce her!"'

For a moment there was nothing other than the sound of them struggling to control their breathing and Suleiman felt the cold coil of anger twisting at his gut as he looked at her.

He swallowed but the action did little to ease the burning sensation which scorched his throat. The acrid taste of guilt couldn't be washed away so easily, he thought bitterly.

He had just seduced the woman who was to marry the Sultan.

He had just committed the ultimate betrayal against his sovereign—and wasn't treason punishable by death?

Had she used him to facilitate her escape? Had she? Had this been a trap into which he had all-too-willingly fallen?

'How many men have you had?' he demanded suddenly.

She stared at him in disbelief. 'Have you heard a

word I've just been saying? How many women have *you* had?'

'That's irrelevant!' he snapped. 'So I shall ask you again, Sara—and this time I want an answer. How many?'

'Oh, hundreds,' she retorted, but the expression on his face made her backtrack and even though she despised herself for wanting to salvage her reputation—it didn't stop her from doing it. 'If you must know—I've had one experience before you. One—and it was awful. An ill-judged foray into the sexual arena with a man I'd convinced myself could mean something to me, but I was wrong.' Just as she'd been wrong about so many things at the time.

'Who was he?'

'You think I'm crazy enough to tell you his name?' She shook her head, not wanting to reveal any more than she had to. She didn't want Suleiman to know that at the time she'd been on a mission—trying to convince herself that there were men other than him. That she'd wanted another man to make her feel the way he did. But she had been hoping in vain because no man had even come close. He affected her in a way she had no control over. Even now, with this terrible atmosphere which had descended upon them, he was still making her *feel* stuff, wasn't he? He still made her feel totally *alive* whenever she was near him.

'I was experimenting,' she said. 'Trying to experience the same things as other women my age, but it didn't work.'

'So you conveniently forgot about your planned marriage?'

'You didn't seem to have much difficulty forgetting it, did you? And surely that's the most glaring hypocrisy of all. It wasn't just me who broke the rules. It took two of us to make love just now, and you were one very willing partner. I'm wondering how that registers on your particular scale of loyalty?'

Something in the atmosphere shifted and changed and his face tightened as he nodded.

'You are right, of course. Thank you for reminding me that my own behaviour certainly doesn't give me the right to censure yours. But before we go, just answer me one thing. Did you set out to seduce me, knowing that having sex with me would put an end to your betrothal?'

She hesitated, but only for a moment. 'No,' she said and then, because it felt like a heavy burden, she told him the truth. 'I planned to do something like that, but in the end I couldn't go through with it.'

'Why not?'

She shrugged and suddenly the threat of tears seemed very real as she thought of the boy who had been sold by his mother. 'Because of what you told me about how you and Murat met. How he'd saved your life and how close you'd been when you were growing up. I realised what a big deal your friendship was and how much it meant to you. That's why I ran away.'

'Only I came after you,' he said slowly. 'And seduced you anyway.'

'Yes.' She kept swallowing—the way they told you

to do in aircraft, to stop your ears from popping. But this was to stop the welling tears from falling down over her face. Because tears wouldn't help anyone, would they? They made a woman look weak and a man take control. And she wasn't going to be that woman. 'Yes, you did.'

'I appreciate your honesty,' he said. 'And at least you've concentrated my mind on what needs to happen next.'

She heard the finality in his tone and guessed what was coming next. 'You mean you'll take me to the airfield?'

'So that you can run away again? I don't think so. Isn't it time that you stopped running and faced up to the consequences of your actions? Maybe it's time we both did.' He gave a grim smile and stood up, magnificent and unashamed in his nakedness. 'My brief was to deliver you to the Sultan and that's exactly what I'm going to do.'

She stared at him in bewilderment and then in fear as his body blocked out the fierce light of the sun. All she could see was the powerful shape of his silhouette and suddenly he seemed more than a little intimidating. 'You're still planning to take me to the Sultan?'

'I am.'

'You can't do that.'

'Just watch me.'

She licked her lips. 'He'll kill me.'

'He'll have to kill me first. Don't be absurd, Sara.' He flicked her a glance. 'And don't move. At least, not yet.'

She didn't know what he meant until he walked over to his horse and took a bottle from his saddle-bag, dousing his headdress with a generous slug of water before coming back to her. His face was grave as he crouched down to wipe her belly clean and Sara felt her cheeks flame, because the peculiar intimacy of having Suleiman removing his dried seed from her skin was curiously poignant.

'Removing all traces of yourself?' she questioned.

'You think it's that easy? I wish.' His bitter tone matched hers and she could see the angry gleam of his eyes. 'Now get dressed, Sara—and we will ride together to the palace.'

CHAPTER SEVEN

THE SUN WAS low in the sky when Sara and Suleiman brought their horses to a dusty halt outside the gates of the Sultan's summer residence. Before them, the vast palace towered majestically—its golden hues reflecting the endless desert sands which surrounded it. It was the first time Sara had ever seen the fabled building, and on any other occasion she might have taken time to admire the magnificent architecture with all its soaring turrets and domes. But today her heart was full of dread as she thought of what lay ahead.

What on earth was she going to say to the man she had now spurned in the most dramatic way possible? She had never loved the Sultan, nor wanted him—but never in a million years had she wanted it to turn out this way. She didn't want to hurt him, or—which was much more likely—hurt his pride.

Would he want to punish her? Punish her brother and his kingdom?

The reality began to soak into her skin, which was still glowing after her passionate encounter with the man who had ridden by her side. No matter what happened next—she wasn't going to regret what had just taken place. It might have been wrong, but the words she had whispered to Suleiman just before he had thrust into her had been true. It had felt so right.

She shot a glance at him as he brought his horse to a halt but his stony profile gave nothing away and she suspected that his body language was deliberately forbidding. He hadn't spoken a word to her since that uncomfortable showdown after they'd made love. He had kept busy with the practicalities of preparing to return. And then he had turned on her and hissed that she was nothing but a temptation, silencing her protests with an angry wave of his hand before phoning ahead to let the Sultan's staff know that they were on their way.

Sara looked up at the wide blue bowl of the desert sky as another band of fear gripped her. If ever she had thought she'd felt trapped before—she was quickly discovering a whole new meaning to the word. Here was one hostile man taking her to confront another—and she had no idea of what the outcome would be.

Her instinct was to turn and head in the opposite direction—but during the ride she had thought about what Suleiman had said.

You've spent your whole life running away?

Had she? It was weird seeing yourself through somebody else's eyes. She'd always thought that she was an intrepid sort of person. That she had shown true backbone by setting up on her own in London, far away from her pampered life. It was disturbing to think that maybe there was a kernel of truth in Suleiman's accusation.

Their approach had obviously been observed from

within the palace complex, for the tall gates silently opened and they walked their horses through onto the gravelled forecourt. Sara became aware of the massed blooms of white flowers and their powerful scent which pervaded the air. A white-robed servant came towards them, briefly bowing to her before turning to Suleiman and speaking to him in Qurhahian.

'The Sultan wishes to extend his warmest greeting, Suleiman Abd al-Aziz. He has instructed me to tell you that your chambers are fully prepared—and that you will both rest and recuperate before joining him for dinner later.'

'No.'

Suleiman's denial rang out so emphatically that Sara was startled, for she knew that the language of the desert was couched in much more formal—sometimes flowery—tones. She saw the look of surprise on the servant's face.

'The princess may wish to avail herself of the Sultan's hospitality,' said Suleiman. 'But it is imperative that I speak to His Imperial Majesty without further delay. Please take me to him now.'

Sara could see the servant's confusion but such was the force of Suleiman's personality that the man merely nodded in bewildered consent. He led them through the huge carved doors, speaking rapidly into an incongruously modern walkie-talkie handset which he pulled from his white robes.

Once inside, where several female servants had gathered together in a small group, Suleiman turned to her, his features shadowed and unreadable. 'You

will go with these women and they will bathe you,'
he instructed.

'But—'

'No buts, Sara. I mean it. This is my territory, not
yours. Let me deal with it.'

Sara opened her mouth, then shut it again as she
felt a wave of relief wash over her. Was it cowardly of
her to want to lean on Suleiman and him to take over?
'Thank you,' she said.

'For what?' he questioned in English, his sudden
switch of language seeming to emphasise the bitterness of his tone. 'For taking what was never mine to
take? Just go. *Go.*'

He stood perfectly still as she turned away, watching her retreat across the wide, marble entrance hall—
his feelings in turmoil; his heart sick with dread. He
found himself taking in the unruliness of her hair and
the crumpled disorder of her robes. He swallowed. If
the Sultan had seen her flushed face, then mightn't he
guess the cause of her untidy appearance?

He turned to follow the servant, his heart heavy.

*How was he going to be able to tell Murat? How
could he possibly admit what had been done? The
worst betrayal in the world, from the two people who
should have been most loyal to the sovereign.*

He was ushered into one of the informal ante-rooms
which he recognised from times past. He lifted his
gaze to the high, arched ceiling with its intricate mosaic, before the Sultan swept in, alone—his black eyes
inscrutable as he subjected his erstwhile emissary to
a long, hard look.

'So, Suleiman,' he said. 'This is indeed an unconventional meeting. I was disturbed from playing backgammon at a crucial point in the game, to be told that you wished to see me immediately. Is this true?'

His eyes were questioning and Suleiman felt a terrible wave of sadness wash over him. Once their relationship had been so close that he might have made a joke about his supposed insubordination. And the Sultan would have laughed softly and made a retort in the same vein. But this was no laughing matter.

'Yes, it's true,' he said heavily.

'And may I ask what has provoked this extraordinary break with protocol?'

Suleiman swallowed. 'I have come to tell you that the Princess Sara will not marry you,' he said.

For a moment, the Sultan did not reply. His hawk-like features gave nothing away. 'And should not the princess have told me this herself?' he questioned softly.

Suleiman felt his heart clench as he realised that years of loyalty and friendship now lay threatened by his one stupid act of disloyalty and lust. He had accused Sara of being headstrong—but was not his own behaviour equally reprehensible?

'Sire, I must tell you that I have—'

'No!' The word cracked from Murat's mouth like the sound of a whip and he held up his palm for silence. 'Hold your tongue, Suleiman. If you tell me something I should not hear, then I will have no option than to have you tried for treason.'

'Then so be it!' declared Suleiman, his heart pounding like a piston. 'If that is to be my fate, then I will accept it like a man.'

The Sultan's mouth hardened but he shook his head. 'You think I would do that? You think that a woman—*any woman*—is worth destroying a rare friendship between two men? One which has endured the test of time and all the challenges of hierarchy?'

'I will accept whatever punishment you see fit to bestow on me.'

'You want to slug it out? Is that it?'

Suleiman stared at Murat and, for a moment, the years melted away. Suddenly they were no longer two powerful men with all the burdens and responsibilities which had come with age, but two eight-year-old boys squaring up to each other in the baked dust of the palace stables. It had been soon after Suleiman had been brought from Samahan and he had punched the young Sultan at the height of an argument which had long since been forgotten.

He remembered seeing the shock on Murat's face. The realisation that here was someone who was prepared to take him on. Even to beat him. Murat had waved away the angry courtiers. But he had gone away and taken boxing lessons and, two weeks later, had fought again and soundly beaten Suleiman. After that, the fight victory rate had been spread out evenly.

Suleiman found himself wondering which of them would win, if they fought now. 'No, I don't want to fight you, Sire,' he said. 'But I am concerned about the fall-out, if this scheduled marriage doesn't go ahead.'

'As well you should be concerned!' said Murat

furiously. 'For you know as well as I do that the union was intended as an alliance between the two countries.'

Suleiman nodded. 'Couldn't an alternative solution be offered instead? A new peace agreement drawn up between Qurhah and Dhi'ban—which could finally banish all the years of unrest. After all, a diplomatic solution is surely more modern and appropriate than an old-fashioned dynastic marriage.'

Murat gave a soft laugh. 'Oh, how I miss your skills of diplomacy, Suleiman. As well as your unerring ability to pick out the most beautiful women on our foreign tours.' He gave a reminiscent sigh. 'Some pretty unforgettable women, as I recall.'

But Suleiman's head was too full of concern to be distracted by memories of the sexual shenanigans of the past. 'Is this a feasible plan, do you think, Sire?'

Murat shrugged. 'It's feasible. It's going to take a lot of backroom work and manoeuvring. But it's doable, yes.'

The two men stared at one another and Suleiman clenched his teeth. 'Now give me my punishment,' he ground out.

There was a brief silence. 'Oh, that's easy. My punishment is for you to take her,' said Murat silkily. 'Take her away with you and do what you will with her. Because I know you—and I know how your mind operates. Countless times I have watched as you grow bored with the inevitable clinginess of the female of the species. She will drive you mad within the month, Suleiman—that much I can guarantee.'

Murat's words were still ringing in Suleiman's ears

as he waited in the sunlit palace courtyard for Sara to
emerge from her ablutions. And when she did, with her
blonde hair still damp and tightly plaited, he could not
prevent the instinctive kick of lust which was quickly
followed by the equally potent feeling of regret.

Her face was pale and her eyes dark with anxiety as
she looked up at him. 'What did he say?'

'He accepts the situation. The wedding is off.'

'Just like that?'

Suleiman's mouth hardened. What would she say
if he told her the truth? That Murat had spoken of her
as if she'd been a poisoned chalice he was passing to
his former aide. That his punishment was to have her,
not to lose her.

He suspected she would never speak to him again.
And he wasn't prepared for that to happen.

Not yet.

'He has agreed to make way for a diplomatic solution instead.'

'He has?' Her eyes were filled with confusion as
if she found something about his reaction difficult to
understand. 'But that's good, isn't it?'

'It is an acceptable compromise, considering the
circumstances,' said Suleiman, holding up a jangling
set of keys which sparked silver in the bright sunlight.
'Now let's go. We're leaving the horses here and taking one of the Sultan's cars.'

Sara tried to keep up with his long-legged stride
as she followed him into the courtyard, but it wasn't
until they were sitting in the blessed cool of the air-

conditioned car that she could pluck up enough courage to ask him.

'Where are we going?'

He didn't answer straight away. In fact, he didn't answer for a good while. Not until they had left the palace far behind them and all that surrounded them was sand and emptiness. Pulling over onto the side of the wide and deserted road, he unfastened his seat belt before leaning over and undoing hers.

'What…are you doing?' she asked.

'I want to kiss you.'

'Suleiman—'

His mouth was hard and hungry and she could feel his anger coming off him in waves. He slid towards her on the front seat of the luxury car, one hand capturing her breast, while the other began to ruck up the slithery silk of her dress. He stopped kissing her long enough to slide his hand up her bare thigh and stare down at her face.

'Suleiman,' she said again—as if saying his name would make some kind of sense of the situation. As if it would remind her that this was dangerous—in so many ways.

'All I can think of is you,' he said. 'All I want is to touch you again. You're driving me crazy.'

She swallowed as he edged his fingertip inside her panties. 'This isn't the answer.'

'Isn't it?'

He had reached her core now, touching her exquisitely aroused flesh so that the scent of her sex overrode the subtle perfume of the rose petals in which she'd bathed.

'No. It's…oh, Suleiman. That's not fair.'

'Who said anything about fairness?'

His finger brushed against the sensitive nub. 'Oh,' she breathed. And again. *'Oh.'*

'Still think this isn't the answer?'

She shook her head and Suleiman felt an undeniable burst of triumph as she fell back against the leather seat and spread her legs for him. But his mouth was grim as he rubbed his finger against her sex and all kinds of dark emotions stirred within him.

He distracted himself by watching her writhe with pleasure. He watched the flush of colour which spread over her skin like wildfire and felt the change in her body as her back began to arch. Her little cries became louder. Her legs stiffened as they stretched out in front of her and he saw a flash of something—was it anger or regret?—before her eyelids fluttered to a close and she cried out his name, even though he got the idea she was trying very hard not to.

Afterwards she smoothed down her tunic with trembling fingers and turned to him and there was a look on her face he'd never seen before. She looked satiated yes, but determined too—her eyes flashing violet fire as she lifted up his robes.

'Now what are you doing?' he questioned.

'You ask too many questions.'

She freed an erection which was so hard that it hurt—and sucked him until he came in her mouth almost immediately. And he had never felt so powerless in his life. Nor so turned on. Afterwards, he opened his eyes to look at her but she was staring straight ahead, her shoulders stiff with tension and her jaw set.

'Sara?' he questioned.

She turned her head and he was shocked by the pallor of her face, which made her eyes look like two glittering violet jewels. 'What?'

He picked up one of her hands, which was lying limply in her lap, and raised it to his lips and kissed it. 'You didn't enjoy that?'

She shrugged. 'On one level, yes, of course I did—as, I imagine, did you. But that wasn't about sex, was it, Suleiman? That seemed to be more about anger than anything else. I think I can understand why you're feeling it, but I don't particularly like it.'

'You were angry too,' he said softly.

She turned her head to look at the endless stretch of sand outside the window. 'I was feeling things other than anger,' she said.

'What things?'

'Oh, you know. Stupid things. Regret. Sadness. The realisation that nothing ever stays the same.' She turned back to him, telling herself to be strong. Telling herself that the friendship they'd shared so long ago had been broken by time and circumstance. And now by desire. And that made her want to bury her face in her hands and weep.

She forced a smile. 'So now we're done—are you going to take me to the airfield so I can go back to England?'

He reached his hand out to touch her face, sliding

his thumb against her parted lips so that they trembled. Leaning over, he hovered his lips over hers. *'Are we done?'*

Briefly, Sara closed her eyes. *Say yes,* she told herself. *It's the only sane solution. You've escaped the marriage and you know there's no future in this.* Her lashes fluttered open to stare straight into the obsidian gleam of his eyes. His mouth was still close enough for her to feel the warmth of his breath and she struggled against the temptation to kiss him.

Were they done?

In her heart, she thought they were.

She ought to go back to England and start again. She should go back to her job at Gabe's—if he would have her—and carry on as before. As if nothing had happened.

She bit her lip, because it wasn't that easy. Because something *had* happened and how could she go back to the way she'd been before? She felt different now because she *was* different. Inevitably. She had been freed from a marriage in which she'd had no say, but she was confused. Her future looked just as bewildering as before and it was all because of Suleiman.

She had tried burying memories of him, but that hadn't worked. And now that she'd made love with him, it had stirred up all the feelings she had repressed for so long. It had stirred up a sexual hunger which was eating away at her even now—minutes after he'd just brought her to orgasm in the front seat of the Sultan's car. It didn't matter what she *thought* she should do—

because, when push came to shove, she was putty in his hands. When Suleiman touched her, he set her on fire.

And maybe that was the answer. Maybe she just needed time to convince herself that his arrogance would be intolerable in the long term. If she tore herself away from him now—before she'd had her fill of him—wouldn't she be caught in the same old cycle of forever wanting him?

'Do you have a better suggestion?' she questioned.

'I do. A much better one.' He stroked his hand down over her plaited hair. 'We could take my plane and fly off somewhere.'

'Where?'

'Anywhere you like. As long as there's a degree of comfort. I'm done with desert sand and making out in the front seat, like a couple of teenagers. I want to take you to bed and stay there for a week.'

CHAPTER EIGHT

'So why Paris?' Sara questioned, her mouth full of croissant.

Suleiman leaned across the rumpled sheets and used the tip of his finger to rescue a stray fragment of pastry which had fallen onto her bare breast. He lifted the finger to his mouth and sucked on it, his dark eyes not leaving her face.

And Sara wanted to kiss him all over again. She wanted to fling her arms around him and press her body against him and close her eyes and have him colour her world wonderful. Because that was what it was like whenever he touched her.

'It's my favourite hotel,' he said. 'And there is a reason why it's known as the city of lovers. We can lie in bed all day and nobody bats an eyelid. We need never set foot outside the door if we don't want to.'

'Well, that's convenient,' said Sara drily. 'Because that's exactly what we've being doing. We've hardly seen any of the sights. In fact, we've been here for three days and I haven't even been up the Eiffel Tower.'

He kissed her nipple. 'And do you want to go up the Eiffel Tower?'

'Maybe.' Sara put her plate down and leant back against the snowy bank of pillows. That thing he was doing to her nipple with his tongue was distracting her from her indolent breakfast in bed, but there were other things on her mind. Questions which kept flitting into her mind and which, no matter how hard she tried, wouldn't seem to flit away again. She had told herself that there was a good reason why you were supposed to live in the present—but sometimes you just couldn't prevent thoughts of the future from starting to darken the edges of your mind. Or the past, come to that...

She kept her voice light and airy. As if she were asking him nothing more uncomplicated than would he please order her a coffee from room service. 'Have you brought other women here?'

There was a pause. The fingers which had been playing with her nipple stilled against the puckered flesh. He slanted her a look which she found more rueful than reassuring. 'What do you want me to say? That you're the first?'

'No, of course not,' she said stiffly. 'I didn't imagine for a moment that I was.'

But the thought of other women lying where she was lying unsettled her more than it should have done. Actually, it didn't unsettle her—it hurt. The thought of Suleiman licking someone *else's* breasts made dark and hateful thoughts crowd into her head. The image of him sliding his tongue between another woman's legs made her feel almost dizzy with rage. And jealousy. And a million other things she had no right to feel.

She should have known this would happen. She should have listened to all the doubts she'd refused to listen to that day in the desert. When she'd been so hungry for him and so impressed—yes, impressed—when he'd offered to fly her anywhere in the world that she'd smiled the smile of a besotted woman and said yes.

And now look what had happened. Her feelings for him hadn't died, that was for sure. She still cared for him—more than she wanted to care for him and more than it was safe to care. Yet deep down she knew that this trip was supposed to be about getting the whole *passion* thing out of their system. For both of them. Something which had begun so messily needed to have a clean ending so that they could both move on; she knew that, too.

So what had happened?

Suleiman had pulled out all the stops—that was what had happened. He was a man she had always adored, and now he had an added wow factor, because his vast self-made wealth gave him an undeniable glamour. And glamour mixed with desire made for a very powerful cocktail indeed.

He had whisked her onto his own, private jet—and she'd got the distinct feeling that he had enjoyed showing it off—and flown her to a city she'd never got around to visiting before. That was the first mistake. Was it a good idea to go to the city of romance if you were trying to convince yourself that you weren't still in love with a man?

He had booked them into the presidential suite at the Georges V, where the staff all seemed to know him by name. Sara had been brought up in a palace, so she knew pretty much everything there was to know about luxury, but she fell in love with the iconic Parisian hotel.

Next he took her shopping. Not just, as he said, because she had brought only a very inappropriate wardrobe with her—but because he wanted to buy her things. She told him that she would prefer to buy things for herself. He told her that simply wasn't acceptable. There was a short stand-off, followed by a making-up session which had involved a bowl of whipped cream and a lot of imagination. And because she felt weak from all their love-making and dizzy just with the sense of *being* there—she went ahead and let him buy her the stuff anyway.

The crisp January weather was cold so he splashed out on an ankle-length sheepskin coat and some thigh-high leather boots.

'But you disapproved when I was wearing a very similar pair back in England,' she had objected.

'Yes, but these are for my eyes only,' he'd purred, pillowing his head against his folded arms as he'd leaned back against the sofa to watch her slide them on when they had arrived back at the hotel with their purchases. 'And they will look very good when worn with nothing but a pair of panties.'

Ah, yes. Panties. That seemed to be another area of his expertise. He indulged her taste for lingerie with tiny, wispy bras designed to highlight her nipples. He bought her an outrageous pair of crotchless panties and later on that day proved just what a time-effective purchase they could be. Silky camiknickers and matching suspender belts were added to the costly pile he accumulated in the city's most exclusive store, with Suleiman displaying an uncanny knack of knowing just what would suit her.

Sara sat up in bed and brushed away the last few crumbs of croissant. 'How many?' she questioned, getting out of bed and feeling acutely aware that he was watching her.

He frowned. 'How many what?'

'Women.' She walked across the room towards the windows, wondering why she had gone ahead and asked him a question she had vowed not to ask.

'Sara,' he said softly. 'It's knowing women as I do which allows me to give you so much pleasure.'

'Yes,' she said, staring fixedly out of the giant windows which commanded a stunning view of the city, where the Eiffel Tower dominated a landscape made light by the shimmering waters of the Seine. 'I imagine it is.'

She listened to the sudden sound of silence which had descended on the room. One of those silences between two people which she'd realised could say so much. Or rather, so little. Silences when she had to fight to bite back the words which were bursting to come out. Words which had been building up inside her for days—years—and which she knew he wouldn't want to hear.

Instead, she stared out at the cityscape in front of

her as if it was the most wonderful thing she'd ever seen, which wasn't easy when her vision was starting to get all blurred.

'Sara?'

She shook her head, praying that he wouldn't pursue it. *Leave me alone. Let me get over it in my own time.*

'Sara, look at me.'

It took a moment or two before she had composed herself enough to turn around and curve him a bright smile. 'What?'

His eyes were narrowed and speculative. 'Are those *tears* I see?'

'No, of course it isn't,' she said, dabbing furiously at her eyes with a bunched fist. 'And if it is, then it's only my damned hormones. You must know all about those.'

'Come here.'

'I don't want to. I'm enjoying the view.'

His gaze slid over her naked body. 'I'm enjoying the view too, but I want you to come back to bed and tell me what's wrong.'

She considered refusing—but what else was she going to do in this vast arena of the bedroom, with Suleiman watching her like that? She felt vulnerable—and not just because she was naked. She felt vulnerable with each hour of every day, knowing she was losing her heart to him.

He held out his arms and she felt as if she'd lost some kind of battle as she went to him, loving the way the flat of his hand smoothed down the spill of her hair as she climbed into bed beside him. She loved the feel of his naked body entwined with hers. She snuggled up to him, hoping that her closeness would distract him enough to stop asking questions she had no desire to answer. But no. He tilted up her chin, so that there was nowhere to look except into the ebony gleam of his eyes.

'Want to talk about it, princess?'

She shook her head. 'Not really.'

'Shall I guess?'

'Please don't, Suleiman. It's not important.'

'I think it is. You're falling in love with me.'

Sara flinched. Maybe she wasn't as good at hiding her feelings as she'd thought. But then, neither was Suleiman as clever as *he* thought. He'd got the sentiment right—but the tense was wrong. She wasn't 'falling' in love with him—she'd *always* been in love with him. Fancy him not knowing that. She gave him a cool smile. 'That's an occupational hazard for you, I expect?'

'Yes,' he said seriously. 'I'm afraid it is.'

She shook her head, laughing in spite of everything. 'You really are the most arrogant man I've ever known.'

'I have never denied my arrogance.'

'Admitting that doesn't make it all right!'

She was trying to wriggle out of his arms, but he was having none of it. He captured both her wrists in his hands, stilling her so that their eyes were on a collision course.

'I can't help who I am, Sara. And I have enough experience—'

'And then some.'

'To recognise when a woman starts to lose her heart

to me. Sweetheart, will you please stop wriggling—and glaring—and listen to what I have to say?'

'I don't want to listen.'

'I think you need to.'

She stilled in his arms, aware of the loud thunder of her heart. His hard thigh was levered between her own and a sadness suddenly swept over her—because wasn't she going to miss being in bed with him like this? Cuddled up in his arms and feeling as if the rest of the world didn't exist. 'I don't want to turn this into a long goodbye,' she whispered.

'And neither do I.' He tucked a strand of hair behind her ear and sighed. 'I thought I did.'

'What do you mean, you thought you did?'

Suleiman stared at her, as if unsure how much to tell her. But this was Sara—and hadn't his relationship with her always been special and unique? The usual rules didn't apply to this blonde-haired beauty he'd known since she was a mixed-up little kid. 'Usually when a woman reaches this stage, I begin to grow wary. Bored.'

'This *stage*?' she spluttered indignantly. 'You mean, as if this is some kind of infectious disease you're incubating!'

He laughed. 'I know that sounds like more arrogance but I'm trying to tell you the truth,' he said. 'Or would you rather me dress it up with lavish compliments and make like you're the only woman I've ever been intimate with?'

'No,' she said, unable to keep the slight sulk from her voice.

'At this stage of an affair,' he said, though his mocking smile didn't lessen the impact of his words, 'I usually recognise that it must come to an end, no matter how much desire I'm feeling. Because an inequality of affection can prove volatile—and I have never wished to play games of emotional cruelty.'

'Good of you,' she said sarcastically. Her heart was beating painfully against her ribcage as she waited to hear what was coming next. But she kept her face as impassive as possible because she wasn't going to give him the chance to reject her. Not a second time. And if that made it seem as if all she cared about was her pride—so what? What else was she going to be left with in the long, lonely hours when he'd gone?

She forced a smile, hoping that she seemed all grown up and reasonable. Because she was not going to be the woman with the red eyes, clinging to his legs as he walked out of the door. 'Look, Suleiman—you've been very honest with me, so let me return the compliment. I've always had a crush on you—ever since I was a young girl. We both know that. That's one of the reasons that kiss when I was eighteen turned into so much more.'

'That kiss changed my life,' he said simply.

Sara felt the clamp of pain around her heart. *Don't tell me things like that, because I'll read into them more than you want me to.* 'This time in Paris has been…great. You know it has. You're the most amazing lover. I'm sure I'm not the first woman to have told you that.' She sucked in a deep breath, because she was sure she wouldn't be the last, either. 'But we both know this isn't going anywhere—and we mustn't make it into more than it is, because that will spoil it. We both know that when something is put out of reach, it makes that something seem much more tantalising. That's why—'

He silenced her by placing his finger over her lips and his black eyes burned into hers. 'I think I love you.'

Sara froze. Wasn't it funny how you could dream of a man saying those words to you? And then he did and it was nothing like how you thought it would be. For a start, he had qualified them. He *thought* he loved her? That was the kind of thing someone said when they took an umbrella out on a sunny day. *I thought it might rain.* She didn't believe him. She didn't dare believe him.

'Don't say that,' she hissed.

He looked startled. 'Even if it's true?'

'Especially if it's true,' she said, and burst into tears.

Perplexed, Suleiman stared at her and tightened his arms around her waist as he felt her tears dripping down his neck. 'What have I done wrong?'

'Nothing!'

'Then why are you crying?'

She shook her head, her words coming out between gulps of swallowed air. Words he could hardly make out but which included 'always', quickly contradicted by 'never' and then, when she'd managed to snatch enough breath back, finishing rather inexplicably with 'hopeless'.

Eventually, she raised a tear-stained face to his. 'Don't you understand, you stupid man?' she whispered. 'I think I love you too.'

'Then why are you crying like that?'

'Because it can never work!' she said fiercely. 'How could it?'

'Why not?'

'Because our lives are totally incompatible, that's why.' She rubbed her hand over her wet cheek. 'You live in Samahan and I live in London. You are an oil baron and I'm a flaky artist.'

'You think those things are insurmountable?' he demanded. 'You don't imagine these are the kind of logistical problems which other couples might have overcome?'

Sara shook her head as all her old fears came crowding back. She thought of her own mother. Love certainly hadn't brought *her* happiness, had it? Because love was just a feeling. A feeling which had no guarantee of lasting. She and Suleiman had both experienced something when they were fixed at a time and in a place which was light years away from their normal lives. How could something like that possibly survive if it was transplanted into the separate worlds which they both inhabited?

'Listen to me, Suleiman,' she said. 'We don't really *know* one another.'

'That's completely untrue. I have known you since you were seven years old. I certainly know you better than I know any other woman.'

'Not as adults. Not properly. We have no idea if we're compatible.'

His hand tightened around her waist; his thumb

traced a provocative little circle. 'I think we're *ve-ry* compatible.'

'That's not the kind of compatibility I was talking about.'

'No?'

'No. I'm not talking about snatched moments of forbidden passion beneath the shade of a rock in the desert. Or sex-filled weekends at one of the best hotels in the world. I'm talking about normal life, Suleiman. Everyday life. The kind of life we all have to lead—whether we're a princess or an oil magnate, or the man who drives the grocery truck.' She pulled away from him so she could look at him properly. 'Tell me what your dream scenario would be. Where you'd like us to go from here—if you had the choice.'

'Well, that bit's easy.' He tugged at the end of a long strand of hair which was tickling his chest. 'You no longer have a job, do you?'

'Not officially, no. I left Gabe a letter on Christmas Eve, saying I'd had to go away suddenly and I wasn't sure when I was coming back. It's not the kind of thing his employees usually do and I'm not sure if he'd ever employ me again. There's a long list of people desperate to fill my shoes. He's the best in the business who could get anyone to work for him. I doubt whether he'd give another chance to someone who could let him down without any warning.'

But if she was hoping to see some sort of remorse on Suleiman's face, she was in for a disappointment. The slow smile which curved his lips made the little hairs on the back of her neck stand up, because she suspected she wasn't going to like what she heard next.

'Perfect,' he said.

'I fail to see what's perfect about leaving my boss in the lurch and not having any kind of secure future to go back to.'

'But that's the point, Sara. You do have a secure future—just a different kind of future from the one you envisaged.' He smiled at her as if he had just discovered that all his shares had risen by ten per cent while they'd been in bed. 'You don't have to go back to working for a large organisation. All that—what do they say?—clocking in and clocking out. Buying your lunch in a paper bag and eating it at your desk.'

'Gabe happens to run a very large staff canteen,' she said coldly. 'And insists on all his staff taking a proper lunch break. And I think it's you who are missing the point. I *want* to go back to work. It's what I do. What else do you suggest I do?'

He tugged on another strand of blonde hair and began to wind it around his finger. 'Simple. You come back to Samahan, with me.'

She stared at him in disbelief. 'Samahan?'

His eyes narrowed. 'The expression on your face looks as if I have suggested that you make your home in Hades. But I think you will find yourself greatly surprised. Samahan has improved greatly since the cross-border wars. The discovery of oil has brought with it much wealth and we are ploughing some of that wealth back into the land.'

He let go of the twisted strand of hair and it dangled in front of her bare breast, in a perfect blonde ringlet.

'My home will not disappoint you, Sara—for it is as vast as any palace and just as beautiful. A world-class architect from Uruguay designed it for me, and I flew in a rose expert from the west coast of America to design my gardens. I stable my horses there—two of them won medals in the last Olympics. I have a great team around me.'

Sara recognised what he was doing. This was the modern equivalent of a male gorilla beating his chest. He was showing her how much he had achieved against the odds—he, the poor boy whose own mother had sold him. He was trying to reassure her that he would treat her like a princess, but that was just what she didn't want. She had hated her life as a princess, which was why she had left it far behind.

'And what would I do all day in this beautiful house of yours?'

'You would make love to me.'

'Obviously that's extremely tempting.' Her smile didn't slip. 'But how about when you're not around? When you're jetting off to the States or swanning off somewhere being an oil baron?'

'You can amuse yourself, for there is much that you will enjoy. Swim in the pool. Explore my extensive library.'

'Just like one long holiday, you mean?' she questioned brightly.

'Not necessarily. You will find a role for yourself there, Sara. I know you will. I think you will find that the desert lands are changing. How long is it since you visited the region?'

'Years,' she said distractedly. 'And I think you'd better stop right there. It's very sweet of you and I'm sure your home is perfectly lovely, but I don't want to go to Samahan. I want to go back to London because there are still loose ends to tie up. I owe Gabe an explanation about what happened and I want to finish up the project I was working on.' Her eyes met his. She realised that she wanted him and loved him enough to want to try to make it work. So why not reverse his question to her? 'But you could come back with me, if you like.'

'With you?' His black eyes were hooded.

'Why not? We can see if we can exist compatibly there—and if we can, then I'll think about giving Samahan a try. Does that sound reasonable?'

She saw the sudden hardening of his lips and realised that 'reasonable' was not on the top of Suleiman's agenda. He wasn't used to having his wishes thwarted, particularly not by a woman. He had expected her to fall in with his plans—without stopping to think that she might have plans of her own.

But was he seriously suggesting she might be happy being ensconced in what sounded like the luxury prison of his desert home? Hadn't that been what she'd spent her whole life rebelling against?

'What do you think?' she questioned tentatively.

He slipped his hand between her legs. 'I think we have wasted enough time talking about geographical escape.'

'Suleiman—'

He bent his head to her neck and kissed it.

'You want me to stop?'

'That's the last thing I want.'

She thought she heard soft triumph in his laugh as he sheathed himself in a condom and then lay back against the mattress with a look of satisfaction on his face. *Like a conquering hero,* she thought as he lifted her up like a trophy, hating the part of her which enjoyed that.

His moan echoed hers as he slid her down slowly onto his erection. With each angled thrust of her hips she took him deeper and deeper and she wondered what he was thinking. She knew he was watching her as her blonde hair swung wild and free—and suddenly she found herself *performing* for him.

Was she trying to prove that she was a match for all those women who had preceded her—by playing with her breasts and biting her lips, her eyes closed as if she was indulging in some wild and secret fantasy?

Whatever it was, it seemed to work because he went crazy for her. Crazier than she'd ever known him. He splayed his dark hands possessively over her hips as he made the penetration deeper still. And each time she was close to orgasm, he stopped. Stopped so that once she actually screamed out loud with pent-up frustration, because he made her build it up all over again.

He did it to her over and over again. Until she begged him to release her and then at last he slid her onto the floor and drove into her, as if it were the very first time all over again. She felt her body shatter with the most powerful orgasm she'd ever known but once it began to recede, she felt a sudden sense of unease.

An unease which grew stronger with every second. Because that had been all about power, hadn't it? Suleiman was a man who was used to getting his own way and by refusing to conform to his wishes she had taken control of the situation. She had taken control and he would use whatever it took to get it back.

Sex.

Power.

Palaces.

Even words of love which sounded wonderful, until you wondered if he actually knew what they meant. Were they just another lever to get her to see things his way? she wondered.

He'd never even seen her in her usual environment. He didn't *know* that very important side of her personality.

'I want to go back to London,' she said stubbornly. 'Do you want to come with me or not?'

CHAPTER NINE

'SAY THAT AGAIN.'

Bathed in the light which flooded into Gabe Steel's enormous penthouse office, Sara met her boss's eyes as he drawled his question. He was leaning back in his chair with a look of curiosity in his grey eyes. And Gabe didn't usually do curiosity. At least, not with his employees. She guessed that leaving him a rather dramatic letter saying she was going away and then asking to be reinstated just a few weeks later was enough to stir anyone's interest. Even your incredibly high-powered and often cynical boss.

'I know it sounds incredible,' she said.

He laughed. 'Incredible is something of an under-statement, Sara. How come you kept it a secret for so long?'

She shrugged. 'Oh, you know. I'd hate to make out that I'm some poor little rich girl—but everyone treats you differently once they know you're a princess.'

'I guess they do.' His pewter eyes narrowed as he twirled a solid gold pen between his long fingers. 'So what's brought about the sudden change of heart?'

Change of heart.

She wondered if Gabe had any idea of how un-cannily accurate that particular phrase was. Prob-ably. You didn't get to be head of one of the world's biggest advertising agencies without having a finely tuned degree of insight.

'I was...' She wondered what he would say if she told him the truth. *I was due to get married to a Sultan, but I put a stop to that particular arrangement by having sex with his closest friend.* Probably not a good idea. Men could be notoriously tribal about that kind of thing and she didn't want to portray Suleiman as some sort of bad guy. And anyway, that wasn't the whole truth, was it? Suleiman wasn't the *reason* be-hind the cancelled wedding. He was just a symptom.

She stared sightlessly out of the penthouse window. A symptom who was currently prowling around her London apartment and making her feel as if she had imprisoned a tiger there.

It was a big apartment—everyone said so. So how come the rooms seemed to have shrunk to the size of matchboxes since Suleiman had accompanied her back from Paris and moved in with her? It had been her mother's apartment and Sara loved every inch of it, a feeling clearly not shared by her lover.

He had walked through the three huge—or so she'd thought—reception rooms, had barely deigned to look at the kitchen and had given the bedrooms only a cursory glance, before turning to demand where the garden was.

She had hated the way her voice had sounded all defensive. 'There isn't one.'

'No garden?' He had sounded incredulous, while all her explanations about the convenience of having a nearby park had fallen on deaf ears.

He had complained about the plumbing—which admittedly *was* fairly ancient—and insisted on having black-out blinds installed in her bedroom. He had commandeered the second bedroom as some kind of makeshift office. Suddenly emails began arriving at odd times of the day and night. Important documents from the US and the Middle East were delivered daily, while a series of efficient sounding staff would ring and she would hear him speaking in his native tongue. She told him it was like living at the United Nations.

He said he was trying to decide whether or not to set up a London headquarters. But that was a big decision which couldn't be made in a hurry, while Sara seemed to get stuck with the smaller, niggling ones.

She'd been forced to find some kind of laundry service since it seemed that Suleiman liked to change his shirt at least twice a day. It helped explain why he always looked so immaculate, but the practicalities of such high sartorial standards were a pain.

But she tried to tell herself that these were just glitches which could easily be sorted out. That Suleiman had never lived with anyone before and neither had she. She convinced herself that all these problems were solvable, but quickly realised there was one which wasn't—and that was the problem of time management. Or rather, *her* time management. Suleiman was obviously used to having women at his beck and call. He didn't like it when she got up at seven each morning to get ready for work. Sometimes it seemed as if he was almost *jealous* of her job.

And that scared her.

It scared her even more than her growing feelings for him.

It was as if the love she felt for Suleiman had started out as a tiny seed, which was in danger of becoming a rampant plant and spreading its tentacles everywhere. His presence was so pervasive and his character so compelling that she felt as if she was being taken over by him. That if she allowed him to, he would take over her whole life and completely dominate her and she would become invisible. And she couldn't allow him to do that.

She didn't dare do that.

So even though she had to fight every loving and lustful instinct in her body, she didn't give in to Suleiman's repeated attempts to push her job into second place.

'Come back to bed,' he would purr, with that tiger-hasn't-been-fed look on his face, as he patted the empty space on the bed beside him.

And Sara would pull on her silk wrap and move to a safe distance away from him. 'I can't do that or I'll be late,' she'd said primly, the third time it happened. 'Haven't you ever been out with a working woman before—and if so, how on earth did you cope?'

His answering smile had been infuriating. Almost, she thought—*smug.*

'Most women can be persuaded to take a sabbatical, if you make it worth their while.'

Sara had felt sick at the lengths to which her sex would go to in order to hang onto a man. Which, of course, made her even more determined not to weaken. Her job meant independence and she'd fought long and hard for it.

She realised that Gabe was still looking at her from the other side of the desk. Still waiting for some kind of explanation. She flashed him a slightly self-conscious smile.

'Actually, it's a man.'

'It usually is,' he offered drily. 'Would that be the reason why you had your skirt on inside out yesterday morning?'

'Oh, Gabe!' She clapped her palms to her flaming cheeks. 'I'm so sorry. I only realised when I came out of the meeting and Alice pointed it out.'

'Forget it. I only mention it because the client did— so perhaps best not to repeat it. Anyway.' He smiled. 'What's his name? This man.'

She could hear her voice softening as she said it. 'It's Suleiman Abd al-Aziz—'

Gabe's eyes narrowed 'The oil baron?'

'You've heard of him?'

He smiled. 'Unlike princesses, global magnates tend not to stay anonymous for very long.'

'No, I suppose not. The thing is, I was thinking...' She twisted her fingers together in her lap and wondered what was making her feel so nervous. Actually, that wasn't true. She knew exactly what was making her nervous. On some instinctive level, she was terrified of Suleiman meeting her powerful and very sexy boss. 'I wanted Suleiman to get a bit of an idea about what my job's about. I told him about the massive campaign we did for that new art gallery in Whitechapel—and I thought that I might bring him along to the opening tonight. If that's all right.'

'Excellent. You do that.' Gabe looked at her expectantly. 'And now, if we're through with all the personal details—can you get me the drawings for the Hudson account?'

Noting the slight reprimand, Sara opened up the folder she'd carried in with her and worked hard on the account for the rest of the afternoon. She sent Alice out for coffee and tried ringing Suleiman to tell him about the gallery opening, but he wasn't answering his phone.

It was gone six by the time she arrived back home to find the apartment filled with the smell of cinnamon and oranges. She wondered if Suleiman had ordered something in and whether he'd just forgotten that she had the opening tonight.

Because mealtimes had proved another stumbling block, mainly because Suleiman was used to having servants cater to his every whim. He liked food to arrive when he wanted it—usually after sex. He was not interested in the mechanics of getting it, not of shopping for it nor having Sara rustle him up a meal. So far they had compromised by eating out every night, but sometimes she just wanted to kick off her shoes and scoff toast on the sofa.

She followed the direction of the aroma out to the

kitchen, and blinked in surprise to see Suleiman leaning over the hob, adding something to a pot. It was
such an incongruous sight—and so rare to see him in
jeans—that for a moment she just stood there, feasting
her eyes on his powerful frame and thick dark hair. The
denim clung to his narrow hips, it hugged the muscular shaft of his long legs and she had to swallow down
her instant feeling of lust.

'Wow. This is a sight for sore eyes,' she said softly.
'What are you doing?'

'Wondering why it's so difficult to buy fresh apri-
cots in central London.' He turned round, his black
eyes glittering as he curved her a smile. 'Actually, I'm
trying to impress my liberated princess by producing
a meal, after she's spent a hard day at the office.'

Putting her handbag down on the counter, she
walked over to him and looped her arms around his
neck. 'I didn't know you cooked.'

'That's because I rarely do these days. But as you
know, I once served in the Qurhahian army,' he said,
bending to brush his mouth over hers. 'Where even
men who had been spoilt by living in palaces were
taught the basics of food prep.'

She laughed, lifting her lips for a proper kiss and
within seconds she was lost in it. And so was he. Suddenly food was forgotten. Everything was forgotten,
except the need to have him as close to her as possible.
Her fingers tugged at his shirt, pulling it open to reveal
his bare chest—not caring that several buttons went
bouncing all over the stone tiles of the kitchen floor.

She tugged impatiently at his belt and he gave a low

laugh as he pushed her up against the door. Rucking up her dress, he ripped her panties apart and her muffled protest was stifled with a hungry kiss. She could hear the rasp of his zip and the buoyant weight of his erection as it sprang free. She reached down to touch him, her fingertips skating over his silken hardness before he removed her hand. Cushioning the weight of her bottom with his hands, he positioned himself where she was hot and wet for him and thrust deep inside her.

Her legs wrapped tightly around his hips, Sara clung to him as they rocked in rhythm, but it was over very quickly. Her head wilted like a cut flower as she leaned it against his shoulder and her voice was sleepy in his ear.

'Nice,' she murmured.

'Is that the best you can do? I was hoping for something a little more lyrical than "nice".'

'Would stupendous work better?'

'Stupendous is a good word,' he said.

'Listen.' She kissed his neck. 'Do you want to go to the opening of that gallery in Whitechapel? The one I told you about? It's tonight.'

He lifted up a handful of hair and brushed his lips against her neck. 'No, I don't—and neither do you. Let's just stay home. I'm making dinner and afterwards I'm sure we can find ways to amuse ourselves.'

Sara could feel the warmth of her orgasm beginning to ebb away. 'Suleiman, I have to go.'

'No, you don't. You don't *have* to go anywhere. You've been working all day as it is.'

'I know I have. But this is my job. Remember?' She

thought of her mother and the way she'd let all her options slide away from her. She thought of the way that men could manoeuvre women into a corner, if you let them. *And she wasn't going to let Suleiman do that to her.* She bent down to pick up the tattered lace which had once been her panties. 'I've been a major part of the whole campaign from the get-go and I want to see the launch. It's expected of me and it would look very odd if I wasn't there. But I asked Gabe whether I could bring you along—and he said yes.'

There was a pause. 'How very generous of him,' he said acidly. 'And you didn't think to give me any notice?'

'Actually, I did.' She tried to ignore the dangerous note in his voice, telling herself that she *had* sprung this on him at the last minute. And why had that been? Because she'd feared just this kind of reaction if she'd said anything about it sooner? 'I tried ringing, but you weren't picking up. Look, you really don't have to go to this, Suleiman, but I do. So I'm going to take a shower and get ready.'

Without another word, she walked into the bedroom and stripped off her clothes before hitting the shower. She half expected Suleiman to follow her, but he didn't.

She was *not* going to feel guilty. Furiously, she lathered shampoo into her hair. If he loved her—as he said he loved her—then shouldn't he be making more of an effort to integrate into her world, and her life?

He could meet Gabe and he'd see Alice again— as well as some of the other graphic designers she'd spoken about. Wasn't that what modern coupledom was all about?

But as she blow-dried her hair in front of the bedroom mirror her fears just wouldn't seem to leave her. She found herself wondering if they were just *playing* at being modern. Pretending that everything was fine, when deep down nothing had really been addressed. At heart, wasn't Suleiman just another old-fashioned desert warrior who was incapable of any real change?

Knowing that the press would be there, as well as the usual smattering of celebrity guests, she was extra generous with the mascara. She could hear the sound of water running in the bathroom next door and moments later Suleiman walked into the bedroom, a towel wrapped around his hips.

He rubbed at his damp hair with a second towel and she thought how powerful his body looked. The whiteness of the towel contrasted against the deep olive of his skin and droplets of water gleamed there, as if he'd been showered with tiny diamonds.

'Oh, good,' she said, and smiled. 'You've decided to come.'

'Reluctantly,' he growled as he pulled a white shirt from the wardrobe.

She watched him from the mirror as she finished fiddling around with her make-up. He looked heart-stoppingly gorgeous in that dark suit which emphasised the blackness of his hair and eyes. She wondered what Alice would say when she saw his name on the guest list. She wondered how he would fit in with all her work colleagues. But her heart was suddenly ridiculously light. He was coming, wasn't he? How could they fail to love him, as she loved him?

She had just slithered her dress over her head, when his words whispered through the air and startled her.

'You're not wearing that?'

She felt the clench of her heart, but she turned round to face him, a sanguine expression on her face. She smoothed her fingers down over the fine gold mesh and smiled. 'I am. Do you like it?'

'No.'

'Well, that's a pity. It's made by one of London's top designers, so it's eminently suitable for tonight's party.'

'It may be, but it is also much too short. You're practically showing your panties.'

The tone of his voice made her heart contract, but she was determined not to back down. She'd thought that they were over all this.

'Don't exaggerate, Suleiman—and please don't come over all heavy on me. The dress is a fashionable length and I'm wearing it. End of story.'

Their eyes met and she became aware of the silent war being waged between them and she tried to see it from his point of view. In Suleiman's world, a woman going out in public wearing a dress this short was sending out a very definite message.

'Look, I know it's the way you've been brought up,' she said. 'But you've really got to lose this idea that women are either saints or scrubbers. I'm wearing gold tights and long boots with it. The boots you bought me in Paris, actually—'

'And I bought those for you to wear in the bedroom.'

'Yes. Well, it may have missed your notice—' she lifted up her leg to reveal the sole of the boot '—but they have real heels made for walking. They weren't designed just for the bedroom! So are you going to lighten up and enjoy the evening?' Her gold bangles jangling, she walked over to him, placing one hand on his shoulder as she tilted her head to one side. 'Are you?'

There was a moment while their eyes fought another silent, clashing battle before Suleiman gave a low growl which was almost a laugh. 'No other woman would dare speak to me the way that you do, Sara.'

'That's why you love me, isn't it?'

'Maybe.' He slid his hand possessively around her waist. 'Come on. Let's go.'

CHAPTER TEN

MOODILY, SULEIMAN GLANCED around the vast art gallery. The cavernous space and endlessly high ceilings made him think that this might have been a warehouse in a former life, though the place certainly bore no resemblance to its humbler origins.

On white walls hung vast canvases sporting naïve splashes of colour which a five-year-old child could have achieved—all bearing price tags far beyond the reach of most ordinary mortals. Stick-thin women and geeky-looking men in glasses stood gazing up at them in rapt concentration, while waitresses dressed like extravagant birds offered trays of exotically coloured cocktails.

He still couldn't believe he was here. He couldn't believe that Sara had brought him here to look at these dull paintings and meet dull people, when she could have been in bed with him instead. He had been cooking her a meal. Didn't she realise that he'd never cooked for a woman before? But instead of switching off her phone and treating him with a little gratitude, she had brought him to this pretentious place. Had given him a plastic glass of very mediocre wine and then had disappeared to greet someone with one of those ridiculous air-kisses he so despised.

She needed to work, she had told him. Just as it seemed she always needed to work. She never stopped. It was as if she couldn't bear to get off the treadmill she'd leapt back on with such enthusiasm when they'd returned from Paris.

He watched her cross the room. The shimmer of her golden dress caressed her body as she moved, while the sinful blonde hair streamed over her shoulders in a silken cascade. Men were watching her, as they had been watching from the moment they'd arrived—even the geeky ones, who didn't particularly look as if they were into women. He wondered if she was aware of that. Was that why she had worn that skimpy little dress—to draw attention to her beauty? Was that what made her walk with such a seductive sway, or was that simply a consequence of wearing those indecently sexy boots?

Why had he bought her those damned boots?

She had stopped to talk to someone and her head was tilted upwards as she listened to what he was saying to her—a tall man with cold grey eyes and a chiselled face. They seemed to be having some kind of animated discussion. They acted as if they knew each other well and Suleiman's eyes narrowed. Who was he? He smiled with polite dismissal at the woman who had attached herself to his side like glue, and walked across the gallery until he had reached them.

Sara looked up as he approached and he noticed that

her cheeks had gone very pink. Had her male companion made her blush? he wondered. He felt the twist of something unfamiliar in his gut. Something dark and nebulous.

'Oh, Suleiman.' She smiled. 'There you are.'

'Here I am.' He looked at the man who stood beside her, with a questioning expression. 'Hello.'

He saw the way Sara's teeth had begun to dig into her bottom lip. Was she nervous, he wondered—and if so, why?

'I'd like to introduce you to my boss,' she was saying. 'This is Gabe Steel and he owns the best and biggest advertising agency in London. Gabe—this is Suleiman Abd al-Aziz and I've known...' She began to blush. 'Well, I've known Suleiman ever since I was a little girl.'

There was a split second as the two men eyed one another before briefly shaking hands and Suleiman found his fingers grasped with a bone-crushing strength which equalled his own. So this was her boss. The tycoon he had heard so much about and the man who had lent her his cottage at Christmas. A man with cold grey eyes and the kind of presence which was attracting almost as much attention from the women in the room as Suleiman himself.

One thought jarred uncomfortably in his head.

Why *had* he lent her his cottage?

'Good to meet you, Suleiman,' said Gabe. 'So tell me, was she a good little girl—or was she very naughty?'

Suleiman froze. He tried telling himself that this

was the normal, jokey kind of statement which existed among work colleagues in the west—but his heart was stubbornly refusing to listen to reason. Instead, his years of conditioning, which had resulted in a very rigid way of thinking, now demanded to be heard. Instead of joining in with the banter, he found himself thinking that this man Steel—no matter how exalted his position—was speaking most impertinently about the Princess of Dhi'ban.

Unless…

Suleiman's heart began to hammer painfully against his ribcage. Unless the relationship went deeper than that of mere workmates. He swallowed. Was it possible that Gabe Steel was the other man she had slept with— the man who had taken her virginity? Hadn't she told him on Christmas Eve that it was Gabe Steel's cottage and that she was *waiting for her lover*?

Had Gabe Steel been her lover?

For a moment he was so overcome by a sweep of jealousy so powerful that he couldn't speak, and when he did his words felt like little splinters of metal being expelled from his mouth.

'I don't think that the princess would wish me to divulge secrets from her past,' he said repressively.

'No, of course not.' Gabe looked startled, before flashing him an easy smile. 'So tell me, what do you think of the paintings?'

'You want my honest opinion?' Suleiman questioned.

'Suleiman's not a great connoisseur of art,' put in Sara hastily, before shooting him a furious look. She put her hand on his arm and pressed it—the sharp dig undeniably warning him not to elaborate. 'Are you, darling?'

Suleiman felt a cold fury begin to rise within him. She was speaking to him as if he were some tame little lapdog she had brought along with her. But he could see that causing a scene here would serve no purpose, except to delay their departure and ensure her fury. Clearly she danced obediently to this man Steel's tune—and when they got home he would do her the favour of pointing it out.

So he merely gave a bland smile as he reached out and drew her against him, a proprietorial thumb moving very deliberately over her ribcage. He felt her shiver beneath his touch and he allowed himself a small smile of satisfaction as he looked at her boss.

'Sara's right, of course. I have never been able to understand the penchant for spending vast sums of money on modern art. Call me old-fashioned—but I prefer something which doesn't look as if a cat has regurgitated its supper all over the canvas.'

'Oh, I think we could certainly call you old-fashioned, Suleiman,' said Sara in a high, bright voice.

'But I can see that your campaign has been successful,' conceded Suleiman, forcing a smile. 'Judging by the amount of people here tonight.'

'Yes, we're very pleased with the turnout,' said Gabe. 'Much of which is down to the talent of your girlfriend, of course. It was her artwork which made people sit up and start taking notice.' He smiled. 'Sara's one of the best creatives I have.'

'I'm sure she is. I just hope you have a good replacement ready to step in to fill her shoes,' said Suleiman.

He could see the look of surprise on Gabe Steel's face and the sudden draining of colour from Sara's.

'Something you're not telling me?' questioned Gabe lightly.

'Nothing that I know of,' she answered as her boss gave a brief nod of his head and walked across the art gallery to talk to a woman on the other side of the room.

'Shall we go home?' questioned Suleiman.

'I think we'd better,' said Sara quietly. 'Before I smash one of those very expensive "regurgitated cat supper" canvasses over your arrogant head.'

'Are you saying you'd like one of those hanging in your living room?'

'I do happen to like some of them, yes, but I'm not going to have a conversation about the artwork.'

Suleiman kept his hand firmly on her waist as he steered her towards the cloakroom, so that she could collect her wrap.

She didn't speak until they were outside and neither did he, but just before he opened the door of the waiting cab he leaned into her, breathing in her scent of jasmine and patchouli oil. 'Just what is your relationship with Steel?'

'Don't,' she snapped back. 'Don't you dare say another word, until we're back at my apartment.' She began speaking to him in Qurhahian then, her heated words coming out in a furious tirade. 'I don't want

the cab driver thinking I'm out with some kind of *Neanderthal*!'

She made no attempt to hide her anger all the way through the constant stop-starting of traffic lights but Suleiman felt nothing but the slow build of sexual hunger in response. The stubborn profile she presented made him want her. Her defiantly tilted chin made him want her even more. He felt the hardening at his groin. He would subdue her fire in the most satisfying way. Subdue her so completely and utterly that she wouldn't ever defy him again. She wouldn't want to...

Feeling more frustrated than he could ever remember, he watched as the orange, green and red of the traffic lights flickered over her face. The flickering kaleidoscope of colour and the sparkle of her golden dress only added to her beauty.

If it had been any other woman, he would have just pulled her in his arms and kissed her. Maybe even brought her to gasping orgasm on the back seat of the cab. But this was not any other woman. It was Sara. Fiery and beautiful Princess Sara. Stubborn and sensual Sara.

The elevator ride up to her apartment was torture. The heat at his groin almost too painful to endure. All he could see was the glimmer of gold as her dress highlighted every curve of her magnificent body, but her shoulders were stiff with tension and her face was still furious.

It seemed to take for ever before the lift pinged to a halt and they were back in her apartment again. The front door had barely closed behind them before she turned on him. 'How *dare* you behave like that?'

'Like what?'

'Coming over all possessive and squaring up to my boss like that!'

'So why the sudden defence of Steel, Sara? Was he your lover? The man to whom you lost your innocence?'

'*Oh!*' Frustratedly, she stared at him for a piercing moment before turning her back and marching into the sitting room, just the way she'd done on Christmas Eve at the cottage. And just like then, he followed her—mesmerised by the shimmering sway of her bottom, until she turned round to glare at him again.

The violet flash in her eyes warned him not to continue with his line of questioning, but Suleiman found he was in the grip of an emotion far bigger than reason. '*Was* he?' he demanded hotly. 'Is that why he lent you his cottage? Why you were so keen to get to the party tonight?'

She shook her head. 'You just don't *get* it, do you? You don't seem to realise that I've been living in England for all these years and I'm just not used to men behaving like this. It's *primitive*. And it's inappropriate.'

'I don't think it's inappropriate,' he ground out. 'You told me that night that you were waiting for your lover and that it was Steel's cottage. Then I discovered that you were not a virgin and so I put two and two together—'

'And came up with a number which seems to have

reached triple figures!' she flared, before taking a deep breath as if she was trying to get her own feelings under control. 'Look, I shouldn't have said that about Gabe that night. I was trying to make you angry—and it seems that I have far exceeded my own expectations. I was hurling out stuff and hoping to get a reaction. But I said all that before we became…involved. For the record, Gabe has never been my lover. But even if he had…*even if he had*…that does not give you the right to just march up to him like that in public and start playing the jealousy card. I just don't get it.'

'What don't you get?' he demanded. 'That a man should feel possessive about the woman he loves? Isn't that a mark of the way he feels about her?'

She shook her head. 'It's got nothing to do with the way he feels about her—it's more a mark of wanting to *own* her! Before you became Mr Oil Baron, you travelled for years on Murat's behalf. Are you trying to tell me that this is the way you behaved whenever you met with some diplomat or politician whose ideas you didn't happen to agree with? Going in with all guns blazing?'

His eyes narrowed. 'On the contrary. One of the reasons I excel at card games is because I have the ability to conceal what I'm thinking.'

Slowly, she nodded her head 'So what happened tonight?'

'You did,' he said. 'You happened.'

'You mean it's something I did?'

He shook his head. 'I'm having trouble working it out for myself. I've never *felt* this way about a woman before, and sometimes it scares the hell out of me. I've never wanted a woman in the way I want you, Sara.'

'But wanting me doesn't give you permission to behave like that towards Gabe. It doesn't give you the right to start treating me like a *thing*. Like a valuable painting or some vase that you own, which nobody else is allowed to look at, because it's *all yours*. I don't want that.'

For a moment there was silence as he looked at her.

'Then just what *do* you want, Sara?' he questioned. 'Because you don't seem to want a normal relationship. Not from where I'm standing.'

'That's funny. A normal relationship? I don't think you'd recognise one if you tripped over it in the street!' she said. 'And how could you? You're possessive and demanding and insanely jealous.'

'And you don't think that you might have fed my instinct to be jealous?'

'I've already explained about Gabe.'

'I'm not talking about Gabe! I'm talking about the fact that ever since I've moved in here, you seem to be pushing me away. It's like you've surrounded yourself with a glass wall and I just can't get through to you.'

She felt the fear licking at the edges of her skin. Was that true—or did Suleiman just want to make her completely his, and to stamp out all her natural fire and independence?

She couldn't risk it.

'Oh, what's the point?' she said tiredly. 'There is no point. We've shone the light on what we've got and seen all the gaping great cracks.'

'I think you've made up your mind that it isn't going to work,' he said. 'And maybe that's the way it has to be. But since you've had your say, then let me have mine. And yes, I hold my hands up to all the charges you've just levelled at me. Yes, I've been "possessive and demanding and insanely jealous". I'm not proud of the way I behaved earlier and I'm sorry. It's been bubbling away for a while now and tonight it just seemed to spill over. But I wonder if you've stopped for a minute to ask yourself why?'

'Because you're still living in the Dark Ages? A typical desert male who will never change?'

He shook his head. 'Let me tell you something else, Sara—that I may have failed to live up to your ideal of the ideal lover tonight, but I've sure as hell tried in other ways.'

'How?' She felt stupid standing there in her golden dress with her bangles dangling from her limp wrist. Like a butterfly which had been speared by a pin. 'How have you tried?'

'*How?* For a start, I have relocated into your poky London apartment—'

'It is *not* poky!'

'Oh, believe me,' he said grimly, 'it is. I've been trying to run a global business from the second bedroom and all I get from you is complaints about the phone ringing at odd hours.'

'Is that *all* you get from me, Suleiman?'

He heard the unconsciously sultry note which had entered her voice and wondered if their angry words had scared her. And turned her on. Because didn't women like to push a man to the brink—even though sometimes they didn't like what happened when they got there?

'No,' he said. 'I get a lot of good stuff, too. The best stuff ever, if you must know—but what we have is not sustainable.'

'Not *sustainable*?'

He hardened his heart against the sudden darkening of her eyes and, even though he wanted to cross the room and pull her into his arms, he stood his ground. 'You think I'm content to continue to be treated as some kind of mild irrelevance, while your job dominates everything?'

'I told you that I needed to work.'

'And I accepted that. I just hadn't realised that you would be living at the office, virtually 24/7—as if you had to prove yourself. I don't know if it was to me, or to your boss—to reassure him that you weren't going to take off again. Or to show me that you're an independent woman in your own right. But whatever it is—you aren't facing up to the truth behind your actions.'

'And you are, right?'

'Maybe I am. And I'll tell you what you seem so determined to ignore, if that's what you want, Sara. Or even if it's not what you want. Because I think you need to hear it.'

'Oh, do you?' She walked over to one of the squashy pink velvet sofas and sat down on it, leaning back with her arms crossed over her chest and a defiant expression on her face. 'Go on, then. I can hardly wait.'

His eyes narrowed, because he could hear the vulnerability she was trying so hard to hide. But he needed to say this. No matter what the consequences. 'I get it that you grew up in an unhappy home and that your mother felt trapped. But you are not your mother. Your circumstances are completely different.'

'Not that different,' she whispered. 'Not when you treated me like that tonight. Like your possession.'

'I've held up my hands for that. I've said sorry. I would tell you truthfully that I would never behave in that way again, but it's too late.'

Her arms fell to her side. 'What do you mean, too late?'

'For us. I've tried to change and to adapt to being with you. I may not have instantly succeeded, but at least I gave it a go. But not you. You've stayed locked inside your own fear. You're scared, Sara. You're scared of who you really are. That's what made you run away from Dhi'ban. That's why you let your job consume you.'

'My father gave me permission to go away to boarding school—I didn't *run away.*'

'But you never go back, do you?'

'Because my life is here.'

'I know it is. But you have family. Your only family, in fact. When did you last see your brother? I heard that you were at his wedding celebrations for less than twenty-four hours.'

Briefly she wondered how he knew something like that. Had he been *spying* on her? 'I couldn't stay for long…I was in the middle of an important job.'

'Sure you were. Just like you always are. But you have vacations like other people, don't you, Sara? Couldn't you have gone over to see him from time to time? Didn't you ever think that being a king can be a lonely job? Hasn't his wife had a baby? Have you even *seen* your niece?'

'I sent them a gift when she was born,' she said defensively, and saw his mouth harden with an expression which suddenly made her feel very uncomfortable.

'You might want to reject your past,' he grated. 'But you can't deny the effect it's had on you. You may hate some things about desert life—but half of you *is* of the desert. Hide from that and you're hiding from yourself—and that's a scary place to be. I know that. You were one of the reasons I knew I could no longer work for Murat, but what happened between us that night made me re-examine my life. I realised that I couldn't continue playing a subordinate role out of some lingering sense of gratitude to a man who had plucked me from poverty.' He looked at her. 'But that's all irrelevant now. I need to pack.'

Her head jerked up as if she were a puppet and somebody had just given the string a particularly violent tug. 'Pack? What for?' She could hear the rising note of panic in her voice. 'What are you packing for?'

'I'm going.' His voice was almost gentle. 'It's over, Sara. We've had good times and bad times, but it's over. I recognise that and sooner or later you will, too. And I don't want to destroy all the good memories by continuing to slug it out, so I'm leaving now.'

She was swallowing convulsively. 'But it's late.'

'I know it is.'

'You could… Couldn't you stay tonight and go in the morning?'

'I can't do that, Sara.'

'No.' She shrugged as if it didn't matter. As if she didn't care. 'No, I guess you can't.'

Her lips were trembling as she watched him turn round and walk from the sitting room. She could hear the sounds he made as he clattered around in the bathroom, presumably clearing away that lethal-looking razor he always used. A terrible sense of sadness—and an even greater sense of failure—washed over her as he appeared in the doorway, carrying his leather overnight bag.

'I'll collect the rest of my stuff tomorrow, while you're at work.'

She stood up. Her legs were unsteady. She wanted to run over to him and tell him to stop. That it had all been a horrible mistake. Like a bad dream which you woke from and discovered that none of it had been real. But this *was* real. Real and very painful.

She wasn't going to be that red-eyed woman clinging onto his leg as he walked out of the door, she reminded herself. *Was she?* And surely they could say goodbye properly. A lifetime of friendship didn't have to end like *this*.

'A last kiss?' she said lightly, sounding like some vacuous socialite he'd just met at a cocktail party.

His mouth hardened. He looked…*appalled.* As if

she had just suggested holding an all-night rave on someone's grave.

'I don't think so,' he said grimly, before turning to slam his way out of her apartment—leaving only a terrible echoing emptiness behind.

CHAPTER ELEVEN

THE APARTMENT FELT bare without him.

Her life felt bare without him.

Sara felt as if she'd woken up on a different planet.

It reminded her of when she'd arrived at her boarding school in England, at the impressionable age of twelve. It had been a bitter September day, and the contrast to the hot desert country she'd left behind couldn't have been more different. She remembered shivering as the leaves began to be ripped from the trees by the wind, and she'd had to get used to the unspeakably stodgy food and cold, dark mornings. And even though she had known that here in England lay the future she had wanted—it had still felt like being on an alien planet for a while.

But that was nothing to the way she felt now that Suleiman had gone.

Hadn't she thought—prayed—that he hadn't meant it? That he would have cooled off by morning. That he would come back and they could make up. She could say sorry, as he had done. They could learn from their mistakes, and work out what they both wanted from their lives and walk forward into the future together.

He didn't come back.

She watched the clock. She checked her phone. She waited in.

And even though her pride tried to stop her—eventually she dialled his number. She was clutching a golden pen she'd found on the floor of the second bedroom—the only reminder that Suleiman had ever used the room as an office. He had loved this pen and would miss it, she convinced herself, even though she knew he had a dozen other pens he could use.

But he didn't pick up. The phone rang through to a brisk-sounding male assistant, who told her that Suleiman was travelling. In as casual a tone as she could manage, she found herself asking where—only to suffer the humiliation of the assistant telling her that security issues meant that he would rather not say.

Where was he travelling to? Sara wondered—as she put the phone down with a trembling hand. Had he gone back to Paris? Was he lying in that penthouse suite with another blonde climbing all over him wearing kinky boots and tiny knickers?

With a shaking hand she put the gold pen down carefully on the desk and then she forced herself to dress and went into the office.

But for the first time in her life, she couldn't concentrate on work.

Alice asked her several questions, which she had to repeat because Sara wasn't paying attention. Then she spilt her coffee over a drawing she'd been working on and completely ruined it. The days seemed to rush past her in a dark stream of heartache. Her thoughts wouldn't focus. She couldn't seem to allocate her time into anything resembling *order*. Everything seemed a mess.

At the end of the week, Gabe called her into the office and asked her to sit down and she could see from his face that he wasn't happy.

'What's wrong?' he questioned bluntly.

'Nothing's wrong.'

'Sara,' he said. 'If you can't do your job properly, then you really shouldn't come to work.'

She swallowed. 'That bad, huh?'

He shrugged. 'Do you want to talk about it?'

Miserably, she shook her head. Gabe was a good boss in many ways but she knew what they said about him—steely by name and steely by nature. 'Not really.'

'Look, take a week off,' he said. 'And for God's sake, sort it out.'

She nodded, thinking that men really *were* very different from women. It was all so black and white to them. What if it couldn't be sorted out? What if Suleiman had gone from her life for good?

She left the building and walked out into the fresh air, where a gust of wind seemed to blow right through her. She hugged her sheepskin coat closer and began to walk, thinking about the things Suleiman had said to her.

Thoughts she'd been trying to block out were now given free rein as she examined them. *Had* she run away from her old life and tried to deny it? Pretended that part of her didn't exist?

Yes, she had.

Had she behaved thoughtlessly, neglecting the only family she had? Rushing away from the wedding celebrations and not even bothering to get on a plane to go and see her new niece?

She closed her eyes.

Yes, again.

She'd thought of herself as so independent and mature, and yet the first thing she had done was to lift up the phone to Suleiman. What had she been planning to say to him? Start whining that she missed him and wanted him to come back to make her feel better?

That wasn't independence, was it? That was more like co-dependence. And you couldn't rely on somebody else to make you feel better about yourself.

She needed to face up to the stuff she'd locked away for so long. She'd been so busy playing the part of Sara Williams who had integrated so well into English life and making sure she fitted in that she had forgotten the other Sara.

The desert princess. The sister. The auntie.

And that other Sara was just as important.

A lump came into her throat as she lifted her hand to hail a cab and during the drive to her apartment she started making plans to try to put it right.

She managed to get a flight out to Dhi'ban later that evening. It meant she would have a two-hour stopover in Qurhah, but she could cope with that. Oddly enough, she wasn't tempted to ask her brother to send a plane to Qurhah to collect her—and she would sooner walk bare-footed across the desert than ask Suleiman to come to her aid.

She spent the intervening hours shopping and packing and then she dressed as conservatively and as unobtrusively as possible, because she didn't want anyone getting wind of her spontaneous visit.

The journey was long and tiring and she blinked with surprise when eventually she arrived at Dhi'ban's main airport, because she hardly recognised it. The terminal buildings had been extended and were now gleaming and modern. There were loads of shops selling cosmetics and beautiful Dhi'banese jewellery and clothes. And there…

She looked up to see a portrait of her brother, the King, and she thought how stern he looked. Sterner than she'd ever seen him, wearing the crown that her father had worn.

Inevitably, she was recognised as she went through Customs, but she waved aside the troubled protestations of the officials, telling them that she had no desire for a red carpet.

'I didn't want any kind of fuss or reception,' she said, smiling as she held up the large pink parcel she had purchased at Qurhah's airport. 'I want this to be a surprise. For my niece, the princess Ayesha.'

The palm-fringed road was reassuringly familiar and when she saw her childhood home appear in the distance, with the morning light bouncing off the white marble, she felt her heart twist with a mixture of pleasure and pain.

She'd never seen the guards outside the main gates look more surprised than when she stepped from the airport cab into the bright sunshine. But today she wasn't impatient when they bowed deeply. Today she recognised that they were just doing their job. They respected her position as Princess—and maybe it was about time that she started respecting it, too.

She walked through the grounds and into the palace. Her watch told her that it was almost two o'clock and she wondered if her brother was working. She realised that she didn't know anything about his life and she barely knew Ella, his wife.

But before she could decide what to do next, there was Haroun walking towards her. His features—a stronger, more masculine version of her own—were initially perplexed and then he broke into a wide smile as he held out his arms.

'Is it really you, Sara?'

'It really is me,' she whispered, glad that he chose that moment to gather her in his arms in a most un-Kingly bear-hug, which meant that she had time to blink away her tears and compose herself.

Within the hour she was sitting with Haroun and his wife Ella and begging their forgiveness. She told them she felt guilty about her absence, but if they were prepared to forgive her—she would like to be part of their lives. And could she please see her niece?

The royal couple looked at one another and smiled with deep satisfaction, before Ella hugged her tightly and said Ayesha was sleeping, and that Sara could see her once they had taken tea.

The three of them sat in the scented bower of the rose garden and drank mint tea. She started to tell them about the Sultan, but of course Haroun knew about the cancelled wedding, because the politicians and diplomats from the two countries were working on a new alliance.

'So you've *seen* Murat?' she asked cautiously.

'I have.'

'And did he…did he seem upset?'

'Not unless your idea of upset is being photographed with a stunning woman,' laughed Haroun.

It was only after gentle prompting that she was persuaded to tell them about Suleiman and how much she loved him. Her voice was shaky as she said it, because she'd realised that the truth was something she couldn't keep running from either.

'But it's over,' she said.

Ella looked at Haroun, and frowned. 'You *like* Suleiman, don't you, darling?'

'I don't like him when I'm playing backgammon,' Haroun growled.

Sara was shown to her old room and there, set between the two gold-framed portraits of her late mother and father, was a book about horses, which Suleiman had bought for her twelfth birthday, just before she'd left for England.

For the brave and fearless Sara, he had written. *Your friend, Suleiman. Always.*

And that was when the sobs began to erupt from her throat, because she had been none of those things, had she? She had not been brave and fearless—she had been a coward who had run away and hidden and neglected her family. She hadn't lived up to Suleiman's expectations of her. She hadn't been a real friend. She hadn't fulfilled her potential in so many ways.

She bathed and changed and dried her eyes and Ella knocked on the door, to take her to the nursery. And that was poignant, too. Shielded from the light by swathed swags of softest tulle lay a sleeping baby in the large, rocking cot she had slept in herself. For a moment Sara touched the side and felt it sway, watching as Ella lifted out the sleepy infant.

Ayesha was soft and smiling, with a mop of silken curls and a pair of deep violet eyes. Sara felt her heart fill with love as she touched her fingertip to the baby's plump and rosy cheek.

'Oh, she's beautiful,' she said. 'How old is she now?'

'Nine months,' said Ella. 'I know. Time flies and all that. And by the way—they say she looks just like you.'

'Do they?'

Ella smiled. 'Check out your baby photos if you don't believe me.'

Sara stared into the baby's eyes and felt the sharp twist of pain. Was it normal to feel wistful for what might have been, but now never would? To imagine what kind of baby she and Suleiman might have produced?

'I wonder if she'd come to me,' she said, pulling a smiley face at the baby as she held out her arms.

But Ayesha wriggled and turned her face away and started to cry.

'Don't worry,' said Ella. 'She'll get used to you.'

It took four days before Ayesha would consent to have her auntie hold her, but once she had—she seemed reluctant to ever let her go. Sara wondered if the baby instinctively guessed how badly she needed the cuddles. Or maybe there was some kind of inbuilt recognition—the primitive bond of shared blood.

She fitted in with Haroun and Ella's routine, and began to relax as she reacquainted herself with Dhi'ban and life at court. She went riding with her brother. She helped Ella with the baby and quickly grew to love her sister-in-law.

One afternoon the two women were wheeling the pram through the palace gardens, their heads covered with shady hats. The week off work which Gabe had given her was almost up and Sara knew that she needed to give some serious thought to her future.

She just hadn't decided what she wanted that future to be.

'Shall we go back now?' questioned Ella, her soft voice breaking into Sara's thoughts.

'Yes, let's.'

Along the scented paths they walked, back towards the palace, but as they grew closer Sara saw a dark figure silhouetted against the white marble building. For a moment her eyes widened, until she forced her troubled mind to listen to reason. *Please stop this,* she prayed silently. *Stop conjuring up hallucinations which make me think I can actually see him.*

She ran her hand across her eyelids, but when she opened them again he was still there and her steps faltered.

'Is something wrong?'

Did Ella's voice contain suppressed laughter—or was she imagining *that*, too?

'For a minute then, I thought I saw Suleiman.'

'Well, that's because you did,' said Ella gently. 'He's here. Suleiman's here.'

The ground seemed suddenly to shift beneath Sara's feet—the way it did when you stepped onto a large ship which looked motionless. She was aware of the rush of blood to her ears and the pounding of her heart in her chest. Questions streamed into her mind but her lips seemed too dry to do anything other than stumble out one bewildered word. 'How?'

But Ella was walking away, wheeling the pram towards one of the side entrances, and Sara was left standing there, feeling exposed and scared and impossibly vulnerable. Now her legs felt heavy. As if her feet had suddenly turned to stone and it was going to be impossible for her to walk. But she *had* to walk. Independent women walked. They didn't stumble—weak-kneed and hopeless—because the man they dreamed of had just appeared, like a blazing dark comet which had fallen to earth.

He didn't move as she went towards him and it was impossible to read the expression on his dark face. Even as she grew closer she still couldn't tell what he was thinking. But hadn't he told her himself that he was famous at the card table for being able to keep a poker-straight face?

She was trying to quell the hope which had risen up inside her—because dashed hopes were surely worse than no hope at all. But she couldn't keep her voice steady as she stood before him, and the pain of wanting to hold him again was almost physical.

'Suleiman,' she said and her voice sounded croaky and unsure. 'What are you doing here?'

'I've come to speak to your brother about the possibility of drilling for oil in Dhi'ban.'

Her heart plummeted. 'Are you being serious?'

He looked at her, an expression of exasperation on his face. 'Of course I'm not being serious. Why do you *think* I might be here, Sara?'

'I don't *know*!'

She was shaking her head and, for the first time, Suleiman saw that she had changed—even if for a moment he couldn't quite work out what that change was. Her skin was a little paler than usual and her lips looked as if they had been bitten into—but beneath all that he could see something else. Something which had been missing for a long time. He swallowed down the sudden lump in his throat as he realised that something was peace. That there was a new strength and resolution which shone out from her shadowed eyes as she looked at him.

And now he began to have doubts of his own. Had Sara found true contentment—*without* him? For a moment he acknowledged that his motives for being here today were entirely selfish. What if she would be better off without him? Had he stopped to consider *that*? Was her need for independence such that she considered a man like him to be an impediment?

His heart turning over with love and pain, he looked

into her beautiful face and suddenly he didn't care. He knew there were no guarantees in this life, but that didn't mean you shouldn't strike out for the things which really mattered. Let Sara tell him that she didn't want him if that was what she truly believed—but let her be in no doubt about his feelings for her.

'I think you do know,' he said softly. 'I'm here because I love you and I can't seem to stop loving you.'

'Did you try?' she questioned, her voice full of pain. 'Is that why you walked away? Why you left my life so utterly when you walked out of my apartment?'

There was a silence for a moment, broken only by the sound of a bird calling from high up in one of the trees. 'I couldn't stay when you were like that,' he told her truthfully. 'When you were too scared to let go and be the woman you really wanted to be. You were pushing me away, Sara—and I couldn't stand that. I knew you needed to come home before you could think about making any kind of home of your own.' He smiled. 'Then I heard on the desert grapevine that you'd come back to Dhi'ban. And I thought that was probably the best thing I'd heard in a long time.'

She turned big violet eyes up at him. 'Did you?'

'Mmm.' He wanted to go to her. To cup her chin in the palm of his hand and hold it safe. To run the edge of his thumb over the tremble of her lips. But he needed her to hear these words before he could touch her again. He owed her his honesty.

'As for the answer to your question. I'm here because you make me feel stuff—stuff I've spent a lifetime trying not to feel.'

'What kind of stuff?'

'Love.'

'Oh. You *think* you love me?' she questioned, echoing the words he had used in Paris.

'No.' His voice was quiet. 'I *love* you—without qualification. I love you fully, completely, utterly and for ever. I'm here because although I'm perfectly capable of living without you, I don't want to. No. That's not entirely true. If you want the truth, I can't bear the thought of living without you, Sara. Because without you I am only half the man I'm capable of being and I want to be whole.'

There was silence for a moment. She lowered her gaze, as if she had found something of immense interest on the gravelled palace forecourt. For a moment he wondered if she was plucking up the courage to tell him that his journey here had been wasted, but when she lifted her face again, Suleiman could see the shimmer of tears in her violet eyes.

'And without you I'm only half the woman I'm capable of being,' she said shakily. 'You've made me whole again, too. You've made me realise that only by facing our biggest fears can we overcome them. You've made me realise that independence is a good thing—but it can never be at the expense of love. Nothing can. Because love is the most important thing of all. And you are the most important thing of all, Suleiman—someone so precious who I thought I'd lost through my own stupidity.'

'Sara,' he said and the word was distorted by the shudder of his breath. 'Sweet Sara. My only love.'

And that was all it took. A declaration torn from somewhere deep inside him. A declaration she returned over and over again in between their frantic kisses, although Suleiman first took the precaution of walking her further into the gardens, away from the natural interest of the servants' eyes.

By the time they returned to the palace—where Ella and Haroun had perceptively put a bottle of champagne on ice—Sara was wearing an enormous emerald engagement ring.

And she couldn't seem to stop smiling.

EPILOGUE

'YOU DO REALISE,' said Sara as she removed her filmy tulle veil and placed it next to the emerald and diamond tiara, which her sister-in-law had lent her, 'that I'm not going to be a traditional desert wife.'

'Shouldn't you have mentioned this *before* we got married?' murmured Suleiman. He was lying naked waiting for his bride to join him on her old childhood bed, and had decided that there was something gloriously decadent about that.

'I did.' She stepped out of her ivory lace gown and hung it over the back of the chair, revelling in the look in his eyes as he ran his gaze over her bridal lingerie. 'Just as long as you know that I meant it.'

'And I meant it when I said that I didn't expect you to be. Just as I did when I said that I will not be a traditional desert husband. I will not try to possess you, Sara—not ever again. I will give you all the freedom you need.'

She gave a happy sigh as she smiled at him. Wasn't it a strange thing that when somebody gave you freedom, it meant you no longer wanted it quite so much?

Suleiman had told her that of course she could carry on working for Gabe—just as long as they came to some compromise over her long hours. The crazy thing was that she no longer wanted to work there—or, at least, not as she'd done before. She had loved her job, but it was part of her past and part of her life as a single woman. She had a different life now and different opportunities. Which was why she had agreed to carry on working for the Steel organisation on a freelance basis. That way, she could travel with her husband and everyone was happy.

She gave a contented sigh. Their wedding had been the best wedding she'd ever been to—although Suleiman told her she was biased. Alice from the office had been invited—and her expression as she'd been shown around the Dhi'ban palace had been priceless. Gabe had been there too—and Sara thought that even her cynical boss had enjoyed all the ancient ritual and ceremony which accompanied the joining of her hand to Suleiman's.

The best bit had been the Sultan's surprise appearance, because it signified that he had forgiven Suleiman—and her—for so radically changing the course of desert history.

'Murat seemed to get on well with Gabe, don't you think?' she questioned as she slid her diamond bracelet onto the dressing table, where it lay coiled like a glittery snake. 'What do you suppose they were talking about?'

'Right now I don't care,' Suleiman murmured.

'About anything other than kissing you again. It seems like an eternity since I had you in my bed.'

'It's almost a week since you had me in your bed—palace protocol being what it is,' she agreed. 'But less than eight hours since you *had* me. *In* the stables, no less—on the eve of my wedding. And I wasn't allowed to make a sound.'

'That was part of the thrill,' he drawled, watching as she kicked off her high-heeled shoes. 'Not very much keeps you quiet, but it seems that at last I've found something which does. Which means that we are going to be indulging in lots of illicit sex in the future, my darling wife.'

She walked over to the bed to join him, still wearing her panties, her bra and her white lace suspender belt and stockings. It felt warm in his embrace, and safe. So very safe.

They were going to honeymoon in Samahan and she was going to learn all about the land of Suleiman's birth. Afterwards, they would decide where they wanted to make their main base.

'It can be anywhere,' he had promised her. 'Anywhere at all.'

She closed her eyes as he tightened his arms around her, because where they lived didn't matter.

This was home.

* * * * *

IN DEFIANCE
OF DUTY

CAITLIN CREWS

*To all the fantastic writers at the 2011 Romantic
Writers of Australia Conference who were
so lovely and welcoming to me, despite my
crippling jet lag. It was such a treat (and an
honour) to get to spend time with you – and
I hope I did justice to your beautiful country!*

*And to my favourite Los Angeles-based
Australian, Kate Rogers, who told me
the truth about magpies.*

USA TODAY bestselling and RITA® Award–
nominated author **Caitlin Crews** loves writing
romance. She teaches her favourite romance novels
in creative writing classes at places like UCLA
Extension's prestigious Writers' Programme,
where she finally gets to utilise the MA and
PhD in English Literature she received from the
University of York in England. She currently lives
in California, with her very own hero and too
many pets. Visit her at www.caitlincrews.com.

CHAPTER ONE

"LOVELY view."

Kiara didn't turn toward the deep, commanding voice, even as it washed over her and somehow into her blood, her bones, making her very nearly shiver. She'd sensed his approach before he'd helped himself to the chair next to hers—there had been a certain expectant stillness in the air around her, a kind of palpable, electrically charged quiet, as if all of Sydney fell silent before him. She'd pictured that easy, confident walk of his, the way his dark, powerful masculinity turned heads wherever he went, the way he'd no doubt been watching her with that intense, consuming focus as he drew near.

But then, she'd been expecting him.

"That's a terrible pickup line," she pointed out, a shade too close to flippant. But she couldn't seem to help herself. She decided she wouldn't look at him unless he earned it. She would pretend to be enchanted by the water of the harbor, the coming sunset. Not by a man like him, no matter how tall, dark and dangerous he might be, even in her peripheral vision. "Especially here. This particular view is famous, I think you'll find. Renowned the world over."

"That should make it all the more lovely, then," he replied, a thread of amusement beneath the steel-and-velvet seduction of his voice. She felt it like heat, pressing into her skin. "Or are you the dreary sort who finds a view is spoiled forever if too many others look upon it?"

Kiara sat at a small outdoor table tucked in on the lower concourse beneath Sydney's glorious, soaring Opera House and the sky above, with full and unfettered access to the famous and beautiful arch of the Harbor Bridge opposite. The setting sun above had just settled into rich and tempting golds, sending the mellow light dancing over the sparkling water of the harbor itself, as if taunting the jutting skyscrapers of the city—as if daring them to look away from the spectacular evening show.

She certainly knew the feeling. And she wasn't even looking at the man who lounged next to her as if he owned the table, the chair, and her, too, though she was *aware* of him in every possible way. In every part of her skin and blood and bones.

"Don't try to change the subject," she said mildly, as if wholly unaffected by him and the great tractor beam of power and charisma that seemed to emanate from him. He was lethal. So compelling it almost hurt not to turn and let herself look at him, drink him in. "You're the one who trotted out a tired old line. I only pointed it out. I don't think that makes me dreary."

She knew intuitively that his particular brand of dark male beauty—so fierce and breathtaking, laced through with all that dizzying masculine power—would be equally dazzling if she dared turn her head and look at it. She could *feel* it. In the way her stomach clenched and, below, ached around a deep, feminine pulse. The way the fine hairs on her arms and the back of her neck stood at attention, almost making her shiver. The way the whole world seemed to shrink to just this table, this chair.

Him.

Instead, she fiddled with the coffee cup she'd drunk

dry a while ago, even toyed with the ends of the wavy light brown hair she'd swept back into a high ponytail, her hands betraying her even as she sat there with such studied carelessness, pretending she was unaware of the great strength of him next to her. The imposing fact of him—ink-black hair against oddly light eyes, the stamp of his Arab ancestry in his fierce features, and that mouthwatering fantasy of a body—that she could grasp even with only the briefest glance from the corner of her eye. The impact on not only her, but the whole of the Opera House Bar around them.

She could see the group of older women at the next table—the way they turned to look at him, then widened their eyes at each other before dissolving into besotted giggles better suited to the girls Kiara imagined they'd been some thirty years before.

"Tell me how to play this game," he said after a moment that seemed overripe with the gold sinking against the water, the murmur of the crowd of tourists all around them, his own dark magnetism spread over them like an umbrella. "Will I woo you with my wit? My appreciation of the local beauty? Perhaps I will tell you a series of pretty lies and convince you to come back to my hotel with me. Just for the night. Anonymous and furtive. Do you think that would work?"

"You won't know until you try," she said, biting back a grin, even as carnal images chased through her head—none of them either anonymous or furtive. All of them spellbinding. Wild with passion. "Though I hardly think laying out your options like that, so coldblooded and matter-of-fact, will do you any favors. You should think in terms of seduction, not spreadsheets." She found she was grinning despite herself then, but still kept from looking at him, staring resolutely ahead at the delicate arch of the bridge as if unable to tear herself away. "If you don't mind a word of advice."

"I relish it, of course." His low voice was cool, ironic, and still managed to kick up fires all along her skin. And deeper. She shifted in her seat, crossing and then recrossing her legs, wishing he did not take up *quite* so much space. He did not seem to move at all, and yet, somehow, she was even more aware of him.

"So far," she continued, her own voice confiding, pitched for his ears alone, "I must tell you that I'm completely unimpressed."

"With the view?" Now his amusement wasn't hidden at all. It moved through his voice even as it moved through her, teasing her with hints of something else beneath his crisp British public school vowels, something that indicated English was only one of his languages. The faintest suggestion that he was nothing simple or easily categorized. "I hope you're not one of those terminally bored socialite types, so shallow and endlessly fatigued by everything the world has to offer."

"And if I am?"

"That would be a great disappointment."

"Luckily," she said drily, "you can hardly have been too invested in something that could only have ended in lies and a furtive hotel visit, could you? I imagine the disappointment will be minor."

"But I am captivated," he protested in an insultingly mild way that made her laugh despite herself.

"By my profile?" She smiled at the bridge, imagined the man, and shook her head. "It's all you've seen of me."

"Perhaps it is your profile superimposed on such a famous view," he suggested. "I'm as awestruck as any run-of-the-mill tourist. If only I'd remembered my camera."

She forgot she didn't mean to look at him and turned her head.

It was looking into the sun. Searing. Dizzying.

He was beautiful—there was no other word for it—but there was nothing in the least bit pretty about him. He was a study in controlled ferocity. He was all sleek muscle and hard, strong lines. His rich black hair, his dark skin, the gleam in his unusual, near-blue eyes. The merciless thrust of his cheekbones, his belligerent jaw. He lounged beside her with seeming nonchalance, but she wasn't fooled.

He was all focus and menace, his rangy, athletic body showcased to perfection in a dark suit and a snow-white shirt that he wore open against his neck, as if he was attempting a casual gesture when everything else about him shouted out the formidable *force* he wore the way another man might wear a jacket. He looked as if there was nothing at all he couldn't do with his disconcertingly elegant hands—and nothing he hadn't already done with them. She could think of several possibilities, and had to swallow against the shocking surge of heat that swept through her then, wild and out of control.

She was sure he could feel the very same flames.

"Hello," he said quietly as their eyes met. Held. His sensual mouth curved into a knowing smile. "I like this view, too."

Kiara forced a jaded sigh. "You really aren't very good at this, are you?"

"Apparently not." His impossible eyes, somewhere between blue and green, or possibly gray, gleamed. "By all means, teach me. I live to serve."

She didn't laugh at that. She didn't need to. His own mouth quirked up in the corner, supremely arrogant and male, as if he was as unable to imagine himself serving anyone or anything as she was.

"For all you know, I could be meeting someone." She forgot about the view; he was far more mesmerizing, especially when his gaze turned darker and something like stormy. She smiled then. "My very jealous lover, for example, who might find you here and take out his aggression all over you. With his fists."

"A risk I feel prepared to take, somehow."

There was no denying the edge of confident menace in his smile then, and she wondered what sort of woman she was to find that as appealing as she did. Surely she ought to be ashamed. She wasn't.

"Is that a threat of violence?" she asked tartly. And then lied. "That's incredibly unattractive."

"That is exactly how you look," he said, the knowing quirk of his hard mouth deepening, his storm-tossed eyes too hot, too sure. "Unattracted."

"Or perhaps I'm simply a single woman out on the town, looking for a date," she continued in the same nonchalant, careless tone. "You seem to want to talk only about the view. Or make depressing remarks about the *furtiveness* of a night of wild, uncontrollable passion. Neither is likely to make me want to date you, is it?"

"Are we talking about a date?" His mouth curved again, as if he was trying not to laugh, and very nearly failing. His almost-blue eyes reminded her of the winter sea, and were as compelling. "I thought this was a negotiation about sex. Endlessly inventive sex, I believe. Or hope, in any case. Not a tedious *date*, all manners and flowers and gentlemanlike behavior."

It took her a moment to breathe through the way he said *sex*, like some kind of incantation. Much less the images he conjured up, and their immediate effect on her body. How could one man be this dangerous? And why was she wholly unable to offer up any kind of defense against him?

"The way this works is that you pretend to be interested only in a date," she told him as if she was *this close* to exasperation but only the kindness of her heart kept her from it. "You *pretend* that you want to get to know me as a person. The more you do that, the more romantic it will all feel. To me, I mean. And that, of course, is the quickest route toward rampant sex in a hotel room." She shrugged her shoulders as if she felt she shouldn't have to be the one to share this with him. As if every other person in Sydney was well aware of this, and she wondered why he wasn't.

"I can't simply ask for rampant sex?" he asked, as if baffled. Possibly even shocked. Though that lazy, indulgent gleam in his eyes said otherwise. "Are you sure?"

"Only if you are planning to purchase it." She eyed him, and the hint of a smile that toyed with that mouth of his, and made her wish all sorts of undignified things. "Which is, of course, perfectly legal here. And no, buying me a drink is not the same thing."

"Your country has so many rules," he said softly, the amusement leaving his gaze as something far hotter took its place. "Mine is far more...direct."

She *felt* the way he looked at her, the fire in it moving over her like a caress, making her wish that she was dressed far more provocatively. Making her wish she could bare her skin to his gaze, to the night falling all around them. The black blazer she wore over a decadently soft black jumper and the dark blue jeans she'd tucked into her favorite black suede books felt confining, suddenly, instead of the casually chic look she'd been going for. She wished she could peel it all off and throw it all in the harbor. She wondered what it was about this man that made such an uncharacteristic urge seem so appealing in the first place.

But she knew.

"Direct?" she echoed, feeling the pull of that hard

face, those unholy eyes. She wanted to move closer to that wicked mouth of his. She wanted it more than was wise. More than she should, out in public like this, where anyone could see. For a moment she forgot the game—*herself*—entirely.

"If I want it," he said quietly, so quietly, but she felt it flood into her as if he'd shouted it, as if he'd licked it into her skin, "I take it."

Kiara felt that hum in her, electric and something like overwhelming. For a moment she could only stare back at him, caught in that knowing gaze of his, as surely as if he'd caged her somehow. Trapped her as surely as if he'd used manacles and heavy iron bars. She shouldn't feel that like a thrill, twisting through her, but she did.

"Then I suppose I should count myself lucky that we are not in your country," she said after a moment, not sure until she spoke that she would be able to at all. She was surprised that her voice sounded so steady. Almost tart. "This is Australia. I'm afraid we're quite civilized."

"All of you in your new, young countries are the same," he said in that low tone, his voice its own dark spell, weaving its way over her, inside of her, as inexorable as the setting sun. "So brash, forever carrying on about your purported civility. But you are all so close, still, to your disreputable pasts, aren't you? All of it welling up from beneath, making a lie of these carefully cultivated facades."

Kiara realized two things simultaneously. One, that she could listen to him talk forever—about countries, about pasts, about whatever he liked. That voice of his triggered something deep inside her, something helpless and wanton, that made her breathless and so wrapped up in him that the world could fall to pieces around her and she wouldn't notice. Or, as now, the sun could disappear entirely beneath the horizon without her registering it, ushering in the inky sweetness of the Sydney night, and she would still see nothing but him.

And two, and more important, that she would die if she didn't touch him. Now.

"As fascinating as your thoughts on young countries and disreputable pasts may be," she said then, keeping her voice a low murmur, her eyes hot on his, "I think that I'd rather dispense with all this meaningless chatter and just get naked. What do you think?"

He smiled again, and she felt it shiver through her and curl her toes. He reached over and took her hand in his, carrying it to his mouth. It was the faintest hint of a kiss, a timeless gesture of chivalry for the benefit of the people all around them, but she felt it like a hard kick. Like a promise.

"There is nothing I would rather do," he said, that gleam of amusement in his eyes turning them something near silver. "But I'm afraid I'm meeting my wife for dinner. I'm sorry to disappoint you."

"I'm sure she'll understand." Kiara played with his strong fingers in hers. "Who would want to stand in the way of acrobatic, inventive sex, after all?"

"She's terribly jealous." He shook his head almost sadly. "It's like a sickness—*ouch*." His gaze turned baleful, and a silver heat gleamed there, while something almost too warm to bear echoed in a kind of sizzle low in Kiara's belly. "Did you just bite me?"

"Don't act like you didn't enjoy it." It was a dare.

He let go of her hand, but shifted closer, reaching over to pull gently on the end of her ponytail, tilting her head up slightly to meet his searing gaze.

"Perhaps I can risk my wife's jealous rages after all," he said musingly. He moved still closer, until their faces were a mere breath apart, his delectable mouth *just* there, *just* out of reach.

Her breath came out ragged, then, as if she'd broken into a run. She felt as if she had. His smile licked over her, into her.

"You look as if you can take it," Kiara agreed, and then she closed the distance between them and kissed him.

His wife, Sheikh Azrin bin Zayed Al Din, Crown Prince of Khatan, reflected with no little amusement, was endlessly delightful to him.

Her lips were soft and sweet against his, hinting at the passion that neither of them could succumb to out in the public eye like this. It was as frustrating as it was delicious. He wanted more than this *hint* of her, after two weeks apart. He wanted to taste her—take her—with a ferocity that might have surprised him, five years after marrying her, had he not been well used to this relentless thirst for her.

A thirst he could not indulge. Not here. Not now.

He pulled away, controlling himself with the ruthlessness that was second nature to him, particularly where his wife was concerned, and smiled again at the dazed look she wore, as if she had forgotten where they were. Azrin could look at her forever. Her pretty oval face with its delicate nose and brows, and her wide, decadent mouth that had been the first thing he'd noticed about her. Her hair was a mix of browns and golds, tumbling down past her shoulders in light waves unless, like tonight, she'd opted to put the heavy weight of it up in one of her sleek, deceptively casual styles. She looked taller than she was, her body firm and toned from her years of athletics and hard work, and she tended to dress conservatively as suited her position, yet with a quiet little flair that was hers alone.

That deep current of wickedness was all for him.

"If you had spoken to me like that when we met," he

said lazily, taunting her, "I doubt I would ever have pursued you at all. So disrespectful and challenging."

She rolled her eyes, as he'd known she would. "I did speak to you like that," she replied. Her generous mouth widened into a smile. "You loved it."

"So I did."

He got to his feet then and took her hand to help her rise. She held on for a moment too long, as if she wanted to cling to even that much contact. He felt the kick of it, of her, deep inside of him. He craved her. He wanted to lick his way over every inch of her skin, relearning her as if the two weeks he'd been without her might have changed her. He wanted to find out for himself. With his mouth, his hands.

She curved into his side as they began to walk back along the concourse toward Sydney's impressive, glittering array of skyscrapers, and the penthouse he kept there that was as much a primary residence as anything could be for two people who traveled as much as they did. He slid his arm around her slender shoulders and contented himself as best he could with a light kiss on the top of her head that barely reached his chin. Her hair smelled of sunshine and flowers, and he could not touch her the way he wanted to.

Not here. Not now. *Not yet*, he thought.

No unrestrained public displays of affection for the Crown Prince of Khatan and his non-Khatanian, scandalous-merely-by-virtue-of-her-foreign-birth princess. Well did Azrin know the rules. The public—particularly in his country—might fight for any possible glimpse of what they called his *modern Cinderella romance*, but that didn't mean they wanted to see anything that wouldn't have suited the family-friendly film of the same name.

There could be nothing that suggested that Azrin was compromised in any way by what many in his country took to be the lax moral code of anyone not from their own part of the world. There could certainly be no hint that the passion between Azrin and his princess was still so intense, so all-encompassing, that some days they did not even get out of bed, even after all this time. He was hoping that this night might lead directly into one of those lost days, even though he knew there was so much to do now, so many details to take care of and so little time to do it all in…

He should tell her now. Immediately. He knew that he should—that there was no real excuse for waiting. There was only his curious inability to speak up as he should. There was only that part of him that didn't want to accept this was happening.

He wanted this one night, that was all. This last, perfect night of the life they'd both enjoyed so much for so long that had let him pretend he was someone else. What was one night more?

"I missed you, Azrin," Kiara whispered, her supple body flush against his, her arm around his waist as they walked. "Two weeks is much too long."

"It was unavoidable." He heard the dark note in his voice and smiled down at her to dispel it. "I didn't care for it, either."

He would be happy when this part of their life was behind them, he thought as they made their way through the usual crowds flocking to Sydney's pretty jewel of a harbor to enjoy the mild evening, the restaurants, the view. He would be more than pleased to do without these weeks of separations that they tried valiantly to keep to ten days or less. The endless grind of international travel to this or that city, in every corner of the globe, to steal a day, a night, even an afternoon together. Meeting up with his wife in hotels that became interchangeable in the cities where they did not have a residence, and hardly noticing which residence was which when they were in one of them. New York, Singapore, Tokyo, Paris, the capital city of his own country, Arjat an-Nahr, on an endlessly repeating cycle. Always having to plan to see his wife around the demands of their calendars, never simply seeing her. Never really able to simply *be* with her.

He would not miss this part of their life at all. He told himself that having this part end would be worth the rest of it. At least they would be together. Surely that was the important thing.

"You should not have stayed so long in Arjat an-Nahr," she was saying, that teasing note in her voice, the one that normally made him smile automatically. "I'm tempted to think that you care more for your country and its demands on your time than your poor, neglected wife."

He knew she was kidding. Of course she was. But still—tonight, it pricked at him. It seemed to suggest things about their future that he knew he didn't want to hear. That he could not accept, not even as an offhanded joke. It cut too deep tonight.

"I will be king one day," he reminded her, keeping his voice light, because he knew—he did—that she was only teasing, the way she often did. The way she always had. Wasn't her very irreverence why he had been so drawn to her in the first place? "Everything will come second to my country then, Kiara. Even you."

And him, of course. Especially him.

She looked up at him, those marvelous brown eyes of hers moving over his face in the dark. He knew that she could read him, and wondered what she saw. Not the truth, of course. He knew even she could not know that, not from a single searching look, no matter how well she could read what she saw. No one knew the truth yet save his father's doctors, his mother and Azrin himself.

"I know who I married," she told him softly, though Azrin did not think she could when he felt so unsure of it himself. "Do you doubt it?" She smiled; soothing, somehow, what felt so raw in him that easily. As if she could sense it without his having to tell her. And then her voice took on that teasing lilt again, encouraging him to follow her back into lighter, shallower waters. "You always take such pains to remind me, after all."

It was only change, he told himself. Everything changed. Even them. Even this. It was neither good nor bad—it was simply the natural order of things.

And more than that, he had always known this day was coming. Why had he imagined otherwise, these past five years? Who had he been trying to fool?

"Do you mean when I request that you keep your voice down while you are pretending that I am merely some overconfident stranger picking you up in a bar, lest the papers feel the need to share this game of yours with the whole world?" He couldn't quite make his voice sound reproving, especially not when her brown eyes were so warm, so challenging, and seemed to connect directly with his sex. And his heart. "Does that count as taking pains, Kiara? Or is it simply a more highly developed sense of self-preservation?"

"Yes, my liege," she murmured in feigned obeisance, laughter thrumming in her voice, just below the surface. She even bowed her head in a mock sign of respect. "Whatever you say, my liege."

His almost equally feigned look of exasperation made her laugh, and the bright, musical sound of it seemed to roll through him like light.

He couldn't regret the past five years. He didn't.

He had always taken his duties as Crown Prince as seriously as he'd taken his position as the managing director of the Khatan Investment Authority, one of the largest sovereign wealth funds in the world. Kiara had always been wholly dedicated to her own role as vice president of her family's famous winery in South Australia's renowned Barossa Valley, a career that took her all over the world and kept her as busy as he was. Theirs had always been a modern marriage, the only one like it in the whole of his family's history.

But then, he had long been his country's emblem of the future, whether he wanted to be or not—and no one had ever asked him his feelings on the subject. His feelings were irrelevant, Azrin knew. While his father was very much and very proudly wedded to the old ways, Azrin was supposed to represent the modern age come to life in the midst of old-world Khatan, his small, oil-rich island nation in the Persian Gulf.

He knew—had always known—that once he took the throne he was expected to usher in the new era of Khatan that his father either could not or did not want to. He was expected to lead his people into a freer, more independent future, without the bloodshed and turmoil some of their neighboring countries had experienced.

And Kiara had been his first step in that direction, little as he might have thought of her in those terms when he'd met her. She was a twenty-first century Western woman in every respect, independent and ambitious, a fourth generation Australian winemaker and wholly impressive in her own right. Marrying her had been a commitment to a very different kind of future than the one his old school father, with his traditional three wives, offered their people.

Together, Azrin and Kiara were considered the new face of a new Khatan. That wouldn't change now—it would only become more analyzed and critiqued. More speculated about. More observed and remarked upon. Their marriage would cease to be theirs; it would become his people's, just as the rest of his life would. It was inevitable.

Azrin had always known this day would come. He just hadn't expected it would come *now*. So soon. And perhaps because he'd thought he would have so many more years left before it happened, he certainly hadn't understood until now how very much he'd dreaded it.

He didn't want to admit that, not even to himself.

"Where have you gone?" she asked now, stopping, and thereby making him stop, too. The busy Sydney Pier bristled with ferries and commuters headed home for the evening, tourist groups and restaurant patrons on their way to an evening out. Her clever eyes met his as her palm curved against his jaw. "You're miles away."

"I am still in Khatan," he said, which was true enough. He took her hand in his, lacing their fingers together, and tugged her along with him as he started to walk again, guiding her around the usual cluster of stalls and street performers making the most of the evening rush and the ever-present tourists. "But I would much rather be in you. Naked, I think you said?"

"I did say that." Her voice was so proper, so demure. Only because he knew her well could he hear the mischief beneath the surface, that touch of wickedness that made him harden in response. "I thought you might have forgotten. My liege."

"I never forget anything that has to do with your naked body, Kiara," he said in a low voice. "Believe me."

He wasn't ready, he thought—and yet he must be. What he wanted, what he felt—none of that mattered any longer. What mattered was who he was, and therefore who he was about to become. He simply had to learn to keep his own desires, his own feelings, in reserve, just as he'd done for years before he'd met Kiara. In truth, it had been nothing but selfishness that had allowed him to spend the past five years pretending it could ever be otherwise.

He handed Kiara into the long black car that idled at the curb once they reached the street and climbed in after her.

Despite the fact that they were a prince and a princess, a royal sheikh and his chosen bride, they had spent years behaving as if they were like any other high-powered couple anywhere else in the world. They'd believed it themselves, Azrin thought. He certainly had.

The Prince and Princess of Khatan were relatable, accessible. *Normal.* They worked hard and didn't get to see as much of each other as they'd like. Theirs was not a story of harems and exoticism, royal excesses and the bizarre lifestyles of the absurdly privileged. They were your everyday, run-of-the-mill power couple, just trying to excel at what they did. *Just like you.*

And yet they were not those couples, and never would be.

They were not normal. They had only been pretending. He told himself it was not a kind of grief that gripped him then—that it was simply reality.

He would be king. She would be his queen. There were greater expectations of those roles than of the ones they'd been playing at all this time. There were different, more complicated considerations. He knew with the kick of something like foreboding, deep in his gut, that there were great sacrifices that both of them would have to make.

It was only change, he told himself again. Everything and everyone changed.

But not tonight.

CHAPTER TWO

It took Kiara long moments after she woke in the wide, plush bed in the center of a room bathed in light to recall that she was in Sydney. In the penthouse in Sydney, she reminded herself as she stretched—that glorious multi-level dwelling high on the top of an exclusive building that only Azrin, who had been raised between several palaces, could call *an apartment*. Her lips curved.

She swung her legs over the side of the platform bed and rose slowly, smiling at the delicious feeling of bone-lessness all throughout her body. That was the Azrin effect. She supposed she should have been used to it by now. Images of the previous night swept through her head, each more erotic than the last. He was a sensualist, her husband; a demanding lover who held nothing back—and took everything in return.

She found herself in the opulent shower with no real idea how she'd got there, humming to herself as she used the delicately scented soap over the skin he'd tasted and touched repeatedly. That was what he did—he made her a besotted, airheaded fool. When he was near, she found she could think of very little else.

Just him. Only him.

She stepped from the great glass shower that she knew from past experience could hold both of them as well as some of Azrin's more inventive fantasies, and toweled herself off, letting her hair down from the clip she'd used to secure it away from the hot spray. Sometimes she felt guilty that she often considered her demanding career a necessary a bit of breathing room between rounds with her far more demanding, far more consuming husband. There was just something about Azrin, she thought, smiling to herself, that encouraged complete surrender.

She found him out in the great room, lounging carelessly on the low sofa that sprawled out in the center of the sleek, modern space, speaking in assured and confident Arabic into the tablet he used for video conferencing. His fierce gaze met hers and though he did not smile, a flash of heat moved through her anyway.

Even after the night they'd shared, she wanted more. Her core warmed anew, ready for him at a glance. Again. Always.

He was lethal.

She made sure to keep out of sight of the camera, slipping into the open-plan gourmet kitchen that neither she nor Azrin had ever cooked in to fix herself a morning coffee from the imposing, gleaming espresso machine. A few minutes later she settled with the fruits of her labor—a flat white in a warm ceramic mug, perfectly made if she said so herself—on one of the chrome bar stools that fetched up to the shiny granite expanse of kitchen counter.

She still did not speak Arabic, though she'd picked up a few phrases over the years, none of them particularly repeatable outside of the bedroom. So she didn't try to figure out what he was talking about in that commanding tone that reminded her that he was a royal prince who some called *my liege* without irony; she let his deep, sure voice wash over her like a caress. She sat and enjoyed a rare moment with nothing to do but look out the wall of floor-to-ceiling glass windows that faced north, the spectacular view stretching across the green lushness of Hyde Park toward the gorgeous Royal Botanic Gardens, the soaring shapes of the Sydney Opera House, and the picturesque Sydney Harbor, all of it bathed in the sweet, golden Australian sunshine.

But she couldn't keep it up. Too soon she was worrying over a problem that had cropped up with the export of one of the Zinfandels they'd been experimenting with in recent years, and wondering if it required a quick, unscheduled call to her mother, the formidable CEO of Frederick Wines and sometime bane of Kiara's existence. Given the complicated cocktail of guilt, love and obligation that characterized Kiara's relationship with her mother as both her daughter and her second-in-command, Kiara usually preferred to handle things like this on her own. She argued the pros and cons in her head, going back and forth again and again.

Sydney preened before her in the abundant sunshine, skyscrapers sparkling in the light and the harbor dotted with sails and ferry boats far below, but Kiara hardly saw them. In her mind, she saw the greens and golds of her beloved Barossa Valley, the rich green vineyards spreading out in all directions, the complacent little towns bristling with Bavarian architecture, built by settlers like Kiara's ancestors who'd fled from religious persecution in Prussia. She saw the family vineyards that had dominated her life since she was a girl—and the grand old chateau that had been in her family for generations.

The winery had taken over her mother's life when she'd found herself there, a widow with an infant, and it was Kiara's life, too, as it could hardly be anything else. At the very least, she had to prove to both her mother and herself that it had all been worth it, didn't she? All the years of sacrifice and struggle on her mother's part to build and maintain Kiara's heritage—surely Kiara owed her, at the very least, her own commitment to that heritage.

She wasn't sure what made her look up to find Azrin watching her then, his conference clearly over and an unusually serious look on his ruthless face.

"Good morning," she said and smiled, pushing her concerns away as she drank him in, as if he could clear her head and vanquish her mother's doubt just by being there in front of her. Instead of halfway across the world somewhere, available only by phone or video chat, which was the way she usually saw him.

She expected him to smile back. But he only looked at her for a long moment, and something twisted inside her—something she didn't entirely understand. She remembered, then, his unusual urgency the night before. The edge to him that had made him even more fierce, even more demanding than usual. Something skittered down her spine, making her sit straighter on the stool. She smoothed the edges of her silk wrapper around her. She didn't look away.

"Why are you looking at me like that?" she asked softly. "What's happened?"

"I am admiring my beautiful wife," he said, though there was a certain rawness in his near-blue eyes. "My princess. My future queen."

Kiara was uneasy, and she didn't know why. He looked as if he'd been up for hours, which was not particularly remarkable, given his many business concerns and the world's various time zones. His dark hair looked rumpled, as if he'd been running his hands through it repeatedly. He hadn't bothered to shave, and the rough shadow along his tough jaw made him look more like the sheikh she sometimes forgot he was and less like the cosmopolitan, sophisticated husband with whom she explored the great modern cities of the world.

For some reason, her throat was dry.

"You could sound a *bit* less complimentary," she pointed out, trying to sound as teasing and as light as she usually did. "If you tried. Though you'd have to work hard at it."

He nearly smiled then, and she had the strange notion that it was against his will. Something sat heavy in the room, making her anxious, and she could see he felt it, too—that it was in him, something grim and hard behind his gaze, making those near-blue eyes grow dark. Making it difficult to breathe.

Kiara prided herself on her ability to close deals and navigate the sometimes treacherous labyrinth of international business concerns in general and the wine industry in particular. Hell, she was good at it. She'd had to be, having had to overcome the usual suspicions that she'd been promoted thanks to her relationship with the boss lady rather than her own hard work, and then, after her wedding, having to stare down everyone who'd sniggered and snidely called her *your highness* or *princess* in the middle of a tense meeting.

She enjoyed confounding expectations, thank you very much. She'd learned how to keep people at arm's length as a defense mechanism against her mother's complete lack of boundaries when she was still a girl. She'd spent her professional life cultivating a little bit of an untouchable ice-queen facade, and becoming a widely photographed and speculated-about princess had only helped make her deliberate shell that much more impenetrable. She liked it that way.

But *this* man was different. *This* man looked at her with some kind of pain in him and she would do anything—dance, tease, crawl, whatever worked—to make it go away.

This was Azrin, and the love she felt for him—the love that had crashed into her and wholly altered the course of her life five years ago—was impossible to hide away behind some smooth mask. He was the one person on earth that she never, ever wanted at arm's length, no matter how wild and unbalanced that sometimes made her feel inside, and no matter how far away from each other they often were.

She was up and on her feet before she knew she meant to move, crossing over to him.

"I have something to tell you," he said, his gaze still so dark, so bleak.

"Then tell me," she said. But she straddled him where he sat, letting her silk wrapper fall open to show that she was naked and still warm from her shower beneath it. "But you'll forgive me if I make the conversation a little more exciting, won't you?"

She wasn't really thinking. She only knew she wanted to soothe him, and to *do* something to make whatever this was better. She felt him harden beneath her, felt his breath against her neck, as if he was as helpless to resist this pull between them as she had always been.

But she knew they both were. It had been this way, outsized and impossible and wholly irresistible, from the very beginning.

"Kiara…" he said, in that tone that was supposed to be reproving, chastising even, but his hands slid beneath the wrapper and onto her bare skin, smoothing over her hips. She arched against him, feeling the scrape of his jaw against the tender slope of her breast. He tilted his head back to look up at her, his hard mouth in an unsmiling line. "What are you doing?"

She thought that was obvious, but she only smiled, and rolled her hips, the heat and strength of him against the softest part of her. She ached as if she'd never had him.

She burned as if he was already deep within her. And his eyes lit with that same fire, and she knew he felt it, too.

Holding his gaze, she reached down between them and released him from his trousers with impatient hands, stroking his silken length, driving herself a little bit wild. Still watching him, those unholy eyes and his fierce, uncompromising face, she shifted up and over him, then sank down, sheathing him hard and deep within her.

"I'm distracting you," she told him, her voice uneven.

"Or possibly killing me," he muttered, taking her mouth with his in a long, hard kiss. "As I suspect is your plan."

She moved against him, rocking him deeper into her, unable to bite back her own small sigh of pleasure. He moved with her until she started to shake, and then he took control. His hands gripped her hips, preventing her from rocking against him when she wanted to tip herself over the edge.

"What are you doing?" she demanded, her voice a mere scrap of ragged sound, and his smile made her shiver.

"Distracting you," he said, his cool eyes glittering with that sensual promise that made her feel nearly giddy. "You'll come when I tell you to, Kiara, and not before."

She wanted to argue, but he moved then, and she could do nothing at all but move with him, surrendering to his hands, his wicked mouth, and his dark, whispered commands. Letting him build the fire between them into an out of control blaze. Letting him take them both exactly where she wanted to go.

And when he finally ordered her to come, she did, screaming out his name.

Azrin could not understand why he didn't simply tell her.

Why he hadn't told her already. Why some part of him didn't want to tell her at all.

They'd had the one last, long night. Drawing it out any further was nothing more than the very kind of selfishness he could no longer allow himself.

She was still in the shower. He could see the shape of her through the steamy glass, and he already regretted having left the warm embrace of the hot water. He could have stayed in there with her, and continued this exercise in pretense, in misdirection, as if they could lose themselves enough in each other that the whole world would go away.

Perhaps that was what he wanted. If he was honest, he knew that it was.

Hadn't that been what Kiara had always been for him? A step away from the expected—an escape from the traditional?

Enjoy yourself while you can, his father had said when he'd married, his creased face canny, knowing. As unsympathetic as ever, the old man as harsh a ruler of his family as he was of his country. *You will pay for it all soon enough, I promise you.*

Because his father had known, too: Kiara was Azrin's way of asserting himself in a life that would too soon be swallowed whole by duty and sacrifice. There would be no escape.

But Kiara had been his. All his. He'd been unable to resist her. She was his most selfish act of all, having nothing whatsoever to do with the things that were expected of him, the things he expected of himself. He had been meant to marry a woman like his own mother—one of the exquisite Khatanian girls who had been trotted out before him at every social opportunity since he was a boy, each more perfect than the last, each competing to show herself to be the most obvious choice for Azrin's future queen.

They were indistinguishably attractive, impeccably mannered and becomingly modest. They were all from powerful, noble families, all raised with the same set of ideals and expectations, all bred to be perfect wives and excellent mothers, all taught from birth to anticipate and tend to a man's every passing whim—and if that man was to be their king? All the better.

Instead, he'd met Kiara in a crowded little laneway in Melbourne. He had been walking off his jet lag as he prepared for a week's worth of meetings with some of the city's financial leaders. He'd ducked into one of the narrow alleys that snaked behind a typical Melbourne street featuring a jumble of sleek modern skyscrapers and Victorian-era facades, and had found his way to a tiny café that had reminded him of one of his favorite spots in Paris. His bodyguard had cleared the way for him to claim a seat at one of the tiny tables overlooking the busy little lane—perhaps a touch overzealously.

"I think you'll find it's customary to *pretend* to apologize when stealing a table from someone else," she had said, a teasing note in her voice that made her sound as if she was about to bubble over into laughter. As if there was something impossibly merry, very nearly golden, inside her just bursting to come out. That had been his first impression of Kiara—that voice.

Then he'd looked up. He'd never been able to account for the way that first look at her, when she'd been a stranger and speaking to him as if she found him both unimpressive in the extreme *and* somewhat ridiculous—not something that had ever happened to him before—had struck him like that. Like an unerring blow straight to the solar plexus.

First he'd seen that mouth. It had hit him. Hard. He'd seen her brown eyes, much too intelligent and direct, with the same arch look in them that he'd heard in her voice. He'd had the impression of her pretty face, her hair thrown back into a careless twist at the back of her head. It had been winter in Melbourne, and she'd dressed for it in boots and tights beneath some kind of flirty little skirt, and a sleek sort of coat with a bright red scarf wrapped about her neck. She had been all edges and color, attitude and mockery, and should not have attracted or interested him in any possible way.

"But as you and your entourage are fairly bristling with self-importance," she'd continued in that same tone, waving a hand at his bodyguard and himself with an obvious lack of the respect he'd usually received, which Azrin had found entirely too intriguing in spite of himself, "I can only assume that you see café tables as one more thing you are compelled to conquer." She'd smiled, which had not detracted from her sarcasm in any way. "In which case, have at. You clearly need it more than I do."

She'd turned to go, and Azrin had found that unbearable. He hadn't allowed himself to question why that should be, or, worse, why he should feel compelled to act on that unprecedented feeling.

"Please," he'd said, shocking his usually unflappable bodyguard almost as much as he'd shocked himself—as Azrin was not known for his interest in sharp-mouthed, clever-eyed girls who took too much pleasure in public dressing-downs. "Join me. You can enumerate my many character flaws, and I will buy you a coffee for your troubles."

She'd turned back to him, a considering sort of light in her captivating eyes, and a smile moving across that generous mouth of hers.

"I can do that alone," she'd pointed out, her smile deepening. "I'm already doing it in my head, as a matter of fact."

"Think of how much more satisfying it will be to abuse

me to my face," he'd said silkily. "How can you resist that kind of challenge?"

As it turned out, she couldn't.

Azrin had spent the rest of the afternoon trying to convince her to join him for dinner at his hotel, and the rest of his time in Melbourne trying to persuade her to go to bed with him. He'd managed only the dinner that night and then a week of the same, and he was not a man who had before then had even a passing acquaintance with failure of any sort.

He hadn't known how to process it. He'd told himself that had been why he'd been so unreasonably obsessed with this woman who had treated him so cavalierly, who had laughed at him when he'd tried to seduce her, and yet whose kisses had nearly taken off the back of his head when she'd condescended to bestow them upon him.

"You want the chase, not me," she'd informed him primly on his last night in Melbourne.

She had just stopped another kiss from going too far, and had even removed herself from Azrin's grasp, stepping back against the wall outside the door to her flat, into which she'd steadfastly refused to invite him. Again.

He'd had the frustrating suspicion that she was about to leave him standing there.

Again.

"What if I want *you*?" he'd asked, that wholly unfamiliar frustration bleeding into his voice and tangling in the air between them. "What if the chase is nothing but an impediment?"

"What a delightful fantasy," she'd replied—though he already knew that was not quite true, that careless tone she adopted. "But I'm afraid that your great, romantic pursuit of me will have to take a backseat to my graduate studies. I'm sure you understand. Dark and brooding princes tend to turn out to be little more than fairy-tale interludes, in my experience—"

"You have vast experience with princes, do you?" His tone had been sardonic, but she'd ignored him anyway.

"—while I really do require my Masters in Wine Technology and Viticulture to get on with my real life." She'd smiled at him, even as he'd registered the way she'd emphasized the word *real*. "I'll understand if you want to throw a little bit of a strop and sulk all the way back to your throne. No one will think any the less of you."

"Kiara," he'd said then, unable to keep his hands off her, and wanting more than just the simple pleasure of his palm over the curve of her upper arm, which was what he'd had to settle for. She was not for him—he'd known that—but he'd been completely incapable of accepting it as he should. "Prepare yourself for the fairy-tale interlude. I may have to go to Khatan tomorrow morning, but I'll be back."

"Of course you will," she'd said, smiling as if she'd known better.

But he'd come back, as promised. Again and again. Until she'd finally started to believe him.

He watched her now, his unexpected princess, as she climbed from the shower and wrapped herself in one of the soft towels. She smiled at him, and he felt something clench inside of him. She had never wanted to be a queen. She hadn't even wanted to be a princess. She'd wanted him, that was all, just as he'd wanted her. Perhaps it had been foolish to imagine that that kind of connection, that impossible need, could be enough.

But foolish or not, this was the bed they'd made.

And now it was time to lie in it, whether he liked it or not. Whether *she* liked it or not.

Whether he wanted to be the King of Khatan or not—

which had never mattered before, he reminded himself
sharply, and certainly didn't matter now. It simply *was*.

"My father's cancer is back," he said abruptly.

"Azrin, no," Kiara breathed, as she tried to process his
words.

He did not move from his position in the doorway. He
leaned against the doorjamb with seeming nonchalance,
beautiful and yet somehow remote, in nothing but dark
trousers he hadn't bothered to fully button. But she could
see the grim lines around his mouth, and the tension gripping his long frame. And the dark gray of his eyes, focused
on her in a way that she could not quite understand.

"He plans to fight it, of course," he said in that same,
oddly detached way, as if he was forcing himself to get
through this by rote. As if this was the preview to something much bigger. Something worse. What that might
be, Kiara did not want to imagine. "He is nothing if not
ornery."

"I'm so sorry," Kiara said, her head spinning. It was
difficult to imagine the old king, Azrin's belligerent and
autocratic father, anything but his demanding and robust
self. It was impossible to imagine that even cancer would
dare try to beat King Zayed, when nothing and no one else
had ever come close to loosening the iron grip he held on
his country, his throne. His only son.

"He does not seem particularly concerned that it will
kill him this time," Azrin continued. He shifted then,
thrusting his hands into the pockets of his trousers. His
mouth twisted. "But then, he has always had an exalted
sense of himself. It is what led to the worst excesses of
his reign. He leaves the wailing and gnashing of teeth to
my mother."

Queen Madihah was the first of the old king's three

wives. That and her production of the Crown Prince rendered her a national treasure. She was the very model of serene, gracious, modestly restrained Khatanian femininity, and as such, had always made Kiara feel distinctly brash and unpolished by comparison. It was impossible to imagine her changing expression, much less wailing.

"He's in excellent health otherwise," she said, thinking of the last time she'd seen her father-in-law, sometime the previous spring. He had insisted she join him for a long walk in the palace gardens, and despite the fact that Kiara regularly put in time on treadmills in gyms all over the world, the pace the older man had set had left her close to winded. That and the way he'd interrogated her, as if he was still suspicious of her relationship with his son and heir, as if he expected her to reveal her true motives at any moment, whatever those might be. "You would never know he was in his seventies..."

Something moved across Azrin's face then, and she let the words trail away.

"He has announced that he is an old man, and has only the weapons to fight one battle left in him," he said. Kiara felt frozen in place, and she didn't understand it. It was something to do with the way he was looking at her, the set to his jaw, that made her...nervous. Much too nervous. "He doesn't think he can care for the kingdom and for himself, not now. Not the way he did the last time."

"Whatever he needs to do to beat it," Kiara said immediately. Staunchly. "And whatever we need to do to help him."

The silence seemed to stretch taut between them.

"He is stepping aside, Kiara," Azrin said. Almost gently, yet with that steel beneath that made a kind of panic curl into something thick and hot in her belly. "Retiring."

For a moment, she didn't know what he meant.

"Of course," she said, when his meaning penetrated. "It will be good practice for you to take the throne while he recovers, won't it?"

"No." Again, that voice. His eyes so hard on hers. As if she was letting him down—had already done so—and she didn't know how that could have happened without her knowing it. Without her meaning to do it. She locked her knees beneath her, afraid, suddenly, that they might tremble and betray the full scope of her agitation.

"No?" she echoed. "It won't be good practice?"

"It won't be temporary. He is stepping aside for good."

She blinked. He waited. Something inside her seemed to go terribly still. As if she could not comprehend what he was telling her. But she did.

"That means—" She stopped herself. She had the urge to laugh then, but knew, somehow, that she did not dare. That he would not forgive her if she did, not now. She shook her head.

"It means I will be the new king of Khatan in six short weeks," Azrin said in that strong, sure voice, as if that hardness was a part of him now, as if it was part of who he was becoming. As if it was a necessary precursor to the throne.

"Six weeks?" Kiara did laugh then, slightly. Her voice seemed too high, too uncertain. "I'd hardly got used to you being a prince over five years of marriage. I can't get my head around you being *king* in a little more than a month!"

She thought he might smile at that, but his mouth remained that flat, stern line. His eyes were the coldest she'd ever seen them. She felt, again, as if she'd been thrown neck deep into something that she ought to understand, but didn't.

"You don't have to get your head around it," he said with a kind of distant formality that made her tense up in response. "I've been getting my head around becoming king my whole life. This was always going to happen— it's just happening a bit more quickly than I'd originally anticipated."

Pull yourself together, Kiara ordered herself then, suddenly aware that she was standing stock still in the middle of the bathroom floor, staring at him as if he'd transformed into some kind of monster before her very eyes. Hardly the way a good, supportive spouse should behave at such a time.

She imagined there was no one in the world who wouldn't feel out of their depth at a moment like this. Thrones! Kings! But this was her husband. This was real. She could sort out her own feelings later. *In private.* She walked over to him, rising on her toes to press a kiss against his hard jaw.

"This can't be easy," she said softly. "But I love you. We'll figure it out."

"I suspect he must be sicker than he wishes to let on," Azrin said, his voice gruff. "He always promised he would die before he abdicated." He let out a sound that was not quite a laugh. "But then, he took the throne when he was all of nineteen. There was only one way to hold it. He came by his ruthlessness honestly."

She kissed him again, determined to ignore that tension simmering in him and all around them. She knew that Azrin's relationship with his father had never been easy. That the king had never been pleased with the way the kingdom viewed Azrin as some kind of savior-in-waiting. Azrin had always said that if his father had only managed to have another son, Azrin would never have remained his heir. But he hadn't.

This is real, she told herself again.

"You can do this," she said. "You've been preparing for years. You're ready."

"Yes, Kiara. I'm ready," he said quietly, his eyes again too dark, his mouth too grim.

Something gripped her then, some kind of terror, but she shoved it aside, annoyed with herself. Again. Was she really so self-involved? She could only stare up at him as he ran a hand over the back of her head, smoothing down her wet hair, gently tipping her head back to gaze at him more fully.

Azrin's mouth curved slightly then, though it was in no way a smile, the way she wanted it to be. His gaze seared into hers, and she was afraid, suddenly, of the things he might see there.

"But are you?" he asked.

CHAPTER THREE

IT WAS a question her own mother echoed a week later when Kiara was back at the winery, trying to handle her responsibilities in one part of her life so she could go to Khatan and do her duty in the other part.

She'd assured Azrin she was ready and willing to do it. Eager, even. She'd been so earnest she'd nearly convinced herself.

Nearly.

"Are you honestly prepared to be a *queen*, Kiara?" her mother asked coolly, as if she'd looked inside and managed to articulate all the dark and unpleasant things Kiara was pretending she didn't feel. "This isn't a game, you know. Khatan's monarchy is not ornamental."

Kiara forced herself to silently count to ten, sitting there in her mother's pretty office with the breathtaking view out across the Frederick vineyards, green and healthy-looking in the afternoon light—not that she could concentrate on that now, though the view usually calmed her down. She had to keep herself from succumbing to the temper she knew her mother would view as a weakness. And, worse, as a confirmation.

Besides, she was all too aware that the temper was just a camouflage for the guilt that lay beneath. A lifetime of guilt, because she knew she was the reason her mother had dedicated her life to this place, these vineyards, after Kiara's father had died. Without Kiara, who knew what Diana might have done with her life?

Was it any wonder that Kiara was in no rush to have any babies herself?

One, two, three...

She eyed her mother across the wide expanse of Diana's always-neat desk, seeing far too much of herself in the older woman. As ever. It was like looking into some version of her future, much as she preferred to deny it to herself. The same narrow shoulders and long-legged frame. The same way of holding themselves, though Kiara knew she would never have her mother's innate elegance. That was all Diana.

Kiara was the only one who had seen beneath her mother's polished exterior. She was the only one who knew what it had cost Diana to give up so much for this place. For Kiara. For the legacy she thought Kiara's father would have wanted to give her himself, if he could have done.

Five, six, seven...

Diana had taken over the Frederick wine business with more determination than skill after her husband's early death, and had ushered it into its current state of prominence by the force of her will alone. She'd hardly been around at all during Kiara's formative years, leaving the day to day raising of her daughter to Kiara's late grandmother, Diana's mother-in-law. And yet none of that prevented Diana from being far too opinionated about the choices she thought Kiara should have made. And judgmental about the ones Kiara actually had made.

Meaning, her mother did not approve of Azrin. At all. Of what he *represented*, as she liked to put it. She thought that Kiara should have married that nice Harry Thompson who'd been her first boyfriend, whose family was also deeply entrenched in the Barossa Valley—and who could, she had always maintained, *understand* Kiara in a way Azrin never would.

And somewhere deep inside, where guilt and obligation mixed into something sharp-edged and prickly, a part of Kiara had always wondered if Diana was right. She wondered it even more today, as she prepared for a role she and Azrin had never discussed in any detail, both assuming it was too far off in the future to bother worrying about.

Was she prepared to be his queen?

She couldn't forgive Diana for asking the question she didn't dare ask herself.

Eight, nine...

"Why wouldn't I be prepared, Mother?" she asked, aware that her voice was more strained than it should have been, clearly indicating that the question had got under her skin. She felt as if she'd lost points before she'd started—an all-too familiar feeling where her mother was concerned. She willed herself to exude the kind of cool poise that she was known for everywhere else but here. "I knew who Azrin was when I married him."

She'd known who he was the moment she'd laid eyes on him. Too powerful. Too dangerous. Too overwhelming and much too ruthless. She might have fallen in love with him, but that didn't change the basic facts about who he was. She'd never lost sight of that. Had she?

"When you married him he was a financier who happened to be a prince, and he was perfectly happy to traipse about the globe with you," Diana said in that seemingly nonchalant way of hers that immediately put Kiara's back up. Nothing about Diana was nonchalant. Not ever. "Now he will be a king, which is not the same thing at all, is it?"

"He was always going to be a king." Kiara's voice was much too cross, and she had to work to produce some approximation of a serene smile to counterbalance it. "A good one, I think. I hope."

"But what kind of queen can you expect to be?" Diana asked, her brows arching high as if astonished Kiara had not raised this issue herself. "You were raised to know about oenology and viticulture, not royal intrigue and matters of state."

"Your faith in me is touching," Kiara said, her smile growing hard to maintain. She stood up then, desperate, suddenly, to avoid getting any deeper into this with her mother. She was afraid of what she might uncover inside herself that she didn't want to know.

Diana only shrugged. "It's not a question of faith," she said. "I talked quite a bit with Queen Madihah at your wedding, you know. She was very open about having been trained to be the king's perfect companion since before she could walk."

Again her dark brows rose. She didn't have to say anything further—it lay there between them as if she'd shouted it.

You are not queen material.

Kiara gathered up her things with as much control as possible, determined not to show Diana how unerring her aim had been, nor how hard she'd managed to strike her target. How did her mother manage to see straight into the heart of her, where she hid her worst fears?

"I don't have time for this," she said as calmly as she could. Which was perhaps not very calm at all. "I have to leave for Khatan early tomorrow. If there's anything else?" She knew her smile was too brittle. "About the business, Mother. Not about my marriage. Please."

"I would just like you to be *realistic* about this, Kiara," Diana said, her flashing brown gaze showing the first hint of emotion Kiara could remember seeing in years. It made her stomach twist, guilt and obligation and something else.

"No, you wouldn't," she replied, temper boiling inside her, rushing in to cover the rest of the things she didn't want to feel. Temper was easier. Cleaner. "You would like me to see things your way. You would like me to *do* things your way."

"Do you imagine that you are the only girl to ever be swept away in some kind of fantasy romance?" Diana retorted. She rose, too, and waved a hand at the window, as if to encompass the vines stretching off toward the hills, the chateau, the whole of their family, their lives, their history. "I was starry-eyed when I met your father, but that hardly prepared me for the reality of running this business, did it? Much less raising a child all on my own when he was gone."

Kiara didn't want to hear this. Not again. This story was imprinted on her bones. It was a story of sacrifice and loss, and then a deep and abiding disappointment that Kiara fell so short of living up to all the things her mother had done for her. Was still doing for her.

It had guided her every step until she'd met Azrin.

"What can any of that possibly matter now?" she asked, her voice low, something dark opening wide inside her that she was afraid to look at too closely. That she knew she needed to close down, hide away, lest it rise up and eat her alive. "I am his wife. His queen. This is happening whether you like it or not, Mother."

Whether you like it or not, too, a small voice whispered inside her—and she immediately hated herself for it. Diana let out a sigh that was loud in the sudden quiet of the office.

"Oh, Kiara," she said, that familiar mix of bafflement and exasperation in her voice, her gaze. And something else—something that made that hard knot inside Kiara seem to swell in response. "None of this is about what *I* want."

Azrin found her out on the private terrace that linked their suites in the family wing of the sprawling palace that sat high on the cliffs above the ancient city of Arjat an-Nahr, where brash skyscrapers now thrust into the skyline along with delicate minarets from centuries past.

She was curled up on one of the deep chaises, her gaze trained out over the dark sea that danced and shimmered far below her. The sun had set but recently, only a line of crimson edged with gold stretched out across the horizon to mark its passing.

Azrin liked that she was here, within reach, mere days since he'd seen her last. The pleasure of it moved through him, so deep and full that the tension of the long day seemed to ease away with every step that brought him closer to her. He liked her here, close by. He'd liked knowing that she had arrived safely and was already in the palace when he finally quit his endless round of meetings and strategy sessions.

She was the single bright spot in a long and complicated day.

She looked over her shoulder toward him as he drew near. There was an expression on her face that he couldn't quite categorize—that he didn't think he'd seen before—but then she smiled. He was already smiling back before he realized that her eyes were darker than they ought to have been.

"I'm glad you're here," he said.

He moved over to the chaise and dropped to sit at the opposite end. The terrace was alive with blooms, bright blossoms by day and the sweet scent of jasmine now that night had fallen. Up above, the stars began to come out. And for a moment, he thought, they could be anyone. Just a woman and a man and the whole night stretched out before them.

He did not allow himself to examine how much he wished that could be true—that they could fall back into that world of pretend they'd lived in all these years. Hidden in, even.

Kiara shifted position against the back of the chaise, and Azrin took the opportunity to arrange her how he wanted her—draping her legs over his lap so he could hold the slender shape of them in his palms. She wore something airy and insubstantial, not quite a dress and not one of her silk wrappers, and her narrow feet were bare. Her hair tumbled around her shoulders, damp from a recent shower, and her face was scrubbed clean of cosmetics.

She was beautiful, and he couldn't understand why she felt so far away when she was right here. When he was touching her.

"How were your meetings?" she asked. Her voice was neutral. Entirely too neutral. He was instantly on guard.

"Much too long," he said. Carefully.

He thought of the bickering ministers, the arguments, the usual pointless intractability from the usual suspects—one of them, sadly, his father. He thought of the inevitable pandering, the concessions, the headaches that were soon to be his alone to deal with. It already felt thankless and dangerous, this relentless push toward progress that he sometimes thought only he supported, and yet there was no stopping it. He had given his word to his people when he was a brash and idealistic twenty-two. He couldn't take it back now, simply because it was harder than he'd anticipated—and happening so much sooner than he'd planned.

And on top of all that was Kiara, with that odd note in

her voice and that remote look in her gaze, as if he'd done something to her when all he'd wanted was to talk all of this out. To hear her perspective—to have someone else on his side. He told himself that he was not disappointed, that she had only just arrived. That there was time enough for the kind of conversations he envisioned. That there was no reason to feel so alone.

"Long and complicated," he added, his voice more curt than it should have been.

"Your aide filled me in on your expectations when I arrived," she replied, her voice noticeably less neutral. "At length. And then your sisters took up where he left off." Something flashed in her dark eyes then, and she moved her legs against him, as if restless. "You think I need lessons in etiquette, Azrin? From a battalion of your sisters? Have I humiliated you in the eyes of all the world and you failed to mention it until now?"

He felt as if he had suddenly found himself standing in the middle of a loaded minefield, a sensation he did not care for at all. He'd thought she would appreciate the advice his sisters could give her on how to comport herself like a Khatanian noble. He fought to keep his temper—too close to the surface, after having been sorely tested all day long—at bay.

"You have no formal training in diplomacy," he said, forcing his tone into something reasonable. He'd been practicing this very same tone of voice all day long, hadn't he? It should have been as familiar to him as a second skin by now. "My sisters are renowned for their impeccable manners. They are the obvious choice to help you."

He searched her face, looking for the Kiara he knew, always so clever and amused, and seeing only those too-dark eyes looking back at him. Waiting for an explanation of his decision to send his sisters to her that should, he thought with a touch of asperity, have already been obvious to her.

"You will be the queen, Kiara," he said. He told himself he sounded far more patient than he felt. "There are things you'll be expected to know—ways you'll be expected to behave. That's all."

"What's wrong with how I behave now?" Her brows rose, challenging him, but with an unfamiliar darkness there, too. "Is there some embarrassing photograph I don't know about? Some tawdry incident I can't recall?"

"Of course not." He reminded himself that it wasn't her fault that his government was an ancient dinosaur that creaked along, arthritic and demanding, and only he could change it—if it could be changed at all. It wasn't her fault he was out of patience, his temper already frayed too thin. "But you will no longer be a princess who can, to some extent, do as she pleases. You will be the symbol of femininity for all of Khatan." His lips curved. "No pressure, of course."

He wanted her to smile, but her gorgeous mouth remained flat, and he felt it like a slap.

"No pressure," she repeated slowly, as if she was working it out in her head, "yet my current behavior is apparently so deficient you had to send your sisters to me the moment I set foot in the palace. When you'd never mentioned this to me at all. I felt ambushed, Azrin."

He sighed then, all the tension and weariness of the day flooding back into him, the exhaustion of every day since his father's announcement swamping him.

"Will you be one more fire I must put out today, Kiara?" he asked, unable to keep the sharp edge from his voice. "One more problem I must solve?"

She stiffened.

"I thought I was having a conversation with my husband," she said, her voice tight. Like a stranger's. "I didn't realize this was an audience with the king."

His hands tightened around her calves when she would have moved her legs from his lap, but he checked his impatience, and let her go. He watched her as she stood, noting the way she brushed invisible lint from her front with angry hands. She didn't look at him, and he hated it. He hated all of this. He thought of the last time they'd met after a separation, in Sydney.

How had they strayed so far from that night? And so fast?

"I assume there's some dinner we need to get ready for," she murmured.

And, of course, there was. There always was. He would have hated that inevitability, too, but it was futile. This was his life.

But Azrin couldn't abide the distance between them—especially not now, when she was in the palace and would remain here. With him. Not just a musical voice on the telephone, a few funny lines of email to read between meetings. He reached over and snagged her wrist in his hand, tugging her toward him. She came without resistance, though her expression was serious as she gazed down at him. Troubled. He couldn't stand that, either.

He brought her face to his, and kissed her as he'd wanted to do since the moment he'd received the news from his aide that she had arrived at the palace.

He teased, he toyed.

He caressed her and seduced her with every weapon in his arsenal. He licked and tasted that mouth of hers that had obsessed him for so long, kissing her until the tension in her body eased—until she was loose and pliable and she sighed against him. Until there was nothing between them but this heat, this unbankable fire, that he wished they had the time to fully explore. Here, now.

When he finally lifted his head she was sitting in his lap, and her face was flushed and warm.

"I need you to do this with me," he whispered against her mouth fiercely. He pulled back, studied her face, wished he understood this need that raged in him. This pulse of something like fury, something hot and intense. "I need your support, Kiara. Now more than ever."

Her gaze was still so serious, despite the heat that lingered there. He had the sudden, unpleasant notion that he was missing something—but he dismissed it. Kiara was open. Direct. She would simply tell him if there was something he needed to know. He was sure of it.

Her mouth crooked into that smile that he had loved since the first moment he'd seen it, so long ago now, in the midst of a wet Melbourne afternoon, and he ignored the lingering sense that there was too much reservation behind it tonight. There were too many other things going on around them, he thought. Too much else to do, and surely she understood that.

She would be fine. She always was.

They always were.

"I'm here, aren't I?" she asked quietly, and he told himself it was what he wanted.

That it was enough.

Kiara became public property overnight. As if she, herself, ceased to exist now that she was meant to be queen in a matter of weeks rather than simply *one day*.

And the more she was regarded as something public, something belonging to anyone and everyone, she registered with a rising tide of panic that worsened every day, the more she seemed to disappear beneath the weight of Azrin's crown.

And he wasn't even king yet.

Every day that passed, every long day during which Azrin's many sisters taught Kiara how ill-suited she was to this role of queen and every night which brought Azrin closer to his father's nearly-relinquished throne, Kiara felt more and more as if an unseen hand was closing around her throat. And tightening.

The worst part was, she had no one to talk to about it.

Azrin was so tired, so distracted. *Overwhelmed*, she thought, and she told herself she understood it. She didn't want to hear him heave another heavy sigh and tell her she was one more fire to put out, did she? She didn't want to be another burden to him. She wanted anything but that, in fact.

And in truth, she didn't know how to raise this sort of issue with him anyway.

They had always been on the same page before now, more or less. They'd fought, as all couples did, but they had always been the sort of fights brought on by stress and exhaustion and too much travel—a short tone or a snapped reply that bloomed into temper, and the resultant hurt feelings that could easily be soothed by a conversation and delicious, reconciliatory sex.

Kiara didn't think that would work this time. What could she say? *It hurts my feelings that you expect me to be your queen? Let's see if we can solve that with a chat?* Of course not.

She couldn't contact the friends she'd become less close with over the years, when what little free time she'd had was filled with Azrin. Her friendships had become little more than the odd catch-up telephone call, a well-received email here and there and happy photographs in the usual online places. Kiara couldn't imagine how she could turn that around now. She would hardly know where to start. And any coworkers she might think to confide in were far too likely to drop hints of any unrest to Diana, and Kiara couldn't bear the idea that she might prove her mother right about her marriage.

She wished she were less proud. More than that, she wished her stoic, loving grandmother were still alive and still able to make the world feel right again with a simple hug, no matter what might have happened.

Azrin had never felt further away, for all that he was geographically closer than he'd been in years. The bittersweet irony of that ate at her. And meanwhile Kiara felt as if she was disappearing under the onslaught of some relentless tide, bit by bit, until she wondered what would be left of her at all.

"It would be better if you were pregnant," King Zayed announced one night, scowling at her from his place at the head of the table.

His words cast an immediate and total hush over the marvelous long table that commanded pride of place in the ornate room of the palace that was only used for private family meals, silencing all the members of the royal family who had gathered around it.

Who all, of course, turned to stare directly at Kiara, in case she was in any doubt about who the old king was addressing.

She was in no doubt. She simply felt sick.

Beside her, she felt Azrin tense, but he remained silent, though she could feel that dark current running through him, humming beneath his skin. She was afraid to look at him—afraid that if she did, she would see that he was as appalled as she was by this and would then be unable to govern herself appropriately.

And more afraid by far that he would not be appalled at all.

"That *would* be ideal," one of King Zayed's highest ministers, who was married to one of Azrin's sisters, agreed at once, as if this was a plan he could launch into action with the force of his agreement.

"The country loves it when the royal family is expecting a child," Queen Madihah chimed in. She aimed her usual calm smile at Kiara. "Especially when it's the queen."

Kiara managed, somehow, to keep from letting her fork drop from her nerveless fingers to clatter against the side of her plate. Or from throwing it at the king.

"Unfortunately," she said when the silence dragged on, when it became clear that Azrin was not planning to speak to his father on her behalf, when she thought she might die if everyone kept staring at her like that and some part of her wished she would, "I am not."

She was so upset she shook slightly, even hours later when she and Azrin returned to their rooms together.

"Why didn't you say something?" she asked.

It took everything she had not to scream at him. Not to simply scream out all the things she was feeling inside, that she was afraid to even look at too closely for fear that even giving them names would allow them to take her over and suck her under, never to be seen again.

"What was there to say?" He did not pretend he didn't know what she was talking about. He shrugged, his expression almost forbidding. "He is still the king. He will always be my father."

"This is *my body*." Kiara shook her head, bewildered. Still feeling something very near to violated by all those eyes on her, all that attention to something that should have been hers and Azrin's alone. "It's *private*."

He looked at her for a long moment, a certain hardness in his gaze that she had never seen before. It made a pit in her stomach open, then gape wide.

"No," he said eventually. She had the impression he was choosing his words carefully, and that hurt too, as if they had become complete strangers to each other in a few short weeks. *As if,* something treacherous and terrified whispered deep within her, *you never knew each other at all*. "It isn't."

She blinked. "What are you talking about?"

"The heir to the kingdom of Khatan will come from your body," he said, his fierce attention dropping to her abdomen as if he could *see* the babies they'd never talked about in concrete terms, always couching it in *someday* and *when we're ready* language.

Kiara's hands crept over her own belly, whether to protect herself or in response to something far more primitive, she didn't know.

"And the sooner that heir exists, the sooner the whole country can breathe a collective sigh of relief," he continued in that same aloof tone. "They are still outraged that I vowed to take only one wife. What if you cannot produce sons? What if the royal line is lost?"

Azrin shrugged and then smiled, and Kiara almost smiled back, because what he was saying was so archaic that it couldn't possibly apply to her. To them. To their life together.

But then she remembered that it did.

"Until all these questions are answered," he said, "I'm afraid your body will be seen to be as much theirs as yours."

"And you accept that," she said softly.

"This is our life, Kiara," he replied, that exhausted sort of look in his eyes that made her feel small and petulant. But that was unfair, wasn't it? This was her life, too. "This is who we are."

This is who you are, she thought, but did not say.

She moved away from him, sinking down to sit in one of the heavily brocaded armchairs, blinking back a searing heat, determined that she would not cry. Not now, when she already felt too vulnerable.

"And maybe they're right," Azrin said after a moment. Kiara felt the world tilt beneath her feet, and she wasn't even standing. She stared at him, unable, in that moment, to speak. He shrugged out of his clothes, baring his beautiful body to her, and for once she felt almost numb. "Maybe we should start thinking about children."

She swallowed, panic licking over her skin, making her head feel heavy.

"Are you saying that as my husband?" she asked, her voice hardly above a whisper. "Or as the king who agrees with his mother that it would foster goodwill with your subjects?"

His gaze grew cold. Unbearably hard. "Can't I be both?"

She didn't know how to answer that. She didn't understand what was happening. She only knew she wanted to curl into a ball and sob, and none of this was helping.

"You told me we could wait until I was ready," she reminded him, a kind of thick dread making her limbs feel heavy. Making her temples pound. "You promised."

"Don't look at me like that, Kiara," he replied, his tone harsh. Or maybe it only felt that way, like one more blow in a long series of them. "We've been married for five years. You know I must have an heir at some point or another. It's not entirely unreasonable to discuss it, is it?"

"Maybe you and your parents and your cabinet ministers should consult with each other, then," she threw at him, feeling wild. Miserable. Attacked. "You can let me know what conclusions you reach. I'll just trot along, obeying your decrees like a happy little brood mare, shall I?"

She regretted it the moment she said it.

His gaze turned dark, and his face seemed to tighten. He stared at her, affront and something worse all over him, and Kiara couldn't seem to do anything but stare back. He muttered something in Arabic that made her flinch even without understanding it, then turned and strode away from her. She heard the water turn on in the adjacent bath, and only then did she let herself breathe, though it sounded more like a sob in the simmering wake of his exit.

A wave of misery flooded through her, and she couldn't stand it. She couldn't even seem to breathe through it. She found herself up and on her feet, then walking into Azrin's bath without knowing she meant to move.

She found him in the shower, steam billowing, bracing himself against the tiled wall as the water beat down on him from above. He turned to look at her as she opened the glass door, and her heart seemed to thud too hard against her ribs.

His eyes were much too dark. His mouth was grim. She felt both reverberate deep inside of her, ripping at her.

"I am not your enemy," he bit out, as if this hurt him, too. As if she did. "Why do you want so badly to be mine?"

But she didn't want to talk. She didn't know what to say that wouldn't hurt them both.

She stepped into the shower fully clothed, and let the hot water wash into her. Over her, wetting her dress, her hair. She put her hands out to touch his slick, hard chest, and when he shifted as if he wanted to talk rather than touch, she gave in to the helpless need clawing at her and slid down to her knees. Slicking her hair back, she knelt before him and kissed her way over the hard ridges of his abdomen, then farther down, her hands gripping the hard muscles of his thighs.

And somewhere along the way she forgot that she meant to quiet him, to apologize somehow, and simply found herself worshiping him. Tasting him. Testing those delicious muscles, that mesmerizing skin, with her mouth, her hands, her tongue.

When she finally moved to his sex, he was hard and inviting, and when she leaned back to look up at him his eyes seemed to glitter with the same tension she felt inside of her. That familiar burn, with a new, desperate edge.

She reached between his legs, letting her hands caress the heavy weight of him, and then she leaned forward and took him deep in her mouth. He said her name like a prayer.

And slowly, deliberately, using her lips and her tongue and the long, slow strokes she knew drove him crazy, Kiara made them both forget.

At least for now.

The night before he took the throne, they hardly slept.

He came into her again and again. He laid her out on the wide bed in the center of his room and stretched out above her, loving his way over every single inch of her skin. She shattered into pieces, he followed. She screamed his name until she thought she might go hoarse.

She took him in and loved him back and neither of them spoke of the desperation, the ferocity, that drove him so hard, that made him near-inexhaustible, that made her eyes well over as she clung to him. That made his mouth seem very nearly grim, even in passion.

That made her wish, so fiercely, that she could take them back to where they'd been before his father's announcement, that she could will away the dawn and everything that she knew would come with it.

But it came anyway, inevitably. A whole nation waited for him. Monarchs and presidents, emirs and prime ministers and cheering crowds of his own people were there to pay their respects to the new King of Khatan. And Kiara would walk slightly behind him, as was tradition, bow her head, accept her own crown and become his queen.

She wondered in that last, stolen moment in their bedroom if he would ever truly be hers again. If he ever had been—or if all of this had simply been borrowed time, after all. She cast the unsettling thought aside. She made herself smile. For him.

All of this was for him. And she doubted he had any idea how hard this was for her, how deeply she feared losing herself entirely to his crown, his country.

Even harder than that was her suspicion that it was something he wouldn't want to know.

"We must go," he said. His voice was too gruff, and there were shadows in his nearly-blue eyes. Kiara did not want to be one of them. Not today. "We must be dressed and prepared and moved into place, like pieces on a chess board."

She ran her hands up over his perfect chest, tilted her head back to look at him, and felt the first real smile she'd had in ages move over her mouth. She did not want to think of her endless lessons in etiquette from the disapproving collective of his sisters, all of whom had made it clear that she could never be the queen he needed. She did not want to think about how cold he had become, how distant. How far away. She did not want to think of chess, either. She wanted to love him, as simple as that. That was all she'd ever wanted.

"The next time we are alone," she said softly, "you will be the king."

She did not say *my king.*

"I will be your husband," he replied, pressing a last kiss to her temple, soft and sweet, making her ache for him. For them. For their perfect past and their uncertain future. "Nothing more and nothing less."

And she wanted, so desperately, to believe him.

CHAPTER FOUR

Some two months after his grand coronation, Azrin escorted his queen with great fanfare and a pervasive sense of relief into a glittering ballroom in Washington, D.C.

Other couples took honeymoons, but the brand-new King and Queen of Khatan had traveled purely to allow Azrin to have long-overdue state visits and hold talks with Khatan's allies around the globe. He had spent a few hours in the Oval Office this afternoon discussing his plans to transition his kingdom toward a constitutional monarchy, and now it was time to make nice with the diplomats. This was the final stop on this particular political tour, and tomorrow they could finally go back home to Khatan.

He could hardly wait.

"You look beautiful," he murmured in Kiara's ear, and she smiled, though she didn't turn into him as she might have once. He felt his eyes narrow.

He was impatient for some kind of real privacy, finally. He wanted to be alone with her, rather than surrounded on all sides by too many people wanting too much of him, day and night. He wanted to lose himself in her without worrying if the walls were thin and the Royal Guard too close—or if he would be called away to some crisis, some call, some piece of news that could not wait for morning.

She looked impossibly regal tonight as she greeted the

assembled dignitaries before them in a gown of rich burgundy, her hair piled high on the top of her head in a complicated arrangement and surrounded with sparkling diamonds that caught the light with her every movement. She laughed politely at something one of the portly, tuxedoed men said to her and he realized, suddenly, that he couldn't recall the last time he'd heard her real laughter—that gorgeous laugh of hers that made him feel as if he basked in the sunshine of it. Of her.

One more thing that needed to change, he thought. One more thing these long, grueling months had taken from them both.

Once through the receiving line, Azrin led her out onto the dance floor and pulled her into his arms. She swayed toward him gracefully, her posture achingly perfect as he led her in the steps of the dance. He gazed down into her face and saw, he thought with a pang, his queen. Smooth, gracious. Perfect. But not his Kiara.

"Do you remember that weekend in Barcelona?" he asked suddenly. Without thought—only the need to reach her, somehow.

She blinked in that way that he was beginning to recognize as a stalling tactic—one that he suspected kept that irreverent tongue of hers under control. He knew he should have been pleased that she'd learned discretion. Hadn't that been why she'd spent all those weeks with his sisters? But instead he felt something entirely too much like loss.

"Which weekend?" she asked lightly. Far too politely, as if he was one of the dignitaries she'd just charmed with so little effort and even less of the real her he knew lurked in there somewhere. It had to. "We've been there any number of times over the years."

"You know which one." He could not pull her close the way he wanted to, and he could not have said why her reticence irritated him so much, so suddenly. He ordered himself to relax. "But I will remind you. We drank far too much sangria and danced for hours. We were the youngest couple in the place by several decades." He moved closer than he should. "And I know you remember it as well as I do."

He remembered her laughter most of all—the way it had poured over them both like water, bathing them both in the joy of it. He remembered the insistent pulse of the music and the fact that they had been soundly out danced by local couples old enough to be his own grandparents. And he remembered walking back to their hotel in the small hours, holding her hand in his and her impractical shoes in the other, as if the streets were theirs alone. He smiled at the memory.

And then she met his gaze, her brown eyes so serious, and his smile faded.

"I remember," she said.

An odd note in her voice made everything go very still inside him.

"Something is the matter." It was more a statement of fact than a question. His hand tightened a fraction around hers. "What is it?"

She shook her head slightly.

"This is hardly the time or the place to talk about anything serious," she said. She indicated the Washington elite surrounding them on all sides, all polite chatter and sharp speculation, with a tilt of her head.

"If that is meant to make me believe that something is *not* wrong," he pointed out, his gaze narrow on hers, "it has failed. Miserably."

She only shook her head again, and smiled that perfect, empty smile. And what could Azrin do? He was the King of Khatan. There was no scenario in which he could have any kind of intimate conversation with his wife in the middle of a dance floor. He couldn't even kiss her the way he wanted to without causing the sort of commotion he preferred to avoid.

He found he hated it.

But he waited.

And as he waited, he watched her, feeling as if he somehow hadn't seen her in a long time, though they had traveled all over the world together in these past weeks, with the whole of their necessary entourage. She was pale beneath her expertly applied cosmetics. And there was a certain kind of brittleness about the way she moved.

"Are you ill?" he asked abruptly when they were finally alone in a suite set aside for visiting heads of state in an exclusive Georgetown hotel, all rich, old wood and faint gestures toward something more art deco.

Kiara stopped walking away from him—toward the master bedroom at the far end of the suite and the sumptuous bath, presumably—her gown whispering around her as she turned back to face him. He watched her for a moment from his position at the top of the steps that led down from the formal foyer into the long, elegant room, trying to see behind that smooth mask he realized she'd been wearing for weeks now.

Trying to understand how she could feel so far away when she was right there, within reach. The tension between them pulled taut, making the vast room seem to contract around them. He hated that, too.

"Of course I'm not ill," she said, her forehead allowing the slightest frown.

"Pregnant?" He didn't know why he'd asked that. To poke at her?

He could see her swallow almost convulsively as he walked down the steps, closing the distance between them.

Her mouth flattened. Her eyes flashed with what he took to be temper, but at least it was better than that mask.

"No. Still not pregnant, should you care to alert the media."

"If there is something wrong—" he began, hearing the impatience in his own voice and unable, somehow, to curtail it.

"What could be wrong?" Her eyes were too bright. She turned her head as if she wanted to hide it, looking out toward the brick terrace that stretched the length of the suite on the other side of the glass windows, the rooftops of Georgetown spread out before them. Deceptively inviting, Azrin thought darkly, in such a deceitful city. "You are a success by any measure. You have been hailed as an innovative and modernizing force for good in a troubled region. A worthy successor to your father in every respect. Surely all of this has turned out exactly as you wanted. As you planned."

"Kiara."

He didn't know what he wanted. He didn't feel like any kind of success, not when she looked away from him, when she seemed so closed off, so far away. He didn't know what moved inside of him, tearing at him. He only knew he couldn't stand this. Whatever this was.

"What else can you possibly want?" she asked him, her voice the faintest whisper. *From me*, he thought she added, but he couldn't be sure. And he didn't know he meant to move until his hands were on her shoulders and his mouth was hard against hers.

"I want you," he growled. He tasted salt and something else, something bitter, but beyond that was simply Kiara, and it took so very little of her to make him drunk. "I always want you."

He dragged his hands through her hair, scattering the

diamonds that had nestled there, digging his fingers into the long tresses, holding her still as he took. Tasted. And took some more.

He was desperate then, and she met him with her own heat, turning his own mad desire back on him—sending them both higher. Hotter. She tugged his coat from his shoulders, his shirt from his trousers. He unhooked her from her gown with more determination than finesse, and then she was pushing him down on the nearest sofa. He twisted her beneath him, settling himself between her thighs as they wrestled off what remained of their clothing and then he found his way into the molten core of her, thrusting hard. Deep.

She gasped, arching up against him, locking her long, smooth legs tight around his hips. He exulted in the heat of her, the lush softness. The perfect fit. The way her hips rose to meet his, then rolled in that particular way that was all Kiara. All his.

He slowed, brushing her hair back from her face and waiting for her eyes to open, to focus on him.

"Tell me what's wrong," he said.

But she only moved her hips against him, her ankles locked in the small of his back. He leaned down and pulled one of her tight, hard nipples into his mouth, making her laugh and then moan.

"Tell me," he said again, and then began to move, his strokes measured and deep, making her shudder against him.

"I've told you in a thousand ways," she said, her voice uneven, her body arching to meet his thrusts. "You need to learn how to listen."

So he listened. He took her other nipple in his mouth, reached down between them to the place where they were joined, and with a single sure touch, threw her right over the edge.

And then he did it all over again.

And again.

Until, he was sure, nothing at all could ever matter but this.

When he woke, it was morning.

He pulled on the nearest thing he could find and made his way out into the long living area of the suite. He found her fully dressed in one of her elegant day dresses and standing by the windows in the great room. She held her morning cup of coffee between her hands, her eyes fixed out the window again, as if the rooftops opposite held secrets she was determined to solve.

"We will not fly out for another few hours," he said, his voice still raspy from sleep. And the lack of it. He was happier than he perhaps should be that the tour was finally over, that he could revel in this morning, empty of his aides and his responsibilities, for now. He leaned down to press a kiss to the back of her neck. "Come back to bed."

"I can't," she said. Then a small sound, as if she sucked in a breath. "I'm not going back to Khatan with you."

"Where are you going?" He felt lazy. Indulgent.

He helped himself to her coffee, pulling the heavy ceramic mug from her hand and taking a pull of it before handing it back to her. She set it down on a nearby accent table and then looked at him, her gaze unreadable.

"Australia."

He nodded absently and turned back toward the bedroom, rubbing a hand over his jaw. He was thinking of the shower, and how good the hot water would feel against his skin. He was wondering how long he could keep any outside thoughts at bay this morning, after such a long and satisfying night—how long he could pretend he was nothing more than a man. Not a king at all today. Not yet.

"Are you planning to visit your mother?" he asked over his shoulder. "When will you return?"

She didn't respond. He turned again, to find her watching him with an expression he didn't recognize on her pretty face. Resigned, perhaps. Some mix of sadness and something else, something like defiance.

"What is it?" he asked, on alert again.

"That's just it, Azrin," she said. "I don't know that I will return."

If it had not been for that terrible, arrested look on his face, the sudden stillness in his powerful body, Kiara might have thought she hadn't spoken out loud.

"I need some time," she said.

She wasn't sure, now, if it was some newfound strength or simple desperation that had chased her from their bed this morning, got her to stop her silent, pointless sobbing in the shower, and wait for him here. Much less actually say what she'd wanted to say for weeks now. She wasn't sure it mattered either way.

She let out the breath she'd been holding, closed her eyes and finished it. "I want a separation."

There was a beat. Then another. Her heart pounded so hard inside her chest that it actually hurt.

"What did you say to me?"

Her eyes snapped to his. They glittered dangerously. He looked particularly wild this morning, his dark hair mussed from sleep, his jaw unshaven, and only those trousers low on his narrow hips. His voice was the iciest she'd ever heard it, a frigid sort of growl that sliced into her like a blade. She had the panicked thought that if she looked down, she would see her own blood.

But she didn't look. She didn't dare. She couldn't tear her gaze away from his. She couldn't do anything but stand there, frozen solid while he seemed to expand to fill the room and she was forced to remember that he was a dangerous, impossibly lethal man.

He only pretended to be tame, she reminded herself, feeling breathless and faintly ill, because it suited him to do so.

"I can't possibly have heard you correctly," he said, his voice that same cold lash.

He didn't move closer to her, but then, he didn't have to. She could see every long, hard line of his big body, so dangerously still, all of that uncompromising male power coiled in him. *Ready*. Sex and command. It was so heady, so intoxicating, that she understood with no little despair that she would always want it—want *him*—no matter how miserable it might make her.

But this was what men like Azrin did. They commanded. They ruled. They blocked out the whole world. They *took*. What had ever made her think she could stand strong and independent, her own person, next to this much power and force? She'd been lucky he'd let her play around in the fantasy of it all this time.

Lucky, she repeated to herself, and it almost made her cry.

"Are you planning to say something else?" he asked, in that dark, impatient tone that made her stomach turn over, hard, even as she felt too hot, too cold. "Am I to draw my own conclusions about this time you need? This separation? Or, let me guess, you are laboring under the delusion that I'll just let you run back to Australia without a fight?"

"I am not happy," Kiara said then, finally, simply, and the words seemed to crack something open inside of her.

As if she'd been afraid to say them, afraid to admit that she felt them, afraid of what would happen once she did…

This, she thought then, wishing she could feel numb. Wishing this could simply be over somehow. Wishing that she had never sat down at that café table all those years ago. *This was exactly what she was afraid of.*

"Are you sure?" His voice was so dark, with such a vicious kick beneath. "You seemed happy enough every time you came in my arms last night. I lost count, Kiara. How many times was it?"

Some sickening mix of temper and desperation swirled in her belly and then pulled tight, giving her just enough false courage to lift her chin, square her shoulders and figure out some way to push the necessary words out of her mouth.

"Yes, Azrin," she said. "You're very good in bed. Congratulations. But that isn't the point, is it?"

He spread his hands out as if in surrender, and she had the despairing thought that he'd never looked less like a supplicant. Even a gesture like this made him look like what he was—a bloody king, indulging her. Patronizing her, on some level, whether he knew it or not.

"Why don't you tell me what the point is," he suggested, and there was less ice in his voice now and more of that deliberate, measured calmness that she found she hated. It smacked of that same indulgence. "You are the one who wants to separate." He said that last word as if it was a vile curse.

"I have done nothing for the past three months but trail around after you," Kiara said, evenly. Rationally. The way she delivered reports in business meetings. "First there was the pre-coronation finishing school with your sisters. Then the months of appearances. Always smiling. Always dignified and silent and polite, entirely without opinions on anything except the flowers. The decor. The weather. That is not what I want from my life."

"That is your job," he said, shrugging, though his eyes remained hard on hers.

"It is *your* job," she retorted, still fighting to keep her voice as calm as she knew it needed to be. "I have an entirely different job, as you know very well. It does not involve acting as if I am nothing more than a repository for opinions you have already vetted. A figure, nothing more. Or, even better, a currently empty uterus that your whole country gets a say in filling, apparently. My actual job involves my *brain*."

His eyes were so dark now, too dark, and seemed to bore into her, seeing all kinds of things she was sure she'd rather keep private. Hidden. But she didn't look away. She knew this was a fight for her life. She knew it with a certainty that should have scared her—that *had* scared her so much that she'd gone almost entirely mute these last weeks rather than risk these words slipping out at some state dinner and shaming them both in front of the whole world.

And because she hadn't wanted this, she admitted to herself. She hadn't wanted to believe that this was happening, even as every day she saw less and less of herself in the mirror.

"I can't believe that you honestly think the Queen of Khatan should—or could—be the vice president of a foreign corporation in her spare time." Azrin's voice was dark and curt.

He shook his head, an impatient expression moving over that ruthless face and telling her quite clearly that he was not taking her seriously. That he had already relegated her to just one more of those daily fires of his, just one more problem to solve. She told herself she shouldn't let it hurt as much as it did. That this—exactly this—was precisely why she had to take this step.

"I don't think you truly think so, either," he continued in the same tone. "I think your feelings are hurt. My attention has been on my responsibilities and you feel ignored. Hence this tantrum."

"This isn't what I signed up for," she said, though it cost her to keep so calm. "And it isn't a tantrum to say so. Pretending that this is a childish display of temper so you don't have to deal with what I'm saying, however, very well might be."

"When you met me I was the Crown Prince of Khatan," Azrin said, the chill back in his voice, that terrible steel in his eyes. "This is, in fact, *exactly* what you signed up for." He laughed slightly, though there was no humor in it. "Sooner than we planned, perhaps, but that's life. Plans change. Sometimes you simply have to do your duty."

"You're talking about *your* life," she said through the constriction in her chest, which she was deathly afraid were the tears she refused to cry. Not in front of him. Not when it was so important he take her seriously. That he *listen*. "*Your* duty. What about mine?"

"What about it?" he asked, every inch of him so arrogant. So incredulous. "This *is* your life, Kiara. Whatever games we played over the past five years, this is reality. The sooner you accept it, the happier you'll be."

And there it was, she thought dully. Painfully. Had she known all along that it would come to this? Had she felt it somehow? Was that why all the pressure to have a baby had rubbed her the wrong way—because she knew this was only a game to him after all?

"Were you playing games all this time?" she asked, unable to keep the catch from her voice. "Because I wasn't.

I have my own responsibilities. My own duties. There are people depending on me, too—"

"I am talking about a kingdom," Azrin said, that impatient edge in his voice again, that cold fury in his gaze. "A government. A country. A whole population. You are talking about grapes."

She felt as if he'd hit her. That dismissive tone in his voice. That look in his eyes. The proof that he had never supported her the way he'd pretended to—that their relationship was nothing but a lie. She felt empty. Hollowed out.

Or, if she was brutally honest, she only wished she did.

How she wished she did.

"No," she said, astonished that she could even speak. Much less manage to sound so calm. So unmoved and unbothered. As if none of this was breaking her heart. "You're talking about your family—and I'm talking about mine."

The silence stretched out between them, ripe with all the things he had to prevent himself from saying. That deliberately even tone of hers slapped at him, infuriated him. Azrin had to fight to keep his temper under control.

"What do you want, Kiara?" he asked when he was certain he could speak without shouting. "How do you see this working out? I am the King of Khatan. You are the Queen. That can't be changed, no matter where you choose to hide."

"I don't know," she said, her voice still so frustratingly even, despite the edge in his. It made him feel wild inside. He saw her hands had balled into fists at her sides, and comforted himself with the knowledge that she was not nearly as cold nor calm as she appeared.

"Do you really think the people will support their

queen's sudden residency in Australia?" He eyed her as if she was a stranger instead of the woman who had bewitched him for years, who he still wanted, even when he was this furious with her, even when he had no idea what to do with all this hopeless rage. "Or is that what you want—that kind of scandal?"

"I said I don't know."

Her head jerked up, and her brown eyes looked very nearly black. He could sense her temper more than see it, and he didn't know what was wrong with him that he should want to goad her into exploding. Into showing him what was beneath all of these impossible, terrible things she was saying, none of which he could believe. Much less accept.

"But by all means, you should keep pushing me about it in that aggressive tone of voice," she said. "I'm sure that will clear everything up."

He realized he was gritting his teeth when his jaw began to ache.

"I will never divorce you," he said softly. Deliberately. "Just so we understand each other."

"You don't get to decide that, Azrin," she retorted, frustration bleeding into the even tone of her voice then. She reached up to massage her temples, as if he was a headache she wanted to rub away. "If I want to end this marriage, I will."

"I see." He moved closer to her without meaning to move, until he was near enough that her scent teased at him, that he could hear the catch in her breath as she eyed him warily. Too warily. And still, none of it was enough. None of this made sense. "So you feel that the promises you made, your vows, are only something you have to keep if and when it's convenient for you. Is that what this is?"

"I have done nothing *but* keep my promises!" she

snapped at him, and he saw a hectic color bloom across her cheekbones. He should not have been so small a man as to feel that like a victory. "You can't say the same. You married *me*, not some Khatanian paragon, crafted from the cradle to serve your every need. You married me knowing exactly who I was—"

"So did you," he retorted. He shook his head as if that might clear it. "What *is* this? You've hardly spoken to me in weeks—"

"You made it perfectly clear that there was no discussion to be had!" She threw the words at him, cutting him off, a bright fury in her brown eyes.

"Are you referring to the many conversations we've had about your unhappiness?" he gritted out. "Of course not, because you've never mentioned it until now. Yet somehow I am to blame because it was never discussed?"

For a moment, they only stared at each other. He could hear the harsh way she breathed, could see the bright heat on her cheeks and the pallor beneath. He wanted to touch her, to soothe her, to *remind* her—but something in the way she looked at him stopped him.

"You should have known better," she said after a long moment, and the rich, deep pain in her voice nearly undid him. A toxic cocktail of shame and blame and anger ripped through him, too much like weakness. "You knew what kind of wife you needed. You should never have pretended it could be me."

He heard the layers of agony in her words. He felt it in the way she looked at him, in the tears that spilled from her dark eyes that she jabbed at with her hands. And he had no idea what to do to fix this, to change it.

"It is you," he said. He let out a hollow sort of laugh. "It is only you."

She shook her head then, looking, if possible, even more miserable.

"Maybe that's the solution," she said. She lifted her chin as if bracing herself. "Maybe you should stop fighting your heritage and your traditions and simply take a more appropriate wife in addition to me. Or two, just like your father."

For a moment it was as if some white-hot kind of electric charge seared through him, so furious did that remark make him. But he reined it in. He shoved it down. Somehow.

"You want a harem, Kiara?" he asked through his teeth. "I will be more than happy to provide you with one. But let's make sure you're clear on how it works. I get to have as many wives as I want. You get to obey me."

"Or, alternatively, I could divorce you and marry Harry Thompson the way my mother always wanted me to," she snapped back, wholly uncowed by him. "He's never been so appealing, frankly."

"Try it," Azrin suggested, his tone nothing short of murderous. "I dare you. See what happens."

Her brown eyes flashed. "Don't threaten me."

And something seemed to crack inside him. He couldn't control the temper that crashed through him, over him. Not anymore. Not when she was so determined to break him into pieces. Not when he no longer seemed to care if she did.

"Don't threaten *me*, Kiara!" He only realized he was shouting when he heard his own voice, so very loud was it. So raw. Her face paled, but he couldn't seem to stop. "Harems? Divorce? *Harry Thompson?* Will you say anything at all to hurt me?"

She had never heard Azrin raise his voice. Ever.

His temper, she would have said, was a cold thing. Layers of ice and that cutting edge in his voice. Not this wild, pulsing fury that still echoed from the walls. That shook her, hard and deep, from the inside out. She had to fight to keep a terrified sort of sob inside, and the worst part was, he had no idea how badly she wanted to take it all back. To fall into bed with him, to smile on command when they were out of bed, and pretend that this wasn't killing her, bit by inexorable bit.

He had no idea how much it cost her to do this. He never would.

"I need to think," she said, no longer caring if her voice was uneven. If the tears fell. "I can't do it in Khatan. I can't do it near you. I need to clear my head."

She didn't realize how hard she was crying until she heard her own voice, thick and distorted with her own sobs.

"Kiara…" He looked at her, his eyes so dark and so raw, and she hated that she'd done this to him. That she hadn't been able to simply handle all of these changes, what they meant, no matter how difficult. That she couldn't love him enough to justify losing herself.

But she couldn't. She just couldn't.

Did that mean she'd never really loved him as she should have? What else *could* it mean? And that, she thought dimly, was entirely on her. It was exactly what she had to figure out.

"Space," she managed to say, though the room was full of darkness and damage and she wasn't sure she could survive this. "You need to give me space."

"What will that accomplish?" His voice was little more than a growl. "We've hardly spoken in weeks and this is the conclusion you've drawn. What will space do but confirm it?" His troubled gaze met hers. "Unless, of course, that's what you want."

"You never gave me any space at all, did you?" She

shook her head, stepping away from him as if to underscore it. "You argued me into dating you. You talked me into sleeping with you. You convinced me to marry you—"

"Spare me the revisionist history, please," he interrupted, his voice little more than a dangerous rasp. "You are no malleable little puppet. You wanted me then. You want me now." His gaze raked over her, into her. "You're standing three feet away from me with your arms crossed in front of you because you can't trust yourself. You know that if I moved any closer—if I touched you—I'd be inside you and *space* would be the very last thing on your mind."

Kiara didn't realize he'd backed her across the room until she felt one of the sofas behind her. She reached out and held on to it, because she was afraid of what she would do if she didn't—because he was right. She wanted to touch him. She always did.

And look where it had got them.

"Yes," she whispered. "We have sex. Maybe that's all we have."

He let out a breath then, jagged and coarse. He moved closer, and it was too much, as it was always too much. She could feel the power and the anger in him, and worse, all of the pain. And still, he was so beautiful. So fierce, so powerful. Her impossible, addictive attraction to him moved in her like some kind of fever. Even now.

He leaned in, holding her hands in his, and then angled his big body down to rest his forehead against hers. Kiara closed her eyes, and it was as if he surrounded her. Completely.

This was killing her.

"You are the only woman I have ever loved," he said quietly.

And she wanted to die.

But even in that moment, even as her mind spun with a

thousand ways she could try to stay and make this work, she knew she couldn't do it. She couldn't disappear any further, or she'd disappear for good. She knew it.

She could feel that intoxicating heat of his, like some kind of fire that burned forever beneath his skin. Enveloping her. Encouraging her to simply lean forward and lose herself in him. She tilted her head back to look up at him, but they were still so close. Close enough to kiss. Close enough that it felt as if they already were.

"If you love me, Azrin," she whispered, because she was desperate. Because she didn't know how else to do this. "Let me go."

He looked at her for a very long time. Kiara wasn't sure either one of them breathed. He took her hands in his, and for a moment she thought he would simply ignore her—simply take her mouth with his and make them both forget. They both knew he could. Some part of her even wanted him to do it, to take this decision out of her hands altogether.

She remembered how she'd loved it once, that he'd made her feel so weak, so overwhelmed, so utterly lost in him. So fascinated. It had been such a contrast to the rest of her life. And she wasn't sure she loved it anymore, but she could feel that same fascination, that same invitation to lose herself in him, as much a part of her now as her own flesh, her own bones. The threat of him as much within her as without.

She understood in that moment that if he did not let her go, she would not be able to make herself leave him. It made her feel hollow inside, that betrayal of herself, but she knew it was true.

And it was amazing how much that part of her wanted him to do it. To make her stay.

"Leave, then," he said, in a voice she hardly recognized, though it broke what was left of her heart into dust.

And then he opened up his hands and let her go.

CHAPTER FIVE

IT WAS shaping up to be a good grape-harvesting season, Kiara told herself with forced cheer as she walked down to breakfast. Despite the fact she'd missed so much of it while she'd been *off playing queen of the castle*, as her mother called it. But it was not even remotely soothing to think about Diana, so Kiara thought about the grapes instead.

When she'd arrived home nearly a month before, they'd been picking the Tempranillo. The grapes were in barrels now, on their way to becoming another excellent Frederick Winery vintage, while the winery turned its attention to the picking of what promised to be a particularly complex and alluring Shiraz.

This was what she was good at, she reminded herself. Grapes and wine. Color, nose and palate. She was home, finally. She was where she belonged. Everything was exactly as it should be, exactly as she'd wanted it.

So why did she feel like a zombie?

She walked, she talked. Kiara was still the vice president of Frederick Winery, but her commitments and tasks had been farmed out to her coworkers when she'd left for Khatan, and there was no way to reclaim her duties without coming clean about the state of her marriage. Luckily, as she'd discovered in her months as queen, she was very good at pretending. She smiled, she laughed, she *acted* as if everything was fine. As if she was on holiday, perhaps.

But inside… Inside she was deathly afraid that there was nothing left of her at all.

Every day, she thought it would be better. Even the littlest bit. She thought she would wake up and feel all that pressure, all that pain, ease. Or at least shift, somehow. She thought she would start to go, say, even five minutes without replaying every word Azrin had said to her in Washington, without seeing that utterly bleak, destroyed look in his stormy eyes. If she could make it through a night without dreaming of him—his breathtaking touch, the sensual thrill of his voice, that approving light in his nearly blue gaze when he looked at her and smiled… But it never happened.

She was beginning to wonder if it ever would.

Through the high, graceful windows that arched along the stairway toward the lower floors of the chateau, Kiara caught the familiar sight of the landscape that had always dominated her life. The lush Frederick vineyards stretched off toward the hills, everything green and gold, in the height of a perfect Barossa Valley summer. This was home, she told herself again. This was not an ancient palace in a foreign city, ripe with ineffable traditions and too many arcane roles she was destined to fail at fulfilling. This was precisely where she belonged. She should be happy—and if not happy, at the very least, content.

And yet she still felt nothing but empty.

Diana was in the kitchen when Kiara entered, looking as casually elegant as ever as she sipped her morning coffee and read the morning paper at the long, wooden table that was the focal point of the bright, cheery room. Kiara's grandmother had made the serviceable kitchen over into the warm center of the great house it was now, and Kiara's girlhood had involved long hours sitting at the table while her gran puttered about at the stove. Diana had made the chateau into a showpiece—somehow unpretentious and luxurious at once, just as she was—but she'd left the kitchen as it was.

Not that it comforted Kiara today. She smiled a polite *good morning* at her mother and then went to fix herself a large cup of coffee.

"You have a visitor," Diana said when she'd finished, and Kiara's heart stopped. It simply stopped. Then pounded so hard she felt light-headed.

He had come. He was here.

She whirled around, her pulse a wild staccato in her throat, to see the speculative way Diana looked at her.

And then she would have given anything to take her reaction back, to hide it away, because her mother saw far too much and was always looking for more—but it was too late.

"It's only Harry," Diana said. Her brows arched. "I hope that's not a disappointment."

"Of course not," Kiara said with as much equanimity as she could muster. She couldn't quite smile. "Why would it be?"

Diana let her paper drop to the scarred surface of the old oak table, focusing in on her daughter with all of her sharp, incisive attention. Kiara steeled herself.

"I'm really not in the mood for an inquisition," she began, but sighed when she saw the look on her mother's face.

"Perhaps it's time to stop wandering about the chateau like a ghost," Diana suggested. Calmly. She was always so calm. It had the immediate effect of making Kiara feel wild and out of control. "Perhaps it's time to reclaim your career. Do more than simply mark time in your life."

"I'm fine," Kiara said. Insisted.

"Clearly," Diana said drily. She shook her head. "You claim there's nothing to discuss, that your marriage is in perfect health though here you sit, with no sign of your royal husband and as far as I know, no plans afoot to see him." She let that sit there for a moment. "*Perfectly fine*, as you say."

"I am not *marking time*," Kiara said, ignoring the rest of what Diana had said. "If you don't want me to stay here, I'm sure I can find a hotel nearby."

"If you want to stay in a hotel rather than in your family's home," Diana replied in the same dry way, which somehow made it worse, "I won't stop you. Though I will, naturally, wonder why it is you would rather hide out in a hotel than face a few innocent and well-meaning questions about a marriage you claim is doing so well."

Kiara took a deep, hard pull of her coffee and wished, not for the first time, that she didn't always feel like this when Diana spoke to her—so torn between that sense of duty mixed with guilt, and that powerful yearning to feel neither.

"My marriage is fine," she said, fighting to keep her voice even. She wished she felt less shaky, the aftermath of that hard kick of misplaced adrenaline making her feel a bit sick to her stomach. "And still off-limits as a discussion topic."

She didn't know what her plan was, she realized as she heard her own voice, her own denials, flying around the kitchen as if she believed them herself. She'd asked Azrin for a separation and he'd, if not precisely agreed, let her go. It had been nearly a month so far, when they'd never gone longer than two weeks without seeing each other. Of course Diana had noticed. Was she simply going to brazen it out? Act as if nothing was wrong when another month slipped by, and then another? How long could she expect that to last realistically?

Why couldn't she admit what had happened? That she and Azrin had separated? Why couldn't she just *say* it?

"Here's what I can't help but notice," Diana said, far too calmly, instead of answering the question. "This is the most animated I've seen you since you arrived back home. Apparently being argumentative suits you. There's a bit of life in your eyes and color in your cheeks."

"This is not animation." Kiara felt something hot slide behind her eyes, and was appalled to think she might crack, might actually cry, right here in the kitchen. And she knew if she did, there would be no hiding the truth from Diana. She would have to tell her mother that the marriage she'd always opposed had failed. And she knew she simply couldn't do it. "This is a desperate bid for you to please, please stop poking at my marriage. I've been begging you to stop for five years!"

Diana gazed at her for a long, simmering sort of moment and Kiara felt something turn over inside her. Hard. She just *knew*, somehow, that whatever her mother was about to say would take recovering from, and she wasn't sure she could recover from anything else just at the moment. She didn't think she could survive Diana's version of home truths. Not now. Not when she was terrified that she was, in fact, the very ghost Diana accused her of being.

"Listen—" she began, but then was saved when Harry Thompson walked in the door from the outside, keen to talk about the conversation he'd just had with the Frederick Winery chief winemaker.

Dear, friendly Harry, Kiara thought, studying him after they'd exchanged greetings.

She supposed he was a good-looking man, though it had been a long time since she'd thought of him in that way.

He was simply Harry. He would one day run his family's wine business. He would raise a few children to follow in his footsteps. He would have good years and bad, as dependent as everyone else was on the vagaries of the Australian weather, the moisture in the soil, the odd heat wave or downpour that could change the year's grape yield. Safe, sweet, dependable Harry.

As Harry and Diana engaged in a friendly debate about their different winemakers' approaches to the Riesling this season, Kiara gripped her coffee and watched them over the brim of the mug.

The truth was, she could understand why Diana still thought Harry was the right choice for Kiara. He'd grown up steeped in wine and the wine business, and for a woman like Diana, who had lost her partner so early and had had to learn the wine business on the run with a small daughter and so many naysayers, he must look like the safest of safe bets. He must look a lot like Kiara imagined her own father must have looked to Diana all those years ago—a kind, loyal family man with deep roots in this valley.

It made Kiara wonder why she had let her romantic relationship with him fizzle, without even a harsh word spoken if she recalled it right, when she'd set off for university. Had she never really wanted *safe*, after all? Despite what she'd told herself before meeting Azrin?

"Are you expecting a big tour group?" Harry asked, stopping in the middle of his lively, friendly argument with Diana to peer out the big kitchen windows that looked out over a portion of the long entry lane leading up to the chateau and the grounds. It wound its way through the vineyards and beneath the small hill where the chateau sat, making the most of the view. "That's quite a convoy."

Kiara followed his gaze with mild interest, but saw nothing but dust kicked up in the air, as whatever vehicles Harry had seen had already disappeared around one of the bends, presumably circling around the final curves toward the front of the chateau.

"No tour group that I'm aware of," Diana said. "But I would be the last to know."

Kiara realized they were both looking at her. "I've no idea," she said. "I haven't given a tour of the winery since I was on my summer holidays from university."

Harry's face cracked into a big smile then, so warm and happy that Kiara found she was unable to do anything but smile back. There was some part of her that mourned the fact that he could never, would never, be the man for her. Surely, she thought, that spoke to defects in her character. Surely she should have wanted him—for all the reasons her mother wanted him for her.

Because if she married Harry or someone like him and lived her life out making wine here, she would be living out the very dream that Diana had wanted for herself—the dream that had been cut short and altered so terribly when Kiara's father died.

And Kiara couldn't help feeling that helpless guilt roll through her again, because she knew it would never happen. Not even if she never laid eyes on Azrin again. Not ever.

"Do you remember that summer right before you started university?" Harry was asking. He turned to Diana. "I don't know how you let us get away with it, to be honest." He launched into a tale of some childhood adventure Kiara had half forgotten.

She was laughing when the door to the outside opened again, as Harry reenacted his own teenage response to the trouble they'd got in. Assuming it was one of the many staff members, Kiara didn't even turn to look.

"That sounds like a delightful story," Azrin said in his

coldest voice, the chill of it slicing through Kiara's laughter, straight into her heart, making her freeze solid and then whip around to take in the impossibility of him standing there, so fierce and hard and with that frigid gleam in his not quite blue eyes. Even so cold, so forbidding, he burned into her, making her momentarily blind. "I'm sorry to interrupt."

He was dressed entirely in black, which only served to make him that much more intimidating, something she would have thought impossible. A black T-shirt hugged his powerful torso and the black trousers he wore beneath did the same, and yet, despite the casual clothes, he was obviously and overpoweringly a king. He looked as regal as he did lethal, like some kind of dangerous angel, conjured up from who knew what kind of erotic dream to loom here, all smooth muscles, hard aristocratic stance, and implied danger. There was no mistaking that masculine threat, that ingrained assumption of dominance. It was written on every hard-packed inch of him.

He never took his gaze from Kiara. And yet that banked sensual menace, that unmistakable air of command, seemed to come off him in waves to blanket the whole of the room.

She could feel him in her bones, as if he had worked his way into the very marrow of her. And she could not seem to tell if what she felt so deep inside, that sweeping, twisting wave of sensation, was jubilation or despair.

Or both.

"Hello, Kiara," Azrin said in that dark, seductive way of his that set off fires inside of her, whole bright blazes she hadn't felt since she'd walked away from him in Washington and couldn't seem to breathe through now. There was only the lick of flames and that mad urge to throw herself directly into them. Into him. His mouth pulled into a crook that was not quite mocking, and yet was entirely too knowing. "My queen."

"Poor Harry," she said, her voice chiding.

It was the first thing she said to him, directly to him, and she didn't stop walking as she said it, she only ushered him into the sitting room on the family side of the chateau as if he was nothing but a guest. One she hardly knew, come to that. Azrin wasn't particularly impressed by that kind of reception from the woman whose absence had tortured him, flayed him alive, and in point of fact still did—but he shoved his own reaction aside.

This was all a means to an end, he told himself as he followed her. His desired end, whatever he had to do to achieve it. Whatever it took.

She turned back toward him once she'd walked all the way into the room, and it hit him then, the weight of the strain between them. It seemed to echo in the air between them, making its own noise. He couldn't help but drink her in, as if he'd been thirsty for her all this time.

He knew it was no more that the truth—he had been. He was.

She was dressed very casually in sand-colored trousers and a top that clung to her mouthwatering curves and was the precise shade of ripe cherries. Her light brown hair was pinned back from her face, but still fell to her shoulders in waves, and it caused him physical pain not to reach over and touch it. Her. He could not have said why he wanted her so terribly, so completely—but it had always been this way. She had always defied reason.

He had to order himself to keep from touching her, little as his own body wanted to obey him. He wanted to drag her mouth to his and end this absurd distance between them. He wanted to take her down to the floor and remind her exactly how good it was between them—but too well did he remember what she'd said in Washington. Her accusations echoed in his ears even now, every bitter word like a separate knife into his gut. That all they had between them was that chemistry, that need.

"Harry who?" he asked, bored by what was obviously a stalling tactic.

"You know exactly who he is." She rolled her eyes. "And he didn't deserve the look you gave him."

Azrin smiled with a benevolence he did not feel, and somehow managed to keep his hands off of her as he lowered himself to lounge on one of the sofas. He barely glanced at the rest of the room, done with that brisk, efficient elegance that so categorized this place. These people. He propped his chin on one hand and eyed Kiara instead as she perched on a nearby chair, clearly determined to keep a safe distance between them. It irritated him beyond measure.

This was his wife. His queen. And she was afraid— or unwilling—to be too near him. He had to lock down the great surge of fury and something else far deeper, far darker, that moved in him then, threatening to take him over.

"I can assure you, Kiara," he said in a voice he could not quite control, "I saw only you."

Her gaze snapped to his for a moment before she looked away again. She moved her shoulders—as if she was bracing herself. As if she had to prepare herself to speak with him, as if she could no longer simply do it. He hated all of it.

"Looming about all menacingly in the kitchen and trying to intimidate everyone around you is not how we do things here," she said in some version of her usual teasing tone. This one, however, was laced through with something far sharper. "Though we certainly have names for it."

"I was not trying to intimidate anyone," he said mildly enough. Which was perhaps not in the least bit mild. "You would know it if I had been, I am certain."

She shook her head as if she despaired of him. He let his gaze travel all over her, and enjoyed it when she flushed. There was so much to say, to work through, and yet all he could seem to concentrate on was the simple satisfaction of being with her again. Of affecting her. Of making her react to him instead of simply walking away from him. He was sure that made him a fool, and he couldn't even bring himself to care.

"You look tired," he pointed out because he knew it would make her eyes narrow in outrage, and it did. "Sleepless nights? An unquiet mind, perhaps, interfering with your rest?"

"Not at all." She met his gaze then with the full force of hers, brown and deep and, he couldn't help but notice, shadowed. She angled her chin up in some kind of defiance. "I've never slept better."

Azrin didn't bother to call her a liar. He didn't have to. He could see the smudges of sleeplessness below her beautiful eyes, like twin bruises. He could see how pale she still was, though that did not seem to diminish either her prettiness or his automatic response to it. He found her as bewitching as ever—more, he acknowledged, because she seemed so unusually vulnerable.

And he was not above feeling it as a kind of victory that her return home had not resulted in an immediate return to her former vitality. That this separation was as terrible for her as it was for him. That she was not blooming into health and happiness without him. What would he have done if she was?

The air between them seemed to stretch, then tighten. Finally, she shifted in her seat, as if the tension was getting to her as much as it was to him. He had the impression it was hard for her to look at him again. Or perhaps he only wanted it to be. As if that might be telling.

"Why are you here?" she asked quietly, staring down at her hands as if they fascinated her suddenly.

"To discuss the terms of our separation, of course." Which was true, in its way. She flinched, then looked toward the open door. He watched her, his eyes narrowing in speculation. Was that guilt? His body thrummed with a kind of anticipation. "Is it a secret?"

"Not a secret, of course. But I haven't got around to telling anyone."

"Meaning it's a secret."

"Meaning I haven't got around to telling anyone," she repeated, frowning at him. "It doesn't mean anything more than that."

He studied her for a moment. "Why not?" When she frowned again, as if she didn't understand him, he sighed. "Why haven't you told anyone? I can understand not wishing to call a press conference, but surely this is precisely the news your mother has waited all these years to hear. Why would you deny her?"

She shook her head, her frown deepening. She pulled in a breath.

"I thought I knew who I was marrying," she said in a small voice. "What I was getting myself into. I thought I knew what I was doing." Her shoulders rose and then fell. "I was wrong."

He let that sit for a moment, ignoring the wild pounding inside of him that wanted only to reject her attempts to distance herself. Even in words.

"Let me understand you," he said coolly, when he could

speak without any hint of temper. Or, worse, that shameful desperation. "Your intention is to simply slip back into your old life? Pretend none of this ever happened?"

The look in her eyes then hurt him.

"I doubt it would work," she said almost ruefully. "But what else can we do?"

"This is the solution you have come up with." It was not exactly a question, and her gaze became wary as she watched him. He leaned back against the sofa, the better to keep himself from reaching out to her. "This is the best you can do, after all of these weeks apart."

"I didn't say I was ready to discuss anything today," she pointed out crisply. "You chose to simply appear here without any warning. You can't possibly expect me to be anything but thrown off balance."

"You have not bothered to keep in touch, Kiara," he said, his hold on his control slipping again, and his temper bleeding through despite his best efforts. "What was I meant to do?"

"You were meant to give me space," she retorted. She shook her head, as if cataloguing all of his shortcomings, all of her complaints. "You seem to have a very hard time listening to the things I want and need, Azrin. It's difficult not to assume that speaks to deep and abiding flaws in our relationship."

"If I recall your comments in Washington correctly," he bit out, "and I am certain I do, there is not a single aspect of our relationship that you don't find flawed. Or did I misunderstand your suggestion that I take a second wife? And perhaps even a third?"

He did not imagine the way she stiffened then, the way her lips pressed tightly together.

"Are you here to tell me you've found a few good candidates?" she asked, and he did not imagine the edge in her voice, either. *Good*, he thought, a dark satisfaction running through him then. Why should he be the only one to take exception to that particular suggestion?

"Perhaps I should ask you the same question," he replied, suddenly far calmer than he'd been. "Wasn't that my supposed replacement I saw out in the kitchen?"

Kiara closed her eyes briefly, then opened them again. They were too bright, but she made no attempt to hide that from him, she only looked at him. He thought he saw the faintest tremor move over her lips, but she rubbed her hand over her jaw and he could not be sure.

"I don't want to do this," she said in a low voice. "I don't want to fight with you. It only proves how little we know each other after all this time, and it breaks my heart." She pulled in a breath. "We come from very different worlds, Azrin, just as everybody warned us. Our parents, the papers, angry strangers on the internet. Maybe we should end this now before we wind up hating each other. I have to think that would be even worse."

He moved then, leaning toward her but not quite closing the distance between them. As ever, he felt the burn of it. The fire, the connection. Her eyes widened, but she didn't shrink away from him. He was desperate enough to think that might be progress.

"What would it take?" he asked. "What do you think could fix this?"

She shrugged helplessly, a gesture of surrender that he found stuck into him like something sharp. He didn't want her to give in, this strong, stubborn woman. To give up. He wanted anything but that.

"I don't think we can, unless you have access to a time machine." She let out a small sound. "How else could we go back and really figure out who we are?"

"Do you think I don't know who you are, Kiara?" he

asked, aware that his voice was little more than a rasp in the quiet room.

"I know you don't," she said, some of the hardness returning to her gaze, her mouth. But then she seemed to shake it off. "But the truth is, I thought you were someone else entirely. I knew a man who was only a prince as an aside. I was completely unprepared for what you'd become when you became a king."

"I am the same man," he said. His voice was too harsh, too sure. The words seemed to fall between them like stones.

"You are not." Her voice was firm. When her eyes met his, he saw the gleam of something he didn't fully understand and certainly didn't like.

This was worse, he thought then—worse even than gestures of defeat. This quiet, soft-spoken talk of the end of them, as if Kiara was conducting a pale, distant postmortem. The wildness was easier; the passion and the pain. The fight. This was intolerable.

"I think you misunderstand me," he managed to say in a voice somewhere near even. "In fact, I know you do."

"See?" She opened her hands wide. "You are making my point for me."

He had to move then and he did, rising from the sofa and somehow not going to her, not touching her, not showing her the vivid truth of them that he could feel arcing between them even now, even as she talked so resolutely about an ending he could not, would not accept. He prowled to the window and stared out, seeing nothing. No acres of vines, no blue sky above, no distant hills.

"What if we could make our own time machine of sorts?" he asked without turning around to face her. "You made a lot of claims in Washington. That I pushed you into dating me, into sleeping with me, into marrying me. What if we dated on your schedule instead?"

There was no sound at all for a beat, then another. Then she made a sort of scoffing noise. Azrin turned then. There was a hectic color splashed across her cheekbones that could as easily be temper or desire. Or some potent combination of both.

He raised his brows at her, daring her, and waited.

"What are you talking about?" she asked after another long moment. "That's ridiculous."

Her voice was cross. Annoyed. But he was sure there was something beneath it. He could feel it. He knew it—because she was wrong. He knew *her*.

"Why is it ridiculous?" he asked, finding to his surprise that he was suddenly able to project a great calm he did not feel. At all.

"We can't just pretend that nothing's happened between us!" she threw at him, her eyes wide, that color deepening in her cheeks. "That we're not married, that you're not... *you*. We can't *date!*"

"We don't have to pretend that we're not who we are—that would defeat the purpose." He spoke with such authority, as if he was not making this up on the spot.

As if this was not a last-ditch attempt to talk her into something he knew neither one of them would ever forgive him for simply taking. Though perhaps only he knew how close he was to doing so—simply throwing her over his shoulder like some kind of barbarian and to hell with what she said she wanted.

"We can pretend that we have just met," he continued like a civilized man would. "You say I don't know you and I say that if that's true, we can fix it. Introduce yourself to me. Tell me who you are." He shrugged. "Perhaps you will find you don't know me as well as you think you do, either. Perhaps we will find there are whole worlds yet to discover between us."

She stared at him.

"You're serious," she breathed.

She swallowed, then shook her head as if she couldn't believe it. As if she doubted what she was seeing, hearing. Or perhaps she only wanted to doubt it.

"Come, now, Kiara," he said silkily. "What do you have to lose?"

CHAPTER SIX

SHE had everything to lose, Kiara thought some time later. But that wasn't something she could tell him, not without admitting how lost he made her feel, or how easily he could have made her stay with him in Washington, had he only pressed the issue.

They sat together out on the wide stone terrace that overlooked the gardens and the winery's busy cellar door, watching the summer tourists come in flocks and buses and even on foot to sample the Frederick wines and the food they served in the small, adjacent restaurant.

The day was impossibly perfect all around them, as if it was colluding with Kiara to show off the beauty of the valley to Azrin, to demand he take notice. They had debated Azrin's absurd idea in the sitting room for a long time, until Kiara had been sure her head was going to break into pieces, and they'd agreed, finally, to take a break from it. A small negotiated oasis of peace.

"Surely," Azrin had drawled in that sardonic way of his, "we are not so lost to each other that we cannot enjoy each other's company. If only for a little while."

There had been no particular reason for that remark to set her teeth on edge, and yet it had.

Nevertheless, Kiara had taken Azrin on a tour of the vineyards, showing him all the ways Frederick Winery had changed since he'd last been here for any serious length of time, back when they'd started dating. She couldn't pretend that there wasn't a huge part of her that was trying to prove something to him as she did it. *Look at the scale of our operation*, perhaps. *Pay attention to how I'm needed here, and why*, she'd said without using the words, with every single vine and barrel she'd pointed out to him.

Azrin, of course, had said nothing. He'd only watched and listened, had seemed to consider the things she'd showed him, with that intense focus of his that made her heart seem to work harder in her chest.

After the impromptu tour, they'd sat down for a simple lunch full of local flavor that Kiara had pulled together from the usual reserves in the chateau's kitchen. She'd put thick slices of freshly baked bread, a few German sausages and a selection of local cheeses on a platter. Then she'd fished a bit of pear chutney from the pantry and, after a moment's thought, a particularly spicy beetroot relish, as well. She'd added small bowls of almonds and olives, and a dish of salted olive oil to dip the bread in.

Neither one of them wanted wine despite the fact there was so much of it available; a necessary precaution in her case, Kiara reasoned, given Azrin's historic ability to run roughshod right over her even without any wine involved.

Or was it more accurate to say it was usually *her* decision to give in to whatever it was he wanted, whether he asked her for her surrender or not? She wasn't sure she liked that thought, and concentrated on the food instead.

For a long time, they simply ate together at one of the small tables nestled there in the shade, in a silence she might have thought was peaceful, even companionable, had she not known better. Had the tension between them not added some kind of indefinable seasoning to each bite she took, a sort of prickle to the breeze that played over the table, even a certain heat to the measuring way his storm-tossed eyes moved over her when he thought she wasn't paying attention.

"You can't really want to walk away from our marriage without at least *trying* to fix it," he said after one such look in that darkly seductive way of his—breaking the silence and the peace between them that easily, though there was a part of Kiara that welcomed it the way she welcomed the onset of a storm after too long beneath threatening clouds. "That doesn't sound like the Kiara I know."

She decided she hated him for that. It explained the acrid taste in the back of her mouth, that unpleasant rolling sensation in her gut. *Hate.* Clearly.

"They will say you could not handle being queen," he continued, seemingly unperturbed. "There will be wild speculation. Is it because you secretly detest my people, my country, as we always suspect Westerners will? Or is it simply because you could not be expected to be sophisticated enough to handle the position, having come from what is, essentially, a glorified farming community?"

She had to bite back the sharp words that crowded her throat—and then she saw that almost silver gleam in his gaze, that slight curve of his hard mouth. *Of course.* He was pushing her. Deliberately.

"You are manipulating me," she said stiffly.

"I am *trying* to manipulate you," he corrected her, his voice suspiciously mild. Was he amused? That made her stomach twist. *Anger,* she told herself. *This is nothing more than anger.*

"Then you've lost your touch completely," she said. "If I cared what other people thought, I wouldn't have married you in the first place, would I? I doubt I would have so much as had that first dinner with you. I'd have been far too cowed by all the dire predictions about harems and compulsory burkhas."

Azrin only smiled, but, in spite of herself, she found herself thinking back to those wild, early days as she looked at him.

She'd fallen for him so hard and so fast that she'd spent months pretending otherwise out of simple fear. Terror, even. That he'd know. That he'd leave. She hadn't been able to decide which would be worse, which would hurt more. She hadn't wanted to find out.

It had been so intense—and so physical. A simple look from him and she'd turned to flame. A kiss, a brush of his fingers, being held against that hard body of his, and she'd detonated. It had been almost overwhelming when she'd realized—when she'd finally allowed herself to believe—that he felt the same way.

Meanwhile, everyone she knew had weighed in with their opinions. Everyone had known a great deal about the predatory nature of the average sheikh, apparently, despite none of them having known any sheikhs personally. She'd heard chapter and verse, again and again. And none of it had done anything at all except convince her that she knew better. That she knew *him*. That Azrin had been worth suffering through whatever silly fantasies her friends and family had wanted to concoct about him, simply because he hadn't grown up with grapevines wrapped around his limbs and a good Shiraz running in his veins.

She'd had so little doubt back then. She'd been so convinced she knew best. She'd been *sure*. Of Azrin, of herself. Of them. When had she lost that? How had it happened? Did the fact that she'd let go of it so easily mean it was never there in the first place?

She shouldn't have been surprised at how sad it made her to think so.

"Are you reconsidering your position?" he asked then, as if he was able to see straight into her memories right along with her. "It's easy to say one cares little about public opinion, and harder, I find, to actually live through it."

"I've lived through it already," she pointed out quietly, as a flash of something bitter snaked through her as if it had been lying in wait, without her knowledge. "I'm living through it as we speak. The updates in the paper about the state of my royal womb, for example."

It was only after she said it, and Azrin only sat there with that expression on his face—as if she'd hauled off and slapped him with all of her strength, straight across the mouth—that Kiara acknowledged the possibility that she perhaps cared a bit more about public opinion than she wanted to admit. She jerked her gaze away from his, and only looked back when he reached over and took her hand in his. She observed, as if from a distance, that so simple a touch sent a jolt straight through her, searing her from neck to ankles.

She missed him. She stared at their joined hands and pretended that wasn't true, that it didn't beat in her like a drum. But she knew better. She missed him so much she made up wild fantasies of hating him to try to distract herself. Fooling no one, least of all herself.

"Do you still love me?" he asked.

His voice was quiet, but the simple question echoed through her as if he'd shouted it. She flinched as if he had. Still, she focused on their hands, not on his face. Not on those too-knowing eyes.

"I'm not sure that matters," she said, aware of how choked she sounded, of how that, in itself, undercut her attempt to shrug this away.

He only waited.

She heard the usual, familiar sounds of summer all

around her. Rainbow lorikeets chattered in the trees above them, while the laughter of the kookaburras floated on the breeze. The tourists at the other tables on the terrace were laughing and talking, reveling in the shade and the sunny day all around them. She could smell fresh cut grass and oak barrels, the tang of grapes and the rich, fertile earth itself, the particular perfume that told her she was here and nowhere else. Home.

But that was not as comforting as it ought to have been. As she thought it should be.

Finally, unable to put it off any longer, unable to stand her own pathetic diversionary tactics, she looked at him.

It shouldn't hurt this much. He shouldn't feel like coming home, when he was anything but that. When he was the opposite of that, in fact, and well had she learned that lesson these past months.

"Do you?" he asked again, a certain implacable note in his low voice, a hint of his formidable will.

She let out a breath. Or it escaped. Either way, she knew he would not stop asking. That there was no hiding from him. From this.

"You know that I do," she whispered, knowing even as she said it that it was a kind of surrender. Or, perhaps, no more than a simple, overdue acceptance of a painful truth that somewhere along the way she'd decided didn't matter anyway.

He knew it, too. She saw the knowledge of it in his gaze, could feel the heat of it between their hands. She only wished she did not wonder if it was some kind of curse. Something they should have run *from*, all those years ago, rather than *toward*.

She supposed this was the time to find out, once and for all.

"I love you, too," Azrin said quietly, all of their history like a rich current pulsing between them, impossible to ignore, as his mouth moved into something not quite as simple as a smile. His hand tightened around hers. The curve of his mouth deepened. "So, Kiara, please. Date me."

"I can't help but notice that this is not Madrid," Kiara said drily.

They stood together out on the nondescript tarmac of what was little more than an airstrip. If she had not been looking out the window as Azrin's private plane had descended toward the shift and roll of the endless desert, she would have had no clue at all to tell her where they were. There were no markings, not even on the faintly military-looking set of buildings off to one side.

The air was hot and shockingly dry, and yet she knew she was lucky it was still winter here; in the summer, in the desert, the temperature climbed so high it would have felt like a physical blow to step into it. The wind whipped into her, around her, and there was the faint sting of sand in it, making her wish she was wearing the headscarf she usually donned when she knew she would be arriving in Khatan.

She'd recognized the towering cliffs and the sea as they'd flown in, circling inland to land on this dusty little tarmac. She knew the picturesque village that was arrayed along one of the gentler cliffs, stretching down toward the pristine white sand beach beneath. She even knew that its name meant something like *beautiful dwelling place* in Arabic.

She should—she'd seen it featured on a thousand post-cards in Arjat an-Nahr, and throughout the rest of the country.

Not that she'd ever been here before. Nor had she had any plans to change that.

"No," Azrin agreed, finally sliding his mobile into his pocket. She couldn't see his eyes behind the dark sunglasses he wore, but she could feel the dark caress of them making her skin prickle. "We are not in Madrid."

He beckoned for her to proceed him as he started across the tarmac. Kiara started walking, noting the absence of the hand he usually held at the small of her back, and finding that she mourned its loss.

"I'm trying to figure out what part of our discussion, in which I clearly stated we should have our so-called first date in Madrid and you agreed, led you to think I instead wanted to come back to Khatan," she said, shoving the odd sense of some kind of grief aside. "Oddly, it's not coming to me."

"Did I agree?" he asked in that mild way that made her far too conscious of that ruthlessness he hid beneath his usually more accessible exterior. "Are you quite sure?"

Kiara opened her mouth to assert that he most certainly had, and then closed it.

She had been the one to talk about Madrid, in fact, once she'd agreed to this plan of his. It was a city they'd barely visited in all their crisscrossing of the globe. A blank canvas, she'd said, on which they could paint anything they liked as they played this little game. Privately, she'd thought it was the perfect choice—it lacked any markers of their complicated personal history, yet was big enough and not too remote, which meant that they could part without too much trouble should either of them wish it.

Should she wish it.

Yet all Azrin had said, now that she thought about it, was that Madrid was, indeed, a lovely city.

"You know I wanted to go to Madrid," she said, as if it was important. As if the city itself mattered, when she knew what truly bothered her was that he he'd made the decision without consulting her.

He looked down at her, and again she *felt* the look in his eyes even if she couldn't see it. She felt it move through her, making her whole body clench around the sensation. His hard mouth curved as if he could feel it, too.

None of this was fair.

"You agreed to the game, Kiara," he said, that heat in his voice seeming to stroke them both. She didn't think that was fair, either. "I merely chose the venue."

They were respectfully handed into the second in a trio of kitted-out jeeps with four-wheel drive by Azrin's usual team of bodyguards, then driven over roads that seemed to Kiara like little more than suggestions or, perhaps, *intentions*, across the high, empty desert. Eventually, they made their way toward the cluster of palm trees and greenery that started at the very edge of the cliffs and then followed the often-photographed village down toward the gleaming sea beyond.

It took long, hard hours to drive across the desert to reach this particular stretch of coastline. There was no commercial airport—until today, Kiara would have said there was no airport at all. Travelers had to be hardy and determined to make their way here, but Kiara could see that it was well worth the trek.

The village boasted a collection of houses that seemed hewn from the cliff face itself, clustered very nearly on top of each other as they straddled the single road that wound through the town. There were two hotels next to each other steps from the bright white sand beach. The locals were reportedly friendly and welcoming, and those who made it here almost universally considered it the jewel of Khatan's mostly inaccessible and proudly inhospitable northern coast.

Kiara had read all about this place in the books she'd devoured while she and Azrin had been dating and then engaged, when she'd been so determined to soak up all the information she could about his country. About him. As if she'd expected there might be some kind of exam.

"I've always wanted to come to this village," she said now, remembering those long nights in her graduate school flat, reading about a place that seemed more fantasy than reality, all shining sun and gleaming sand, as the Melbourne winter had thrown rain and fog against her windows. "Though I did not imagine you would have to abduct me to make that happen."

Next to her in the backseat of the Jeep, Azrin merely shrugged. He had one hand braced against the door as the vehicle jolted down the rough cliff side road while he frowned down at the mobile that was once again in his other hand.

"You got on the plane of your own volition," he pointed out, that undercurrent of amusement making his dark voice rich in the confines of the Jeep. He didn't bother to look at her as he said it. He didn't have to.

Kiara rolled her eyes. She should be furious. She should feel betrayed, kidnapped, taken advantage of. But she was forced to admit to herself that she felt none of those things. What she felt was vulnerable. And she knew herself well enough to know that it didn't matter what corner of the world they might have gone to for this little game Azrin wanted to play. It was Azrin himself who made her feel so...at risk. So threatened.

And not by him but, far worse, by her own damned feelings.

She'd thought for some reason that a big, bustling city might dampen her reaction—might help dissipate the intensity of it—though she realized now that that had just been wishful thinking. When had the location made a bit of difference? It didn't matter if they were in Hong Kong or the Napa Valley. Azrin was like some kind of sorcery, and she was, apparently, helpless to resist him.

She could feel him, as usual, taking up too much space in the back of the Jeep. Dominating all of the air around him as well as the seat itself. He even sat with that air of total command, his lean and powerful body seeming to infringe upon her, to take her over, without his having to move a muscle in her direction. And Kiara knew that it was all of this that she feared, all of this that made her feel so terribly weak.

It was not that he touched her, she knew; it was that she surrendered to that touch so completely. So totally. Without a single moment's hesitation or forethought. It was not that he demanded she forget everything that mattered to her when she looked at him; it was that she let herself forget it. She let herself fall.

She couldn't help but think that it was a terrifyingly easy step from submitting to the sensual spell he wove with so little effort to surrendering to him totally—completely disappearing into him until she did nothing at all but smile politely and wait for him, forgetting that she had ever wanted more than that for herself. She'd felt that like a noose around her neck by the time they'd reached Washington—her own eradication happening all around her with every state dinner, every smile she aimed at a different dignitary she had to be so careful not to offend. What would be left of her? Anything at all?

Her mother had said as much before Kiara left.

"When will you be back?" Diana had asked from the door of Kiara's bedroom. Kiara had started, and then had wondered just how long her mother had been standing there. If she'd seen, for example, how emotional Kiara was valiantly attempting not to be.

"I'm not sure," she'd said, frowning down at the clothes she'd laid out before her as if it required fierce concentration to put together a small suitcase. As if, after all those years of constant travel, she couldn't do this sort of thing in her sleep. "I'll let you know as soon as I have a reasonable estimate, of course."

She had been speaking to her boss, not her mother. She'd been assuming that Diana had wanted that information so that she could continue to monitor Kiara's workload in her absence. She should have known better.

"Kiara…" Diana's voice had trailed away, uncharacteristically, and when Kiara had looked over at her, she'd been shocked to see a strange sort of expression on her mother's face. As if Diana had been lost for words. Or simply lost. It had made Kiara feel knocked off balance. "You don't have to go with him. You don't have to do anything you don't want to do. You can stay here as long as you like. Stay a ghost, even. Until you work out whatever it is you need to work out."

There was a part of her that had yearned to accept that invitation—that had seen it as the olive branch it was undoubtedly meant to be. And it was even a good, short-term solution. Let Diana chase Azrin off while Kiara hid in her room like a child and licked her wounds. It certainly held great appeal. She'd already been doing it for a month.

But the rest of her had been far too wary of what it meant to give up control to Diana—and what Diana herself would have made of it if she did. Diana had never ceded control to anyone. Diana had created an empire out of sheer bloody-mindedness. Why couldn't Kiara do the same?

Not to mention, there was that stubborn core of her that

couldn't bear Diana to think ill of Azrin, even by impli-
cation.

"Do you think so little of me that you think Azrin is
bullying me into leaving with him?" she had asked, more
sharply than was fair. "That I'm letting him?"

Guilt swamped her as soon as she said the words. She
despaired of herself. It was easier to give in to her anger; it
masked how truly conflicted she felt in her mother's presence and always had. But that didn't make it right.

"Of course not," Diana had said impatiently. "He's certainly an intimidating, formidable man, but you've never
seemed remotely overwhelmed by it. I rather thought that
was one of the things you liked about him."

"He's my husband," Kiara had said, fighting to keep
her turbulent emotions under control. "I like a great many
things about him."

Diana had sighed. "I was eighteen when I met your father," she'd said quietly. Too quietly. As if this was not the
same old story she trotted out to reestablish their roles—to
underscore her sacrifices and Kiara's failure to live up to
them. "Only twenty when we had you. Before I met him
I'd had all kinds of different dreams. I wanted to paint. I
wanted a degree. I thought I'd travel. I had an enduring
fantasy of running a bed-and-breakfast somewhere desperately remote, where I could go weeks without seeing
another living soul." She'd shifted where she stood, smiling slightly, as if at her own memories. "I'd never thought
twice about wine. I don't think I could have picked out a
vineyard if I'd been lost in one, much less the difference
between the grapes. But I loved your father, and this was
where he had to be, so this is where I came."

Kiara had stopped pretending that her clothes were so
difficult to pack, that they'd required her full attention, and
had turned to face her mother then, crossing her arms as

she did it. As if she'd expected some kind of body blow. She'd never heard this before. She'd never heard Diana express anything even remotely approaching *regret*.

"It was hard," Diana had said softly, her much too similar brown eyes meeting Kiara's. "Much harder than I expected."

Kiara had shaken her head, refusing to give in to the confusing emotional storm that pounded through her then, making her question everything. Her mother. Herself.

Anger was easier. Safer.

"You've always said that the two of you were happy," she'd pointed out, fighting to keep that harsh edge from her voice. "Wildly happy, in fact."

"I'm not saying we weren't," Diana had countered. "I'm saying it was hard. More for me than for your father. He simply led the life he'd been raised to lead, while I had to learn how to be a part of it. But I still had my own dreams. Even after you were born. I thought I'd leave the winery to your father and pursue them on my own." She'd looked at Kiara for a long, uncomfortable moment. "But then he died."

Kiara had felt as if something had reached straight into her and had wrapped impossibly strong hands around her heart, her lungs, her stomach. And then had started to squeeze. She'd felt a surge of something she wanted to call fury, but it had been far too dark for that, far too edged with a deep current that felt too much like misery. And she'd refused to explore any of it. She'd understood with cold certainty that she didn't want to know.

"Let me see if I can parse this one out," she'd said instead, all of that anguish inside of her sharpening as she spoke, making her stand there like an ice sculpture and glare at Diana. "Either this is an anecdote about the perils of loving a man and moving with him into his predetermined life, or it's a rather more sentimental story about the need to follow my hopes and dreams despite my marriage. Which is it?"

As usual, Diana had seemed completely impervious to any show of temper. Or any insult. Also as usual, that had had the direct result of making Kiara feel like a toddler in midtantrum.

But that had been far preferable to what lay beneath. It always was.

"What I'm telling you is simple," Diana had said instead, with a little laugh that had sent Kiara's blood pressure skyrocketing. "After your father died, there were times that I looked around and wondered how on earth I'd ended up hip-deep in all of this wine when I'd never wanted anything to do with it. I'm lucky in that I've found that I'm quite good at it, but that's not always how this kind of story ends." She raised her elegant shoulders and then let them fall. "I know that becoming the Queen of Khatan is a role you took on as the price you had to pay to be with Azrin. I don't want you to look back on the choices you make now and find you regret them, Kiara." She'd shrugged again, but there was something so sad about it that it made Kiara's throat seem to close. "That's all."

Kiara had felt a great wave swell in her then, and she'd been terrified it might be a sob, or the start of a great many sobs. It had rolled through her body and made her come much too close to shaking. Or worse. She'd hugged herself, hard, her fingers digging into her own flesh, and managed somehow to keep her eyes steady on Diana's.

"You make a lot of assumptions," she'd managed to say in a voice that was a good approximation of normal, even as it had been laced through with a lifetime of never feeling good enough for this woman, no matter what she did or didn't do. Of always falling short of Diana's endless sacrifices. And of the despair that lay like a thick pool beneath. "For all you know, the wine business was the price I had to pay to make you treat me like a daughter every once in a while, instead of just another employee."

Needless to say, Kiara thought now, staring broodingly out the window as the small convoy kept on moving past the pretty little village and along the barely perceptible trail that hugged the base of the towering cliffs, that exchange had not improved her relationship with her mother. It had only made her feel terrible about her own capacity for cruelty.

Kiara was forced to face the unflattering reality that she'd reacted as strongly as she had because Diana had managed, as ever, to push the hottest of Kiara's buttons. A simple story about losing her dreams in favor of her husband's, and Kiara had gone off like a rocket. Wasn't that why she'd left Azrin in Washington? Because she'd felt trapped, claustrophobic and muted in her new role? Because she'd been terrified that if she didn't leave, she would lose the will to try, and would be stuck forever in a position she hated, empty and useless, a figure standing always behind her husband with nothing of her own at all?

She felt the panic beat at her again, making her pulse race. She looked around the inside of the Jeep, taking in Azrin, the armed guards in front, the tinted windows that concealed them from the outside world. She should not have agreed to this foolishness. It was one more case of her thinking she could have her cake and eat it, too. She couldn't. She'd tried.

It didn't matter how much she loved Azrin, or how much he loved her. None of that changed anything. None of that even mattered, not really. None of that made him less a king, or made her any more suited to being the kind of queen he required.

She turned her head to tell him so, once and for all, and found him smiling a sweet, almost nostalgic smile. Not at her, she realized almost at once, even as her heart hitched in her chest. No, his gaze was directed out the window, at what looked to Kiara like a shadow in the great rock face that loomed above them.

As if he felt her gaze on him, he looked over at her, and Kiara felt something clutch inside her again. He looked... *carefree*, she thought, with some amazement. She couldn't remember the last time she'd seen such light in his fierce face, such uncomplicated joy.

It made her want to cry.

"This is my favorite part," he said, which didn't make any sense to her at all.

But before she could ask him what he meant, the Jeep in front of them took what should have been an impossible, suicidal right turn. Directly into the cliff. Instead of smashing into rock, it disappeared as if it had been sucked straight into it, and Kiara only realized that the shadow was the entrance to a narrow canyon as their own Jeep took the same turn.

"Just wait," Azrin said calmly, as Kiara realized she must have gasped. "It gets better."

The narrow road twisted and zigzagged, hardly seeming wide enough for the Jeeps that very nearly scraped the jutting rock on either side as they performed a series of turns at speeds that indicated they were very familiar with this route. Or completely insane. Kiara craned her head around to look up, to see that there was only a faint ribbon of sky visible far above, the sheer walls of the canyon almost closing them in.

She should have felt trapped. Perhaps she did. She took a breath, then another, and still they drove on, heading deeper into the rocks, into what was surely the heart of the cliffs themselves. Were they headed underground? Into some kind of bunker? Did he want to attempt to *date* her, as he put it, in some kind of medieval Khatanian jail?

They drove on and on. It was gloomy this far inside the rocky cliffs, this far away from that sliver of sunlight far above them—gloomy and cold. And still they drove, the mountain seeming to loom all around them, the road they followed hardly deserving of the name.

"Azrin…" she began when she couldn't take it another moment, when she thought the immensity of the rock, its implacable weight and the relentless chill on all sides, might actually send her into a panic from which she'd never recover.

He reached over and took her hand, taking it to his mouth for a kiss that seemed, she registered, almost absent, even if the touch of his lips slid through her like the brush of velvet across her skin. He kept his eyes trained ahead, and after a long moment, then another, he smiled.

"It's only scary the first time," he told her, that indulgent tone too buoyant with that same joyfulness for it to grate, and then he nodded toward the window. "Because every other time, you know that the ride is worth it."

Kiara frowned at him, but she turned as he'd directed her, and lost her breath all over again.

Because on the other side of the window, spreading out before her as the tiny canyon widened and sunlight poured down from above, was paradise.

The narrow little canyon opened up into a wide gorge, where palm trees and other vegetation clustered and beckoned over a series of inexpressibly beautiful aquamarine pools. The glorious waters seemed lit from within, as well as from the sunlight pouring down from high above. Here, inside the protected valley, the sun warmed the rocks—

the forbidding chill of the narrow approach an immediate distant memory.

Kiara hardly knew where to look first, and found herself sitting up and leaning forward like an overawed child.

The pools lay in a straight line along the floor of the canyon, each one larger than the one before it, seeming to dead-end at what appeared to be the farthest reach of the great hidden valley. And that was when Kiara actually let out a gasp, amazed. What could only be some kind of palace seemed to hang in the very air, as if carved from the rock itself, a five-story fortress garnished with balustrades and terraces, balconies and delicate arches, all of it jutting out over the water of the farthest, largest pool as if it had sprung full-grown from the side of the mountain.

As if it had always been there.

"It is called the Palace of the Ten Pools," Azrin told her, pride and a kind of reverence in his voice. "It was considered a holy place for many ages, and then became the favored summer retreat of my great-grandfather. Very few know of it."

"It's beautiful," Kiara whispered, though she could hardly speak past the sudden lump in her throat.

It was more than beautiful. The impossible, nearly belligerent thrust of the palace out from the rock cliff made her chest feel tight. It was a fierce, implacable building that shouldn't exist. It called to mind some warrior's mixture of gingerbread houses and medieval keeps, all jumbled together into what looked like a series of vertical rock sculptures, piled haphazardly on the side of a dizzyingly sheer cliff.

Azrin turned toward her, smiling, and it was like sensory overload. She couldn't tell what her body was doing, what she wanted, she could only tell that it was *too much*. A secret palace, mysterious pools inside a mountain…

how was she supposed to resist something like this? How was she meant to truly analyze what had become of them, of their marriage, if every time she turned her head, the beauty of their surroundings made her want to weep?

If he did?

"It hardly seems smart, though," she pointed out. She sat back and eyed him critically. "Bringing out your big guns so early on."

"Afraid you can't handle it?" he asked, that teasing light in his gaze.

He appeared perfectly at ease, lounging back against the seat as if he hadn't a care in the world as the Jeep brought them closer and closer to the impossible rock palace that some part of her still whispered couldn't possibly be real.

"I can handle it," she assured him. She waved her hand, encompassing the beauty of the pools, the fall of sunlight that seemed to bounce off the mountainsides, the dream-like palace itself. "But what are you going to do for a second date?"

CHAPTER SEVEN

HE WAITED for her out on the highest of the wide balconies as the afternoon edged toward evening. Up above, the sky was beginning to ease into a darker blue, and the skeleton staff they'd brought along to run the palace had already lit all the lights that hung like lanterns around the stone and iron perimeter.

Azrin never tired of this place. Of the mysterious echoes against the rocks. Of the way he seemed able to breathe deeper here, the air clear and sweet. Of the enchanted pools themselves, so deep and beautiful, no matter the season. They soothed him, even when he did no more than gaze upon them. He'd swum in them as a child, sat beside them as an adult, allowed them to work their quiet magic on his soul.

Tonight they made him believe that all of this would work out precisely the way he wanted it to work out. The way it should.

The way it must, he thought, and pretended he did not notice his own urgency.

He sensed her before he heard the faint scuff of her foot against the stone, and turned as she walked out onto the balcony, and then, after the slightest, barely perceptible hesitation, toward him. He leaned back against the high iron rail and watched her approach.

His wife. His queen.

Kiara wore a flowing magenta tunic over loose fitting trousers, and only thin sandals on her feet. She had a wrap over her shoulders, in deference to the mild winter evening that was already cooling the air around them. Her hair swung free in loose waves that his fingers itched to touch, and when she drifted closer he saw she wore only minimal cosmetics, letting her natural beauty shine forth. Captivating him as he was sure she intended.

Or perhaps, he thought ruefully, she simply captivated him as she always had, no intention necessary.

He made no move to reach for her as she walked to the railing and stood next to him but not quite touching him, not quite allowing her thigh to brush against his. She gazed out over the rail at the hidden gorge spread out before them. He made no move at all, and it nearly killed him.

"I count only five pools," she said after a moment, her voice soft. Almost shy, he would have said, though that didn't make any sense at all. "Shouldn't there be ten?"

"There are ten."

She looked at him, her brows raised in query, and he smiled, awash in the simple pleasure of looking at her when she was not frowning back at him, not obviously sad or distant, her eyes that clear, gorgeous brown he'd loved for so long now and not filled with the anguish that he, somehow, always seemed to put there despite his own best intentions.

"There are two pools in a cave deeper inside the mountain," he said, nodding toward the sheer cliff that faced him and stretched up toward the desert floor far above them. "They are fed by a hot spring and are accessible only from the second level of the palace." He waved a hand to his left. "If you were to swim down beneath the waterfall at the end of this pool, you could access the small passage that leads to three further pools. Two small ones that have only rocks and towering cliffs and one that is really more properly a lake, complete with a small, rocky beach." He wanted to lean in closer. He wanted to capture her face in his hands and taste that wide, compelling mouth. He did neither, and he wasn't at all certain where the strength for that came from. "In total, ten pools."

She looked away again, and he watched the way her hands clenched at her sides, as if she fought off her demons even as she stood there, looking otherwise relaxed. He understood then that it was a great talent of hers—one he should have recognized as the warning it was much earlier.

"It doesn't seem real here," she said in that same soft voice, with that same curious reticence. "It feels as if a place like this shouldn't exist."

He gave in to his urges and reached over then, pulling a strand of her brown-and-gold hair between his fingers, feeling the raw silk of it against his skin. She smelled of citrus and spice, a kind of delicate perfume that was only hers, and he knew that whatever she thought was happening here, whatever she believed this game might prove between them, that he would never, could never let her go. He didn't have it in him. She had always been the one thing he was wholly, unrepentantly selfish about, his one weakness, and he didn't imagine that anything could change that simple fact.

No matter how distant they had become these last months. No matter what.

He supposed that made him as manipulative as she'd accused him of being, after all, and he couldn't bring himself to regret that as he should have done. As a better man would have done, he was sure.

"Are we already on our date?" she asked, her voice a shade or two too husky. But at least that hint of shyness was gone. At least she sounded like herself. "If so, you should know that it's incredibly forward to just grab someone's hair when you hardly know them. In some cultures that could get you killed."

"Lucky, then, that I'm the king of this one."

He gestured toward the small seating area arranged behind them, jutting out from the wall of the palace. There was a construction of canopies above to shield them from the sun by day and thick, heavy rugs to take the chill from the stones beneath them now, like some majestic, luxurious cabana. Large, colorful pillows were scattered about the floor, circling a wide, low table of inlaid mosaic tiles in shades of blue, green and black.

Azrin watched as Kiara lowered herself to the pillows with that absentminded, matter-of-fact grace of hers that he found so intoxicating. He threw himself down on the other side, unable to take his eyes from her pretty face. She tucked her hair behind her ears in a gesture that betrayed her nervousness, he thought—with a certain satisfaction that he could still affect her. That he still got under her skin.

If he was the better man he thought he should have been, he might have had some compunction about enjoying that. But he did not.

"We should lay down some rules," she said, her gaze touching his, then skittering away. "Before we begin this dating experiment of yours."

"You think we need rules?" He could think of other things they needed, none of which were appropriate for the moment. But they moved in him like heat. Like something narcotic, straight into the bloodstream.

"I do." Her brows rose again, but this time in something far more mocking, far less nervous. This was the Kiara he recognized. "Particularly if you are going to lounge about like that, like some kind of dissolute pasha."

He vastly preferred her like this, he thought. Despite any marks that sharp mouth of hers might leave on his skin.

"Were Khatan still under the rule of the Ottoman Empire," he drawled, "I would indeed be a pasha, as many of my ancestors were before me."

He eyed her across the table. She returned his gaze for a long moment, and he saw faint color spread across her cheekbones. He saw the way she swallowed, long and hard. He wondered for a moment if she would crumble, what it might mean if she did, but her eyes remained clear.

"Noted," she said quietly. "Rule number one—no flippant references." She sighed. "And we'll have to talk about sex, of course."

"This is the best date I've ever been on," he replied with silken delight, only partially feigned for effect. "Is that an invitation? My answer is an enthusiastic yes, of course."

"I don't think we should have any," she said primly, as if he hadn't spoken.

"This feels like déjà vu, Kiara." He felt that dark amusement ignite within him. "We might as well be in Melbourne five years ago. You will put up a token protest, we will fall into bed anyway, and you will marry me all over again. I had no idea we could sort all of this out so easily."

"I'm serious," she said, and he could hear the chill in her voice. The defensiveness. It kindled his banked temper into a bright blaze in an instant, fierce and hot. He slammed it back down as best he could.

"Of course you don't want to have any sex." He leaned back against the pillows and regarded her evenly. "You think that I use your body against you, confuse you with our sexual chemistry, control you somehow with it, whatever." He let that sit there for a moment, then raised a brow, daring her. "Isn't that right?"

"Speaking of flippant references," she said, her voice sounding faintly strangled. The color had deepened across her cheeks, making her seem to glow with the strength of her feelings.

"As a matter of fact," he said, "*I* don't think we should have any, either."

"You don't." Her voice was patently disbelieving. As if he was a wild animal instead of the man—*the husband*—who loved her to a distraction five years and incalculable complications into this marriage. It was infuriating. *She* was infuriating.

"I don't," he said, his voice hardening as he spoke, "because I grow tired of the way I am painted in this fantasy you have of our marriage. I think your sexual appetite is as voracious and encompassing as mine, which you used to admit freely. Revel in, even. But it does not suit you to think of it in those terms any longer. You prefer to be the victim, for reasons I'm sure you'd prefer I not speculate about."

"I don't want to be a victim!" Her voice was some mixture of shock and fury, and she sat up straighter, her eyes blazing across the table at him. "I'm not one!"

"You use sex as a weapon, Kiara," Azrin said matter-of-factly, propping himself up on an elbow to level a look at her. Her cheeks were wild with color now, and there was a hectic sort of look in her eyes, nearly black now with emotion. Or the burn of her temper. He was happy enough with either, whatever that might make him. "You claim it's all we have when the truth is, you make sure it's all we *can* have. I think it makes you feel safer. More in control."

"You use sex in place of conversation, in place of emotion, in place of what should be a real, healthy relationship!" she hurled back at him. There was no doubt she was furious—the air crackled with it, and Azrin thought that now, maybe, they could get somewhere. Now that her mask was off, that polite veneer tossed aside. "You never asked me how I felt about any of the changes that you threw at me—that were thrown at both of us—you just demanded I do as you said and then acted as if sex would fix the rest of it!"

"Then we agree," he said smoothly, tamping down his own temper, telling himself that this was neither the place nor the time. It was the rawness of what they still felt that had to matter, not all the analysis of what they'd each done to the other. It had to matter, he thought, or nothing did, and *that* was something he refused to accept. "No sex, unless it is a gift. Unless it is honest. No hiding from unpleasant truths or uncomfortable realities. And no wielding it as a weapon designed to make the other the villain."

"This is ridiculous," she snapped. "You might as well simply claim that up is down and day is night."

"Have you any other rules, Kiara?" he asked, hearing the edge in his voice despite his best efforts to soften it. "Any other reasons to drag this out?" He stared at her coolly. "It tempts me to wonder if you don't really want to get to know me, after all, as we agreed. It might contradict all these stories you tell yourself."

She jerked her gaze away from his, and there was nothing but silence for a long while.

Azrin watched her. He listened to the sounds of the pools all around them—the water lapping against the rocks, the splashing of the waterfall, the breeze that moved through the palm trees and made them rustle as if they, too, were restless. She was breathing too hard, too fast, her gaze directed straight down into her lap, and he suspected that if he could see her hands beneath the table they would be clenched into fists.

The shadows had lengthened into full dusk by the time she looked at him again, her brown eyes clear once more. Too clear, perhaps. She shifted where she sat, pulling her wrap tighter around her shoulders and smoothing it over her arms. She even smiled, for all that it was one of her meaningless, well-practiced political smiles.

He didn't let it get beneath his skin. Not tonight. He was happy enough to see a smile, any smile—and more than happy to take up the challenge that it entailed.

"So tell me," she said, her voice light, easy.

A sharp-edged mockery of first-date conversation, and well did he know it. And enjoy it. She propped her chin up with her hands as she leaned her elbows on the table, and gazed at him with an attention that bordered on the fatuous and almost made him laugh.

"Do you come here often?" she asked.

Game on, my love, he thought, and began.

"I've already told you what I do," Azrin said politely. So politely.

His voice was intelligent and amused, deep and dark and sexy, and seemed to smooth its way down her spine and then wrap around into the very core of her. She'd always been entirely too susceptible to that voice. Hadn't that been one of the reasons she'd sat down at that café table in Melbourne? Any sane person would have walked away, or so she'd often told herself.

"You are the king," she said, as if reminding them both. Or herself, anyway. "Lord of all you survey, et cetera. That must be fun. Smiting your enemies, plundering and pillaging." She waited for his brows to arch in protest and smiled. "Figuratively speaking, of course."

"It is not fun at all," he said, his voice lower, then. More serious, suddenly, though he smiled slightly, as if to conceal it. "It is many things, and often rewarding, but no. There is nothing *fun* about it."

He glanced over his shoulder toward the palace then and waved a peremptory hand in the air. Kiara sat back and watched as his staff poured out from the nearby, arched entrance at that regal command, bearing trays piled high with all kinds of Khatanian delicacies.

There were dishes of rice, platters of grilled fish and a selection of carved meats. Delicate, flaky pastries that Kiara knew would be filled with combinations of meats and cheeses, spices and sugar. There was a plate of the most tender lamb, sliced open to show that it was stuffed with rice, eggs and onions, and was temptingly fragrant with the unusual combination of spices that Kiara knew to be traditionally Khatanian.

There were tall drinks of thick yogurt that would be flavored with cardamom or pistachio, and would perfectly complement the savory flavors of the rest of the food served. There were dishes filled to near overflowing with the ubiquitous dates and olives and almonds that grew everywhere, handmade hummus and tabbouleh, and plates piled high with the special Khatanian flatbread that shared characteristics with a Mediterranean pita or an Indian naan but was better than either, whether it was plain, roasted with garlic and olive oil, or stuffed full of coconut and dried fruit.

Kiara's mouth watered.

"Come on now," she said when his staff had bowed their way back indoors, leaving them to an expertly prepared feast to eat surrounded by candles and lanterns and the clear night sky above them, in the most magical place she'd ever seen. Or even dreamed. "You have to think some of this is fun."

Azrin only shot her a dark look she couldn't quite read as he reached for the flatbread and tore himself a thick piece.

"Feasts delivered at your command," she continued. "Jetting about the globe in a private plane. Palaces scattered about several countries, yours to occupy at will. This is the third one I know about in Khatan alone. And when I met you in Melbourne you drove that Ferrari and I know you thought *that* was fun."

She'd thought it was fun too, though she hardly let herself think about things like that any longer. She'd been so determined to think only about the difficulties, the impossibilities. The expectations and demands. The agony of all of this.

But beneath all of that, she still remembered the way the sleek, luxury car had hugged the famous curves along the Great Ocean Road. She remembered how Azrin had held one hand on the steering wheel and one resting high on her thigh, and how close she'd felt to flying there, the limestone cliffs on one side and the aching beauty of the sea against the rocks on the other.

She'd had the notion that she was as close to really flying free as she would ever get with this breathtakingly beautiful man, in such a heart-stoppingly perfect machine, on the very edge of the world. *Together*, she'd thought then, and it had felt as if they were truly soaring, the powerful car racing beneath them, as smooth and as sexy as he was and yes, fun.

When was the last time she'd thought about fun?

"You are talking about the privileges of wealth," Azrin said after a moment. He reached forward to dip his bread in the hummus. "That is not the same thing as being a king."

"Isn't it?" She was skeptical.

And she had to remind herself to breathe again, her heart racing as if she was still in that car, five whole years and half the world away on the prettiest road she knew, falling head over heels in love with the man who'd driven them with such easy grace and careless competence. She had to shake her head slightly to remind herself where she was, and more than that, *when*.

"There are a great many wealthy men who are responsible to no one but themselves," Azrin pointed out. "That is not an option when you have a country to run and would prefer not to run it into the ground."

His eyes narrowed slightly, as if he could see how far away she was, and where she'd gone. Which, she told herself sharply, he certainly could not.

"So what you notice most about your throne is the weight of it," she said, focusing back on this conversation, and not the phantom weight and heat of his elegant hand holding her against her seat so many years ago now, both promise and sensual threat. "Not the bowing and scraping. Not the fact that your every word is both command and law. Not the great good fortune of having access to all that wealth, that kingdom, the palaces that go along with it."

"What makes you think all of that is not, in itself, the weight I mean?" he asked softly.

Kiara didn't like the way that question resonated inside her, and directed her attention to the food instead, ignoring the small voice within that whispered she was little more than a coward. That she didn't want to know any more than she already did—that what she knew already was too much and would take too much getting over as it was.

She started with forkfuls of a fish she couldn't identify, grilled to perfection with the tang of lime and deeper, more complex flavors beneath. She closed her eyes for a moment, savoring it.

"And you?" he asked. She opened her eyes to find him regarding her with heat in his gaze, kicking up an answering fire inside her. His mouth crooked. "What is it you do?"

"I'm a winemaker," she said.

She heard the way she said it, with that undercurrent of something very near belligerence, and saw that he heard it, too. But he only looked at her. She felt herself flush, and was unsure if it was from some kind of embarrassment or something else, something more closely tied to that molten heat that moved in her simply because he was near, no matter how she wanted to deny it.

"How did you become a winemaker?" he asked.

As anyone on a date would, she supposed. There was no reason it should have agitated her the way it did, like a splinter into flesh.

"It's the family business," she said automatically, shifting against the pillows. "I grew up on a vineyard." She let out a sigh as that impossible heat and everything else inside her seemed overwhelming suddenly—or was it that she felt too exposed? "This feels silly, Azrin. You know all of this. I know all of this. Nothing we're going to say tonight is going to change the fact that you want things I can't give you."

She had the impression he sighed, too, though she couldn't hear it over the sound of the white noise in her head.

"You have been my wife for five years," he pointed out, his voice even. "It only became too onerous for you, apparently, in the past four months. Why are you so certain those four months outweigh the previous five years altogether? I'm not sure I agree with that assessment." He shook his head when she started to speak. "But this is hardly appropriate first date conversation, Kiara. Don't force me to conclude that you want to sabotage this experiment before we even start."

She fumed. There was no other word for it. She stared at her plate for a moment and ordered herself to be calm. To breathe. She avoided looking at him for long moments as she loaded up her plate again. Fragrant rice, neither too soft nor too sticky. Perfectly cooked lamb with so many flavors packed into it. Tangy, rich olives, creamy hummus, and her favorite flatbread with garlic.

It was all so tempting, but she couldn't bring herself to take another bite.

"So what are you looking for in a queen?" she asked, instead of all the things she wanted to say, all of which seemed to crowd her throat. "If that's the kind of thing kings like to talk about on first dates. With perfect strangers like me."

His eyes gleamed silver, as if he found her amusing or possibly edible, and she had to repress a shiver of automatic reaction to either possibility.

"I like wine," he said, his mouth curving.

"Congratulations," Kiara replied crisply, refusing to find that comment endearing on any level. Damn him. "If that is your only criteria, you should have no trouble finding the perfect queen. You need only click your fingers and a queue will appear before you, wineglasses at the ready."

"You are right, of course."

He drew up one knee and leaned his arm against it. He could not have looked more like what he was—a mysterious desert sheikh, king of everything around them and for miles in all directions—if he'd tried. Perhaps he had tried.

He was dressed in the loose linen trousers he favored in private and a short-sleeved, buttoned shirt in the same whisper-soft fabric, both in shades of deep cream that made his olive skin seem that much darker, his long body that much more sleekly muscled. He looked cool, confident. Power seemed to emanate from him like heat, as if even his own casual clothes did not dare attempt to contain him.

Kiara found her throat was dry.

"My queen will be a symbol," he said after a moment. "Whether she wants to be or not. She must acknowledge the traditional values of my country, yet infuse her role with her own modern flair, her own achievements and strength. I want both and I would not be happy with anything or anyone less."

"And what if this…*infusion* can't exist?" Kiara asked, her voice harsher than it should have been, than she wanted it to be. "What if real women cannot be symbols, only imperfect spouses, and your lofty expectations will crush her where she stands?"

"My queen must be strong," Azrin said, his voice as quiet as his eyes were intent on hers. His voice seemed to ring in her, through her.

"Strong enough to be rendered completely silent?" Kiara countered. "Strong enough to be marginalized and forgotten, shoved aside, unable to complain or even comment on what is happening to her for fear she will be told she is *but one more fire* her king—not her husband—must put out?"

"Strong enough to know that none of those things are happening, even if it feels as if they are in a time of such confusion, right as her husband takes the throne," he retorted, his voice even, his gaze hot. Direct. Nothing so simple as anger there, she thought almost helplessly, but something deeper, far more raw. It made goose flesh rise over her arms, the back of her neck. "Strong enough to wait. Strong enough to keep from running."

"Most women are not psychic, Azrin," Kiara told him, her voice low and shaking with all the things she was trying so hard not to say. Not to scream. "They cannot divine intention from the ether, only from behavior. From what you say and how you treat them, in fact. And then act accordingly."

"Some women, upon marrying the crown prince to a kingdom, would not be quite so surprised when he became a king," Azrin said, his voice deliberately slow, as if she might have trouble understanding him. Trying to provoke her, she was sure, and seethed. "It is in the job description, after all. It's right there in the title, the kingdom. The simple fact of who I am."

"While some princes, upon marrying a woman not from their culture, might make it clear what their expectations are *before* there is any risk of ascending a throne."

"You make it sound as if you were chained to my ankle and dragged along in my wake," Azrin snapped then, his control clearly deserting him, which Kiara should not have felt like some kind of victory.

Hadn't she watched him really lose control in Washington—and hated it? What was the matter with her? She felt as if some great wave was rising in her, about to crest, but she had no idea what it was. She didn't *want* to know.

"I don't recall all this torture and torment, Kiara. When was this great silencing? Did I ask it of you or did you decide it all on your own? All I asked was that you support me. Was that really too much for you?"

"I don't want to be your mother!" she cried, the words ripped from somewhere inside her. The wave crashed into her, over her. The words she hadn't known she meant to say seemed to echo back from the night sky, the rock walls, even the pools. She lifted her hands in the air and then dropped them back down to the table. "I'm sorry, but I don't. It's as if she exists only as a projection of your father. A painting of his, maybe. A shadow. I don't want to be like that. Or like your sisters." She shook her head. "I won't."

"Nor do you seem particularly interested in being your own mother." He leaned forward then, and his dark eyes pinned her to her seat, made her feel paralyzed. And he knew it. She knew he did. "Yet isn't that exactly what you're doing? Choosing that vineyard above all else, and damn the consequences? Damn me, damn our marriage— when you don't even really know that it's what you want, after all?"

"Of course it's what I want!" But she felt breathless, suddenly, as if she'd run a race, and with that churning in her stomach, too, as if she'd lost. By miles. "It's what I've always wanted!"

Yet even as she said it she remembered what she'd said to her mother in her old bedroom in the chateau—what she'd all but hurled at Diana's head. And she couldn't help wondering if it was possible that Azrin knew things about her that she didn't, however much she wanted to deny that he could. Did he see the things she'd always been too afraid to say before? Did he know, somehow, exactly what she'd said to Diana? *Maybe the wine business was the price I had to pay to make you treat me like a daughter every once in a while.*

But she hadn't meant any of that, had she? She'd only wanted to strike out, strike back, at her mother. She'd only wanted to make a point. An unkind one, perhaps, but that didn't make what she'd said *true*.

Of course she hadn't meant it. Not really.

Azrin's gaze was pitiless then. And still so uncomfortably direct, seeing deep into her. Far too deep. Seeing things she would have sworn weren't there. *Because they aren't there*, she told herself fiercely.

She watched, holding her breath now, as an expression she didn't recognize moved over his face. Something she might have called sadness, had that made any kind of sense. As if he grieved for something, and she was suddenly much too afraid to ask herself what that could be.

He ran a hand over his face as if he was tired. When he looked at her again, his eyes were almost kind. And she thought he might have shattered her heart, just like that.

"Is it really what you've always wanted?" he asked quietly. "Are you sure?"

CHAPTER EIGHT

KIARA barely slept.

At a certain point, tired of turning this way and that without end, the fine linen sheets wrapped around her like instruments of torture, she'd stopped trying.

She'd half expected Azrin to appear with the dawn to start in with his particular brand of torment all over again. She'd braced herself for it, scowling hollow-eyed and sleepless at the gently billowing canopy that hung above her until the light outside her windows was the blue of just before dawn and she'd finally fallen into an exhausted, restless sort of doze.

But he didn't come. Not when her attendant brought her a steaming cup of strong, dark Khatanian coffee to herald the start of the new day. Not as the morning wore on, the sun streaming in the old windows, lighting up the oddly shaped chamber with its one wall of wholly unfinished rock, the rest seeming to simply hang from the mountainside, old woods and fine tapestries scattered here and there and thick, colorful rugs stretched over the smooth floors.

The night had ended abruptly. She'd simply stood up and walked away without another word, leaving him at the table without so much as a backward glance. She told herself now that it had been necessary—that once again, she'd needed space. From him. From the things he made her think about. Both.

"Until tomorrow, then," he'd murmured, the dark irony in his low voice following her as she'd retreated, yet another fresh hell to add to her collection.

Kiara told herself she was thrilled that he was otherwise occupied today. Delighted, in fact. She could lounge about this lovely, sun-drenched suite of rooms she'd been given, stuff herself with figs and almonds and sweet dates drenched in honey, and not spend a moment turning over everything that had been said the night before in her head.

But that, of course, proved impossible.

She found her way outside, onto the small, private balcony off her suite. She welcomed the day's warmth in the stones beneath her bare feet, a simple pleasure that felt more healing, perhaps, than she wanted to admit. She couldn't help but sigh as she looked out over the series of pools, a breathtaking view down the canyon that had grown no less stunning, even if she knew to expect it this time. She rested her hands on top of the sun-baked iron railing, and let the light from high above dance over her face.

And admitted to herself that she had never felt so lost. So alone. And empty, too—as if she'd been hollowed out, as if she was no more than a shell erected around all the things she'd held to be true, all the beliefs she'd had about herself. Her whole life and all she'd worked for. Her goals, her dreams. Azrin and this marriage of theirs. Even the past few months.

Did she use sex as a weapon, as he'd claimed? Did she really not know what she wanted from her life? Was she truly as uninterested in being like Diana as she was in becoming Queen Madihah, and if so, what did that mean?

The questions seemed to thud through her like heavy stones, one after the next.

Azrin was a forceful, commanding man. He had been groomed since birth to lead. To be the king of this country and all that entailed. To rule. He was dark sometimes, even brooding. He had a temper, certainly. He was fierce. Demanding. Arrogant and ruthless. What he wanted he took, he'd told her once, and she knew it was true. She'd experienced it personally. But he was more than all of that—there was that flashing intelligence, that dry wit. His intense, shattering sensuality. His strong sense of duty. His kindness. He was a complicated man, by any reckoning. On some level, still a mystery to her.

But she had never known him to be anything but honest.

She didn't want to think about what that must mean. There were so very many things, she realized then, that she didn't want to think about. That she went out of her way to keep from thinking about, in fact. Not that it worked. Not entirely.

Strong enough to wait. Strong enough to keep from running.

That was what he'd said he wanted from his queen. From her. But she hadn't given him that, had she? She hadn't waited. She hadn't even attempted to give him the benefit of the doubt. She'd left on the very first morning she could without causing an international scandal, right after their official tour was finished. She'd run, despite the fact she'd always believed herself to be the kind of person who would never do such a thing. Yet she didn't know what she was basing that belief on, when she'd run again, last night. When in every way that mattered, she was still running.

So the only question was, what, exactly, had she been running from?

And where would it end? Where would she stop?

She didn't know. As ever, she wasn't sure she *wanted* to know.

But she did know she couldn't sit here, marinating in all of these revelations, without exploding. Or worse. She had to do something to escape her own head.

Kiara studied the collection of statues in the high-ceilinged, arched gallery that snaked along the outer lip of one of the lower levels of the palace. She'd wandered out of her rooms and through the palace, following whatever passage seemed most appealing, and had ended up here.

It was a striking, impressively unique room. The interior walls were rough and old, but the rest of the gallery was a modern confection of latticework and glass, showing the old clay statuary and assorted relics within to their best advantage. She leaned closer to a display of ancient-looking daggers, still deadly so many centuries since they'd been made.

And when she straightened, Azrin was beside her.

Her skin seemed to tighten over her bones, even as that familiar heat bloomed within her. Her body had no confusion where Azrin was concerned. Her body simply *wanted*.

"You have your very own museum here," she said before she knew she meant to speak, surprised to hear that light, sunny tone she would have said was lost to her trip from her lips so easily.

"It is part of the family collection," Azrin replied. When she glanced at him beside her, his gaze was narrow on hers. Considering. "Periodically we show pieces of it in the Royal Museum in Arjat an-Nahr." He reached down and ran a fingertip along the edge of an ancient scabbard. Kiara felt sensation swirl inside of her as if he'd touched her instead. "Though some pieces have been here for centuries."

He looked tired, she thought, her traitorous heart melting, even as her stomach twisted in a guilty little knot. His near-blue eyes seemed too dark, and his black hair looked rumpled, as if he'd been running his fingers through it. He wore another version of his all-black casual uniform, more warrior today than desert king—a pair of dark trousers and another torso-hugging T-shirt that made her hands itch to touch him. She smoothed down the front of the floor-length, casual sundress she wore instead, and found it a poor substitute.

"You certainly know how to hit on a girl." She tilted her head back and smiled slightly as she gazed at him. "Who can resist a man who claims an entire museum is only *part* of his family's private collection?"

His eyes met hers. Held. A moment passed, then another. Then, slowly, that almost-blue gaze began to gleam silver.

"It takes artifacts to win you, does it?" He spread out his hands, taking in the whole of the gallery. "Then I am your man." His mouth curved. "I can offer you the plunder of *several* museums."

"Tell me more," she said, aware of the way her heart beat a little bit harder, a little bit faster. She decided she might as well play the game the way they used to. Bold lies and brash claims. Whatever came to mind, purely to entertain. "I am nothing if not avaricious. I might as well be a magpie."

"My favorite quality in a woman," he said drily.

"I should think so," she agreed, and even laughed. "After all, you always know where you stand, don't you? When in doubt, throw some more priceless gems into the mix."

"Be still my heart."

She hadn't meant to move, hadn't realized they'd started walking together, until Azrin was gesturing for her to precede him out of the great glass doors that led out to a patio ringed with tall shade trees and a tall, gurgling fountain in the center. Kiara couldn't help but sigh in pleasure.

She walked to the fountain and sat on the wide lip of its basin, then trailed her fingers in the clear water. It was cool against her skin, but when she looked up at Azrin again, she knew the water was not why she had to restrain a shiver.

He stood with his hands thrust deep in his pockets, his uncompromisingly fierce face intense, his hard mouth merely hinting at the possibility of a curve. And his gaze seemed to move inside her like her own overheated blood. He was too beautiful, and somehow forbidding, too, and she couldn't quite bring herself to look away as she thought she should.

"I like that you're a king," she said in that flippant way that usually made him smile, and nearly did today. "It matches the palace. It's all very fairy tale-ish. And as a stereotypical magpie, I can't help but approve of all the implied royal shininess."

"Fairy tales tend to be inhabited by princes, not kings." There was that silver glint in his gaze, his mouth that little bit softer. "I think you have your happily ever afters confused."

"Are you saying I'm not Cinderella?" she asked in mock horror. She looked down at her sundress, the bright red fabric threaded through with hints of white flowers, all cascading to the feet she'd slipped into thonged sandals. "Does that make me Little Red Riding Hood instead?" She arched her brows when she looked back at him. "I think we both know what that makes you."

"You have no idea," he said, his voice like silk, as warm as the bright sun far above.

Time seemed to slip, to heat, to disappear into that sensual promise that hummed between them. Kiara had to look away to gain her balance. To remind herself why she should not—could not—sink into that promise and disappear.

"It must be better to be a king than a prince," she said instead, her voice huskier than it should have been. She found her teasing tone and matching smile hard to come by, but she managed both, somehow. "Everybody loves an upgrade."

Azrin looked at her for another long moment, this one threaded through with something far darker, a kind of smoke across the more familiar terrain of their wild chemistry.

"I'll share this with you," he said, as she'd begun to wonder if he planned to speak at all, "since you are a complete stranger to me. Just a girl I met in a museum, by chance, yes? It will be like confessing to the wind."

"You'll never see me again," she agreed, smiling. "As of tomorrow morning it will be like I never existed. You can tell me anything."

He rocked back on his heels, a curious sort of look on that powerful face, and a tension she didn't understand drawing the magnificent lines of his body tight. She felt her smile falter. He shrugged then, though he never looked away, and made a sound that was near enough to a laugh.

"I don't want to be king."

It was such a simple sentence. Such unremarkable words. He said it so quietly, almost casually, but Kiara knew better. She could feel the words like the bullets they were, one after the next. She felt every hair on her body seem to stand on end, and found it suddenly hard to swallow.

"But this is your destiny," she said, her voice little more than a whisper. "You have been preparing for it all of your life."

"It is my duty," he corrected her. His mouth curved then, but it was not a smile. "I have always done my duty, you understand. It defines me. Cambridge, Harvard Business School, the Khatan Investment Authority—all of these were carefully calculated steps toward the throne, decided upon by my father and his advisors, to make sure to craft me into a just and capable monarch, a credit to my family name in every respect." His hard mouth twisted. "My every move has been mapped out for me since the day I was born."

"Lucky for you that you excelled at all of those things," she said, trying to keep her tone light and not sure she succeeded.

"It wasn't luck," he said, not arrogant then so much as matter-of-fact, which made her heart seem to contract, then ache. "It was what was expected."

"Then I suppose we should be happy that you are so good at living up to expectations." She smiled again, though she suspected it was not a happy smile. "Some of us are not."

She searched his face, hardly recognizing the expression he wore, barely understanding the way he was looking at her.

"And then one day I met a girl in a café," he said quietly. Devastatingly. More bullets, and these hit hard, burrowed deep. "And she was completely unexpected."

"You should be careful about these girls you meet in all these public places." It was hard to sound teasing, mildly chastising, when there was such a great lump in her throat.

When her chest hurt. "It can't possibly end well—and your reputation is sure to suffer."

"You are the only thing I ever wanted purely for myself," Azrin said, cutting through the game that easily, that sharply. Cutting it off. "The only thing that was not simply expected of me." His gaze was like fire, searing into her, until she felt all but cauterized. And breathless from the sting of it. He did not look away. He did not seem to move at all. "You are the only thing *I* chose."

She opened her mouth to speak, but no words came. And she felt that panic inside her, pushing through her limbs, making her shaky. Making her feel impossibly fragile. She wanted to move, to outrun it before it drowned her completely.

And she knew in a moment of perfect clarity that if he had not called her on it just the night before, she would have closed the distance between them and tried to soothe his words away with her mouth. Her hands. Any weapon at her disposal.

The revelation that he was absolutely right stunned her.

She had to blink it away like hot tears, burning at the backs of her eyes. Her heart was pounding too hard now, echoing in her ears and making her feel as if the whole earth, the stone palace and the pools beyond, rocked wildly beneath her. Even though she knew they did not. Even when she could hear the cheerful, oblivious splash of the fountain, like a merry little song that mocked what was happening inside her. She found herself on her feet, braced to run again, to bolt.

Only the fact he'd called her on that, too, stopped her.

And Azrin simply stood there, entirely too close, his arms crossed over his chest now, and watched her as if he could see this fight writ large across her face. She had no doubt that he could and that, too, made her wonder how she could possibly keep all the tears inside.

"You made me wish I could be a different man, Kiara," he said in that low voice that rolled through her, setting off more of those small earthquakes, leaving only debris and rubble behind. "I let myself imagine that we could simply be normal. Like anyone else. You made me forget, for five years, why that could never be. Left to my own devices, I would have played that game with you forever."

His gaze was hot, far hotter than the warm winter sun above them, and seemed to incinerate Kiara where she stood. She felt it—him—like a touch. As if he'd taken his elegant hands and run them all over her body. And as if he really had done exactly that, she felt her breasts grow heavy, the core of her grow damp. She felt that deep, low ache that only he could ease.

As if she could only process how much she wanted him, all the different layers of it, through the simplest, most direct method. As if sex could say everything she couldn't. As if it could bridge all of the spaces between them.

She felt frozen there before him, as surely as if he held her in his palms. Or pinned her to some wall somewhere.

He sighed slightly, as if he'd lost his own battle. As if he recognized hers. Then he reached over and curled his hands around her upper arms.

Don't, she thought desperately. *Please don't.*

But she didn't say the words out loud. Because she had no idea if they were directed to him—or to herself.

She could have moved away from him. She could have told him to stop. She knew she should have.

"Azrin…" she whispered.

But she didn't know whether she meant to beg him to stop, or to never stop, and the fact that she didn't know—that she couldn't tell—made her shake inside.

Again. Anew.

And that was when he bent and fixed his mouth to hers, hot and sweet and irresistible, and everything went wild and white.

He should not have tasted her. It was madness. He was a fool.

But he couldn't bring himself to stop.

He only knew that it took forever to claim her mouth with his. It had been so long. Too long. An eternity since he'd kissed her, held her. He exulted in the perfect fit of her against him, the sweetness of her curves beneath his hands, the promise in the tiny noises she whimpered into him as he slanted his mouth over hers and drank deep.

What could possibly matter, save this?

His body shouted the usual demands, as desperate for her as ever. But this time, he ignored the wild clamor of need. The driving beat of that passion that he could feel burning between them. The overpowering urge to drive deep inside of her and ride them both into blissful oblivion.

This time, he simply kissed her.

He sank his hands into the soft waves of her hair, anchoring her head into place, angling her face so he could find the perfect, slick fit of his mouth against hers. He let the kiss slow, go deep. She moved even closer, looping her arms around his neck and pressing her pert, plump breasts against his chest, making that demanding fire within him blaze ever higher, ever brighter.

He loved all of it. *Her.* He wanted to taste her from head to toe. He wanted to take that bright sundress off with his teeth. The ways he wanted her played on an endless, infinite loop inside of him, stoking that burning need, making him harder and wilder and that much more desperate for her.

And still he kissed her. As if there was nothing at all but this. But them.

As if there was no world at all, no demands. No throne. No winery. No hotel room in Washington, shrouded in all that bitterness.

Only the shimmering, magical pools, the quiet song of the fountain behind them. Only the taste of her mouth. Only the perfection of the curve of her cheek beneath his palm.

Skin to skin. Her mouth under his. The sun and the sky and this. *Them.*

Her hands moved to stroke his jaw, his neck. He let one of his hands make that dangerous descent from the back of her head to the wickedly tempting line of her spine, tracing his way down until his fingers rested proprietarily at the small of her back.

My wife, he thought, a fierce and almost savage feeling pumping through him. *My queen.*

And he kissed her, over and over, endlessly, until he was drunk with it, intoxicated by her taste, by her closeness, by the small sounds she made, by the way he could not help but want her, love her, need her.

My Kiara.

He moved her away from him, settling her against the edge of the fountain again and moving to kneel before her. He ran his hands down her legs, all the way to her ankles, where he found his way beneath the hem of her dress. Then he retraced his path, skin against skin this time, and heard the ragged way she pulled in her next breath—so ragged it nearly qualified as a moan.

He'd take it.

He pulled the dress out of his way, baring her long, silky legs to his view. He followed the elegant line of one, using his lips and tongue, finding his way over the perfection of her calf to the sweet curve of her knee—and the delicate place behind it that made her shiver when he stroked it with his fingers. Then he moved higher, kissing his way up the delectable curve of her inner thigh. He found the scrap of silk and lace that stretched across her hips and pulled it down and then off, tossing it aside.

He looked up at her then. Her chest was heaving, her eyes wide. Her hands gripped the lip of the fountain so hard he could see a hint of white at her knuckles, and he could feel the way she trembled. He ran his palms up her legs again, shifting her slightly as he moved closer, then pulled up her legs to drape them over his shoulders, opening the very heart of her femininity to him.

She made a noise that could have been his name, her brown eyes black with passion. With the same need that clawed at him, dragging steel-tipped talons through his gut and demanding he take her, taste her, glut himself on her.

He leaned forward and licked his way into the molten core of her.

She shuddered and shook. She sobbed out his name, unmistakable this time. She moved against his mouth, riding his tongue, and he loved it, all of her. He anchored her hips with his hands and let her go wild against him, her back arching as her lovely body tensed. He worshipped her, lips and tongue and the faintest hint of his teeth, reveling in her incomparable taste. Her scent. Her hot, writhing pleasure.

She cried out his name once more—louder—and then she burst into flames all around him, nearly incinerating him, too, in the force of her sweet release.

It was not enough, Azrin thought then, as she slumped against him. It was never enough.

He moved to sit on the edge of the fountain beside her, letting her lean heavily against his shoulder as she fought to come back to him.

It took two breaths. One, then another, and then her face paled.

She sat upright, pushing herself away from him. Her beautiful eyes darkened, and not with passion this time. She made a small, panicked sort of noise that seemed to hurt her, and thus him, and then she shoved herself away from him. She staggered slightly as she got to her feet, and the male in him found that leftover reaction far more satisfying than perhaps he should.

"Where are you going?" He could still taste her. It made him hard and edgy, neither of which he suspected would help him here. He wanted to pull her back against him and hold her, pull her down to the ground and take her until they were both limp and happy, but he imagined she wouldn't want that, either.

"Is this your plan?" she asked, her voice shaking. Her dark eyes looked haunted, despite the sunshine that poured down from above them. "You predicted this, didn't you? My token protest followed by sex… Isn't that what you said? How pleased you must be that I've fallen into line, just as you expected I would."

"Kiara."

There were spots of color high on her cheekbones now, and he saw the way she shivered, though it was nowhere near cold in the patio. She ignored him.

"Worst of all, you broke our agreement," she said in the same uneven voice. Her lips trembled. "And I let you."

"Was this not a gift?" he asked. "It was the very definition of a gift, I would have said."

"You know perfectly well that it was not." She bit at her lower lip. "The strings attached are practically visible."

"Kiara…" He said it again, as if her name would soothe her. Reach her. He had to order himself not to move, to simply sit and wait, and not use his body in a way she would claim was deliberate. As she claimed everything he did was deliberate. And so he only watched her, even as temper galloped through him, burning him alive. "I can't pretend I'm not in love with you."

He watched what looked too much like pure misery wash over her face, before she stepped back—as if she couldn't handle the words and needed to physically put space between her and their source. She shook her head slightly, as if she wanted to unhear them. As if she could. He saw her eyes grow bright and glassy, and knew she was fighting back tears. Her lips pressed together as if she was afraid of what she might say—or holding back sobs.

It killed him to see her like this.

"This shouldn't have happened," she rasped out.

"Is it really so terrible?"

He had the sense she was too fragile, now; too breakable, and he had to fight back everything inside of him that wanted to go to her, to protect her from whatever hurt her—even if it was herself. Or, worse, him.

"This is the problem," she managed to say after a moment, though her voice was choked. "No matter what I want, no matter what I think is right, I just…surrender to you. As if I have no will at all. I make a mockery of everything I believe to be true about myself every time I let you near me."

He ran his hands over his face, temper and protectiveness in a pitched battle inside of him. She looked at him through bruised eyes, as if he truly was the big, bad wolf of all those European fables, and he found himself torn between the need to prove to her that he was not—and the more primal urge to simply show her his teeth.

"Kiara," he said, torn between a kind of exasperated amusement and something else, something deeper and, he thought, far sadder, "this is passion. This is love. This is what people all over the planet search for, fight for, kill for. How can you believe it's a problem?"

"It's easy for you to say that, isn't it?" She wrapped her arms around herself, as if she could ward off the shivers that way. Or him. "You always end up getting exactly what you want."

The things he wanted were so mundane, he thought, looking back at her from only a foot or two away, and yet, so far.

They were always so far away from each other.

He felt a profound sense of futility move through him then, and he shoved it aside. He refused to give up, to accept it. He wanted Kiara, in a hundred different ways. That was all. In his arms. In his bed. In his kingdom. But most of all—in his life. Why didn't she want the same things? Why was he the only one fighting for the two of them, for their marriage, while she seemed perfectly content to keep fighting him?

"You cannot honestly believe that any of this is *what I want*," he bit out, and there was no controlling the edge in his voice then. He didn't even try.

Her face seemed to crumple, and she took another step back. She shook her head again, as if trying to steady it, and she didn't meet his gaze.

He hated this. All of it. Himself most of all.

"I can't do this," she said in a low, thick voice. "I just can't."

He should let her go, he knew, though every part of him revolted at the very idea of it. She turned and started for the glass doors, hurrying as if she expected to be hauled back—or to collapse into tears. He knew he should say nothing at all. He should let her regroup, let her come up with a new suit of armor to wear around him. Let her build new walls. Produce new battalions to fight this endless war he was beginning to wonder if either of them would ever win.

He simply couldn't do it.

"Tell me," he said, his voice pitched to carry, laden with command, enough that she stopped in her tracks, one hand on the glass door in front of her. "When do you think we'll discuss the real issue here?"

She turned slowly. Carefully. It took her one breath, then another, to meet his gaze. Azrin stretched his legs out before him, crossing his ankles. He folded his arms over his chest. He watched her take that in, then gulp, and he accepted the possibility that he did not look as relaxed or inviting as he wished to appear.

"We've done nothing but discuss the real issues," she said after a moment, her head tilted slightly as if she was trying to read him. "Over and over again, in fact. We clearly do nothing save hurt each other. In the end, it's all a terribly painful waste of time."

"I couldn't agree more." Anticipation burned in him then, low and bright, and he felt everything in him still. Wait. Focus. She flinched slightly as if he'd surprised her.

"Right." She looked confused for a moment, then inexpressibly sad, but she pulled it all in and managed to produce that neutral, unassuming expression instead. The one she'd worn all over the world, charming everyone in her wake. The one he knew was nothing but a mask. "I'm glad."

"Let's put an end to it, shall we?" He could hear the darkness in his own voice, the kick of his temper beneath it. He had no doubt she could, too. "Why bother to keep fighting? As you say, it does nothing at all but make everything worse. We had a lovely five years, didn't we?"

He almost stopped then, as a terrible look flashed through her beautiful eyes. Something far worse than simple pain or temper. It almost undid him. But she wiped it away. She squared her shoulders and tilted up her chin, as if she expected he might swing at her next. As if he already had.

"We did," she said, that telling huskiness in her voice.

"Then all I require of you is one simple thing," he said. As if it would be easy. "The answer to a single question. No more and no less, and then we can be done with this. Once and for all."

"Ask it." Her voice bordered on harsh, but he could hear the emotion that simmered beneath it. He could see it in the places her mask failed, somehow, to cover. He smiled.

And then he lifted one hand and beckoned her close with a regal flick of his fingers. "Come here," he said.

He didn't pretend it was anything less than a command. And she didn't pretend she wasn't aware of it. He could see the trembling she fought to keep under control. He could see the shifting tides of feeling in her dark brown gaze. He watched the war she fought with herself—to take that next breath, to walk toward him with something less than her usual grace, to keep moving toward him when he knew very well it was the last thing she wanted to do.

"Closer," he said when she stopped a few feet away. He could read the mutinous expression on her face then, easily. "You look as if you expect me to bite you."

"I'm not ruling it out." But she set her jaw visibly and took the necessary steps toward him, putting herself within arm's reach.

She stood there, her hands at her sides even as every single part of her vibrated with tension. And that underlying panic. He could see it as clearly as if she'd hung signs announcing it around her neck. He was tempted to let her stew in it. He almost did.

"There," he said finally. With entirely too much satisfaction. "Was that so hard?"

"As a matter of fact, it was." She shifted from one foot to the other. "Is that your question?"

"Not exactly." He wanted to touch her. He forced himself to restrain the urge. "Though it will lead us into it nicely."

"I don't want to play this game, whatever it is." Her voice was hoarse again. It made him wonder what showed on his face. What she saw of that darkness he was holding tight within him. That fury.

"One question," he said softly. Almost kindly. "That's all. You need only answer it honestly and I'll set you free, if that is what you want."

Again, that misery that she fought so hard to hide moved over her face, but she nodded anyway. As if she had to fight herself to do even that.

"It's very simple." He leaned in close and made sure every word counted. Made sure she was watching him. Hearing him. Made sure there could be no mistake about this. "Just tell me what it is you're running from."

CHAPTER NINE

IT WAS if he'd sucked all the air out of the world.

Kiara stared at him, stricken. And then her heart pounded into her stomach like a sledgehammer, and she wondered if she was going to be sick. One beat, then another, and she still wasn't sure. She felt a wild, terrible heat engulf her. It was as if he'd pried her open and exposed the deepest, darkest parts of her to a blistering light, and she hated it. She hated it, she hated him, *she couldn't breathe*—

She swayed on her feet, battling what seemed like stars behind her eyes. She wanted to back away from him, but knew that would only prove his point. It was harder to stand there, harder to *keep* standing there, than it should have been. Than it was to do anything else, including keeping herself upright and in one piece, somehow, despite the stunning blow he'd dealt her.

She still couldn't seem to catch her breath.

How does he know? some voice inside her asked in a panic, but the part of her that wasn't surprised—the part of her that had, perhaps, been expecting something like this on some level—simply *hurt*.

"I'm not running," she managed to say in someone else's voice, though she knew those were her lips that moved. That forced out automatic denials even she did not believe. "I'm right here."

But Azrin only watched her, his storm-tossed eyes entirely too knowing, and she let out a small noise that was much too close to a sob.

She felt dizzy again. *Still.* Her mind flooded with a burst of images, memories, cascading through her, one on top of the next. All those things she didn't want to think about. All those difficult truths she didn't want to face. Everything that had brought her here. It all seemed to whirl inside her like some kind of vicious tornado, spinning around, coiling tighter, ever more dangerous and out of control—until she thought she might burst.

Until she thought she *wanted* to burst, because that might stop the awful spinning.

"You're the one who changed, Azrin," she whispered, desperate to say or do *something* that might ease the pressure inside her. Terrified that if she didn't push it away somehow, it would eat her alive. Far too worried that it already had. "I didn't change at all. Things were perfect the way they were."

She hardly knew what she was saying, but she couldn't seem to stop herself. Azrin shifted then, lifting a hand to stroke his hard jaw, his eyes glittering as they narrowed in on her.

"I thought so, as well," he said, and she didn't know why she thought he was so calm when she could hear that harsh undercurrent in his voice, when she could see the darkness in that near-blue gaze. When she could feel it sear into her skin, like some kind of brand. "But was it really?"

"Do we have to tear apart our history, too?" she demanded, that great emptiness yawning open inside of her again, this time with teeth. "Are you determined to see to it that we have nothing to salvage from this at all?"

She raised her hands to smooth down her dress, as if that would save her, and was surprised to feel that they trembled. And she remembered with perfect, unpleasant clarity that sense of relief she'd often felt when she'd left Azrin in some or other city to return to her career, that feeling she'd tried so hard to stuff down deep inside her and pretend wasn't happening.

Because he was so demanding. So...*much*. Because she lost her head over him so easily, so totally.

The guilt swamped her now as if it was new. And she couldn't pretend that she didn't know what it was, that primal urge to return to the life she knew and could control, the life she already knew all the twists and turns of, having watched her mother live it once already. She remembered how decadent it had always felt to spend more than a few days with him at any one time, how far she'd felt herself fall into him whenever he was near—and yet how she'd never forgot that it was always only temporary. She'd wanted it to stay that way. She'd made sure to keep it that way, hadn't she?

She'd never wanted to disappear so far into him that she'd be unable to find her way back. She'd never let herself come close.

"What are you so afraid of?" he asked now. She could hear the torment in that low, commanding tone. She felt a matching agony twist inside her, stealing what little breath she could manage.

And suddenly it was as if she could speak now, or die of it.

As if there was no other choice.

"You." It was barely a whisper, barely audible, but she knew he heard her. When he only watched her, his eyes hooded and painfully dark, one of her hands crept up to press hard against her chest as if she could soothe the frantic beating of her heart. "Me, when I'm with you." She searched his face, so fierce and proud. "But I think you already know that."

She backed up then, no longer caring what it proved about her. One step, then another, and still Azrin did nothing but watch her do it. *Let* her do it. And the scant bit of breathing room didn't help at all. She might as well have been caged between his palms. Threaded around his elegant fingers.

Some part of her was, she knew. And always would be, no matter what happened here.

Why did acknowledging that inevitability make her want to weep?

"I have been proving myself to you since the day we met," he said, a certain hardness in his voice now, betraying that cold temper of his she could sense if not see. "But it doesn't matter, does it? You decided long ago that I would leave you, and you have been punishing me for it ever since."

"That's not true!" She flung the words at him, her knees weak beneath her, her stomach lurching. "We have wholly incompatible lives!"

Azrin shook his head. A single, definitive jerk. Dismissing her protests that easily.

"If I could give up this kingdom for you, I would," he said, his gaze connecting with hers and making her shiver. "I would grow grapes in your precious valley. I would learn the land. And it would be a good life, Kiara. Don't think for a moment I haven't thought about it."

"You have not," she hissed at him, shaking off the images his words conjured in her head, refusing to let herself dwell on them—or on the part of her that balked at the idea of this proud, regal man in any role but the one he had. He was a king, not a winemaker. The idea that he would consider the alternative made her angry, suddenly. "You want me to believe you have fantasies of turning into Harry Thompson? Of course you don't. Don't patronize me."

"I'm not that man," he bit out, the price of his iron control visible in every hard line of his body, his tight jaw, the arms that seemed to clench where he still held them crossed over his chest. All of that temper he managed to hold in reserve, she thought, when she felt utterly undone. "I can't be. I can't abandon this country, no matter how much I love you. But there's one thing I can't manage to understand, Kiara, no matter how many times I work this all through in my head."

He paused, as if to make sure she was listening to him. She had to grit her teeth against the roar of the tornado inside her, the way it clawed to get out, the things she was afraid she might say. His head tilted slightly to one side, studying her.

"Why don't you love me enough to consider the same sacrifice?" he asked.

It felt as if an electric current pulsed through her, making everything burn bright and then scream with the same deep ache. And she was no longer at all sure that she was going to survive this.

"I love you enough to think we should do better than tear each other apart!" she threw at him, that wild storm bursting out of her, no longer something she could even pretend to control. "I love you enough to know I can't be what you want—and that you want far more than I'm able to give. I love you enough—"

"Kiara."

Her name was a brisk, implacable command this time, and she despaired of herself when she heeded it and fell silent. He was so still, all that seething ruthlessness firmly held in check, right there, right in front of her, behind his dangerous gaze. All that intense male power focused on her, until she felt crowded out of her own body. Panic beat in her, through her. That harsh electricity burned.

"Hear me," he ordered her, very distinctly. Every inch of him the king. Nothing soft. All fierce lines and ruthless certainty. "I am not your father."

And it was too much.

Finally.

It was as if those words detonated a bomb deep inside her, and everything simply *exploded*. It was all the worse because it was so silent, and so total. Her toes to her hip bones to her elbows to her head—all blown away. All lost.

The buzzing in her ears shifted, liquid and sickening, to intense dizziness. Her knees gave out from beneath her. And for the first time in her life, Kiara stopped fighting and simply...fell.

But Azrin caught her.

She never saw him move. She simply found herself in his arms, cradled against the immovable wall of his chest. She realized she was crying, then; great, body-racking sobs that she thought might wreck her completely—might tear her into a thousand pieces were he only to loosen his hold.

But he didn't.

He stooped and swept her into his arms, and then carried her over to the bench that stood in a corner of the patio, shaded from the sun above with a straight view out over the sparkling pools below.

And he sat there, holding her, for what seemed to Kiara like a very long time.

She simply cried.

She let it all out, things she hadn't known she was holding on to and the things she'd planned to keep her fingers tightly clenched around forever. She sobbed against his chest, her hands over her face as if she could hide, now, when he'd already seen everything. The very worst of her. She simply wept, while he whispered soothing Arabic words she didn't understand and kissed her gently, softly on her temple. Her cheek. The backs of the hands she tried to use as some kind of shield.

She cried until she felt empty of it all, hollowed out, but this time not in that terrible, aching way. As if she had finally cleared the space. As if she was made new somehow. And when she opened her eyes again and pulled in a deep breath, there was Azrin.

Waiting for her, as he always did. The truth of that seemed to move over her, through her, like light.

"They planned out their whole life," she said, her voice thick with the aftereffects of so many tears. So much poison. She wiped at her face, curling toward him even more, as if she could never be close enough. "They were going to work in the vineyards together, raise a family. Live off the land and turn it into something bigger than them. My father was the one with all the dreams." She shook her head. "And they ended up with so little time together. Not even three years."

He smoothed a hand over her hair, and pressed a new kiss to her forehead.

"I expect you to disappear," she whispered. "All it takes is one car accident, and everything is changed. Forever."

"I know." He held her closer, tighter. "I know."

And there was a peace, somehow, in the promises he didn't make, the future he didn't pretend to know. The tacit admission that no one could know. It seemed to soothe something raw that had lived inside her for far too long.

His strong, magnificent body surrounded her, and Kiara couldn't help but revel in it. She might have been conflicted all this time, but her body was not. As ever, it molded to him, took his strength and heat and wrapped it around her, making her feel safe. Protected. *Loved*.

She understood, then, what she hadn't before. What all their heat, their white-hot chemistry and deep sensual connection, had disguised. Or helped confuse. That she had always felt safe with this man, from the moment she'd met him, or she would never have let him buy her that long-ago coffee.

And it was that very feeling that had always terrified her so profoundly. Because if she lost the man who made her feel like this, as if she was finally home whenever and wherever they were so long as he was near, then what? How could she recover from that kind of body blow? Look at what had happened to her mother. How shut down and closed off she'd become, even from her own daughter.

So she had prepared for his loss in advance. She had kept herself at arm's length, emotionally and physically, which had been easy to do with their demanding schedules over the years. They'd been on a perpetual honeymoon. But come the real marriage, the day-to-day living together, the reality of duties and responsibilities with no escape? It had all become that much more dangerous for her. That much more terrifying.

She'd had to face the fact that if she let herself go—if she relinquished her escape hatch—she would be entirely at the mercy of this man. Utterly submerged in him, as she'd always fought so hard to prevent.

And if he left when she'd given up everything else? When she'd finally let herself become dependent on him emotionally—finally allowed herself to trust him? How could she possibly survive it? She'd never wanted to find out.

The insight shook her down her toes.

"Azrin..."

She said his name as if she was tasting it for the first time, and his hard mouth curved. His near-blue eyes saw too deep, too far, but this time, she didn't fear what he might find. This was the beginning of their marriage, she thought. Five years later than it should be, a bit hard-won and battle scarred, but it was theirs.

And she would fight for it with everything she had. Everything she was.

Even if she didn't know how.

"I don't even know what to promise you," she whispered now, holding his beloved face in her hands. "I don't even know where to start."

"Try to do this with me without running away from me every time you get scared." His voice was rough, his gaze intense. He brushed her hair from her face, then pressed a slow, sweet, intoxicating kiss to her mouth. It was like a vow. "All you have to do is try, Kiara. That's where we start."

And so she tried. They tried together.

One day bled into the next, golden sun and crisp blue sky. They ate grand Khatanian feasts in the shade and swam in the pools. They sat out on the balconies and wrapped themselves around each other every night as they slept together in the grand old bedroom reserved for the king.

They talked. Of everything and nothing. They played their old, familiar games and they carefully, cautiously, built new bridges between them in the fragile peace they'd found. And they *wanted*. She knew exactly how much he wanted her, because she wanted him in the same way. It was sex and need and that tautly wound, inexhaustible passion that burned between them and was never fully sated. Never burned out.

And they loved each other with it, again and again. They explored each other's bodies as if they were brand-new to each other. Azrin took her with his usual command and inventive flair wherever they found themselves. She had her way with him in the dark, intimate embrace of the hot pools deep in the mountainside, quiet and fierce, surrounded by a hundred candles. He returned the favor in the bright white heat of midday, her hands braced against the balustrade while Azrin moved, so hot and so devastatingly sensual, behind her.

And all the while, the pools sighed and murmured all around them. Birds sang strange and lovely choruses from the trees and the winter sun beamed down bright and warm, surrounding them in a bright cocoon of sunshine and song. It was magical. Some kind of sorcery, and he was in the center of it.

Kiara felt as if she'd been transported to a different world. A fantasy world, where a place like this could exist at all and a man like this could look at her with that silver gleam in his eyes that she knew was a smile, and she could let herself feel nothing at all but treasured. She had to keep reminding herself that this was no fantasy—this was real. This was their life.

This is where it starts, she told herself every day, like a prayer. *This is our marriage.*

And slowly, carefully, she started to let herself believe that it might work. That she could trust him, and love him, and that there was no need to hold some part of her in reserve. That she could trust in what they had enough to do without her escape route.

Every day they spent together, she believed it a little bit more.

Then, one day, as they sat together on the great slab of smooth rock that served as the palace's beach, beneath the rustling palm trees, there was a noise from high above them. At first it didn't make sense, to hear such a strange,

mechanical sound in the midst of so much natural splen-
dor. Kiara had the mad notion that it was her heart, so
loud this time that even he heard it and frowned. But then
she recognized the sound she was hearing and looked up.

A helicopter. Sleek and black and clearly military.

And it was coming down for a landing.

By the time it did, Azrin had turned to stone. It didn't
matter that he wore nothing but a swimming costume. He
might as well have been draped in finery and sitting amidst
the gold and precious stones in his throne room, complete
with his crown and a selection of royal advisors.

He was once and again the king, Kiara thought. The
reality of their lives had intruded once more. *As it always
will*, she reminded herself. She watched the way he stood
there, so coldly regal and detached, waiting to hear whatever terrible news they had come in so dramatic fashion
to deliver to him here in this secret corner of his kingdom.

And this time, when she told herself she could do it,
she believed she really could. *She would.* Because what
mattered was not what life threw at them, but that they
lived it together.

Surely if she'd learned anything, it was that.

"Your Majesties," the soldier intoned respectfully, sinking to his knees in front of them when he climbed out of
the helicopter, but when he lifted his gaze from the ground
he looked only at Azrin. Who nodded as only a king could,
no more than a supremely arrogant tilt of his head.

"A thousand apologies for disturbing you, Sire, but
you are wanted in Arjat an-Nahr." The soldier cleared his
throat, his agitation plain, making Kiara clench her hands
into fists against the tension—but Azrin only waited, as
if he already knew whatever news the man brought. As if
nothing could shock him. "It is your father."

* * *

The old king had slipped into a coma, far sicker, it turned out, than he had been prepared to admit when he'd relinquished the throne.

"It is difficult to say," the doctor told Azrin as they stood next to the old man's bed. Azrin could hardly look at the frail figure before him; in his head, his father was still so large, so colorful. Belligerent and bombastic. Occasionally cruel. Not this tiny man, finally succumbing to an illness he'd already beat back once before, reduced to tubes and machines and hovering medical personnel. "It's possible he could pull out of this, but it would only be a reprieve. Your father, Your Majesty, is gravely ill."

"How ill?" he asked, his tone short. The doctor did not seem to notice—or think it unusual if he did.

"I would be shocked if he wakes up from this coma," the doctor said after a brief pause. The man shifted position, as if he fully expected to be struck down for what he was about to say, but squared his shoulders and went ahead anyway, and Azrin found he liked him for it. "And it would be nothing short of miraculous if he lives out the week."

Azrin stared down at his father for a long time.

"I understand," he said.

And he did. He understood his role, his place, his duty, in a way he hadn't before. It was as if a fog had suddenly lifted to reveal the bright glare of the desert sun, and he could see clearly for the first time in years. He could see exactly what he was doing, and what he needed to do.

He could see far too much.

It had been a shock for him to take the throne so soon, when he hadn't thought he'd have to face that responsibility for years. Decades, even. Perhaps he'd even panicked, loath as he was to admit that even to himself. He had lost himself in those five years with Kiara, and he couldn't regret it even now. He'd loved that fantasy version of himself—a man who could travel the world on some kind of an extended honeymoon, only intermittently accountable to his people. Before her, there had been only his duty and his future. But with her, he'd wanted nothing at all save that beautiful present to continue indefinitely.

He had let himself forget.

And then, when it was time, he had taken the crown knowing full well his father was still here. Sick, but capable of offering his opinions, the canny insights that had helped make him so formidable over the course of his reign. Even if Azrin disagreed with him or thought him depressingly hidebound, as he often did, the old man was there. It wasn't all Azrin's responsibility. For all intents and purposes, he'd had a king in reserve.

It had allowed him to make promises about reforms while concentrating instead on his own marriage above all things. On some level, he had still been lost. Still behaving like the prince he'd been.

But now there was only Azrin. It was life without a safety net, a reign all his own, whether he was ready for it or not.

He stood back as his father's wives came into the room. He caught his mother's gaze, not surprised to see she'd broken with her customary impassivity and was sobbing like the others. She came to him, burying her face against his shoulder. He almost wished he could allow himself that kind of release, but then, he was no longer a son, a brother, a husband.

He was the king. First, last, always. It was time he came to terms with that.

"I am lost!" his mother wailed against his shoulder. "We are all lost!"

Azrin murmured something soothing, his eyes on his father's other two wives. They, too, looked as destroyed as his own mother sounded. It was more than grief, he thought; it was a sharp, encompassing panic, and an anguish, as if they were lying in that bed along with Zayed. Or as if they wanted to be.

"We will get through this," he told his mother, as more of that unwelcome clarity hit him.

"There is no *through*," she said dully, her face twisting into something unrecognizable. And Azrin realized he had never seen his mother without his father. That she was unintelligible to him without the force of his father behind her. "What am I without him?"

He could not answer her.

Out in the private waiting room the hospital had set aside for the royal family, all of his sisters gathered with their husbands and children, all of them focused on each other and their shared worry, their grief. Some of his sisters wept. His brothers-in-law, most of them high-ranking members of his government, spoke in low voices to each other. They were indistinguishable from one another in their particular high-class Khatanian way. He could close his eyes and pick out their roles, each person's status, their place in the family, simply by the way they spoke.

And in the corner, sitting on her own, her hands clenched tightly before her, standing out from the crowd like a beacon of light, *his* light, was Kiara.

She would never fit in here, not completely, and there was no pretending that was not precisely why he'd been so drawn to her. She would never blend. She'd been a vibrant splash of color against the wet and gray of the Melbourne laneway all those years ago. Against the demands of his life. She still was.

She was nothing like his sisters, his mother, his father's other wives. She was not from this world, *his world*, and she never would be. She had been right to accuse him of trying to force her into a role that didn't fit her at all. She'd been right about a lot of things.

I don't want to be your mother, she'd told him.

And if he was honest, if he listened to her rather than his own selfish need for her, he didn't want her to be his mother, either. He didn't want her to face the prospect of his own death with so little strength at her disposal. He didn't want her to face anything like that. He wanted her strength, her fire. He couldn't imagine her without it.

If you love me, she had told him in Washington, *let me go*.

He had still been holding on to so many things then, and she was one of them. She was the emblem of the life he might have lived if he was someone else. And he'd had the opportunity to live it for five glorious, perfect years. But there were far greater concerns than his heart. It should never have been a factor in the first place.

It was long past time he grew up.

As if Kiara could feel him, her gaze rose and met his from across the room, and he felt it like a touch. Like her hands across his skin, teasing and tormenting him, bringing him ever closer to that sweet madness. Like those perfect, endless days at the pools that he understood, too late now, were their last.

Because he knew what he had to do. What he should have done from the start, had he not been so weak. So inexcusably, damagingly selfish.

"Your Majesty," an attendant said respectfully as Kiara arrived back at the palace after another long day at hospital. "Your mother waits for you in your chamber."

Kiara had smiled automatically as the woman started to speak, but it took long moments for the words to penetrate. Even when they did, they made no sense.

"My mother?" Kiara asked, baffled. "Here?"

The attendant only nodded, and Kiara walked the rest of the way to her rooms rather more quickly than she might have otherwise, mystified.

Sure enough, Diana stood out on the private terrace that linked Kiara's suite to Azrin's, gazing out over the sea. Kiara blinked, unable to make sense of her mother's presence in a place thousands of miles and halfway across the globe from where it ought to be. She repressed the urge to rub at her eyes.

Diana turned as Kiara walked out through the glass doors and smiled in her enigmatic way, looking as elegant and unreachable in a flowing caftan as she did in her denim jeans or occasional ball gowns back in Australia. The stars seemed particularly bright above them, as if in counterpoint to the jutting skyscrapers that trumpeted Khatan's wealth and financial prowess from the city center far below the palace.

"It really is lovely here," Diana said with a smile that seemed almost bittersweet.

Kiara closed the distance between them, frowning. She could think of too many horrible reasons for her mother to appear in person here, rather than simply sending one of her usual emails or even making a phone call. Too many to count.

"What are you doing here?" she asked, tripping over her words as her imagination ran away with all the possibilities. "Has something happened?"

It was Diana who frowned then, her elegant brow wrinkling in apparent confusion. She shifted back as Kiara approached, and tilted her head slightly to one side, as if Kiara was behaving oddly and required observation.

"Azrin had me come," she said. Her tone indicated this

should have been common knowledge. "I didn't think it was meant to be a surprise, was it?"

"Because of his father?" Kiara couldn't remember her mother and King Zayed ever speaking, aside from a few formalities at the wedding. Why would she come to see him at hospital? More to the point, why would Azrin ask her to come?

"No, Kiara." Diana's frown deepened. "Because of you."

Her gaze turned something very like *kind* then, and far too knowing, and Kiara felt a cold chill wash over her, into her, down deep into her bones.

No.

She could think of only one good reason that her mother would look at her like that. Only one. But it was impossible. Not after everything they'd been through. Not now, when she'd finally stopped wanting exactly this.

"I'm fine," she said, as if to stave it off, this thing that was happening here, but there was a deafening sort of buzzing sound, and it took her longer than it should have to realize it was only in her head.

Diana smiled then, with compassion—but no surprise. No surprise at all.

But it was impossible.

Kiara didn't realize she'd spoken out loud, until her mother's smile deepened.

"No, darling," Diana said gently. "Don't you see? He's finally set you free."

CHAPTER TEN

No.

The word cracked in her like a thunderclap. Kiara stared at her mother for a single, stunned moment, then abruptly she turned on her heel and started for the doors to her room. Fury and purpose coursed through her blood, heating her from the inside out.

"I'm sorry you came all this way," she said over her shoulder, but there was no helping it. Not when everything inside her was focused on what Azrin must have said—what he must have been thinking—to get Diana to come here. And here she had been trying to give him distance to deal with his father's condition! "I'm afraid it was a wasted trip."

She was almost to the door that led back out into the main part of the palace when her mother caught up with her.

"Kiara!"

The way Diana said her name suggested she'd said it more than once. Kiara stiffened, but she turned back around anyway—though it went against everything inside her to do it when adrenaline was pumping through her, making her feel jittery. Making her want to run through the palace and find him. Fight him.

No, she thought again, furiously. *He is not doing this. He is* not *doing this.*

"Perhaps you should take a moment," Diana suggested, in that carefully neutral tone of hers that indicated she expected Kiara to erupt into temper. Or that she thought Kiara already had. "And really think things through."

"What do you think I need to think through?" Kiara asked, fighting to keep all that adrenaline out of her voice, all of her mounting tension to herself. She saw her mother's expression and accepted that she'd failed.

Diana pulled in an audible breath, and a wave of sadness—or perhaps it was regret—washed over Kiara as it occurred to her that her mother was nervous. That they were both so eternally nervous around each other.

"It seems to me that your relationship with Azrin has been, since the start, based very much on spontaneous, emotional decisions," Diana said, her voice neutral as ever—only that quick breath before to betray her. She held up a hand as if staving off an argument. "That is not a judgment. Merely an observation." She took another breath. "Perhaps you have an opportunity here to pause and reflect. To think about what you really want."

Kiara remembered, then, the way she'd left things with her mother. The terrible thing she'd said to her—even if, a small voice whispered, it might have been true. And yet despite that, Azrin had called her and she had come. Kiara supposed that said more about her mother than she had ever been willing to admit to herself. That Diana loved her in her own way. That she always had.

It made her profoundly sad that it was such a novel thought. And there was no reason at all that she shouldn't face this relationship with honesty, too. No reason she shouldn't try to see if she could make it that little bit better between them. If it was possible.

"You and I are so much alike, aren't we?" she asked softly. Diana's eyebrows shot high, and her careful expression melted away into something…honest, at least. If wary. Kiara lifted a shoulder. "Neither one of us was asked if we'd like to take over Frederick Winery. You felt you had to live up to the Frederick legacy. So do I—except I feel I have to live up to all of that and your expectations. The sacrifices you made for me."

"My sacrifices were my choice," Diana said stiffly. "But it was never my intention to force you into a role you hated. I could have sworn you enjoyed what you did, Kiara. I know you did."

"I did," Kiara agreed evenly. "I like the business world. I like working. I particularly like the wine business." Diana had begun to nod, as if Kiara was making her argument for her. Kiara shook her head. "But I am the Queen of Khatan."

It was the first time she'd said it like that. As if she was claiming it. She felt a deep kick of something like power, as if she was connecting, finally, with what this new life, this marriage, would entail. As if she was finally accepting that this was hers.

He was not doing this to her. Not now.

"Kiara…" Diana began, frowning the way she did when she was searching for another line of argument. Another approach, another rationalization.

"Why do we both have such a narrow view of things?" Kiara asked then. "Why do we both assume that because something has always been done one way, it can only be done that way? That's not how we make our best wines, is it?"

Diana only gazed back at her, no doubt trying to figure out where she was going, what she meant. Kiara wasn't sure she knew, but she pressed on.

"I can't be the vice president of Frederick Winery and also the queen of Khatan," Kiara said, and she knew it was true. Some part of her mourned that deeply. Some part of her wanted to cling to that old life out of fear, just as she always had. But the rest of her wanted whatever came next—as long as it came with Azrin. "But that's not to say I can't sit on the board of directors. I just can't be as involved in the day-to-day running of the winery as I used to be. It's not all or nothing, is it? As if without me as vice president, Frederick Winery will fall off the face of the planet?" She laughed quietly. "It's been running just fine without me these last months, hasn't it? Too well, one might say."

Diana let out a small breath that could have been a sigh. She was still impossible to read. Kiara reminded herself that she would always be Diana, no matter what understanding they might reach.

"Do you think this will make you happy?" Diana asked after a moment, shaking her head as if Kiara had disappointed her yet again. But, Kiara thought, if she had—that was all on Diana. There was nothing she could do about it. And she could no longer tear herself apart in the trying. "Disappearing into this world of his?"

"Did it make you happy when you did it?" Kiara countered, and then felt a sharp pang of instant regret when her mother blanched. "I'm not trying to be cruel," she continued, though she felt uneven, off balance and wasn't entirely sure what she was trying to do. "I promise you, I don't want to disappear. And you don't have to, either, you know. If you don't want to anymore. You can choose something else."

And so can I, she thought, and it was as if she was finally giving herself permission. Or forgiveness.

It was Diana's turn to blink. To stare at Kiara for a long

moment, as if she didn't know who Kiara was—or had no idea what she was talking about.

"You had dreams," Kiara reminded her, her voice urgent with emotions she couldn't name—she could only feel the long overdue truth of them. "You can still make them come true."

"Because you think the fairies will come and run the winery, do you?" Diana asked, but Kiara heard the thickness in her voice that she was trying to conceal beneath that touch of asperity.

"Go find a bed-and-breakfast on a lonely spit of land somewhere and see what happens," Kiara suggested in a voice gone hoarse. "The winery will be fine. We'll make sure it's fine."

She felt the surge of heat at the back of her eyes, and could see an answering brightness in her mother's, and for the first time in her life, wished that they were the sort of women who embraced.

But maybe this was where it all started, the relationship they should have had all these years. This moment, right here.

"You don't have to prove anything in those vineyards any longer, Mum," she whispered, using the familiar name she hadn't said out loud since she was a child. And there might have been tears that they were both too stubborn to let fall, but they were both smiling, too. "And neither do I."

She found him in his private study, hidden away in the diplomatic wing of the palace, where she had never known him to go except in the daytime. She stood in the doorway for a moment, taking a breath or two to simply drink him in.

He looked far too tired, if still so beautiful, his fierce face looking more weary than ferocious tonight, his hard

mouth a firm, grim sort of line. He was sprawled back in
the oversized armchair that sat at an angle before a fire-
place. He was wearing one of his exquisite dark suits and
he hadn't even bothered to loosen his tie.

He was staring straight ahead, as if he saw ghosts standing before him in the empty room. As if he was the lone-
liest man alive.

"You should be gone by now," he said without looking
up. Kiara's heart gave a great thump in her chest.

"I'm not being sent off in the night," she replied tartly.
"Under cover of darkness, as if I should be ashamed."

"Tomorrow morning, then." Still, he did not look at
her. Though she saw the way his mouth tightened, and
she could sense the way his temper coiled in him, raw and
close to the surface.

"What happened to the two of us doing this together?"
she demanded. "With no one running away?" She thought
he meant to speak, but then he seemed to think better of
it. She moved farther into the room. "Instead you called
my mother?" she asked, her tone one of utter disbelief.

He made a noise then that was somewhere between a
snort and a laugh.

"I imagined her triumph at the end of our marriage
would make the long flight seem to race by," he said in a
voice too dark to truly be dry.

Kiara kept moving until she stood before him, looking
down at that marvelous body of his, long and lean and
sleek. What was wrong with her, she wondered, that he
could order her away with every appearance of sincerity
and she could still want him so badly?

He took his time raising his gaze to hers. She felt the
heat of it, the way he dragged his eyes along every curve
of her body. The tailored dress she'd worn to the hospital suddenly felt unduly confining. The modest neck and

fashionably cinched waist seemed impossibly constricting, as if it was shrinking against her skin as she stood there.

But she knew better. She knew it was Azrin.

He finally met her gaze, his own dark, stormy. His harsh mouth betrayed no curve, not even the faintest hint of one. He looked edgy and dangerous tonight, too much a warrior, too unpredictable a man.

"Do you need to hear me say it?" he asked, in a tone she hardly knew, harsh and almost cold. "I release you." His voice was distinct. Precise. "Go. Be whatever you want, wherever you want. This time I will not follow you. This time I will let you be. You have my word."

She would have been heartsick to hear him say such things, she recognized from some distant place, had she had any intention at all of obeying him. As it was, she only stood there, staring down at him—challenging him.

"You're giving up?" she asked. Her brows arched up. "After all your talk at the pools. Is this is your revenge?"

"The pools are not reality." His voice was frigid, but his eyes were hot. He sat forward as if to emphasize the point. "And neither are we."

"But I thought—"

"What is this?" He sounded impatient, but the way he looked at her said something else, and she clung to that. He rose from the chair then, so they were standing too close together, and frowned down at her. "I thought you would rejoice in your freedom. I thought this would give you the excuse you needed to leave here and never look back."

"You thought wrong," she retorted. She wanted to touch him, but held herself in check. "Not the first time."

"I've finally realized that none of this matters, Kiara," he growled down at her. "You, me—this was nothing more than a fantasy." His jaw was like granite. "I've always known exactly what my life must be, what it will entail and what I will have to do to serve this country as my family has done for generations."

His mouth twisted then, and it was still no smile. It made Kiara's stomach turn over. He reached over and took her upper arms in his hands, but not, she understood, in a particularly tender manner. She still bloomed beneath his touch.

"I am a selfish man," he said bitterly. "I always have been where you are concerned. And you were right. I knew what kind of woman I should have married. One who would have understood what was expected. One who would have welcomed the weight of it all. But I had to have you instead."

He leaned closer, and his eyes were the blackest she'd ever seen them. They made her shiver.

"And look what I've done to you," he whispered, his voice like a lash.

He let go of her then and she fell back a step, feeling dizzy. She was not prepared for this. For what it meant if he gave up. If he stopped fighting for this, for them. For her. But she remembered everything that had happened at the pools, everything they'd discovered, and she knew that if she had to be the one to fight, she would. For him. For them.

For as long as it took.

"I don't want you to let me go." She searched his face as he stared at her. She watched the way he raked his fingers through his thick black hair. The way he shook his head. The way he yanked his tie from around his neck as if he, too, felt constricted.

Perversely, that gave her hope.

"I may not have choices," he said in a low voice, "but you do. If you stay here, I can't promise that these roles won't eat us alive. I expect they will. They already have. And then what?"

"I don't want to disappear." She moved toward him, deliberately, forcing his gaze to hers. "But I'm not afraid of that any longer, not the way I was. You asked me to trust you, Azrin, and I do."

"You say that," he said quietly, his voice laced with regret, and that underlying bitterness, too, "but we both know that's not so."

"Maybe it's a work in progress," she admitted. "But it's happening."

"Then what about children?" he asked in the same quiet tone. He smiled slightly—sadly—when she winced in surprise. "Why do you flinch away in horror whenever the topic arises? You will not even have the conversation, Kiara. Why do you think that is?"

She could see that he knew why it was. But so did she.

And she was no longer afraid.

"Yes," she said, very distinctly. "The very idea of a baby made me feel trapped—choked. Look what happened to my mother! If she hadn't had me, she could have done anything." She reached over then and put her hands on his chest. She felt him stiffen, but he didn't step away. "But I'm letting go of that, Azrin. I'm not my mother. *You* have to trust *me*."

"Kiara—" But he cut himself off, as if he didn't know what to say for once, and Kiara felt compassion flood through her. His father was dying. He was not only a son coming to terms with his new role in his family, but a king coming to terms with what this must mean for his country. It was not so surprising that he'd done this, when she thought about it that way.

"It's all right," she told him, letting her hands stroke

him. Soothing him. Calming him. As she knew only she ever did. Or could. "You don't have to be the king for me, Azrin. You can panic. We're both safe here."

A great shudder worked through his big body, and his eyes closed for a moment. But he opened them again almost at once, and reached down to hold her hands in his—less in a romantic way than to keep her from caressing him, she understood. She didn't protest it.

"What do you want?" he asked, his voice a dark thread of sound. "It never even occurred to me to set you free until now, Kiara. It may never occur to me again. You already know you hate this life. Be very clear about what you want from this."

From me, his dark gaze added. *From any of this*, she thought.

But she knew.

"I'm going to be a terrible queen," she told him, holding his gaze. "I will try hard, but fail you in a thousand ways, because I will never be the kind of woman you *should* have married." She shrugged philosophically. "We will have to find the humor in it."

"And what will you do, as my terrible queen?" He moved his thumbs over the backs of her hands, as if he couldn't quite help himself. She bit back a smile. "Aside from embarrassing me at home and abroad with your antics?"

"Maybe I'll buy a hundred wineries," she said, her pulse leaping beneath her skin when his lips twitched. "Maybe I'll start some new kind of business more appropriate for queens." She was intrigued by the considering gleam in his eyes then, but couldn't let herself get sidetracked. "Maybe I'll figure it out as I go along. But the only thing I know I want, have always wanted, is you."

He looked down at her for a beat of her heart, then another. For a terrible moment she thought he would pull away, but then he drew her hands to his chest instead, and held them there.

"You have always had that," he whispered. "I told you. From that very first moment."

"I love you, Azrin," she whispered back, her voice harsh with emotion. With regret and with promise. With everything they'd come through, together. "I don't want to leave you."

"Then if you love me—" he replied in the same tone, an echo of another time, her own words in that awful hotel room. A past she never wanted to revisit "—don't leave me. Ever again."

She lifted herself on her toes and pressed her mouth to his. Making it real. Feeling the way she trembled all over, and sighing as his arms came around her, strong and hard and true.

He kissed her. He kissed her again and again, as if testing out all the angles for the first time, and she tasted him in the same way, as if she could never get enough of him. Knowing she would never get enough of him. He sank his hands in her hair and she wrapped herself around him, desperate. Demanding.

And in his arms again. Finally.

He shrugged out of his jacket, his shirt. Then he took his time peeling her clothes from her body and worshipping every inch of skin he uncovered. They knelt together on the wide, soft rug and lost themselves in each other. Each touch, each taste, a reaffirmation. A vow.

"Being with you isn't disappearing," Kiara whispered, kissing her way across his chest, his belly. "It's finally being found."

"I will never lose you again," he told her, laying her out

on the floor and crawling over her, tasting his way to the center of her feminine heat. "Never."

And then he kissed his way into her, and tore her apart.

Kiara slowly came back to earth. Azrin stripped the rest of his clothes off and then stretched out next to her, deliciously naked. It was enough to make her rise up, her languor forgotten as she climbed over him and took the hard length of him inside of her.

So deep. So good.

Azrin whispered love words in Arabic and English as he began to move. Kiara rode him, heat in her eyes and his hands so demanding on her hips, until he threw her over the edge again and followed her there, calling her name.

And she knew that they were both exactly where they belonged.

Azrin found the bar in Sydney's tony Hyde Park neighborhood almost empty.

He pushed in through the heavy glass doors and shook the wet Australian weather from his clothes. He glanced around at the bartender who stood idly by, polishing glasses, and several waiters in a cluster near the kitchens, all of whom respectfully averted their eyes.

He dismissed them, prowling over to the great windows that looked down on Sydney Harbor, gray and rainy this afternoon. He lowered himself into one of the low leather chairs and only then looked at the effortlessly beautiful woman who sat in the other, still gazing out at the view as if she hadn't noticed him at all.

Though he knew better.

"Let me guess," she said, her voice a throaty sort of murmur that teased over him like a caress, like an open flame. "You are a very boring sort of businessman. Sales, no doubt. In town for a tedious conference of one sort or another and thought you'd pop out for a drink."

"It's as if you are psychic."

He let his gaze play over her. She was exquisite. She sat with perfect, if relaxed, posture in the seat next to his. She was elegance and an impossibly pretty face packed into a black dress that nodded toward the conservative yet still managed to emphasize her sleekly athletic figure, and all of it balanced on wicked, wicked shoes. Her hair was twisted into a smooth chignon, and she had accented both her hair and her ears with the hint of pearls. She looked sleek. And edible.

Mine, he thought.

And still she didn't look at him.

"It's a pity you have so little to recommend you," she said as if she was truly saddened. "I'm in from a lovely visit to the Barossa Valley. I need to find someone at least as exciting as the board meeting I just attended."

She recrossed her legs, drawing his attention to the silken length of them, and those dangerous heels. He pictured them wrapped around his hips and smiled.

"I'm afraid I am not at all exciting," he murmured. "I am a very poor salesman, as it happens. Far duller than a board meeting."

"I should tell you that I'm a single woman on the prowl, in the market for no-strings-attached, mind-altering sex." She let out a disappointed sigh. "Clearly you don't fit the bill."

"What if I make you an offer?" he asked, leaning closer. She turned her head to look at him then and they both smiled. Her brown eyes were merry and mischievous.

And that mouth. How he loved her mouth.

"Hello," she said. And then, her tone turning serious, "I'm listening."

"I'm a married man." He tapped his fingers against the arm of his chair and watched the way her eyes tracked his movements. Hungrily. "But if you like that kind of danger, I can promise you acrobatics. A fierce attention to detail. My wife has insatiable demands."

Her smile widened. She propped her elbow on the wide, flat arm of her leather chair, then rested her chin on her hand as she regarded him. He reached over and traced the fine bones of her wrist, then the line of her forearm.

"Do you mean proper gymnastics?" she asked. "Cartwheels and backflips? Or is that more of a metaphor?"

"The choice is yours." His voice was gallant.

"Meaning it *could* be proper gymnastics." She laughed. "Not an offer you're likely to get just anywhere, I'd think."

"I am a king among men."

She smiled in delight. "So you are."

"Come home with me," he said, ignoring the game completely, his fingers wrapping around her hand and tugging it to his mouth to press a kiss against it. "I want to be inside you more than I want my next breath."

"I love you, too," she said, her own breath catching as she spoke. "But they've cleared out this whole restaurant for us. It would be rude to—"

She broke off as he stood abruptly, and laughed as he offered her his hand.

"Or not," she said. Her mouth curved. "It really is good to be king."

"How is your mother?" he asked when she was standing, her heels putting her right at eye level, all of Sydney laid out behind her, wet and cloudy and at her feet.

"We will always rub each other wrong, I think," Kiara said, but then shrugged it away. "She says she may never come back from Iceland, anyway. She loves it there. And we do very well indeed with all the world between us."

Azrin leaned in and kissed her lightly on that decadent mouth of hers, far more appropriately than he wanted to do. But cleared out restaurant or not, there were still people here. It was still not private. And they were still, and ever, the King and Queen of Khatan. She pulled away from him, smiling ruefully, as if she could read his thoughts.

"Have you thought about the job offer?" he asked.

"It turns out I could probably be a much better consultant than I ever was a vice president." Her eyes sparkled as she looked at him. "But I'm an even better queen."

And so she was. She was not traditional, of course, but as Khatan held its first elections and started down the path toward democracy, there was no need for her to be. If she'd wanted to, she could have been as busy as she'd been before, with all the charities that vied for her patronage and all the places that invited her to speak.

They'd both grown so much this past year. His father's death had forced him to take a cold, hard look at a lot of things. And so had Kiara. It was hard for him to think back to that dark period right after he'd taken the throne. It was hard to imagine he'd come so close to losing her.

He started toward the door, his arm around her. That would never happen again, he vowed. Never.

"I think I'm finally ready," she whispered as they walked, her face shining as she looked at him, as she leaned in close against his shoulder. "To start trying."

"Ready?" he repeated, but then, suddenly, he knew.

He smiled as a new kind if joy shot through him, and laced his fingers into hers. Holding her tight. He wanted to run his hands over her flat belly, to celebrate the babies they would finally make together, but he couldn't do it here. Not while there were still eyes on them.

But there were a thousand ways to love this woman, his Kiara, and touching her was only part of it.

"I will alert the Khatanian media at once," he teased her instead, grinning when her brown eyes gleamed.

"Don't be silly," she said in the same tone, her cheeks flushed with pleasure. "I've assured your entire extended family they'll be the first to know. Preferably over dinner."

Azrin laughed, and then, at last they headed home. Together.

* * * * *

TO DEFY A SHEIKH

MAISEY YATES

*To Megan Crane, who said 'obviously you
have to write this book' when I told her about
my idea. There are few things that are more
valuable than the encouragement of friends.*

Maisey Yates is a *USA TODAY* bestselling author
of more than thirty romance novels. She has a
coffee habit she has no interest in kicking, and
a slight Pinterest addiction. She lives with her
husband and children in the Pacific Northwest.
When Maisey isn't writing she can be found
singing in the grocery store, shopping for shoes
online and probably not doing dishes.

Check out her website: www.maiseyyates.com.

CHAPTER ONE

SHEIKH FERRAN BASHAR, ruler of Khadra, would not survive the night. He didn't know it yet, but it was true.

Killing a man was never going to be easy. But that was why she'd trained, why she'd practiced the moves over and over again. So that they became muscle memory. So that when the time came there would be no hesitation. No regret.

She waited by the door of the sheikh's bedchamber, a cloth soaked in chloroform in one hand, a knife stowed securely in her robe. There could be no noise. And she would have to surprise him.

How could she have regret? When she knew what his legacy had brought onto hers. Tradition as old as their kingdoms demanded this. Demanded that his line end with him.

As hers had ended with her father. With one lone, surviving daughter who could never carry the name. With a kingdom that had lost its crown and suffered years of turmoil as a result.

But now was no time for emotion. No time for anything but action. She'd gotten herself hired on at the palace a month ago for this very purpose. And Ferran had been no wiser. Of course he hadn't. Why would he ever look at her? Why would he ever recognize her?

But she recognized him. And now, she'd observed him. Learned him.

Sheikh Ferran was a large man, tall and lean with hard

muscle and impressive strength. She'd watched him burn off energy in the courtyard, hitting a punching bag over and over again. She knew how he moved. She knew his endurance level.

She would be merciful. He would feel nothing.

He would not know it was coming. He would not beg for his life. He wouldn't wait in a cell for his life to end, as her father had. It would simply end.

Yes, unlike him, she would show mercy in that way at least.

And she knew that tonight, she would win.

Or she would be the one who didn't live to see morning. It was a risk she was willing to take. It was one she had to take.

She waited, her muscles tense, everything in her on high alert. She heard footsteps, heavy and even. It was Ferran, she was almost positive. As sure as she could be with footsteps alone.

She took a deep breath and waited for the door to open. It did, a sliver of light sliding across the high-gloss marble floor. She could see his reflection in it. Broad, tall. Alone.

Perfect.

She just needed to wait for him to close the door.

She held her breath and waited. He closed the door, and she knew she had to move immediately.

Samarah said a prayer just before she moved from the shadow. One for justice. One for forgiveness. And one for death, that it would come swiftly. For Ferran, or for her.

He turned as she was poised to overtake him, and her eyes met his. It stopped her, dead in her tracks, the glittering in those dark depths so alive. So vibrant. He was striking, beautiful even.

So very familiar.

In spite of all the years, she *knew* him. And in that moment, all she could do was stare, motionless. Breathless.

That moment was all it took.

Ferran stepped to the side, reaching out and grabbing her arm. She lifted and twisted her wrist, tugging it through the weak point of his hand where his fingers overlapped, as she crossed one leg behind the other and dipped toward the floor, lowering her profile and moving herself out of harm's way.

She turned and sidestepped, grabbing his shoulder and using his thigh as a step up to his back. She swung herself around, her forearm around his neck, the chloroform soaked rag in her hand.

He grabbed her wrist, a growl on his lips, and she fought to tug out of his grasp, but this time, he held fast. This time, he was expecting her escape.

She growled in return, tightening her hold on his neck with her other arm. He backed them both up against the wall, the impact of the hard stone surface knocking the air from her.

She swore and held fast, her thighs tight around his waist, ankles locked together at his chest. His hand wrapped around her wrist, he took her arm and hit it against the wall. She dropped the rag and swore, fighting against him.

But her surprise was lost, and while she was a skilled fighter, she was outmatched in strength. She'd forfeited her advantage.

She closed her eyes and imagined her home. Not the streets of Jahar, but the palace. One she and her mother had been evicted from after the death of her father. After the sanctioned execution of her father. Sanctioned by Ferran.

Adrenaline shot through her and she twisted to the side, using her body weight to put more pressure on his neck. He stumbled across the room, flipped her over his shoulders. She landed on her back on the floor, the braided rug doing little to cushion her fall, the breath knocked from her body.

She had to get up. This would be the death of her, and

she knew it. Ferran was ruthless, as was his father before him, and the evidence of that was the legacy of her entire life. He would think nothing of breaking her neck, and she well knew it.

He leaned over her and she put her feet up, bracing them on his chest and pushing back, before planting her feet on the floor and leveraging herself into a standing position, her center low, her hands up, ready to block or attack.

He moved and she sidestepped, sweeping her foot across his face. He stumbled and she used the opportunity to her advantage, pushing him to the ground and straddling him, her knees planted on his shoulders, one hand at his throat.

Still, she could see his eyes, glittering in the dark.

She would have to do it while she faced him now. And without the benefit of chloroform either putting him out cold or deadening his senses. She pushed back at the one last stab of doubt as she reached into her robe for her knife.

There was no time to doubt. No time to hesitate. He certainly hadn't done either when he'd passed that judgment on her father. There was no time for humanity when your enemy had none.

She whipped the knife out of her robe and held it up. Ferran grabbed both of her wrists and on a low, intense growl pushed her backward and propelled them both up against the side of the bed. He pushed her hand back, the knife blade flicking her cheek, parting the flesh there. A stream of blood trickled into her mouth.

She fisted his hair and his head fell back. She tried to bring the blade forward, but he grabbed her arm again, reversing their positions. He had her trapped against the bed, her hands flat over the mattress, bent a near-impossible direction. The tendons in her shoulders screamed, the cut on her face burning hot.

"Who sent you?" he asked, his voice a low rasp.

"I sent myself," she said, spitting out the blood that had pooled in her mouth onto the floor beside them.

"And what is it you're here to do?"

"Kill you, obviously."

He growled again and twisted her arm, forcing her to drop the knife. And still he held her fast. "You've failed," he said.

"So far."

"And forever," he said, his tone dripping with disdain. "What I want to know is why a woman is hiding in my bedchamber ready to end my life."

"I would have thought this happened to you quite often."

"Not in my memory."

"A life for a life," she said. "And as you only have the one, I will take it. Though you owe more."

"Is that so?"

"I'm not here to debate with you."

"No, you're here to kill me. But as that isn't going to happen—tonight or any other night—you may perhaps begin to make the case as to why I should not have you executed. For an attempt at assassinating a world leader. For treason. I could. At the very least I can have you thrown in jail right this moment. All it takes is a call."

"Then why haven't you made it?"

"Because I have not stayed sheikh, through changes in the world, civil unrest and assassination attempts, without learning that all things, no matter how bad, can be exploited to my advantage if I know where to look."

"I will not be used to your advantage."

"Then enjoy prison."

Samarah hesitated. Because she wouldn't forge an alliance with Ferran. It was an impossible ask. He had destroyed her life. He had toppled the government in her country. Left the remainder of her family on the run like dogs.

Left her and her mother on the streets to fend for themselves until her mother had died.

He had taken everything. And she had spent her life with one goal in mind. To ensure that he didn't get away with it. To ensure his line wouldn't continue while hers withered.

And she was failing.

Unless she stopped. Unless she listened. Unless she did what Ferran claimed to do. Turn every situation to her advantage.

"And what do I need to give in exchange for my freedom?"

"I haven't decided yet," he said. "I haven't decided if, in fact, your freedom is on the table. But the power is with me, is it not?"

"Isn't it always?" she asked. "You're the sheikh."

"This is true."

"Will you release me?"

He reached behind her, and when he drew his hand back into her line of vision, she saw he was now holding the knife. "I don't trust you, little desert viper."

"So well you shouldn't, Your Highness, as I would cut your throat if given the chance."

"Yet I have your knife. And you're the only one who bled. I will release you for the moment, only if you agree to follow my instructions."

"That depends on what they are."

"I want you to get on the bed, in the center, and stay there."

She stiffened, a new kind of fear entering her body. Death she'd been prepared for. But she had not, even for a moment, given adequate thought and concern to the idea of him putting his hands on her body.

No. Death first. She would fight him at all cost. She would not allow him to further dishonor her and her family. She would die fighting, but she would not allow him inside of her body.

Better a knife blade than him.

Ferran wouldn't...

She shook that thought off quickly. Ferran was capable of anything. And he had no loyalty. It didn't matter what he'd been like in that other life, in that other time. Not when he had proven all of that to be false.

She didn't move, and neither did he.

"Do we have an agreement?" he asked.

"You will not touch me," she said, her voice trembling now.

"I have no desire to touch you," he said. "I simply need you where I can see you. You're small, certainly, and a woman. But you are strong, and you are clearly a better fighter than I am, or I would have had you easily beaten. As it is, I had no choice but to use my size advantage against you. Now I have the size advantage and weapon. However, I still don't trust you. So get on the bed, in the center, hands in your lap. I have no desire to degrade or humiliate you further, neither am I in the mood for sex. On that score, you are safe."

"I would die first."

"And I would kill you first, so there we have an agreement of sorts. Now get up onto the bed and sit for a moment."

He moved away from her, slowly releasing his hold on her, the knife still in his hand. She obeyed his command, climbing up onto the bed and moving to the center of the massive mattress. Beds like this had come from another lifetime. She scarcely remembered them.

Since being exiled from the palace in Jahar she'd slept on raised cots, skins stretched over a wooden frame and one rough blanket. In the backs of shops. In the upstairs room of the martial arts studio she'd trained in. And when she was unlucky, on the dirt in an alley. When she'd arrived in the Khadran palace, as a servant, she'd slept in her first bed since losing her childhood room sixteen years ago.

The bed here, for servants, was much more luxurious than the sleep surfaces she'd been enjoying. Sized for one person, but soft and with two pillows. It was a luxury she'd forgotten. And it had felt wrong to enjoy it. The first week she'd slept on the floor in defiance, though that hadn't lasted.

And now she was on Ferran's bed. It made her skin crawl.

She put her hands in her lap and waited. She had no reason to trust his word, not when his blood had been found so lacking in honor. And not when he'd carried that dishonor to its conclusion himself.

The execution of her father. The order had been his. And no vow of bonds between royal families, or smiles between friends had changed his course.

As a result, she did not trust his vow not to touch her either.

"I'll ask you again," he said. "Who sent you?"

He still thought her a pawn. He still did not realize.

"I am acting of my own accord, as I said before."

"For what purpose?"

"Revenge."

"I see, and what is it I have not done to your liking?"

"You killed my king, Sheikh Ferran, and it was very much not to my liking."

"I do not make a habit of killing people," he said, his tone steel.

"Perhaps not with your hands, but you did set up the trial that ended in the execution of Jahar's sheikh. And it is rumored you had part in the overtaking of the Jahari palace that happened after. So much violence…I remember that day all too well."

He froze, the lines in his body tensing, his fist tightening around the knife. And for the first time, she truly feared. For the first time, she looked at the man and saw the ruthless desert warrior she had long heard spoken of. Thirty days in the palace and she had seen a man much more civilized than she anticipated. But not here. Not now.

"There were no survivors in the raid on the Jahari palace," he said, his voice rough.

"Too bad for you, there were. I see you know from where I come."

"The entire royal family, and all loyal servants were killed," he said, his voice rough. "That was the report that was sent back to me."

"They were wrong. And for my safety it was in my best interest that they continued to think so. But I am alive. If only to ensure that you will not be."

He laughed, but there was no humor to the sound. "You are a reaper come to collect then, are you? My angel of death here to lead me to hell?"

"Yes," she said.

"Very interesting."

"I should think I'm more than interesting."

He stilled. "You made me fear. There are not many on earth who have done so."

"That is a great achievement for me then, and yet, I still find I'm unsatisfied."

"You want blood."

She lifted her chin, defiant. "I require it. For this is my vengeance. And it is all about blood."

"I am sorry that I could not oblige you tonight."

"No more sorry than I."

"Why am I the object of your vengeance?" he asked. "Why not the new regime? Why not the people who stormed the palace and killed the royal family. The sheikha and her daughter."

"You mean the revolutionaries who were aided by your men?"

"They were not. Not I, nor anyone else in Khadra, had part in the overthrowing of the Jahari royal family. I had a country to run. I had no interest in damaging yours."

"You left us unprotected. You left us without a king."

"I did no such thing."

"You had the king of Jahar tried and executed in Khadra," she spat, venom on her tongue. "You left the rest of us to die when he was taken. Forced from our home. Servants, soldiers…everyone who did not turn to the new leader was killed. And those who escaped…only a half life was ever possible. There was no border crossing to be had, unless you just wanted to wander out into the desert and hope to God you found the sea, or the next country." As her mother had done one day. Wandered out into the desert never to return. At least, in recent years it had eased. That was how she'd been able to finally make her way to Khadra.

"I am not responsible for Sheikh Rashad's fate. He paid for sins committed. It was justice. Still, I am regretful of the way things unfolded."

"Are you?" she spat. "I find I am more than regretful, as it cost me everything."

"It has been sixteen years."

"Perhaps the passage of time matters to you, but I find that for me it does not."

"I say again, I did not give the order to have your people killed. It is a small comfort, certainly, as they are gone, but it is not something I did. You aren't the only one who doesn't believe. I am plagued by the ramifications of the past."

She curled her lip. "Plagued by it? I imagine it has been very hard for you. I'm not certain why I'm complaining about the fate of my country. Not when it has been so hard for you. In your palace with all of your power."

"It is hard when your legacy is defined by a human rights violation you did not commit," he bit out. "Make no mistake, I am often blamed for the hostile takeover of your country. But I did not send anyone into the palace to overthrow your government. Where have I benefited? Where is my hand in your country? What happened after was beyond my reach. And yet, I find I am in many ways responsible for it."

"You cannot have it both ways, Sheikh. You did it, or you did not."

"I had choices to make. To stand strong for my people, for my father, for my blood. Had I foreseen the outcome, as I should have done, my choices might have been different."

"Are you God then?"

"I am sheikh. It is very close to being the same."

"Then you are a flawed god indeed."

"And you? Do you aspire to be the goddess?" he asked, moving to the foot of the bed, standing, tall, proud and straight. He was an imposing figure, and in many ways she couldn't believe that she had dared touch him. Not when he so obviously outmatched her in strength and weight. Not when he was so clearly a deadly weapon all on his own.

"Just the angel of death, as you said. I have no higher aspiration than that. It isn't power I seek, but justice."

"And you think justice comes with yet more death?"

"Who sent the king of Jahar to trial, Sheikh? Who left my country without a ruler?" *Who left me without a father?* She didn't voice the last part. It was too weak. And she refused to show weakness.

"I did," he said, his tone hard, firm. "Lest we forget the blood of the king of Khadra was on his hands. And that is not a metaphor."

"At least Khadra had an heir!"

His expression turned to granite. "And lacked an angry,

disillusioned populace. Certainly the loss of the king affected Jahar, but had the people not been suffering…"

"I am not here to debate politics with you."

"No, it is your wish to cut my throat. And I must say, even politics seems preferable to that."

"I am not so certain." She looked away for a moment, just a moment, to try and gather her thoughts. To try and catch her breath. "You left a little girl with no protection. A queen without her husband."

"And was I to let the Jahari king walk after taking the life of my father? The life of my mother."

"He did not…"

"We will not speak of my mother," he said, his tone fierce. "I forbid it."

"And so we find ourselves here," she said, her tone soft.

"So we do indeed."

"Will you have me killed?" she asked. "As I am also an inconvenience?"

"You, little viper, have attempted to murder me. At this point you are much more than an inconvenience."

"As you see it, Sheikh. The only problem I see is that I have failed."

"You do not speak as someone who values their preservation."

"Do I not?"

"No. You ask if I aim to kill you and then you express your desire to see me dead. All things considered, I suppose I should order your lovely head to be separated from your neck."

She put her hand to her throat. A reflex. A cowardly one. She didn't like it.

"However," he said dryly. "I find I have no stomach for killing teenage girls."

"I am not a teenage girl."

"Semantics. You cannot be over twenty."

"Twenty-one," she said, clenching her teeth.

"Fine then. I have no stomach for the murder of a twenty-one-year-old girl. And as such I would much rather find a way for you to be useful to me." He slid his thumb along the flat of her blade. "But where I could keep an eye on you, as I would rather this not end up in my back."

"I make no promises, Sheikh."

"Again, we must work on your self-preservation."

"Forgive me. I don't quite believe I have a chance at it."

Something in his face changed, his eyebrows drawing tightly together. "Samarah. Not a servant girl, or just an angry citizen. You are Samarah."

He'd recognized her. At last. She'd hoped he wouldn't. Not when she was supposed to be dead. Not when he hadn't seen her since she was a child of six.

She met his eyes. "Sheikha Samarah Al-Azem, of Jahar. A princess with no palace. And I am here for what is owed me."

"You think that is blood, little Samarah?"

"You will not call me little. I just kicked you in the head."

"Indeed you did, but to me, you are still little."

"Try such insolence when I have my blade back, and I will cut your throat, Sheikh."

"Noted," he said, regarding her closely. "You have changed."

"I ought to have. I'm no longer six."

"I cannot give you blood," he said. "For I am rather attached to having it in my veins, as you can well imagine."

"Self-preservation is something of an instinct."

"For most," he said, dryly.

"Different when you have nothing to lose."

"And is that the position you're in?"

"Why else would I invade the palace and attempt an assassination? Obviously I have no great attachments to this life."

His eyes flattened, his jaw tightening. "I cannot give you blood, Samarah. But you feel you were robbed of a legacy. Of a palace. And that, I can perhaps see you given."

"Can you?"

"Yes. I have indeed thought of a use for you. By this time next week, I shall present you to the world as my intended bride."

CHAPTER TWO

"No."

Ferran looked down at the woman kneeling in the center of his mattress. The woman was, if she was to be believed, if his own recognition could be believed, Samarah Al-Azem. Come back from the dead.

For surely the princess had been killed. The dark-eyed, smiling child he remembered so well, gone in the flood of violence that had started in the Khadran palace, ending in the death of Jahar's sheikh. What started as a domestic dispute cut a swath across the borders, into Jahar. The brunt of it falling on the Jahari palace.

It was the king of Jahar who had started the violence. Storming the Khadran palace, as punishment for his wife's affair with Ferran's father. An affair that had begun when Samarah was a young child and Ferran was a teenager. When the duty to country was served by both rulers, having supplied their spouses with children. Or so the story went. But it had not ended there. It had burned out of hand.

And countless casualties had been left.

Among them, the world had been led to believe, Samarah.

Was she truly the princess?

A girl he'd thought long dead. A death he had, by extension, caused. Was it possible she lived?

She was small. Dark-haired. At least from what he could

tell. A veil covered her head, her brows the only indicator of hair coloring. It was not required for women in employment of the palace to cover their heads or faces. But he was certain she was an employee here. Though not one who had been working for the palace long. There were many workers in the palace, and he didn't make it his business to memorize their faces.

Though, when one tried to kill him in his own bedchamber, he felt exceptions could be made. And when one was possibly the girl who had never left his mind, not ever, in sixteen years...

He truly had exceptions to make.

He was torn between rage and a vicious kind of amusement. That reckoning had come, and it had come in this form. Lithe, soft and vulnerable. The most innocent victim of all, come to claim his life. It was a testament, in many ways, to just how badly justice had been miscarried on that day.

Though he was not the one to answer for it. His justice had been the key to her demise. And yet, there was nothing he could do to change it. How could he spare the man who had robbed his country of a leader, installed a boy in place of the man.

The man who had killed his family for revenge.

They were two sides to the same coin. And depending upon which side you looked at, you had a different picture entirely.

Also, depending on which version of events you heard...

He shook off the thoughts, focused back on the present. On the woman. Samarah. "No?" he asked.

"You heard me. I will not ally myself with you."

"Then you will ally yourself with whomever you share a cell with. I firmly hope you find it enjoyable."

"You say that like you believe I'm frightened."

"Are you not?"

She raised her head, dark eyes meeting his. "I was prepared for whatever came."

"Obviously not, as you have rejected my offer. You do realize that I am aware you didn't act on your own. And that I will find who put you up to this, one way or the other. Whether you agree to this or not. However, if you do… things could go better for you."

"An alliance with you? That's better?"

"You do remember," he said, speaking the words slowly, softly, and hating himself with each syllable, "how I handle those who threaten the crown."

"I remember well. I remember how you flew the Khadran flag high and celebrated after the execution of my father," she said, her tone ice.

"Necessary," he bit out. "For I could not allow what happened in Jahar to happen here."

"But you see, what happened in Jahar had not happened yet. It wasn't until the sheikh was gone, the army scattered and all of us left without protection that we were taken. That we were slaughtered by revolutionaries who thought nothing of their perceived freedom coming at the price of our lives."

"Thus is war," he said. "And history. Individuals are rarely taken into account. Only result."

"A shame then that we must live our lives as individuals and not causes."

"Do we?" he asked. "It doesn't appear to me that you have. And I certainly don't. That is why I'm proposing marriage to you."

"That's like telling me two plus two equals camel. I have no idea what you're saying."

He laughed, though he still found nothing about the situation overly amusing. "The division between Khadra and Jahar has long been a source of unrest here. Violence at the borders is an issue, as I'm sure you well know. This could change that. Erase it. It's black-and-white. That's how I live my life. In a world of absolutes. There is no room for gray areas."

"To what end for me, Sheikh Ferran? I will never have my rightful position back, not in a meaningful way. The royal family of Jahar will never be restored, not in my lifetime."

"How have you lived since you left the palace?"

"Poorly," she said, dark eyes meeting his.

"This would get you back on the throne."

"I will not marry you."

"Then you will enjoy prison."

The look on her face nearly destroyed what little was left of his humanity. A foolish thing, to pity the woman who'd just tried to kill him. And she could have succeeded. She was not a novice fighter. He had no illusion of her being a joke just because he was a man and she a woman. He had no doubt that the only thing that had kept him from a slit throat was her bare moment of hesitation. Seconds had made the difference between his life and death.

He should not pity her. He should not care that he'd known her since she was a baby. That he could clearly picture her as a bubbly, spoiled little princess who had been beautiful beyond measure. A treasure to her country.

That was not who she was now. As he was not the haughty teenage boy he'd been. Not the entitled prince who thought only of women and what party he might sneak into, what trouble he might find on his father's yachts.

Life had hit them both, harsh and real, at too young an age. He had learned a hard lesson about human weakness. About his own weaknesses. Secrets revealed that had sent her father into the palace in a murderous rage…one that had, in the end, dissolved a lineage, destroyed a nation that was still rebuilding.

She was a product of that, as was he. And her actions

now had nothing to do with that connection from back then. He should throw her in a jail cell and show her no mercy.

And yet he didn't want to.

It made no sense. There was no room for loyalty to a would-be assassin. No room for pity. Putting your faith in the wrong person could have a disastrous end, and he knew it well. If he was wrong now...

No. He would not be wrong.

This was not ordinary compassion leading him. There was potential political gain to be had. Yes, Jahar had suffered the most change during that dark time sixteen years ago, but Khadra had suffered, too. They had lost their sheikh and sheikha, they had been rocked by violence. Their security shaken to its core.

The palace had been breached.

Their centuries-old alliance with their closest neighbors shattered. It had changed everything in a single instance. For him, and for millions of people who called his country home.

He had never taken that lightly. It was why he never faltered. It was why he showed her no mercy.

But this was an opportunity for something else. For healing. One thing he knew. More blood, more arrests, would not fix the hurts from the past.

It had to end. And it had to end with them.

"Can you kill me instead?" she asked.

"You ask for death?"

"Rather than a prison cell?"

"Rather than marriage," he said.

Her nostrils flared, dark eyes intense. "I will not become your property."

"I do not intend to make you my property, but answer me this, Samarah. What will this do to our countries?"

"I almost bet it will do nothing to mine."

"Do you think? Are you a fool? No one will believe one girl was acting alone."

"I am not a girl."

"You are barely more than a child as far as I'm concerned."

"Had I been raised in the palace that might be true, but as it is, I lived on the streets. I slept in doorways and on steps. I holed up in the back rooms of shops when I could. I had to take care of a mother who went slowly mad. I had to endure starvation, dehydration, the constant threat of theft or rape. I am not a child. I am years older than you will ever live to be," she spat.

He hated to imagine her in that position. In the gutter. In danger. But she had clearly survived. Though, he could see it was a survival fueled by anger.

"If you kill me," he said, "make no mistake, Khadra will make Jahar pay. If I imprison you…how long do you suppose it will take for those loyal to the royal family to threaten war on me? But if we are engaged…"

"What will the current regime in Jahar think?"

"I suppose they will simply be happy to have you in my monarchy, rather than establishing a new one there. I suspect it will keep you much safer than a prison cell might. If you are engaged to marry me, your intentions are clear. If you are in jail…who knows what your ultimate plans might have been? To overthrow me and take command of both countries?"

"Don't be silly," she said, her voice deceptively soft. "At best, I'm a lone woman. Just a weak, small ex-royal, who is nothing due to her gender and her gentle upbringing. At worst…well, I'm a ghost. Everyone believes me dead."

"I am holding a knife that says you're far more than that."

"But no one will believe otherwise."

"Perhaps not. But it is a risk."

"What do you have to gain?" she asked.

It was a good question. And the main answer was balm for his guilt, and he had no idea where that answer had come from. The past was the past. And yes, he had regretted her death—a child—when he'd thought she'd been killed. But it had not been at his hand. He would have protected her.

He would protect her now. And in the process, himself, and hopefully aid the healing of a nation too long under a shadow.

"Healing," he said. "What I want is to heal the wounds. Not tear them open again. I will not have more blood running through this palace. I will not have more death. Not even yours," he said, a vow in many ways.

Sheikha Samarah Al-Azem was a part of a past long gone. Tainted with blood and pain. And he wanted to change something about it. He wanted more than to simply cover it, and here she presented the opportunity to fix some of it.

Because it had not been her fault. It had been his. The truth of it, no matter how much he wanted to deny it, was that it was all his fault.

It was logic. It was not emotion, but a burning sense of honor and duty that compelled it. He didn't believe in emotion. Only right and wrong. Only justice.

"What's it to be, Samarah?" he asked, crossing his arms over his chest.

"Prison," she said.

Anger fired through him, stark and hot. Was she a fool? He was offering her a chance to fix some of this, a chance at freedom. And she was opting for jail.

She was not allowing him to make this right. And he found he didn't like it.

"So be it," he growled, throwing the knife to the side

and stalking to the bed, throwing her over his shoulder in one fluid moment.

She shrieked. Then twisted, hissed and spit like a cat. He locked his arms over hers, and her legs, but she still did her best to kick his chest.

"I think, perhaps, *habibti,* a night in the dungeon will cool your temper."

He stalked to the far wall of his room and moved a painting, then keyed in a code. The bookshelf swung open. "We've modernized a bit here in Khadra, as you can see," he bit out, walking through the open doorway and into a narrow passageway. "Though these tunnels are quite new."

"Get your hands off of me!"

"And give you a chance to cut my throat? I highly doubt it. You were given another option and you chose not to take it. No one will hear you scream, by the way. But even if they did…I am the sheikh. And you are an intruder."

He knew every passage that ran through the palace. Knew every secret. A boy up to no good would have to know them, of course, and a sheikh with a well-earned bit of paranoia would, naturally, ensure the passages were always kept up. That he knew the layout of the castle better than anyone, so that the upper hand would always be his in the event of an attack.

He had lived through one, and he was the only member of his family who had. He felt he had earned his feelings on the matter.

In any case, he was well versed on where every dark, nondescript tunnel in the palace led. And he knew how to get down to the dungeon. It wasn't used. Hadn't been in ages, generations. But he would be using it tonight.

Because if he left her free, she would no doubt kill him in his sleep. And that he could not have. Either she formed an alliance with him, or he put her under lock and key. It was very simple. Black-and-white, as the world, when all was in working order, should be.

"I will kill you the moment I get the chance!" she spat, kicking against his chest.

"I know," he said. "I am confident in that fact."

He shifted his hold on her, his hand skimming the rounded curve of her bottom as he tried to get a better grip on her. The contact shot through him like lightning. This was the closest he'd been to a woman in…much too long. He wouldn't count how long.

You know just how long. And if you marry her…

He shut off the thought. He was not a slave to his body. He was not a slave to desire. He was a slave to nothing. He was ice. All the way down.

He took them both down a flight of stone steps that led beneath the palace, and down into the dungeon. Unused and medieval, but still in working order.

"Let me go."

"You just threatened to kill me. I strongly doubt I'm letting you go anytime soon."

He grabbed a key ring from the hooks on the back wall, then kicked the wrought iron door to the nearest cell open. Then he reached down and picked up a leg iron and clamped it around her ankle.

She swore, a violent, loud string of profanity that echoed off the walls.

He ignored her, slung her down onto the bench and moved quickly away from her range of movement before shutting the door behind him.

"You bastard!" she said.

He wrapped his fingers around the bars, his knuckles aching from the tight grip. "No, I am pure royal blood, Sheikha, and you of all people should know it."

"Is the leg shackle necessary?"

"I didn't especially want to find myself overpowered and put in the cell myself."

She closed her mouth, a dark brow raised, her lips pursed. A haughty, mutinous expression that did indeed remind him of Samarah the child.

"You do not deny you would have." He walked to the side of the cell so that he could stand nearer to her. "Do you?"

"Of course not," she said.

"Come to the bars and I will undo the leg shackle. It is unnecessary now that you're secured."

"Do you think so?" she asked.

He stared at her, at those glittering eyes, black as midnight in the dim lighting of the dungeon. "Perhaps I do not now. You truly need to work on your self-preservation. I would have made you more comfortable."

Her lip curled, baring her white teeth, a little growl rumbling in her chest. "I will never be comfortable in your prison."

"Suit yourself. Prison is in your future, but you may choose the cell. A room in the palace, a position as sheikha, or you may rot in here. It is no concern of mine. But you will decide by sunset tomorrow."

"Sunset? What is this, some bad version of *Arabian Nights?*"

"You're the one who turned back the clock. Pursuing vengeance in order to end my bloodline. Don't get angry with me for playing along." He turned away from her, heading back out of the dungeon. "If you want to do it like this, we will. If you want to play with antiquated rules, I am all for that. But I intend for it to go my way. I intend to make you my wife, and I doubt, in the end, you will refuse."

CHAPTER THREE

FERRAN PACED THE length of his room. He hated himself in this moment, with Samarah behind the secret passage doors, down in the dungeon.

She did not deserve such treatment. At least, the little girl he'd known had not.

Of course, if they were all paying for the sins of their fathers, she deserved the dungeon and then some. But he didn't believe in that. Every man paved his own road to hell. And he'd secured his sixteen years ago.

And if he hadn't then, surely now he had.

Marriage. He had no idea what he'd been thinking. On a personal level, anyway. On a political level he'd been thinking quite clearly.

But Samarah Al-Azem, in his life, in his bed, was the last thing he'd been looking for. In part because he'd thought she was dead.

Though he needed a wife, and he knew it. He was long past due. And yet…and yet he'd never even started his search. Because he was too busy. Because he had no time to focus on such matters.

Much easier to marry Samarah. Heal the rift between the countries, ensure she was cared for. His pound of flesh. Because it wasn't as though he wanted this for himself.

But then, it was better that way. He didn't allow himself to want.

This was about atonement. About making things right.

Want didn't come into it. For Ferran, it never had. And it never would.

Samarah woke up. She had no idea what time it was. There was no natural light in the dungeon. If there had been a torch on the wall, she wouldn't have been terribly surprised.

But then, that might have been a kindness too many. Not that Ferran owed her a kindness at this point.

Not all things considered.

But she hadn't been looking to repair bridges. She'd been looking to finish it all.

You can't finish it from in here...

"No," she said out loud. "Fair enough."

But the alternative was to agree to marry him. Or to give the appearance of an alliance.

Anger, revulsion, burned in her blood.

She could not ally herself with him. But...

But every predator knew that in order to catch prey successfully, there was a certain amount of lying in wait involved.

She squeezed her hands into fists, her nails digging into her palms, the manacle heavy on her ankle. Diplomacy was, perhaps not her strongest point. But she knew about lying in wait. As she'd done in his room last night.

This would be an extended version of that. She would have to make him trust her. She would have to play along. And then...then she could have her revenge before the world if she chose.

The idea had appeal. Though, putting herself in proximity with Ferran, pretending to be his fiancée, did not.

She lay back down on the bench, one knee curled into her chest, the chained leg held out straight. She closed her eyes again, and when she opened them, it was to the sound of a door swinging open.

"Have you made up your mind?"

She knew who the voice belonged to. She didn't even have to look.

She sat up, trying to shake out the chill that had settled into her bones. She looked at Ferran's outline in the darkness. "I will marry you," she said.

The room Ferran showed her to after her acceptance was a far cry from the dungeon. But Samarah was very aware of the fact that it was only a sparkling version of a cell. A fact Ferran underlined as he left her.

"You will not escape," he said. "There are guards around the perimeter. And there will be no border crossing possible for you as my patrol will be put on alert. You will be trapped in the country should you decide to try and leave, and from there, I will find you. And you will have lost your reprieve."

He was foolish for worrying, though. She had nothing to go back to. No one waiting for her. And she had arrived at her goal point. Why would she go back to Jahar with nothing accomplished?

It was true that Jahar was not as dangerous for her as it had once been. In the past five years there had been something of an uneasy transition from a totalitarian rule established by the revolutionaries, who had truly only wanted power for themselves, into a democracy. Though it was a young democracy, and as such, there were still many lingering issues.

Still, the deposition of the other leaders had meant that she no longer had a target on her back, at least. But she had no place, either.

That meant she was perfectly happy to stay here, right in Ferran's home, while she thought of her next move.

Well, perhaps perfectly happy was an overstatement,

but it was better than being back in an old room in a shop in Jahar.

She looked around, a strange tightness in her chest. This was so very familiar, this room. She wondered if it was, perhaps, the same room she'd sometimes stayed in when she and her family had come to visit the Bashar family. In happier times. Times that hardly seemed to matter, given how it had all ended.

Lush fabrics were draped over marble walls, the glittering red and jade silks offering a peek at the obsidian and gold beneath. Richness layered over unfathomable richness. The bed was the same. Draped yards of fabric in bold colors, the frame constructed around the bed decorated with yet more.

Divans, pillows, rugs, all of it served to add softness to a room constructed from stone and precious gems.

And the view—a tall, tower room that looked beyond the walls of the palace gardens, beyond the walls of the city and out to the vast dunes. An orange sun casting burning gold onto the sands.

There was a knock on the grand, carved double doors and she turned. "Yes?"

One door opened and a small woman came in. Samarah knew her as Lydia, another woman who worked in the palace, and with whom Samarah had had some interaction over the course of the past month.

"Sheikha," Lydia said, bowing her head.

So it had begun. Samarah couldn't deny the small flash of…pleasure that arched through her when the other woman said her title. Though it had been more years gone than she'd been with it, it was a title that was in her blood.

Still, she was a bit disturbed by the idea of Lydia knowing any details of what had passed between Ferran and herself. More disturbing though was just what she'd been led to believe about their relationship.

The idea of being Ferran's wife...his lover...it was re-volting.

She thought of the man he was. Strong, powerful. Broad shoulders, lean waist. Sharp dark eyes, a square jaw. He was clean shaven, unusual for a man in his part of the world, but she couldn't blame him. For he no doubt used his looks to his advantage in all things.

He was extraordinarily handsome, which was not a point in his favor as far as she was concerned. It was merely an observation about her enemy.

Beauty meant little. Beauty was often deceitful.

She knew that she was considered a great beauty, like her mother before her. And men often took that to mean she was soft, easy to manipulate, easy to take advantage of. As a result some men had found themselves with a sword trained at vulnerable parts of their body.

Yes, she knew beauty could be used to hide strength and cunning. She suspected Ferran knew that, as well.

She had spent the past month observing his physical strength, but she feared she may have underestimated the brilliance of her adversary.

"I have brought you clothes," Lydia said, "at the sheikh's instruction. And he says that you are to join him for dinner when the sun sinks below the dunes."

She narrowed her eyes. "Did he really say it like that?"

"He did, my lady."

"Do you not find it odd?"

A small smile tugged at Lydia's lips. "I am not at liberty to say."

"I see," Samarah said, pacing the width of the room. The beautifully appointed room that, like Ferran and herself, was merely using its beauty to cover what it really was.

A cage. For a tigress.

"And what," Samarah continued, "did he say about me and my change in station?"

"Not much, my lady. He simply said we were to address you as sheikha and install you in this wing of the palace. And that you are not to leave."

"Ah yes, that sounds about right." She was relieved, in many ways, that he hadn't divulged many details. "So I am to dress for him and appear at this magical twilit hour?"

"I shall draw you a bath first."

Samarah looked down at herself and put a hand to her cheek, her thumb drifting over the small cut inflicted by her own knife. She imagined she was a bit worse for wear after having spent the night in a dungeon. So a bath was likely in order.

"Thank you. I shall look forward to it."

Minutes later, Samarah was submerged to her chin in a sunken mosaic tub filled with hot water and essential oils. It stretched the length of the bath chamber, larger than many swimming pools. There were pillars interspersed throughout, and carvings of naked women and men, lounging and tangled together.

She looked away from the scenes. She'd never been comfortable with such things. Not after the way her family had dissolved. Not when she'd spent so many years guarding her body from men who sought to use her.

And certainly not when she was in the captivity of her enemy. An enemy who intended to marry her and…beget his heirs on her. In that naked, entwined fashion. It was far too much to bear.

She leaned her head back against the pillow that had been provided for her and closed her eyes. This was, indeed, preferable to the dungeon. Furthermore, it was preferable to every living situation she'd had since leaving her family's palace.

And of course he'd planned it that way. Of course he would know how to appeal to certain weaknesses.

She couldn't forget what he was.

When she was finished, she got out and wrapped herself in a plush robe, wandering back into her room.

"My lady," Lydia said. "I would have helped you."

"I don't need help, Lydia. In fact, and this is no offense meant to you, I would like some time alone before I go and see the sheikh."

Lydia blinked. "Of course, Sheikha." Samarah could tell Lydia was trying to decide whom she should obey.

Ultimately, the other woman inclined her head and walked out of the chamber.

Samarah felt slightly guilty dismissing her, but honestly, the idea of being dressed seemed ridiculous. Palatial surroundings or not. She picked up the dark blue dress that had been laid out on her bed. It was a heavy fabric, with a runner of silver beads down the front, and a scattering of them across. Stars in a night sky. Along with that were some silken under things. A light bra with little padding, and, she imagined, little support, and a pair of panties to match.

She doubted anyone dressed Ferran. He didn't seem the type.

She pondered that while she put the underwear and dress on. He had not turned out the way she might have imagined. First, he hadn't transformed into a monster. She'd imagined that he might have. Since, in her mind, he was the man who killed her father.

He also hadn't become the man she'd imagined he might, based on what she remembered of him when he'd been a teenage boy.

He'd been mouthy, sullen when forced to attend palace dinners and behave. And he'd often pulled practical jokes on palace staff.

He didn't seem like a man who would joke about much now.

Well, except for his 'when the sun sinks beneath the dune' humor. She snorted. As if she would be amused.

She considered the light veil that had been included with the dress. She'd chosen to wear one while on staff, but in general she did not. Unless she was headed into the heart of the Jahari capital. Then she often opted to wear one simply to avoid notice.

She would not wear one tonight. Instead, she wandered to the ornate jewelry box that was situated on the vanity and opened it. Inside, she found bangles, earrings and an elaborate head chain with a bright center gem designed to rest against her forehead.

She braided her long dark hair and fastened the chain in place, then put on the rest of the jewelry. Beauty to disguise herself. A metaphor that seemed to be carrying through today.

She found that there was makeup, as well, and she applied it quickly, the foundation doing something to hide the cut on her cheek. It enraged her to see it. Better it was covered. She painted dark liner around her eyes, stained her lips red.

She looked at herself and scarcely knew the woman she saw. Everything she was wearing was heavy, and of a fine quality she could never have afforded in her life on the street. She blinked, then looked away, turning her focus to the window, where she could see the sun sinking below the dunes.

It was time.

She lifted the front of her dress, her bangles clinking together, all of her other jewels moving with each step, giving her a theme song composed in precious metals as she made her way from the room and down the long corridor.

She rounded a corner and went down a sweeping staircase into a sitting area of the palace. There were men there, dressed in crisp, white tunics nearly as ornate as her dress.

"Sheikha," one said, "this way to dinner."

She inclined her head. "Thank you."

She followed him into the next room. The dining area was immaculate, a tall table with a white tablecloth and chairs placed around. It was large enough to seat fifty, but currently only seated Ferran. There were windows behind him that looked out into the gardens, lush, green. A sign of immeasurable wealth. So much water in the desert being given to plants.

"You came," he said, not bothering to stand when she entered.

"Of course. The sun has sunken. Behind the dunes."

"So it has."

"I should not like to disobey a direct order," she said.

"No," he responded, "clearly not. You are so very biddable."

"I find that I am." She walked down the edge of the table, her fingertips brushing the backs of the chairs as she made her way toward him. "Merciful even."

"Merciful?" he asked, raising his brows. "I had not thought that an accurate description. Perhaps...thwarted?"

She stopped moving, her eyes snapping up to his. "Perhaps," she bit out.

"Sit," he commanded.

She continued walking, to the head of the table, around the back of him, lifting her hand the so she was careful to avoid contact with him. She watched his shoulders stiffen, his body, his instincts on high alert.

He knew he had not tamed her. Good.

She took a seat to his left, her eyes on the plate in front of her. "I do hope there will be food soon. I'm starving. It seems I was detained for most of the day."

"Ah yes," he said, "I recall. And don't worry. It's on its way."

As if on cue, six men came in, carrying trays laden

with clay pots, and clear jars full of frosted, brightly colored juice.

All of the trays were laid out before them, the tall lids on the tagines removed with great drama and flair.

Her stomach growled and she really hoped he wasn't planning on poisoning her, because she just wanted to eat some couscous, vegetables and spiced lamb. She'd spent many nights trying to sleep in spite of the aching emptiness in her stomach.

And she didn't have the patience for it, not now.

She needed a full stomach to deal with Ferran.

"We are to serve ourselves," Ferran said, as the staff walked from the room. "I often prefer to eat this way. I find I get everything to my liking when I do it myself." His eyes met hers. "And I find I am much happier when I am in control of a situation."

She arched a brow and reached for a wooden utensil, dipping it into the couscous and serving herself a generous portion. "That could be a problem," she said, going back for some lamb. "As I feel much the same way, and I don't think either of us can have complete control at any given time."

"Do you ever have control, Samarah?"

She paused. "As much as one can have, Sheikh. Of course, the desert is always king, no matter what position in life you hold. No one can stop a drought. Or a monsoon. Or a sandstorm."

"I take it that's your way of excusing your powerlessness."

She took a sharp breath and turned her focus to her dinner. "I am not powerless. No matter the situation, no matter the chains, you can never make me powerless. I will always have choices, and my strength is here." She put her hand on her chest. "Not even you can reach in and take my heart, Sheikh Ferran Bashar. And so, you will never truly have power over me."

"You are perhaps the bravest person I've ever met," he said. "And the most foolish."

She smiled. "I take both as the sincerest of compliments."

"I should like to discuss our plan."

"I should like to eat—this is very good. I don't think the servants eat the same food as you do."

"Do they not? I had not realized. I'll ask the chef if it's too labor intensive or if it's possible everyone eat as I do."

"I imagine it isn't possible, and it would only make more work for the cook. Cooking in mass quantities is a bit different than cooking for one sheikh and his prisoner."

"I've never cooked," he said. "I wouldn't know."

"I haven't often cooked, but I have been in the food lines in Jahar. I know what mass-produced food is."

"Tell me," he said, leaning on one elbow. "How did you survive?"

"After we left the palace—" she would not speak of that night, not to him "—we sought asylum with sympathizers, though they were nearly impossible to find. We went from house to house. We didn't want people to know we'd survived."

"It was reported you were among the dead."

She nodded. "I know. A favor granted to my mother by a servant who wanted to live. She feigned loyalty to the new regime, but she secretly helped my mother and I escape, then told the new *president*—" she said the word with utter disdain "—that we had been killed with the rest."

"After that," she said, "we were often homeless. Sometimes getting work in shops. Then we could sleep on the steps, with minimal shelter provided from the overhang of the roof. Or, if the shopkeeper was truly kind, a small room in the back."

"And then?" he asked.

"My mother died when I was thirteen. At least…I as-

sume she did. She left one day and didn't return. I think…
I think she walked out into the desert and simply kept
walking. She was never the same after. She never smiled."

"I think that day had that effect on us all. But I'm sorry
to hear that."

"You apologize frequently for what happened. Do you
mean it?"

"I wouldn't say it if I didn't."

"But do you feel it?" she asked. He was so monotone.
Even now, even in this.

"I don't feel anything."

"That's not true," she said, her eyes locked with his.
"You felt fear last night. *I* made you fear."

"So you did," he said. "But we are not talking about me.
Tell me how you went on after your mother died."

"I continued on the way I always had. But I ended up
finding work at a martial arts studio, of all places. Master
Ahn was not in Jahar at the time of the unrest, and he had
no qualms about taking me in. Part of my payment was
training along with my room and board."

"I see now why you had such an easy time ambushing
me," he said.

"I have a black belt in Hapkido. Don't be too hard on
yourself."

"A Jaharan princess who is a master in martial arts."

She lifted a shoulder. "Strange times we live in."

"I should say. You know someone tried to murder me in
my bedchamber last night."

"Is that so?" she asked, taking a bite of lamb.

"I myself spent the ensuing years in the palace. Now
that we're caught up, I think we should discuss our engagement."

"Do you really see this working?" she asked.

"I never expected to love my wife, Samarah. I have long
expected to marry a woman who would advance me in a

political fashion and help my country in some way. That is part of being a ruler, and I know you share that. You are currently a sheikha without a throne or a people, and I aim to give you both. So yes, I do see this working. I don't see why it shouldn't."

"I tried to kill you," she said. "That could possibly be a reason it wouldn't work."

"Don't most wives consider that at some point? I grant you, usually several years of marriage have passed first, but even so, it's hardly that unusual."

"And you think this will…change what happened? You think what happened *can* be changed?" she asked. And she found she was honestly curious. She shouldn't be. She shouldn't really want to hear any of what he had to say.

"Everything can be changed. Enough water can change an entire landscape. It can reshape stone. Why can't we re-shape what is left?"

She found that something in her, something traitorous and hopeful, something she'd never imagined would have survived all her years living in the worst parts of Jahar, enduring the worst sorts of fear and starvation and loss, wanted to believe him.

That the pieces of her life could somehow be reshaped. That she could have something more than cold. More than anger and revenge. More than a driving need to inflict pain, as it had been inflicted on her.

"And if not," he said. "I still find the outcome prefera-ble to having my throat cut. And you will have something infinitely nicer than a storeroom to sleep in. That should be enough."

And just like that, the warm hopefulness was extin-guished.

Because he was talking as though a soft bed would fix the pain she'd suffered. The loss of her family, the loss of her home.

He didn't know. And she would have to force him to understand. She would make him look at her pain, her suffering. And endure it as she had done.

"Yes," she said, smiling, a careful, practiced smile, "why not indeed?"

CHAPTER FOUR

NOT FOR THE first time since striking the deal with Samarah, Ferran had reservations. Beautiful she was, biddable she would never be.

She was descended from a warrior people, and she had transformed herself into a foot soldier. One he'd rather have on his side than plotting his death.

She'd been a little hermit the past few days. But he was under no illusion. She was just a viper in her burrow, and he would have to reach in and take her out carefully.

Barring that, he would smoke her out. Metaphorically. He wasn't above an ironhanded approach. He supposed, in many ways, he was already implementing one. But the little serpent had tried to kill him.

There was hardly an overreaction to that. Though, there was a foolish reaction. Proposing marriage might be it. And there were the reservations.

He walked up to the entry of her bedchamber and considered entering without knocking. Then he decided he liked his head attached to his shoulders and signaled his intent to enter with a heavy rap on wooden doors.

"Yes?"

"It's Ferran," he said.

He was met with silence.

"If you have forgotten," he said, "I am the sheikh of Khadra and your fiancé. Oh, also your mortal enemy."

The left door opened a crack, and he could see one brown eye glaring at him through it. "I have not forgotten."

"I haven't seen you in days, so I was concerned."

She blinked twice. "I've been ill."

"Have you?"

"Well, I haven't felt very well."

"I see," he said.

"Because we're engaged."

"Did my proposal give you a cold?"

The eye narrowed. "What do you want?"

"I did not propose to you so you could nest in one of the rooms in my palace. We have serious issues to attend to. Namely, announcing our engagement to the world. Which will involve letting the world know that the long-lost, long-mourned sheikha of Jahar lives."

"Can't you write up a press release?"

"Let me in, Samarah, or I will push past you."

"Would you like to try?"

"Let me in," he repeated.

She obeyed this time, the door swinging open. She held it, her arm extended, a dark brow raised. "Enter."

"Why is it you make me feel like I'm a guest in my own palace?"

"These are my quarters. In them, you are a guest."

"This is my country, and in it, you are a prisoner." Her shoulders stiffened, her nostrils flaring. "Such an uncomfortable truth."

"I can think of a few things more uncomfortable."

He arched a brow. "Such as?"

"If I planted my foot between your ribs," she said, practically hissing.

"You and I shall have to spar sometime. When I'm certain you don't want me killed."

"You'll be waiting a long time."

"Careful. Some men might consider this verbal foreplay." He said it to get a reaction. What disturbed him was that it did seem that way. It made his blood run hotter. Made him think of what it had felt like to hold her over his shoulder, all soft curves and deadly rage.

He gritted his teeth. He was not a slave to his body. He was a slave to nothing. He was master. He was sheikh. And with that mastery, he served his people. Not himself. That meant there was no time for this sort of reaction.

Her upper lip curled into a snarl. "You disgust me. Do you think I would sleep with the man who ordered my father killed?"

"For the good of our people? I would sleep with the woman whose father caused the death of my parents." The man who had wrenched the bars open that held Ferran's demons back from the world. The man who revealed what it was Ferran could be with the restraints broken.

He ignored those memories. He ignored the heat that pooled in his gut at the thought of what sleeping with her would mean.

She blinked. "I feel as though we have an impossible legacy to negotiate. I have, in fact, been thinking that for the past few days."

"To what end?"

"To the end that in many ways I understand what you did." Her dark eyes looked wounded, angry. "But I don't have to condone it. Or forgive it."

"Your father killed mine. Face-to-face and in cold blood. My mother…"

"I know," she said. "And…it is a difficult set of circumstances we find ourselves in. I realize that."

"Not so difficult. Marriage is fairly straightforward." It was a contractual agreement, nothing more. And as long as he thought of it in those terms, he could find a place for it in his ordered world.

Both brows shot up. "Is it? As our parents' deaths were

a result of marital infidelity I think it's a bit more complex than you're giving it credit for."

"Passion is more complex than people give it credit for. Passion is dangerous. Marriage on the other hand is a legal agreement, and not dangerous in the least. Not on its own. Add passion and you have fire to your gasoline."

"Okay, I see your point. But are you honestly telling me you act without passion?"

He lifted a shoulder. "Yes. If I acted based on passion I would have had your pretty head for what you tried to do. Lucky for you, I think things through. I never act before considering all possible outcomes." He studied her, her petite frame hinted at by a red, beaded tunic that hung to her knees, her legs covered by matching pants. Her dark hair was pulled back again, the top of her head covered by a golden chain that was laced over her crown. He wondered what her hair might look like loose. Falling in glossy black waves over her shoulders.

And then he stopped wondering. Because it was irrelevant. Because her hair, her beauty, had nothing to do with their arrangement. It had nothing to do with anything.

"Are you passionate?" he asked, instead of contemplating her hair for another moment.

She cocked her head to the side, a frown tugging down the corners of her lips. "About some things," she said. "Survival being chief among them. I don't think I could have lived through what I lived through without a certain measure of passion for breathing. If I hadn't felt burning desire to keep on doing it, I probably would have walked out to the desert, lain down on a dune and stopped. And then there was revenge. I've felt passion for that."

"And that's where we differ. I don't want revenge, because the purpose it serves is small. I want to serve a broader purpose. And that's why thinking is better than passion." Passion was dangerous. Emotion was vulnerability. He believed in neither.

"Until you need passion to keep air in your lungs," she said, so succinct and loud in the stillness of the room. "Then you might rethink your stance on it."

"Perhaps. Until then…in my memory, passion ends in screams, and blood, and the near destruction of a nation. So I find I'm not overly warm to the subject."

"But you don't anticipate us having a marriage with passion?" she asked.

He looked at her again. She was beautiful, there was no question, and now that she didn't have a knife in her hands it was possible to truly appreciate that beauty. She had no makeup on today, but she was as stunning without it as she'd been with her heavily lined eyes and ruby lips.

"Perhaps a physical attraction," he said.

He wasn't sure how he felt about that. The truth of the matter was, he'd given up women and sex that day his family had been killed. That day he'd been handed the responsibility of a nation full of people.

His father had been too busy indulging his sexual desires to guard his family. To guard his palace. And then he had seen what happened when all control gave way. When it shifted into unimaginable violence. When passion became death.

He'd turned away from it for that reason. But he'd known that when he married he wouldn't continue to be celibate. He hadn't given it a lot of thought.

But he was giving it thought now. Far too much.

Those beautiful eyes flew wide. "I hardly think so."

"Why is that?"

"I despise you."

"That has nothing to do with sex, *habibti*. Sex is about bodies. It is black-and-white, like everything else." She looked away from him, her cheeks pink. "You expect a celibate union? Because that will not happen.We need children."

Something changed on her face then. Her expression going from stark terror, to wonder, to disgust so quickly he wondered if he was mistaking them all. Or if he'd simply hallucinated it. "Children?"

"Heirs."

Now her unpainted lips were white. "Your children."

"And yours," he said. "There is no greater bond than that. No greater way to truly unite the nations."

"I…"

Samarah was at a loss for words. She'd been thrown off balance by Ferran's sudden appearance, and then…and then this talk of marriage. Of passion and sex. And then finally…children.

The word hit her square in the chest with the force of a gun blast.

Terror at first, because it was such a foreign idea.

Then…she'd almost, for one moment, wanted to weep with the beauty of it. Of the idea that her love might go on and change. That it might not end in a jail cell of Ferran's making. That she might be a mother.

On the heels of the fantasy, had come the realization that it would mean carrying her enemy's baby. Letting the man who had ordered her father's death touch her, be inside of her. Then producing children that would carry his blood.

Your blood.

You wouldn't be alone.

No. She couldn't. Couldn't fathom it.

And yet, there was one thing that kept her here. That kept her from fashioning a hair pick into a weapon and ending him.

When he'd said, cold, blunt, that her father had killed his, that he had been responsible for the death of his mother as well, she'd realized something for the first time.

She would have done the same thing he had done. Given the chaos her father had caused, were she in Ferran's position, the newly appointed leader of a country...she would have had her father executed, too.

That shouldn't matter. The only thing that should matter was satisfying honor with blood. She could have sympathy for his position without offering him forgiveness or an olive branch of any kind.

But it sat uncomfortably with her. Like a burr beneath her rib cage. And she didn't like it. But then, she liked this whole marriage thing even less than the murder thing.

She was undecided on both issues presently.

And he'd confused her. With his comfy mattresses, delicious food and offers of a life she'd never imagined she could have.

A chance to be a sheikha. To do good in the world. To remember what it was to be poor, starving and homeless, and to have a chance to make it better for those in this country who were currently suffering in poverty.

A chance to be a mother.

A chance to live in a palace with everything that had been stolen from her.

She would not feel guilty for wanting that. Not even a little. Not when she'd spent so many years as she had. She'd been spoiled once, and after all the deprivation, she felt she could use a return to spoiling.

It was all so tempting. Like a poisoned apple.

But she knew it was poisoned. Knew that while it looked sweet it would rot inside of her.

"I can't discuss this just now," she said.

"You've already agreed. It's the only reason I've not had you arrested."

Yes, she had agreed. But inside she didn't feel as if it was a done deal yet. It didn't feel real, this change in her fate. She'd done nothing but focus on her revenge for so many years. Revenge and survival. They'd kept her going. They were her passion. She had nothing else; she cared for nothing else. Food, shelter, safety, sleep, repeat. All in the aim of making it here, and from there? She'd had no plan. She'd imagined…well, she'd hardly imagined she would survive this.

He was offering her something she'd never once imagined for herself: a future. One that consisted of so much more than those basic things. One that gave her the chance to add something to the world instead of simply taking Ferran from it.

He wasn't a monster. And that she'd known since she first came to live at the palace a month ago. It had been uncomfortable to face that. That it was a man she fought against, not a mythical being who was all terror and anguish. Not the specter of death himself, come to destroy her family.

She hated this. She hated it all. She hated how it tempted her.

"I suppose I have," she said, "but I'm still processing what it means."

It was the most honest thing she'd said to him in regards to the marriage. There were implications so far-reaching that it was hard for her to see them all from her room here in the palace.

"As am I. But one thing I do know is that marriage means heirs. I'm a royal, so there is no other aspect of marriage that's more important."

"Certainly not affection," she said.

"Certainly not. I doubt my father had much if any for my mother. If he did, he would not have been with your mother."

"Or perhaps they were simply greedy." She looked down, unsure if she should say the words that were pounding through her head. Because why talk to him at all? Why discuss anything with him? "I think my mother loved them both."

It was a strange thing to say. Especially when love had been utterly lacking in her life. But this was, in part, her theory why.

"What?"

"I think she loved my father and yours. She was devastated to lose them both. That her husband, whom she loved, was killed in the same few days that her lover was killed...I don't think she ever recovered. I don't know that she ever loved anything as much as she loved the two of them." Certainly not her.

He paused for a long moment, his eyes on the back wall. "That's where you're wrong."

"Is it?"

"Yes. I don't think your mother ever loved anyone more than she loved herself."

"You aren't fit to comment on her," she said, but there was something about his words that hit her in a strange way. Something that felt more real than she would like.

"Perhaps not." The light in his eyes changed, and for a moment, she thought she almost saw something soft. "No child should have to see what you did."

She looked away. "I hardly remember it."

Except she had. She and her mother had been staying at the palace. Visiting. Of course, she figured out that meant they'd been sneaking time in for their affair. At the time it had all been so confusing. She'd been a child who hadn't known anything about what had passed between the sheikh and sheikha and why it had caused the fallout that it had.

Honestly, at twenty-one, she was barely wiser about it than she'd been then.

In her mind, male desire wasn't a positive thing. It was something she feared. Deeply. Living unprotected as she had, she'd had to respond with fierce, single-mindedness to any advances.

It didn't take long for the men in the city to learn that she wasn't worth hassling.

And in her life, there had been no place, no time, for sexual feelings.

It made it hard to understand what had driven their parents to such extremes. What had made her mother feel her husband, her only daughter weren't enough for her. What had made her cast off a lifetime of perfect behavior, a marriage to a man she'd seemed to love, and for her father to react with mindless violence. She'd long been afraid that desire like that was some sort of demon that possessed you and left you with little choice in the matter.

But she didn't fear it now. Obviously, it wasn't a concern for her. Particularly not with a man like him.

"I am glad for you," he said. "I remember it with far too much clarity."

"You didn't…you didn't see…"

He swallowed, his eyes still focused on a point behind her. "I saw enough."

All she could remember was being pushed behind a heavy curtain. She'd stayed there. And she'd heard too much.

But she hadn't seen. She'd been spared that much.

"What is your timeline for this marriage?"

"The sooner the better. You're certain no one is going to come for you?"

"You mean am I sure no one will come and save me? Yes, I'm certain. There is no one like that in my life." What a lonely thought. She'd always known it, but saying it out loud made it that much more real, sharpened the contrast between what he offered with marriage, and what she would get if she used him and went ahead with her plan.

It was simple. A chance at a future, or nothing at all.

The offer of a future was so shiny, so tempting, so breathtakingly beautiful....

"That is not what I meant."

"What did you mean?"

"Are any of the old regime, the revolutionaries, still after you in any regard?"

"Not that I'm aware of. The old leader was killed by one of his own, and that ushered in a completely new political era in Jahar. Things are better. But there is still no place for me."

"As a symbol, you would shine beautifully," he said.

The compliment settled strangely in her chest. Lodged between rage and fear. "Thank you." The words nearly choked her.

"It is true. I think people would look at you, at us, and see echoes of a peaceful time. Of a time when our nations were friends. Sure, you won't be sheikha of Jahar, but you will still matter to the people there. They suffered when the royal family was deposed. They will be happy to know that you've risen up from that dark time, as will they. As they have."

"It is an idealistic picture you paint."

"I'm not given to idealism. This is how it will be."

"You seem very sure," she said.

He lifted a shoulder. "I am the sheikh. So let be written, et cetera."

"I didn't imagine you would have a sense of humor."

"I don't have much of one."

"It's dry as the desert, but it's there."

The left side of his mouth curved upward into a smile. "I see, and what did you imagine I would be like?"

"I had imagined you were a *ghul*."

"Did you?"

She shifted uncomfortably. Because sadly, it was true.

In her mind, he'd become a great, shape-shifting creature. A blood-drinking monster.

"Yes."

He reached his hand out, and she swiped it away with a block. He lowered his head, his dark eyes intent. "Permit me," he said, his voice hard.

She froze and he lifted his hand again. She stayed there, watching him. He rested his hand on her cheek, his thumb sliding over her cheekbone, over the cut he'd inflicted on her.

"I suppose," he said. "To a child who saw me as the one who took her father from her, as the one who stole her life, I would seem like a monster."

"Are you not?" she asked, unable to breathe for some reason, heat flooding her face, her limbs shaking.

With one quick movement, she could remove his hand from her face. She could break his thumb in the process. But she didn't. She allowed this, and she wasn't sure why.

Perhaps because it felt like something from another time. When Ferran hadn't been scary at all. When she hadn't hated him. When he'd simply been the handsome, smiling older son of her parents' best friends.

But he isn't that boy. That boy was a lie. And he's now a man who must answer for his sins.

"I suppose it depends," he said. "I am a man with many responsibilities. Millions of them. And I always do what I must to serve my people. From the moment I took power." He lowered his hand, heat leaching from her face, retreating with his touch. "I will always act in the best interest of my people. It depends on which side of me you fall on. If you are my enemy…if you hurt those I am here to protect, then I am most certainly a monster."

"And that," she said, her words clipped, "is something I can respect."

It was true, and it didn't hurt to say. There was honor

in him, and she accepted that. The only problem was, it clashed with the honor in her. With her idea of what honor needed in order to be satisfied.

"Get yourself ready," he said.

"What?"

"I intend to take you out into the city."

"But…no announcements have been made."

"I am well aware of this. But a limo ride with a woman who is hardly recognizable as the child sheikha who disappeared sixteen years ago isn't going to start a riot."

"A limo ride?"

"Yes. A limo."

"I haven't been in a car…well, I rode beneath the tarps in a truck to get across the border into Khadra. Then I got a horse from some bedouins out in the desert and rode here."

"What became of the horse?"

"I sold him. Got a return on the money I spent on him."

"Enterprising."

"I am a woman who's had to create resources, even when there were none. Other than that ride in the truck though, I've not been in a motorized vehicle in years."

"You haven't?"

"I walk in Jahar. I rarely leave the area I live in."

"Then decide what you think would be best for a limo ride. And by all means, Samarah Al-Azem, try to enjoy yourself."

CHAPTER FIVE

SAMARAH MADE HERSELF well beyond beautiful for their outing into Khajem, the city that surrounded the palace. It was hard to believe that the child he had known had grown into the viper that had tried to end him. And harder still to believe that the viper could look so soft and breathtaking when she chose. Hard to believe that if he leaned in to claim her mouth he would probably find himself run through with a hairpin.

Today she was in jade, hair constrained, a silver chain woven through it, and over her head, a matching stone resting in the center of her forehead.

"This is all so different to how I remember it," she said, once they were well away from the palace.

"It is," he said. "Khadra has been blessed with wealth. All I've had to do is…"

"You've been responsible with it. You could have hoarded it. God knows my country had wealth, and it was so badly diminished by the regime that came after my parents. Spent on all manner of things, but none of them ever managing to benefit the people."

"As you can see, we've followed some of what Dubai has done with development. New buildings, a more urban feel."

"But around the palace everything seems so…preserved."

"I wanted to build on our culture, not erase what came

before. But Khadra has become a technology center. Some of the bigger advances are starting to come from here, and no one would have ever thought that possible ten years ago. The amount of Khadrans going to university has increased, and not universities overseas, to take jobs overseas, but here. Some of the change has been mine, but I can't take credit for that."

"I wish very much Jahar could have benefited from this," she said, her words vacant. As though she had to detach herself in order to speak them. "You have done…well."

"You didn't know about the development happening here, did you?"

"I saw from a distance. From in the palace, but I didn't know the scope of it. I didn't know what these buildings accomplished." She leaned against the window and looked up at a high-rise building they were passing. "How could I have known? We were cut off from the world for years, not just my mother and I, but the entire country. We were behind an iron curtain, as it were. And in the years since it's lifted…well, the rest of the country may have made a return to seeing the world, but mine has stayed very small."

"I think it's time it grew a little, don't you?"

"Why are you doing this?" she asked, turning to look at him.

It was a good question, and he knew she didn't mean why had he improved his country, but why was he showing her. Why was he trying to change her mind about him.

It had less to do with self-preservation than he'd like to believe.

Perhaps it was because he wanted to return something to her that, no matter how justified he thought it might be, he'd taken from her.

Perhaps it was simply a desire to see some of the sparkle return to her dark eyes.

Or maybe it was just that he truly didn't want a wife

who had more fantasies about killing him than she had of him in bed.

Would he truly make her his wife? In every sense of the word?

He looked at the elegant line of her neck, her smooth, golden skin, dark glossy hair. And her lips. Red or plain, they were incredible. Lush and perfectly shaped. He had not looked at a woman in this way in so long. He hadn't allowed himself to remember what desire was. What it was to want.

So dangerous. So very tempting.

If he married her, it would be his duty. His heart rate quickened, breathing becoming more difficult.

Yes, he would make her his wife. In every sense. He was decided.

She would be perfect. Because of who she was. Because she knew. She knew about the danger of passion. She would be the kind of wife he needed. The kind of wife that Khadra needed.

"Have I suitably impressed you?" he asked.

She nodded slowly. "In some ways. It cannot be denied. But I find I'm in need of...something."

"What is that?"

"I've been idle for too many days. You promised me a sparring match. I think I will have it now."

He looked at the lovely, immaculate creature sitting across from him, her elegant fingers clasped in her lap as she asked him to spar with her in much the same tone she might have used to ask him to afternoon tea.

He thought of what she would look like if they sparred. Her hair in disarray, sweat beading on her brow. He gritted his teeth and fought to suppress the rising tide of need that threatened to wash him away.

"If you think you're ready, Sheikha."

"Only if you think you are, Sheikh."

* * *

Samarah was surprised to discover that Ferran had provided her with clothes. Well, he'd already been providing her with clothes, so she didn't mean it that way. But the fact that he'd provided her with clothes for the gym was surprising.

A pair of simple black shorts and a matching tank top. After all the layers she was used to—for protection on the streets, for her disguise in the palace, and then...with all of her beaded gowns now she was in position as Ferran's... whatever—she felt nearly naked in the brief clothing.

She opened the door to her chambers and saw Lydia just outside. "How do I get to the gym?"

"The general facility or Sheikh Ferran's private facility?"

"I...assume the sheikh's private facility."

"Near his quarters. Down this hall, and down the staircase, all the way at the far end. It's the last set of doors."

Dear Lord, he'd put her a league away from him. Probably because he feared for his safety. The thought made her smile as she started the trek down to his quarters. That she had succeeded in unsettling him would do for now. It wasn't revenge, but it was in the right vein.

She moved to the red double doors and pushed them open slowly. And stopped cold when she saw Ferran, his back to her as he punched the large bag hanging from the ceiling.

He wasn't wearing a shirt. The only clothing on his body was a pair of black shorts that looked a lot like hers. Though, they covered more of his legs.

His back was broad. Shockingly so, tapering down to a slim waist. Everything on him was solid. Ridges of muscle shifting beneath skin as gold as desert sand.

She'd known he was strong. She'd come up against him already and seen just what a worthy opponent he was, but seeing him now…she could see why her hesitation had meant the end of her plan.

She could see it in every line of his body as his fist hit the bag and sent it swinging. He was powerful. A weapon. That was the basis upon which she admired him. What warrior, what martial artist, would not appreciate such a finely honed instrument? That was why she stared. It could be the only reason.

Samarah took a breath and assumed her stance, raising her leg high, bringing it down softly between his shoulder blades. A muted outside crescent kick.

He whirled around, reaching out and grabbing her wrist, tugging her forward, her free arm pinned against his solid chest.

"You're here," he said, cocking his head to the side, his eyes glittering.

"You had your back to the door."

"So I did. I suppose I deserved that."

"I could have hurt you," she said. "I didn't skim you on accident."

"I understand that," he said, his breath coming in hard bursts from the exertion, fanning hot across her cheek.

"Are you ready?"

"Just quickly." He released his hold on her and ran his hands over her curves, light and fast. Her heart slammed against her breastbone when his fingertips grazed the sides of her breasts. "I had to check," he said.

Her breath escaped her throat in a rush. "Check what?"

"To see if you had a weapon."

"I have honor," she said. "If I was going to kill you, it wouldn't be during a planned sparring match."

"I see. You'd do it while I slept then."

"Honor," she repeated.

"Clearly. Shall we go to the center of the mats?"

He gestured to the blue-floored open room and turned away from her again, walking to the center of the mats.

She followed and took her position across from him, her hands up, ready to strike or block. "Are you ready?" she asked.

"When you are."

"Are you giving me the handicap because I'm a woman?"

"No, I'm giving you the handicap because you're tiny and I must outweigh you by a hundred pounds."

"I'll make you regret it," she said.

She faked a punch and he blocked high. She used the opportunity to score a point with a side kick to his midsection and a follow-up palm strike to his chin. She wasn't hitting with full force, because she honored the fact that this was for points, not for blood.

He blocked her next hit, gripping her arm and holding it out, miming a blow that would have broken her bones at the elbow if he'd followed through.

One for him, two for her. Her mental score sheet had her in the lead, and she was happy with that, but unhappy that, in reality, that would have been a disabling hit. Points aside, had it been a real battle, she would have crumpled to the ground screaming.

They hit gridlock, throwing hits, blocking them, then one of them would slip a blow through.

He was using a mixed fighting style, while she was true to her discipline. Her training was more refined, but his was deadly.

She was faster.

Only a few minutes in, she had him breathing hard, sweat running down the center of his chest, between hard pectoral muscles. She watched a droplet roll over his abs, and she was rewarded with a swipe of the back of his hand across her face.

She let out a feral growl and turned, treating him to a spinning back kick that connected with the side of his cheek. It wasn't as pulled as she'd meant it to be, and his head jerked to the side, a red mark the lingering evidence of the contact.

He growled in return, gripping her forearm and flipping her over his back. She hit the soft mat and rolled backward, coming to her feet behind him and treating him to a sweep kick under his feet so that he kissed the mat just as she'd done.

He got to his feet more slowly than she had, and she was facing him when he came up, her breathing coming sharp and fast now. She hadn't fought anyone this hard in a long time. Maybe ever. Sparring in the studio had never been quite this intense. There had never been so much on the line.

She wasn't sure exactly what was happening here. Only that it seemed essential she show him who she was. That she was strong. That she wasn't someone he could simply manipulate and domesticate. That no matter that she was, for now, going with his plan, he should never take for granted that she was tame.

It was a warning to him. A reminder to herself. She might have put on some beautiful dresses this week; she might have been impressed with the changes he'd made in the city. She might enjoy the soft bed she had now.

But she could not forget. She was not a princess anymore. Life had hardened her into more. She was a warrior first. And she could never forget that.

She prepared to strike again, and he reached out, his hands lightning fast, his fists curled around her forearms, pushing her arms above her head.

She roared and pulled her hands down, twisting them as she did, but he was expecting it. She'd done this to him once before, and she wasn't able to break through his hold.

She pulled her *kiai* from deep inside her, her voice filling the gym. The sound startled him enough that she was able to pull one hand free, and she used it to land another palm strike against his cheek.

He twisted her captured arm behind her back and propelled her forward so that she hit the thankfully padded wall.

She was pinned.

She twisted, scraped her foot along his instep—somewhat ineffectively since she was barefoot. But she was able to use his surprise again to free herself and reverse the positions. His back was to the wall, his arms in her hold. But that wasn't what kept him still, and she well knew it.

It was her knee. Poised between his thighs, ready to be lifted and to connect hard with a very delicate part of his anatomy.

"I would keep still if I were you," she said.

"We're sparring," he said, his chest rising and falling hard with each breath. "You're not supposed to do full contact hits."

"But I could," she said, smiling.

He leaned forward, angling his head and she stopped breathing for a moment. He was making eye contact with her, and it made something in her feel tight and strange. She looked down, her vision following a drop of sweat again, this time as it rolled from his neck, down his chest.

She found herself fascinated by his chest. By each cut muscle. By the way the hair spread over his skin. So unique to a man's body. These shapes, the hair, the hardness of the muscle.

She looked down farther. At the well-defined abs, the line of hair that disappeared beneath the waistband of his shorts. And she nearly choked.

She'd never been this close to a man. Not for this long. She'd fought them off before, but this was different.

She looked back up at his face, breathing even harder now. Her limbs tingling a bit. From the lack of oxygen, she was certain. Since she was breathing hard. And there was certainly no other explanation.

He leaned forward and bit her neck. It wasn't painful, the sensation of his teeth scraping against her skin. It was something else entirely. Something that made her flail, stumble and fall backward onto the mat.

"I say we call it even, little viper," he said, looking down at her.

Rage filled her and she popped back to her feet. "Of course you'd say that because I won. That was...not a move I recognize."

"You didn't say no biting."

"One shouldn't have to say that!"

"Apparently one did," he said, breathing out hard, the muscles in his stomach rippling.

"I demand a rematch."

"Later," he said, "when I can breathe again. You are a fierce opponent. And considering I do have a major size advantage, I cannot overlook the fact that, were we the same size, you would have destroyed me."

"I very nearly destroyed you as it is," she hissed.

"Very nearly."

"Don't sound so dry. I could have ended you."

"But you will not," he said. "Not now."

"You don't think?"

"No," he said, shaking his head. "Because I can offer you life. Ending me means ending yourself, too."

Her throat tightened, her palms slick. "I was prepared for that."

"I understand," he said, his tone grave. "But I think now that you've been given another opportunity you might see things differently?"

She looked down, hating that the war inside her was

transparent to him. Hating that he could see her weakness. That he could see she *wanted*. That his poisoned apple was indeed shiny and tempting.

A future. One with power. One where she wasn't starving, or freezing or afraid.

One where she lived.

Yes, she was starting to want that. But what it came with…that she wasn't sure of. But the cost would be her honor. The cost would be letting her enemy into her bed.

If it's for the greater good?

That was hard. She'd never much thought of the greater good. Only her own. That was what survival mode did to a person.

But this served the greater good and her personal good.

Weakness. Are you certain this isn't just weakness?

It very likely was. But then, she was tired of being strong. At least in this way. Tired of having to be so strong she didn't care for anything but living to the next sunrise, but living long enough so her life could end in Khadra when she'd ended Khadra's ruler.

Perhaps, in the end, that was the weakness. To aspire to nothing more than revenge, because wanting anything more had always seemed impossible. Too far out of her reach.

She shoved that thought aside.

"Perhaps," she said. "You have to admit, life is a very enticing reward."

"It is," he said. "I was personally prepared to beg for it sixteen years ago."

She blinked. "Were you?"

"It turned out I didn't have to," he said. "I simply hid… and I was able to escape."

She nodded slowly. "That's what I did."

"You were a child."

"You were young."

"I did my best to atone," he said. "Though, in the end it was too late."

"You couldn't have saved them. If your father wasn't strong enough to save them, a boy of fifteen with no fighting skills certainly couldn't have."

It was nothing more than the truth, and she wasn't sure why she was speaking it. Wasn't sure exactly why she wasn't letting him marinate in his guilt. Only that, from a purely logical standpoint, he was wrong. Because, had he not hidden, as she and her mother had done, he would not have lived.

She took a sharp breath and continued. "It would have done your country no good to have you killed that day."

The left corner of his mouth lifted. "Perhaps not. But it would have saved you a trip."

CHAPTER SIX

It was time for him to announce his impending marriage. And Ferran could only hope his viper bride cooperated with him.

She'd been in the palace for nearly a week, and their contact had been minimal since that day in the gym. Partly because he'd found the physical contact a temptation he did not need.

It had put a fire in his blood that he didn't like to remember existed. When he'd been a boy, he'd been all about himself. All about pleasure. Lust, and satisfying that lust.

But then he'd seen the devastation such things could bring. So he'd stopped acting that way. He'd stopped indulging his flesh.

Now Samarah was unearthing feelings, desires, best left buried.

Her father wasn't the only man he'd killed that day. He'd destroyed everything he'd been, everything he'd imagined he could be, in that moment too.

His rage had been regrettable but no matter how things played out, the end would have meant death for her father. But he had never been able to forgive himself for the deaths of Samarah and their mother.

Finding out she was still alive gave him a chance to soothe parts of him he'd thought would never heal.

But attraction, like the kind he'd felt in the gym, sparring with her, biting her...that had no place in this arrangement. They had no place in him.

They would have to consummate, and they would have to have children, but beyond that, Samarah would be free to live as she chose, and to be the symbol he needed.

He hardly needed her in his bed. He ignored the kick of heat that went through his body at the thought. When they'd fought, she'd been passion personified. And it had been beautiful and terrifying in equal measures. Because there was more conviction in her movements than existed in his entire body.

But then, he didn't need conviction. He just needed to do right. He needed to do better than his father. He needed to do better than he'd done at fifteen.

He'd lied to Samarah when he'd spoken of her father's fate. When he'd spoken of simple justice and black and white. So much of that reasoning had come from rage.

Ferran curled his hands into a fist, a spike of anger sending adrenaline through his veins. When he thought of his mother...cold and lifeless... Innocent in every way.

And then he thought of the spare moments before that. When Samarah's father had wrapped his fingers around her throat and Ferran had acted. For his mother. And for him.

But he had been too late. His violent rage utterly useless. In the end, none of his life was the same. Nothing of those whom he loved remained. Not even the good pieces of himself.

That day had destroyed so many things. And it was why he had to guard his emotions, why he must never allow his demons free rein. Ever again.

He rapped on Samarah's door and it opened slowly. Lydia, the maid, peered out. "Sheikh," she said, inclining her head.

"Is the lady ready?" he asked.

"Yes, Sheikh."

"I can speak for myself." Samarah's voice came from beyond the door.

"Leave us please, Lydia," he said.

The other woman nodded and scurried out of Samarah's chamber and down the hall. He walked in, and she looked at him with an expression reminiscent of someone who'd been stunned.

"What?"

"You're in a suit."

"So I am," he said, looking down at his black tie and jacket. "This shocks you?"

"I didn't expect Western attire."

She was elegant, in a long-sleeved black dress with a swath of white silk draped across the skirt and a gold belt around her waist. Matching gold decorated the cuffs of her sleeves, and there was gold chain woven through her hair. Which was still back in a braid.

He felt like making it a personal mission to see her hair loose.

Though, he shouldn't care about her hair. It had nothing at all to do with honor.

"You look perfect in Eastern attire," he said.

She pursed her lips. "I would think you might have liked us to look united."

"Perhaps you wanted it to look as though we got dressed together?"

Her cheeks turned a burnished rose. "That is not what I meant."

"Perhaps one day we will dress together." Though there would be no purpose behind that in their marriage, either. He would go to her at night when it was necessary. They wouldn't share a life. Not in those ways.

"This is not…an appropriate…I don't…"

"Do I fluster you, Samarah?" He did, he could see it. And he had no idea why he enjoyed it. Only that he did.

And he enjoyed so few things, he felt driven to chase it. If only for the moment.

"No," she said, dark eyes locking with his, her expression fierce. "It would take much more than you to fluster me, Ferran Bashar. I remember you as a naughty boy, not simply the man you are now."

"And I remember you as a girl, but I think we're both rather far removed from those days, are we not?"

"Maybe."

"I think we're a whole regime change, an execution and a revenge plot away from who we were."

"And a marriage proposal," she said.

"Yes, there is that. Though you seem to object to all mentions of marital related activities."

"I'm not ready to think about it," she said.

"I see." Heat burned through him, reckless and strange. Nothing like he'd experienced in his memory. Arousal was familiar. But there was a way he handled it now. And that was: alone.

He didn't act on reckless impulse. He didn't try to make the heat burn brighter. He extinguished it as quickly as possible. By working out until he dropped from exhaustion. By submerging himself in cold water.

He'd managed to diminish the desire for release until it was simply a physical need. Like hunger for food, thirst for water. There was no need for fanfare or flirtation. He had successfully managed without another person for years.

But there was a reality before him now. A woman he would marry. A woman who he would share his body with. And he was fascinated by her, by the thought. Now that sex was on the horizon he was finding it a difficult desire to ignore.

Especially with all the questions he had about her hair. How long it was. How it would feel sifting through his fingers.

Yes, he was curious about many things. He looked at her, at the exquisite line of her neck, the curve of her lips. His heart rate sped up. His fingers itching with the need to touch her.

"Tell me, Samarah," he said, ignoring his reservations and chasing the fire, "in all of your time spent on vengeance training and nurturing your rage, did you make time for men?"

She blinked. "No."

"Women?"

She blinked again. "No."

"Have you ever been kissed, Samarah?"

She stepped back as if she'd been shocked, her eyes wide. And he should be thankful she had. Or years of restraint would have been undone. "We're going to be late."

"The press will wait. We're what they're there for."

"I don't like to be late." She strode past him and out the door. "Are you coming?" she asked, out of view.

"Yes," he said, trying to calm the heat that was rioting through him.

They had to present a united front for the nation. He only hoped she didn't decide to attempt to give him a public execution.

Samarah looked out at the sea of reporters and felt the strong desire to scurry off the podium and escape so she could indeed do what Ferran had already accused her of doing. Nesting in the palace. Hiding away from everyone and everything.

She wasn't used to being visible like this. It felt wrong. It felt like an affront to survival.

But then, this pounding, wild fear she was experiencing was much better than the strange, heated fear she'd felt in her bedroom.

Have you ever been kissed, Samarah?

What kind of question was that? And why did it make her feel like this? Edgy and restless, a bit tingly. If this was rage, it was a new kind. One she was unfamiliar with. And she didn't like it one bit.

"It is with great happiness," Ferran said, his tone serious and grave and not reflecting happiness in the least, "that I announce my upcoming marriage. It is happy, not only because marriage is a blessed union—" Samarah nearly choked "—but because I am to marry my childhood friend—" she mentally rolled her eyes at his exaggeration "—who was long thought dead. Sheikha Samarah Al-Azen."

The room erupted into a frenzy, a volley of questions hitting like arrows. Samarah hadn't been the focus of so much attention in her memory. As a child, she'd been shielded from the press, and as an adult, she'd spent her life in hiding.

This wasn't anything she was prepared for. Fear had a limited place in her life. It acted only as a survival aid. To be heeded when she needed to heed it, and ignored when something larger than survival commanded she ignore it.

She never felt as if she was a slave to it.

Until now. Until she found herself doing something that went beyond explanation.

She put her hand on Ferran's arm, her fingers curling into his firm, warm flesh, and she drew nearer to him, concealing part of herself behind his body.

She felt him tense beneath her touch, saw a near-imperceptible shift in the muscles on his face. "I will take no questions now," he said. "I will add only this. I am regretful of the history that has passed between Khadra and Jahar. As are we all. I hope that this ushers in a new time. A new era. We are neighbors. And when children come from this union, blood. And while things will never be as they were, perhaps we can at least forge a truce, if not an alliance."

He put his hand on her back, the touch firm, burning her through her dress. He propelled her from the podium and away from the crowd, who were being managed now by his staff. "I have briefed them on what to say," he said when they were back in the corridor. "They have a nice story about how we reconnected at a small event we both attended in Morocco six months ago."

"That's quite the tale," she said, feeling shivery now, though she wasn't sure why.

"You have not been in front of people in that way before, have you?"

"I'm used to being anonymous," she said. "Actually, I'm used to needing anonymity for survival. This runs...counter to everything that I've learned."

That was a truer statement than she'd realized it was going to be. A far deeper-reaching statement.

Everything she'd been experiencing here this past week countered everything she knew about life. Everything she'd known about Ferran.

And about herself.

It was a lot to take in.

"This is my world," he said. "Everything I do needs a press conference."

"I'm not sure how I feel about that. Well, no, that's not true. I'm certain I don't like it." Because if she was really doing this sheikha thing, she wasn't sure how she would survive something like that all the time. "I feel too exposed."

"You're perfectly safe," he said.

"I'm standing there being useless in formal attire and I'm not at all ready to defend myself if something should happen."

He frowned and took a step toward her, and she took a step back, her bottom hitting the wall behind her. "It's something you'll have to get used to. This is only the beginning. We'll be planning a formal ball after this, to celebrate our upcoming marriage. And then the wedding. I am not going to hurt you," he said. "Stop preparing to collapse my windpipe."

"Should the need arise, I must be prepared."

One dark brow shot up. "The need will not arise."

"Says you."

He planted a hand by her head, leaning in. "I am here to protect you. I swear upon my life. In that room, where the conference is being held, there are always guards. They are ready to defend us should anything happen. And if they should fail, I am there. And I will guard you. I failed you once, Samarah. I let you die, and now that you've come back from the grave I will not allow you to return to it."

She felt the vow coming from his soul, from that place of honor he prized so dearly, and she knew he spoke the truth. So strange to hear this vow when part of her had still been ready to exact the revenge she'd come to deliver from the first.

She looked up and met his gaze. It was granite. And she felt caught there, between the marble wall and the hardness in his eyes. Between the honor he had shown since her return, and the growing respect she felt for that honor, and the years-long desire for a way to repay the devastation he'd been part of wreaking on her life. She couldn't look away, and she didn't know why. She was sent right back to the moment in his room, when she'd been poised, ready to take his life, and she'd seen his eyes.

There was just something about his eyes.

"I have never been able to trust my safety to another person," she said. Even when she'd had her mother with her, she'd often felt like the one doing the protecting. The parenting.

"Entrust it to me," he said. "I've already entrusted mine to you."

She turned that over for a moment. "I suppose that's true. But then, I am a prisoner of sorts."

"Instead of a leg shackle you'll have a ring."

"Sparklier anyway," she said, flexing her fingers, trying hard not to picture what it might feel like to wear a man's ring.

"You don't sound thrilled."

"Jewelry was never an aspiration of mine."

"I dare say it wasn't."

"So you can hardly expect for me to get all girlish over it, now can you?"

"Oh, Samarah, I don't expect that. No matter how much you make yourself glitter, I'm not fooled."

"Good," she said.

"You are a feral creature," he said, leaning in slightly, the motion pulling the breath from her lungs.

"And you think you'll tame me?"

He put his hand on her cheek, his thumb tracing the line of her lower lip. She could do nothing. Nothing but simply let him touch her. Nothing but see what he might do. She was fascinated, in the way one might be of something utterly terrifying. Something hideous and dark that all decent people would turn away from. Her stomach twisted tight, her lungs crushed, unable to expand.

"Have you ever seen exotic animals that were caged?" he asked. She shook her head. "The way they pace back and forth against the bars. It's disturbing. To see all that power, all that wildness, locked away. To see every instinct stolen from them. I do not seek to tame you. For those very reasons. But I do hope we might at least come to exist beside one another."

"We might," she said, the words strangled.

"I will take that as an enthusiastic agreement coming from you. I know this is not ideal but can't you simply..."

"Endure for the greater good?" she asked.

"Yes."

"Is that what you will be doing?"

"It's what I've always done," he said. "It's what I must do. This is the burden of a crown, Samarah. If you do it right, you're under the power of the people, not the other way around."

"Let me ask you this, Ferran," she said. And she didn't know why she was keeping the conversation going. Didn't know why she was standing in the hall with him, backed against a wall, allowing him to keep his hand on her cheek. But she was.

She knew she was extending the moment, extending the contact, but as confused as she was by her motivations, she didn't feel ashamed.

"Ask away," he said.

"You consider me feral."

"I do."

"Does this mean you're domesticated? As you've been brought up in captivity?"

"Of course I am," he said. "I'm the ruler of this country, and I have to be a diplomat. A leader. I have to be a man who acts rationally. With his mind, with his knowledge of right and wrong."

She narrowed her eyes and tilted her head, the motion causing his fingers to drift downward to her jawline. He traced the bone there. Slowly. It felt like the long slow draw of a match. Burning. Sparking.

"That's not what I see," she said.

"Oh no?" he asked. "What is it you see?"

"A tiger pacing the bars."

CHAPTER SEVEN

Samarah was in the garden doing martial arts forms when Ferran found her.

"I'm pleased to see you're out enjoying the scorching heat," he said.

She wiped the sweat from her forehead. "It's the desert. There is no other sort of weather to enjoy. It's this or monsoons."

"You don't get so much of the torrential rains here. But if you go west, toward the bedouin camps…there you find your monsoons."

"Then I suppose here at the palace, heat is my only option."

"Mostly."

He watched her for a moment longer. Every graceful movement. Precise and deadly. She was a thing of beauty. A thing of poisoned beauty.

He was much more attracted to her than he'd anticipated. Because he hadn't anticipated it at all. This strange, slow burn that hit him in the gut whenever she was near. He'd never experienced anything like it. He wasn't the kind of man who burned for one woman. For any woman.

He scarcely remembered his past lovers. He'd had one year of his life devoted to the discovery of women. At fifteen, he hadn't been able to get enough. Such a spoiled, stupid boy he'd been. He'd been granted almost his full height then, and he'd had more money and power than a boy his age knew how to wield. That had meant he'd discovered sex earlier than he might have otherwise.

But women had only been a means to him finding release, and nothing more. He'd never wanted one much more than any other.

But here and now, he burned.

It was not at all what he wanted.

Then there was her bit of insight.

A tiger pacing the bars.

When she'd said that, he'd wanted to show her—while he kept himself leashed, he was not in a cage. He could slip it at will, and he'd had the strong desire to make sure she realized that.

To press her head against the wall and let her feel just what he was feeling. To tilt her head back and take her lips with his.

To show her just what manner of man he was.

But that was passion driving that desire. And he didn't bow down to passion. It was too exposing. And he would not open himself up in that way again.

This deadly, encroaching *feeling* had fueled his plan for the day, too. It was time for both of them to get out of this palace, this mausoleum that held so many of their dead.

He would get them both out into an open space for a while.

"I had thought you might like a chance to go out in it for a while."

"Out in it?"

"The heat," he said.

"Oh." She stopped her exercise. "For what purpose?"

"There is a large bedouin tribe that camps a few hours east of the palace at this time of year, and I always like to pay them a visit. See that their needs are being met, what has changed. They have an ambassador, but I like to keep personal touch, as well."

"Oh. And you would…bring me?"

"You're to be my wife. This will be a part of your duties. You will be part of this country."

"It's hard to imagine being a part of Khadra," she said. "Being somehow a part of you."

"And yet, that is to be our future," he said.

"So it appears."

"So it is."

"So let it be written, et cetera."

He smiled. "Yes. I think you just bantered with me."

She frowned in return, the golden skin on her forehead creasing. "I did not banter with you."

"You did. For a moment there, you thought of me as a human being and not a target you'd like to put an arrow through."

"Lies. I am imagining breaking your nose as we speak."

"I don't think you are, princess."

"Don't let my naturally sweet demeanor fool you."

"There is no chance of that," he said.

He didn't know why, but he wanted to tease her. He wanted to make her smile. Because she never did. It was less perturbing than wanting to feel how soft her skin was beneath his fingers, anyway. So perhaps for now he would just focus on the smile.

"How will we get there?" she asked.

"By camel."

An air-conditioned, luxury four-wheel drive SUV was hardly a camel. She realized, the moment the vehicle pulled up to the front of the palace, that Ferran had been…teasing her.

Strange.

He probably wasn't afraid of her anymore, since he

seemed content to poke at her with a stick. Which, all things considered, wasn't the worst thing. That he wasn't afraid of her, not that he felt at liberty to stick-poke her.

Though, she couldn't remember the last time someone had teased her. Maybe no one ever had. Dimly, she recalled a nanny who had been very happy. Smiling and singing a lot. But Samarah couldn't even remember the woman's name. And she was more a misty dream than an actual memory.

Master Ahn had been kind. But he hadn't had much in the way of a sense of humor. He'd been quiet, though, almost serene and it had made a nice counterweight for Samarah's anger. He'd helped her channel it. He'd helped her find some measure of peace. Had helped her put things in their proper compartments.

But he hadn't teased her.

Ferran held the door for her and she got inside, the rush of cold air a nice change from the arid heat. She wasn't used to being able to find this kind of reprieve from the midday sun. It was…luxury.

"This is not a camel," she said.

"Disappointed?" he asked, as he took his place in the driver's seat and turned the engine over.

He maneuvered the car out of the gates and toward and around back behind the palace, where the city thinned out, and there was a gap in the walls. Walls that were left over from medieval times. More of the old mixed with the new.

"I'm not particularly disappointed by the lack of camel, no."

"They aren't so bad once you learn to lean into the gait."

"They are so bad, Ferran. I remember."

"Do you?"

She leaned back against the seat and closed her eyes. "Vaguely. We did a…caravan once. We rode camels. And picnicked out in the sand beneath canopies. It seems like…

like maybe it was a dream. Or another person told me this story. It hardly seems like me. But I remember the rocking motion of the camel so…if I know that, then it had to have been real, right?"

He nodded. "It was real. Your father hosted a picnic like that for visiting dignitaries every year."

"Oh, is that it? I couldn't remember. Weird how you know more about my past than I do. I was so young and my mother never talked about it."

Weird was…too light of a word. It was…everything. Horribly sad. Happy, in a strange way, to hear about her past finally instead of just having vague memories seen through the lens of a child.

But so odd that she was dependent on the man she saw as her enemy to learn the information.

"We used to go to the palace by the seaside," she said. "My parents' home. Mine now. Ours. Or it will be."

Her stomach tightened. "I'm not sure if I want to go there."

"Why not?"

"I was so happy there," she said, closing her eyes. "It almost hurts to think about it. Like someone scooped out my stomach." She opened her eyes again and looked out at the desert. "I don't think I want to go," she said again.

They were silent for the rest of the drive. Samarah trying to focus on the view and the air-conditioning, rather than the heat the man beside her seemed to radiate. It was stupid. His body temperature should be ninety-eight point six, just like hers. So why did he always feel so damn hot? It was irritating beyond measure.

So were the feelings that he called up out of her. Effortless. Like he was some sort of emotional magician. Creating emotions when there had been none, at least no refined, squishy ones, for years.

"Do you see?" he asked.

She looked up and out the front windshield at the tents in the distance. "Yes."

"That's the encampment. And there's smoke. Likely they're cooking for us. If not, we're in trouble because it means they aren't happy with me."

"Do they have reason to be unhappy with you?"

"People are unhappy with the leader of their country most of the time for various reasons, are they not?"

"I suppose they are. Though, I've had more reason to be unhappy with mine than most."

"Given the circumstances, yes."

"They stole my life from me," she said, looking up and meeting his gaze. "They stole my life."

"*They* did?"

And not him. She didn't miss the unspoken part of the sentence.

"Do not read too much into that. It was a complex situation, that's for sure," she said. "Many people could be assigned portions of blame. Except for me," she said, feeling the familiar anger welling up in her. "I was a child. I was six. It wasn't my fault. And I've still had to live it."

"You have," he said. "And it is a crime, because you're right. You had no fault in it. You had no part in the play and yet you were forced to deal with the consequences. So now…accept this. Accept this life. Live something different."

His words curled around her heart. Sticky, warm tentacles that wrapped her up tight and made her feel secure. And trapped. And she wasn't sure if she should fight or give in.

"Are you ready?" She knew he was talking about getting out and meeting the people, but it had another meaning for her.

She nodded slowly. "I'm ready."

She thought, for the first time, she might truly mean it.

* * *

The people did rush to greet them. And there was dinner prepared. They hurried to make a spot at the head of the table not just for Ferran, but for Samarah.

Ferran was pleased that everyone here seemed happy with his choice of bride. Because for the desert people who often traveled near the borders of the neighboring countries, the relations between Khadra and surrounding nations was even more important than to those who lived in the cities.

For them it wasn't about trade. Or import tax. Or the ability to holiday where they pleased. For these people, it was often about survival. To be able to depend on the friendliness of their neighbors for food, shelter, water if there was an emergency. Medical help. It was essential.

For his part, Ferran provided what he could, but if there was ever an emergency on the fringes, then there would be no way for the government to provide aid in time.

He looked at Samarah, who was curled up next to him, her feet tucked beneath her bottom, her hands in her lap. She looked much more at ease in this setting than she had at the press conference, but he still wondered if all of the people looking at her with obvious interest were bothering her.

He didn't like for her to be afraid. That realization hit him hard. But he wasn't sure why it did. Of course he shouldn't want her to be afraid. She was to be his wife, and it was his duty to ensure his wife was protected, regardless of how they'd gotten their start.

Perhaps you find it strange because you know you can't really protect her?

Not from the truth. Not if it ever came out.

He shut down his thoughts and focused on what was happening around them. Most of the tribe was sitting in the mobile courtyard area for dinner. Families in clusters, children talking and laughing, running around on the out-skirts of the seating area.

The elders were seated with him and Samarah, on cush-ions, their food in front of them on a wooden mat that would be easy to roll up and transport. It was nothing like the heavy, grand dining table in the palace that his father had had brought in. So formal. Custom made in Europe.

Ferran found that in many ways, he liked this better. This spoke of Khadra. Of its people. Its history.

"Sheikha."

Ferran watched Samarah's dark head snap up when the tribal elder to his right addressed her. "Yes," she said, seem-ingly shocked to have been spoken to.

"How do you find the political climate in Jahar at pres-ent?"

She blinked rapidly. "I… It has improved," she said. "The sheikhdom is never going to be restored, not as it was. The new way of doing things is imperfect. But since the death of the previous leader, there is something of a more…legitimate democracy in place. All things consid-ered, that is perhaps best for the country."

"And do you think this will unite the countries again?"

Her brow creased. "It's difficult to say. But I do think that the current government won't perceive me as a threat now that I'm marrying into the Bashar family and making my home here. So that is helpful for me. As for everyone else? I think if nothing else it will help old wounds heal."

Ferran nodded slowly. "If she can forgive me, then per-haps Jahar can forgive."

"And," she said, her words slow and steady, "if Fer-ran can lay aside the pain my family caused him, perhaps Khadra can forgive the pain, too."

"It was a great loss, that of your mother and father," the elder said to Ferran.

"Yes," he said. "It was."

"But you have done well. You've made them proud. You've made us all proud."

Ferran watched Samarah's face. He wondered if she thought he'd done well. Or if she still thought he was the worst sort of man.

The funny thing was, Samarah was more right about him than any of the leaders here. Yes, he'd done some good for his country. That was true. But in many ways he was no less than the murderer Samarah believed him to be.

"You do well in your choice of bride," the man continued. "It is truly a wise choice for us all."

"That," Ferran said, "I will wholeheartedly agree with you on."

And he did. Samarah was a choice he couldn't have foreseen having the chance to make. And she was certainly the best one.

"Well," she said. "Thank you."

"It's the truth," Ferran said.

The other man turned his attention back to the man to his right and Ferran continued to keep his focus on Samarah.

"I'm pleased to be a handy political pawn."

"Better than an instigator of war. You see what might have become of these people if you'd succeeded in executing me? Or if I'd imprisoned you. Marriage is preferable to either of those things."

"Marriage is preferable to death or imprisonment? Someone should embroider than onto a pillow."

"Poetic, I think."

"Very."

"Neither you or I are romantics," he said, watching her very closely, trying to gauge her response. She was so very hard to read. Such a guarded creature. And he shouldn't care about whether or not he was able to break that guard.

It had nothing to do with their arrangement. And neither did his fascination with her. Though, being able to read her might come in handy, just in case she ever got it in her mind to try and kill him again.

"Obviously not," she said, her face remaining impassive.

"Do you ever smile, *habibti*?" he asked.

"That's…an improvement over *little viper,* so I won't push the issue. And no, I don't often smile.

"I think that's too bad."

"Do you ever smile, Ferran?"

"Not often."

"Then don't concern yourself with my smile. I thought you said you weren't a romantic."

"Is smiling a romantic notion now?"

"Maybe just a luxury you and I haven't been able to afford?" she asked, cocking her head to the side.

"Perhaps that. Though, I am a sheikh,"

"As you've reminded me many times."

"It is the most defining part of me."

"Is it?"

"Yes," he said. "If I weren't a sheikh…things would be very different. But I am. And as such I can afford a great many things. Perhaps I should invest in smiling."

"Investing in frivolity? That seems like a recipe for disaster."

"Or at the least a recipe for…shenanigans."

The left side of her mouth twitched. "Shenanigans?"

"Yes."

"You said *shenanigans.*"

"I did," he said.

"Have you ever said that word before in your life?"

"No. I haven't had occasion to."

"It's a good word," she said. "And you got up to a lot of them when you were a teenager. I…I remember."

"I hope you don't remember in very great detail," he said. "I wasn't the best version of myself then."

She frowned. "So…this is the best version of you then?"

"Obviously." Her shoulders shook, her lips turning upward, a choked noise escaping. "Did you just…laugh at me? Is that what that was?"

"I think so," she said.

"You nearly smiled."

"I…did." She looked confused by that.

"I wish for you to do that again," he said. And he meant it. Not because he was being emotional, but because it wasn't fair that a woman like her, one so beautiful, one who should have been happy, had ended up with so few things to smile about.

"Perhaps I shall."

"Consider it at least." The corner of her mouth twitched again. "We will retire to bed soon."

Her eyes flew wide. "We?"

"I have brought my own tent, and it was graciously set up for us. Don't worry, it has rooms. And you will get your own."

"I had better."

"You will have to get over your aversion to sleeping with me." His pulse quickened. He was quickly discovering he had no aversions to sleeping with her. And why should he? Marriage made sex expected. It justified the desire.

As long as desire didn't rule in him, as long as he kept control over his weaknesses, there was no harm in being with his wife.

Her eyebrows lowered. "I am not having this conversation with you," she said, her voice a furious whisper, "sitting next to all these men."

"Your point is taken," he said. "But I come back to the issue of smiling."

She looked hesitant for a moment. As if she was trying to decide if she should say something else to him or bolt off into the desert. "What about it?"

"I should like the chance to try and make you smile tomorrow." Because he wanted to give her something. To give her more than he'd taken away.

"How will you do that?"

"There is an oasis not far from here. It is a place I frequent. I would like to show you."

"I…" He could tell she was considering telling him where to put his offer. But she swallowed her initial response. "All right," she said.

"We will have to ride horses, though, as you cannot drive in with a car."

"Horses?" she asked.

"Yes, horses. Can you ride?"

"I…I don't know."

"Well, you can share mine. I intend to ask for the use of one here."

"All…all right."

"No argument?"

She shook her head. "No. I think…perhaps I might make an attempt to smile."

CHAPTER EIGHT

SAMARAH HESITATED NEXT to the big black horse that was saddled and ready for their ride to the oasis. Ferran was already seated and she was meant to…get on there with him somehow. There was no way to avoid physical contact.

And frankly, physical contact with him was disturbing.

Though, the fact that it was disturbing…disturbed her. Because there was no reason for it to be quite so unsettling.

Sure there is. He ordered your father to his death. He's partly responsible for much of the misery in your life. Of course it's uncomfortable.

Yes, but it wasn't only that.

She wasn't used to touching men. And he was very much a man. So very different from the way she was built. So hard. So…so warm. She always came back to how damn warm he was. Perhaps he had a fever.

He lowered his hand and she stared at it.

"You're meant to take it," he said.

"Take it where?" she asked, crossing her arms beneath her breasts and turning her shoulders in.

"Grasp my hand, Samarah."

She reached out and curled her fingers around his, heat exploding against her palm and streaking up her arm. She didn't even have time to process it before she found herself getting hauled up onto the horse, behind Ferran.

Reflexively, she wrapped her arms around his waist and

leaned into him. Then she started to ponder which was more frightening. The idea of falling onto the sand, or continuing to cling to Ferran and his unnaturally warm back.

His back won. For now.

She should have asked to sit in front. It might have been a bit less disturbing.

But then...then she could have been between his thighs. Though, for the moment, he was between hers. There really was no winning in this situation. At least the current seating arrangement gave her an upper hand of sorts. If she wanted to jump off and run, she could. That was a comforting thought.

"It is not a long ride," he said, "an hour perhaps."

"I'm not concerned," she said, holding her head away from the hollow between his shoulder blades that looked like a very nice place to rest her cheek.

But she would not. She didn't need to use him as a headrest.

"You seem stiff," he said, spurring the horse into a trot.

"I am on a horse. How would you like me to behave?"

"Rest against me."

"I hardly think that's necessary."

"Suit yourself."

"Nothing about this suits me," she said.

"That's not good. Because I'm attempting to make you smile, and if nothing suits you, I won't be able to accomplish that."

"You're making me sound difficult."

"That's not my intent. You are much less difficult than when we first met and you attempted to stab me. That considered, I would hate to get on your bad side again."

"Who said you were off of it?"

Their conversation faded out and she settled into the horse's gait. And eventually, she settled into him. Her neck got stiff, a kink forming in the side, and she looked at the perfect pocket, just there, between his shoulder blades.

It would alleviate the pain. If she could just rest against him for a second.

She lowered her head. He was solid, but it wasn't uncomfortable at all. The fabric of his shirt was damp with sweat, and she didn't find it at all disagreeable.

That only increased her discomfort.

She could hear his heart, thundering in his chest. Could feel the shift of his muscles as he moved with the horse over the desert sand.

She turned her face slightly and caught the scent of his skin. Of the sweat. Really, none of it was disagreeable at all. Which…made it disagreeable in its way.

Samarah shifted and tightened her hold on him, her palms flat against his stomach. He was hard there, too. And she could feel his muscles, the definition of them, even with the fabric of his shirt separating her hands from his flesh.

She'd seen his muscles, so she knew just how very defined they looked. And she also knew about the body hair. Which she found much more fascinating than she should.

She stared at the horizon line after that, trying her best not to think too hard about Ferran's body, and the way it felt beneath her hands. Or the way it looked without his shirt.

It was only because she was trapped against him that she was thinking this way.

The ride stretched on forever. She got hotter, and she got more restless. And her thoughts weren't calming down. Her body wasn't, either. She would have thought you just got used to being pressed against someone eventually, but apparently you didn't.

At least not when that someone was Ferran.

"We're here," Ferran said, his tone hard, tugging back on the horse's reins, bringing his behind pressing hard between her thighs and sending a jolt through her body.

She curled her fingers into his shirt, desperate to hold on to him. And desperate to jump off and run screaming into the desert until she could figure out what the hell was wrong with her.

She looked around his shoulder, and her body slowly released the tension it was holding fast to. The oasis was beautiful. A lush green blot of ink against a dry, pristine background of bone-white sky and pale sand.

"Hang on to the saddle," he said.

She obeyed and he slid down off the horse, then held his hands out.

"Seriously?" she asked.

"What?"

She swung her leg over the side of the horse and slid down onto the sand, landing deftly on her feet. "I'm not a delicate flower, Ferran. Do not treat me like one."

"I wouldn't dream of it."

"You just tried. Now, where is it we're staying?"

"Are you wilting?"

"Be careful, or I will bite you. I believe I owe you on that score."

His expression sharpened, the look in his eyes intensifying. "I can't say I'm entirely opposed to you biting me."

"That makes no sense."

"Perhaps not to you, *habibti*. But if I conduct our marriage in the proper manner, it will make sense to you soon."

"I don't see how it could."

He just looked at her, and he appeared to be amused. And she felt heat—both anger and other sorts of heat, sorts she didn't want to contemplate—rising in her.

"Your imagination is sadly lacking."

"You bit me once already," she said. "I felt nothing."

Her stomach pitched, both because she was lying, and because she was reliving the scrape of his teeth over her skin. It was such an intimate thing. And right then, she started connecting all the dots.

"Surely people don't bite each other when they…" She snapped her mouth shut.

"Not always. And I meant no more than I said."

"I don't believe that," she said. "About there being no hidden meaning, not…not about the biting. I believe that, I just… Where are you going?" He'd taken the horse by the reins and started leading him away.

"I thought you wanted to see where we were sleeping tonight?"

"Fine. Lead the way."

"I am."

They walked farther into the oasis, shielded by a rock formation, and by a thick growth of trees that grew taller as they edged closer to the waterline.

The water was like a sheet of glass. Reflecting the trees, the sky and sun from the still surface.

"This is incredible," she said. "Are there…don't a lot of animals come here?"

"I've never seen many, not when I have a fire going at night. And it's rained recently, so this isn't the only water. Though, you should watch for snakes."

"I don't like snakes," she said, her focus going to the ground as she watched the placement of each of her steps.

"I'm not a huge fan of them, to be honest, but for the most part, you won't be bothered by them."

"Yes, well, sometimes in floods, they would slither into the rooms I was staying in. Fortunately, not usually poisonous ones. But…but sometimes the odd viper would pay me a visit. So, your nickname for me is somewhat fitting."

"You don't have to worry about snakes tonight," he said. "I'll build a fire now."

"It's hot still."

"A precaution. The tent is this way."

She followed him down the well-worn trail that led deeper into the trees, and out to the far side of the small lake. She stopped when she saw it. "It is not exactly a tent."

The "tent" had permanent walls, with windows, and what appeared to be a broad canvas stretched over the roof and anchored into the ground. There was a small deck off the front that went over the water.

"What is this?" she asked.

"My escape, I suppose. Something much simpler than the palace. And quiet. I come out here whenever I visit the tribe. And sometimes for no reason at all."

"Do you bring women here?"

She was curious. Fascinated by who Ferran was as a man. Not as the monster she'd built up in her head, and not even as the man he was around her. But the man he'd been for the past sixteen years. The man who, apparently, had a retreat. And who knew biting was a thing that could be exciting. And who undoubtedly *had* been kissed many times. And had lovers.

Yes, she was very curious all of a sudden, who this man was. Because she had to know her enemy. The enemy she was preparing to ally herself with.

"No," he said. "I don't bring women here."

"Where do you bring women?" she asked.

She was curious now. And she wanted to know the answer. She wanted to know about these women, who knew about how it felt to be pressed up against his back, and to feel his stomach. And...more.

She despised the fascination. It was like giving in to the desire to watch a fight breaking out on the streets. To take in the horror, the anger and blood. To be both drawn to and repulsed by what she was seeing.

"Why do you want to know?" he asked.

"Because I do."

"Why?"

"Because...because I am supposed to be your wife." It was the first time she'd said it. The first time she'd felt like that position might matter. Like it might really be real. Like she was making real steps toward their treaty, rather than just standing in a holding pattern, contemplating the merit of escaping, or exacting revenge of some kind. "It seems like I should know these things about you."

"I don't," he said, his tone hard.

"What?"

"I don't...conduct affairs."

"Never?" she asked.

"No."

"I...I don't..."

He swept past her and into the dwelling.

She looked inside. "This is very much not a tent. Just as your car was not a camel."

Yes, the ceiling was swaths of draped fabric; beneath it stretched canvas that she imagined was completely waterproof, but that did not make it a tent.

There was formal furniture. It was spare, but very expensive looking. Wood and plush fabrics. Nothing as ornate as the palace. This seemed to speak more of Ferran, and not the rulers that had come before him. This was the man, and not the legacy.

At least, it was a piece of him.

She was digging for other pieces.

"I confess, calling it a tent was slightly misleading."

"And the car?"

"Yes, that, too."

"You're telling me you don't conduct relationships with women?" she asked. "I assumed..."

"Why would you assume, Samarah?"

Her cheeks heated. "I would have thought a man such as yourself would have lovers. Several of them. I remember how you were. Though, I suppose being naked with someone makes you very vulnerable to them. Sleeping with someone—they could kill you while you dreamed. I suppose…I suppose that means you have to be selective about lovers."

She wanted to know the answer because if she really was to be married to this man then it seemed like this was important information for her. It seemed she should know how he viewed sex. Why he had no lovers. If he was being truthful. Because if they were going to be married, they would share the marriage bed and all the intimacies that entailed.

Intimacies she was woefully uneducated about.

She'd heard sex spoken of in vile, crude terms. Had heard men make threats that were disgusting. Had heard prostitutes make allusions to things she hadn't fully understood.

She hoped there was more to marital activities than all of that. Really, she knew there had to be, because it was the thing that had driven their families to destruction.

That was the part that scared her. The part of her that feared she would become a slave to it…the part that feared there was a part of herself that was undiscovered that would change completely when she finally found it.

"Being naked with someone does not really make you all that vulnerable to them. And I never slept with any of my lovers."

"You didn't? I was under the impression that…" She trailed off, not liking how innocent she was revealing herself to be.

In so many ways she had no innocence. She'd been in the palace during all that horrible destruction. And then, back at home she'd survived the siege. There had been so much violence on both of those days. She'd survived homelessness, hunger, cold, heat, fear. Grief. So much more grief than one person could be expected to bear.

But she didn't understand the kind of connection that

drove two people to pursue a romantic relationship. She didn't understand sexual desire. Not in a specific way that existed between two lovers.

It was her only piece of innocence really. Her physical innocence. Her emotions were jaded, her mind inundated with the cold ugliness of the world. It was only her body that remained untouched and she had fought fiercely for that. For her body was the one thing she had left that hadn't been violated by the world.

Still, she didn't especially want him to know all of that. *Have you ever been kissed, Samarah?*

She had a feeling he might know already. But she didn't need to go revealing herself.

"You do not have to sleep with someone just because you have sex with them. Though, perhaps in your case, since you lacked a steady bed it was easier to stay."

She didn't know what to say to that. She wasn't sure if he was digging for information or not. And she wasn't sure if she wanted to give him any.

"We aren't talking abut me," she said.

"No. We are not. But that should answer your questions."

"It doesn't really."

"Then perhaps you should speak more plainly so I can answer them. I am not playing guessing games with you, Samarah."

"When you say you do not conduct affairs…you are not…I mean, you have been with…"

"I am not a virgin," he said, the word dripping with incredulity. "I slept with enough women that they blurred together during my teenage years, but there was an inciting incident that put me off passion. I had a job to do, and I have not had the time to lose myself in pleasure since I overtook the throne." His expression was hard, a dark, frightening rage filling his eyes. "Do you now feel suitably informed, Samarah?"

No. Now she wanted to ask about the pleasure. The pleasure he was afraid to lose himself in. Wanted to ask what that meant to a man like him. Sixteen years of celibacy. What it would mean when he broke it. And if he really intended to break it with her. For them to… Now she wanted to ask a whole lot of questions, but she was stuck because if she did then she really would give herself away. And then she would be standing in a remote location talking about sex with the man who was caught in a fog in her brain. Somewhere between enemy and ally. Somewhere between monster and fiancé.

It was all too weird.

"I feel more informed. Yes. Are you going to start a fire?"

"Yes," he said. "I'll bring you your things. Why don't you get settled."

"Where is my room?" She wondered for a moment if he would suggest they share. And that terrified her. And made her feel something else that she couldn't quite place.

"Whichever one you choose, I will take the other. Does that suit?"

"As much as anything in this arrangement does."

"You flatter me," he said, his voice clipped.

Now he sounded annoyed with her, and she couldn't for the life of her figure out what she'd done. And she shouldn't care. So she wouldn't.

"All right, I will arrange my things. Enjoy building your fire."

"I'll see you again for dinner," he said. "If it rains, I will cook indoors."

"Do you expect it to rain?"

"I always prepare for a potential catastrophe. Rain, flooding."

"All right," she said, waving her hand, already going off to explore other rooms of the house. She badly needed a reprieve from his presence. He was making her say—and think—crazy things.

She needed to get her head on straight. She needed to remember what it was she was doing here.

That thought deflated her. She sank to the couch. What she was doing here was marrying Ferran Bashar, the man she'd sworn to kill. Because it was the right thing to do. For their countries. It was a greater good she couldn't simply ignore.

This was a true sacrificial act, not just something that would assuage the burning anguish inside of her. She'd talked herself into thinking his murder, and her subsequent death, a death she'd been nearly certain of, would be sacrificial. But perhaps not. Perhaps it had only been an act born of blinding rage and desperation.

The same sort of rage that had driven her father.

The thought hit her hard, a realization she slid sickly through her veins like cold tar. She was not her father. She was not a mindless rage machine who would destroy all simply to get revenge upon his wife and her new lover.

And on the heels of that realization, the other was cemented.

She was going to marry Ferran. She was going to be his wife.

God help her. It was real.

A tear slid down her cheek and dropped onto her hand. And for the first time since her mother wandered into the desert and never returned, Samarah Al-Azem let herself cry.

When she stumbled outside an hour later, she didn't feel any less stunned, but she did feel a renewed sense of purpose. Determination. She felt...she felt as if she was truly on a new path. As if she'd reconciled this change.

At least in part.

She looked up at the sun, which was resting low over the horizon now. A chill spread over the desert sand, along with a hazy blue blanket that seemed to thicken the air. Gnats swarmed over the reeds, and she batted them away from her face as she walked through the tall plants down to the water.

She grabbed a large stick and let it go before her, doing a sweep for snakes as she went along.

Thankfully, none had seen the need to get in her path.

She came to the damp, cold mud and stopped, looking out at the water. The surface rippled, then broke, and Ferran appeared. He stood, his back to her, water droplets rolling through the valleys in his flesh, created by the hard-cut muscles that she'd been enjoying on the ride over.

He took a step up toward the bank that was to the left, and the waterline lowered on his body, so that it revealed two deep grooves in his lower back before showing his…oh.

He took another step and the water slid off his skin. And she could see now that he was naked. And he was…

She'd never really looked at a man's butt before. Not like this. Not one that was bare, and muscular and…well, bare.

More importantly, she'd never been given to the urge to simply stare at a man like this, clothed or not. As a man and not a threat. As a man and not a mere weapon. But flesh and blood. He was fascinating. Especially with their earlier conversation playing through her mind, combined with the close proximity of the horse ride.

And her recent acceptance, full acceptance, of the fact that she was to be his wife.

Yes, it was all that that had her there, staring and unable to stop. Her mouth was agape. Truly. Her face felt like it was on fire and her heart…her heart was beating faster than she'd thought was physically possible.

The only time it had ever come close to this was in moments of sheer, unadulterated terror. Those she'd had.

Those she was familiar with. This? This was something else. Something new. Something that had nothing to do with the past.

He turned to the side and she couldn't breathe. It all just gathered in her chest like a ball and stopped. She was completely frozen, held captive by him. She wanted to see him. All of him. She wanted so badly for the mystery to be solved. To know now what he looked like. All over. Because not knowing…it made her more afraid of the future. She just needed to know.

She tried to swallow, but it got caught with the knot of air.

Then he turned to face her, dark eyes boring into hers. But she only met his gaze for a moment. Then, completely without thought, she was looking down.

She bit her lip, taking the moment to study him in detail. It was her first glimpse of a naked man and she found she could only stare. And that she could not remain wholly detached.

"See something you're interested in."

She wasn't sure *interested* was the word. She forced her gaze back to his. "I'm sorry."

He lifted one shoulder and the muscles in his chest shifted. Fascinating. "No need to apologize. I didn't hang a sign out."

"Do you…do you have a sign?" she asked, feeling slow, her brain processing things at half the speed. The lack of oxygen was probably to blame.

"No, I don't have a sign."

"It would be the best way to warn people."

"I could have sent you a text."

She blinked slowly. "I don't have a phone."

"That will change."

"Will it?"

"Of course," he said, still standing there. Casually naked.

She didn't feel casual at all. There was so much skin on display it made her want to slip out of her own and run away.

"There's no *of course* about any of this. Not to me and I—I can't just stand here and talk to you while you're naked."

"That will change, too."

"I do not think," she said, turning around and heading back up the path, sweeping her stick through the grass and quickly following behind.

She had no desire to run away from a naked man, only to step on a snake. Out of the frying pan and all that.

And it wasn't as if Ferran's nakedness put her in any danger.

The heat in her cheeks, the pounding of her heart, said otherwise. It felt a lot like fear. She knew fear well. Much more intimately than most.

Though, there were subtle differences to this feeling.

Such as the not entirely unpleasant feeling between her thighs.

She wasn't that innocent. She knew what that was. Why was this happening to her now? With him?

You are marrying him....

Yes, but she'd intended to deny sex as part of the equation for as long as possible and then submit to it when she had no other option. Her plan, thus far, hazy as it was, had been to just lie there and think of Jahar, so to speak. As far ahead as she'd thought in the past hour, when she'd finally decided that yes, she would be his wife. Really. Not just as a reprieve to a sentence or until she could kill him.

Even so, she wasn't ready to contend with the idea that she might...desire him.

No. This was just garden variety, biologically inspired arousal that had nothing to do with desire. It was the first time she'd been exposed to a man, an attractive man, and not been worried about him being something of a threat in the back of her mind.

So that was all it was.

She frowned as she shut the door to the dwelling. When had she stopped perceiving Ferran as a threat? She was certain he wouldn't harm her. Certain he would never force himself on her. And she wasn't sure what he'd done to earn that measure of trust, when only two weeks ago she'd cowered in the middle of his bed, her own weapon in his hands, fearing he would kill her or use her body.

She didn't now. Not in the least.

Strange how things had changed. How they were changing.

Now, that made her feel afraid. Because without all the anger at Ferran, she wasn't sure what she had left. It had insulated her, consumed her, for so long, she felt almost bereft without it.

"I apologize that my body offended you."

She turned and saw Ferran in the doorway, tugging his shirt over his head. His pants were already on, riding low on his lean hips. Not that any of it helped now, since she could so clearly visualize how he looked without the clothes on. Problematic.

"It was not…offensive," she said. "I just am not accustomed to having conversations with nude men. Out in the open."

"You only have conversations with them in the enclosed?"

"Well, where else would I have them?" she asked.

"Outside, it turns out."

"No. That's why I came in."

"Stubborn creature. Since you're in an enclosed space now, I could always take my clothes off again as I know you find this preferable."

She held up her hands, her heart scurrying into her throat. "No!"

"Then perhaps you might like to come outside and have dinner."

"Clothed?"

"Only if you want. I have no such rules about women and nudity."

She narrowed her eyes. "But you aren't naked with women at all, if what you say is true."

"Come back outside, Samarah."

"I will require we both remain clothed." She walked out the door and followed the rising smoke, back down to the pond where he'd been swimming only a few moments earlier. The ground was damp here, but there were blankets and pillows spread out already. There was a pan over the fire, resting on a grate.

"You've cooked?"

"I come here alone often, as I said. I could cook inside, but I quite like to eat out here." He took the pan from the grate and moved it to a small, low table that was next to his seat.

"Obviously."

There was rice and meat in the pan, and he handed her a bowl filled to the top. It was much simpler than the way they ate at the palace. She liked it. It reminded her of who she was apart from all the comforts. Of the way she'd grown up.

But this was a piece of that memory with the absence of that wary feeling. The fear. The anger. This was different. This felt like they were totally set apart from the world. From reality.

It was nice, because she'd had far too much reality in her life.

Something about this felt much more like a fantasy. Strange, because never in all her life away from the palace had she imagined spending time with Ferran being part of a fantasy. In her life at the palace, perhaps. She'd been fascinated by him then. The handsome prince who was always in trouble. Always up to mischief.

He lifted his head, and the disappearing sunlight cast a glow on his face. She remembered then. An image pulled from deep in her mind. Standing in the palace in Khadra, watching him stride into the room. The way he'd smiled. He'd reached out his hand on her head and ruffled her hair.

And she'd been certain he was the most beautiful person she'd ever seen.

She didn't know why she was only remembering this now.

Or maybe she did. Maybe because her anger, her determination for revenge, wouldn't let her have a memory of him that was so…precious.

It was precious because it was a part of where she'd started, and she had so few memories of that time in her life. The time where things had been right. Before it had all gone to hell.

"I remember you," she said, allowing real memories to mingle with her words. Allowing herself, for the first time, to really remember the people they had been. Before their parents had destroyed everything.

"You should. I've been sitting here with you the whole time."

"From before," she said. "I remember you." It made her feel so strange. To connect him, suddenly, much more strongly with that boy than with the monster she'd made in her mind.

"And what do you remember?"

"I thought…I thought you were beautiful." They were true words, forgotten thoughts that rose up in her mind and poured from her lips, filled her chest with a strange warmth.

"Did you?" he asked. "That is…not the description one might hope for."

"I was a little girl. I thought you were fascinating." She looked down into her bowl. "And you were very nice to me." Little wonder she hadn't let herself remember that. Because it did not fit with the stories she'd told herself about Ferran the monster. But here and now, those legends were being overridden with something more powerful. With memory.

"It was impossible not to be. You would not be ignored, and being unkind would have been like kicking a puppy."

In this moment, she decided she would pretend there was nothing away from this fire. She would allow them to have nothing but these good, shared memories. A truce.

"Well, I appreciate it, anyway. I had a…nice memory just now. I'm short on those. I don't remember very much about my life before my father died. And I think a lot of that isn't so much because I was too young—I was six. I feel I should remember some things—but because I forced myself to stop trying to remember. Because it hurt so bad. Because it…made me hate where I was even more. Those memories didn't serve a purpose, so I didn't let myself have them." She looked up. "I'd like to have them again. I'd like to have…something normal."

"I'm afraid I'm not the man for that," he said.

Of course he wasn't. How could he be? Given the way things were all tangled up, he couldn't be. And still, she pressed. "Why?"

"I'm not sure I know what normal is. Though, I'm not sure either version of our lives, on this side of the tragedy or the other, were normal."

"Maybe not. But one was happy. In one, I did smile."

"And you're looking for your smile."

"I am. Currently seeking any emotion other than anger

or fear, actually. That's basically been my life for the past sixteen years."

His expression changed, hardened. "I cannot imagine all that you've been through."

"It's okay. I mean, it's not okay. But it's what is. And there is nothing that can be done about it now."

"I wish there was more I could do."

She laughed suddenly. So suddenly not even she expected it. "It's so strange. I never thought I would sit across from a campfire with you while you offered to try and fix things for me. Not so long ago, I would have cried death before dishonor but...I feel like I was wrong about you."

"Samarah..."

"I don't see how either of us could have won in the situations we were put in, Ferran. You were a new ruler and you had to act as a king. And that day my father did not act as a king. He was simply a jealous man. Ruled by emotion." She took a breath and tried to loosen the tightness in her chest. "He was tried fairly, and found guilty of a crime he absolutely committed. What happened to my mother and I was less just, but it wasn't by your hand."

It nearly pained her to say it. But there was no honor in misdirected rage. She knew that better than most. And yet she had spent sixteen years clinging to it.

It didn't make her friends with Ferran, but...but it made her feel as though a truce that extended beyond the moment might be possible.

"Samarah," he said again, "there are things... I am not a hero."

"Neither am I. I'm a victim. And I think you are, too. But isn't it time to stop?"

"You're not a victim now," he said, the words coming slowly. "You will never be again. You're a sheikha. And you have power in this country. You have power now."

"I think I've proven that I've always had power. Though,

it's nice to have that power backed up by…the law. And the army."

"Don't get too power mad."

"I can make no guarantees." She looked out across the water, dark blue now with the sun gone behind the horizon line. "Do you know, these past weeks with you…before them, I can't remember the last time I sat and just had a conversation with someone. I can't remember when I had the time for something so casual. Master Ahn was very good to me. The closest thing I ever had to a friend, but we didn't have many conversations. He instilled in me the will to survive, the sense to think with my head and to act with honor in all things. To know what was right, so deeply that it would be an instinct to act upon what's right when the time comes…." She paused. "Maybe…maybe that's why I hesitated in your room that night. Because something in me knew it was wrong. Because something in me knew I couldn't possibly be serving justice if I hurt you."

"A bold statement, Samarah."

"I realized something today. I was allowing rage to dictate my action. And in that, I was no better than my father. For all that I wished to avenge his death, I have never condoned his actions. My anger was for me. For my mother and our country. But revenge was never going to make that right. Rage would never do anything but lead to more devastation. I'm ready to let go. Even if that makes me weak." She looked down at her food, then back up at him. "Does it make me weak?"

"You have never been weak," he said. "Never."

"You say that with such confidence. But I've always been scared."

"Is that a weakness?"

"Not when it keeps you alive, I suppose."

He set his food down, then stood. "I'm going to bed,"

he said. "Tomorrow we'll stay for breakfast and then head back to the bedouin camp."

For some reason, the thought of leaving made her feel sad. "Okay."

"See you tomorrow, Samarah."

Another chance to simply sit. To be with another person. To live. She found she was looking forward to it.

CHAPTER NINE

SAMARAH WOKE UP to the sound of rain on the canvas rooftop. She slipped out of bed and looked outside. It was gray out, the sun trying to pierce through the heavy blanket of clouds that had rolled in overnight.

She ran her fingers through her hair and leaned forward, the silken strands sliding over her shoulders.

She looked out the window, at the rain pelting down, hitting the parched earth, large droplets creating ripples on the surface of the lake. And she had the sudden urge to go out in it.

She'd hated the rainy season when she'd lived in Jahar. Hated having to hide in rooms that were muddy and flooded. Hated looking for shelter during the day wherever she could find it, or more often, just spending most of the afternoon feeling like a drowned rat.

But it was different now. She wasn't forced to stand out in the rain. She had a choice. She could stay in here where it was dry, or she could dance in the water drops. It was up to her. Because she had a home now. She had shelter.

Everything had changed. There was more than survival. There was…enjoyment. Happiness. Something about yesterday's realization, yesterday's acceptance, had allowed her to capture these things. Or at the very least the possibility of them.

She stood and walked to the window, pressing her palm

against the glass. Then she turned and walked out into the living area. It was still hazy, and the house was dark. She hadn't checked the time but it had to be early.

She padded to the front door and pressed down on the handle before going out onto the deck. She was wearing only a nightgown, a soft, silken one with very little in the way of adornment. It had been provided for her at the palace and she'd packed it for the trip. It wasn't designed to be flashy, just to be comfortable.

Normally, she wouldn't go walking outside in it. And she wouldn't go walking out with her hair down, simply because there was too much of it, and letting it free was much more trouble than it was worth.

But right now she didn't care.

She stepped down onto the wet sand; it stuck to her feet while the raindrops poured down over her body, making her nightgown stick to her skin. She looked up and let the rain drop onto her face, sliding down her cheeks and her neck.

How different it was to stand in the rain when it was your choice. When you knew you could go back inside and get dry.

She spun in a circle, her arms held out wide. She felt like the child she had been. As if she was free. As if rain was just rain, and she didn't have to worry about the cold, or the discomfort, the mold or the damp. All of the cares she normally carried were washed away.

She walked along the path they'd taken last night, to the ashes of the fire from the night before, and to the edge of the water. She looked out across the surface, continually being shattered by heavy drops of rain and tilted her face upward again.

"You'll catch your death."

She turned and saw Ferran, and immediately the child-like joy, the simplicity of it, faded. And she realized she was

standing there with nothing but a thin nightshirt clinging
to her body, and her hair wet and stringy down her back.

"You're out here, too," she said.

And in nothing but a pair of jeans. He was wearing jeans.
And no shirt. But he hadn't worn jeans to bed so that must
have meant he'd been…well, he'd likely slipped the jeans
on before coming outside.

"Yes, but you're…you're beautiful," he said.

"I'm wet."

"Yes." He took a step toward her and she looked behind
herself, her heel at the edge of the water. There was no
backing away from him. And she didn't feel very inclined
toward punching him in the face, either. Which was new.
He extended his hand and took a strand of her hair between
his thumb and forefinger, twisting it lightly. "I wondered
what your hair looked like down."

"It is also wet. Therefore not the most flattering repre-
sentation."

"I disagree," he said, leaning in closer. "Do you know
how much of your body I can see through that nightshirt?"

She looked down at the fabric, which had shaped itself
to her figure. She could clearly see her nipples, hardened
from the cold. The nightgown provided no coverage there.

"I have an idea," she said, looking back up.

"And do you know what it does to me?"

She started to speak, then closed her mouth. Then she
blinked and shook her head. "No."

"I have not touched a woman in sixteen years. I… Right
now I feel like the ground here. Like I've been too long
without water, and it's finally here in front of me."

"Oh…Ferran…I don't…I…" She didn't know what to
do. She wasn't sure what he wanted. She wasn't sure she
could give it.

He hadn't touched a woman in sixteen years, and now
he was here, his hands on her hair. Touching her. So much

pressure on her, when she had no idea what might happen next.

"I'm going to ask you again, Samarah." His dark eyes were level with hers. "Have you ever been kissed?"

She felt as if the breath had been pulled from her lungs. "Not exactly," she said.

"And by that you mean?"

Samarah hesitated, her heart fluttering in her chest. She knew this admission would change things. That in a few moments, the answer to the question *have you ever been kissed*, would not be the same. Even with no experience, she knew it. In her bones. In her blood. And she wanted it. "Not by anyone other than my family. Never by a man. Never in the way you mean."

He put his hands on her cheeks and brushed the water drops away. Was she really going to let him kiss her?

He's going to be your husband.

He was your enemy.

He'll be your lover.

Her brain was fighting with itself. And she had no idea which voice to listen to. But she felt her lips parting, her eyes slipping closed as she tilted her face upward.

To know what was right, so deeply, that it would be an instinct to act upon what's right when the time comes...

"I have waited for this," he said, his voice a growl, "for longer than you can imagine."

And then his lips met with hers. They were hot beneath the sheen of rain that covered them. Slick from the water. And firm. But more so than she'd imagined they might be. He held her face steady, then tilted his head, opening his mouth and touching the center of her upper lip with the tip of his tongue.

A simple, delicate touch that sent a flash of heat, like lightning, through her body.

He pulled back slightly, his hands still on her face, holding her. "Kiss me back, Samarah."

"I don't know…how. I don't know…" Desperation grew wings and fluttered in her chest, fear and need gripping her tight.

"What do you want to do?"

"I…" She looked at his chest, at his stomach, and she put her hands on him, one palm resting against the hard ridge of his abs, the other just above his heart. She wanted to touch him. To feel those muscles with no clothing between them. She'd known that for a while now, even though she hadn't quite understood it.

Or, more to the point, she hadn't wanted to understand it.

Now she did. Now she wanted to understand it all. All this depth and nuance of being human, of being alive. This rich tapestry that existed beyond mere survival.

There was so much more than just drawing breath. There was the feel of Ferran's skin beneath hers. The rough hair, the heat of his body, the hard definition of his muscles. And there was the need it created in her. Reckless and heady. A high like nothing else she'd ever experienced. The adrenaline rush that accompanied fear coupled with a much more pleasant emotion.

So this was lust. Real, raw lust, so much more potent than she'd ever imagined it could be. Even though she'd known it must be something so very strong, there was a difference from knowing that and having lived it. She was living it now.

She leaned in and kissed him, freezing when her mouth touched his, a raindrop rolling between their lips and sliding onto her tongue. She laughed, then pulled back. "Sorry, I don't think you're supposed to laugh when you kiss."

He moved his hands from her face and wrapped them around her waist, pulling her against his body. "Why not?" he asked. "I like that you're finally smiling."

He closed the distance between them, his kiss harder this time. His lips moved over hers, his tongue sliding against the seam of her mouth before she opened and gave him entry. Then he took her deep, long. The sensual friction sending a deep, sharp pang of longing through her. An arrow of pleasure that shot straight to her core and left a hollow pain in its wake.

She fought to free her hands from where they were trapped between their bodies and wrapped her arms around his neck, holding him to her. She tried to match his movements, to make her lips fit against his. He adjusted some of what he was doing, and she adjusted, too. And then they found a way to make their lips fit together just right.

He moved his hands down over her back, her butt, and down to her thighs. Then he gripped her tight, tugging her up into his arms, the blunt tips of his fingers digging into her flesh, the points of pressure adding pain into the mix with the pleasure.

She clung to him, wrapped her legs around his waist so that she didn't fall back down to the ground, and the motion brought the heart of her into contact with his hard stomach. A short, shocked moan climbed her throat and escaped.

He growled and angled his head, biting the side of her neck, harder even than he'd done back in the gym.

She whimpered, and he slid his tongue over the spot, soothing the sting, ramping up her arousal. She kissed him back, feeling confident now. Maybe because he seemed as if he was on the edge of control, too. She certainly was. Because this wasn't necessary, or useful. And yet it felt essential. And she wanted it. More than she could ever remember wanting anything.

He cupped her bottom and pulled her hard against him. At the same time he bit her lip, then soothed it away. Pleasure rocketed through her. She curled her fingers tightly into his shoulders, understanding perfectly now why some people actually enjoyed biting.

There was so much more to this than she'd ever thought possible. To wanting a man. To sexual desire. It wasn't just nice feelings, or pleasure, or whatever it was she'd imagined it might be.

It was need, so deep and intense it made you burn. It was pain. Pain because there was too much pleasure, pain because you wanted more.

Kissing Ferran was both the best and the worst kind of torture.

It was everything. It filled up the moment. It filled her up. And yet, it wasn't enough. It hinted at things she didn't know about, made her desire things she didn't understand. Made her body crave something she wasn't certain existed. Tipped her beliefs on right and wrong onto their heads and twisted her into a stranger she didn't know, and wasn't certain she liked.

But she didn't care.

She rocked her hips against him and a low, feral growl rumbled in his chest. He moved quickly, decisively, lowering them both down to the ground. To the sand. And she didn't care that she was going to get dirty. That she would get wetter. It didn't matter as long as he kept kissing her.

He adjusted their positions, forking his hands through her hair, tilting her head back, tugging slightly. He slid one hand down her back, cupping her rear and lifting her up against him. And she wasn't pressed against his stomach anymore, but the hard line of his shaft. She'd seen him naked yesterday, but it hadn't prepared her for this. He hadn't been aroused yesterday in the lake.

Instinct, and need, had her flexing her hips against him, each movement making the ache inside her build, grow, until she thought she was going to die.

She was sure no one could withstand this kind of sensual assault. The rough sand beneath her; Ferran, hot and hard above her; the rain, cold against her skin.

He moved his hand to cup her breast, drawing his thumb slowly across her nipple, before pinching her lightly. She was still covered by the damp fabric of her gown. He lowered his head and sucked her deep into his mouth.

He pushed against her, the hard ridge of his arousal hitting her just where she needed it.

And the dam burst inside of her. A hoarse cry escaped her lips, much like the sound she made when she fought. Raw, passionate, bold.

Pleasure poured through every part of her. She arched against him, holding tight to his shoulders as the waves crashed over her, her eyes squeezed shut, her fingernails digging into his shoulders.

She just lay there for a moment, feeling spent, the fog slowly clearing. And then she started to feel other things. Shame. Embarrassment.

He moved against her again, kissing her neck, his hands firm on her breasts.

She shoved at his chest.

"What?" he asked. "Samarah, did I hurt you?"

"No…I…no…"

She couldn't tell him. She couldn't tell him that she'd had what she suspected was an orgasm from kissing him. That was…it was terrifying and way past the point of embarrassing straight into humiliating. Because how could that be? How? With him…with anyone, but especially with him.

This was not lying back and thinking of Jahar. This was not a truce. It was somewhere far over that line, and it was one she couldn't believe she had crossed.

He moved away from her and she scrabbled to her feet, her nightgown sticking to her legs, tugging upward, the sand caked over her skin, in her hair. "I just…I have to go back inside now."

"You do?" he asked, still on the ground, breathing hard. He looked nearly as shocked as he had the night she'd tried to kill him.

"Yes. I do. I…thank you. For the kiss. I have to go. I'm cold."

She turned away from him, her arms wrapped around her waist, and she ran back toward the house, then into the bathroom. She locked the door behind her and turned the water on, stepping inside fully clothed and watching the sand wash down the drain.

Then she started to shiver.

She'd never felt anything like this before. And it was much too big for her to deal with. Too big for her to process.

There was a whole new depth to life, and she'd just discovered it. And now she was terrified by what might come next. By what it meant about who she was.

Because once upon a time, Ferran might have been able to have lovers without feeling connection. But in that moment she knew for certain that *she* couldn't.

She thought of her mother, the author of her own destruction, and everyone else's, so desperately in love with two men that she couldn't give either of them up.

As much as she didn't want to be her father, she didn't want to be her mother. And God help her, she would not be a fool over Ferran Bashar.. And until she figured out how to get a handle on her emotions, she couldn't allow Ferran to touch her again. It was as simple as that.

Ferran called himself every kind of bastard as he kicked over the cooking grate that was still set up over the dead coals from last night's fire.

He was an animal. Of the worst kind. He'd known she was a virgin, hell, he knew she'd never been kissed. She'd been badly handled all of her life. Thrown out onto the streets when she was a child so that she could escape a grisly death.

He was responsible for every bad thing that had happened in her life. And now he'd added another thing to the incredibly long list.

He'd allowed himself to be ruled by passion. Had let the floodgates open after keeping them firmly closed for so many years.

No.

He was not that man. Not anymore. He would not allow it. Not again.

He had been rough with her. He'd been ready to take her, take her virginity, in the sand, in the rain. Without talking to her. Without making sure she was ready.

You're using your need for control to hold her captive.

He shrugged the thought off, turning his self-disgust to the more specific events at hand.

He'd led with his own desire, and had given no thought to anything else. He'd thought he was better than that now. He had to be. The alternative was unthinkable.

He stalked into the water, in spite of the fact that he was already wet, and submerged himself. It was much colder today, with the sun behind the clouds and the rain pouring down.

It didn't do anything to assuage his arousal. He was still so hard it hurt, need coursing through him like a current. He ground his teeth together and walked back out of the water, his jeans heavy and tugging downward, chafing against his erection.

That had been a stupid, damn idea. And it hadn't even worked.

He walked back toward the house and shrugged his jeans off at the door. Hopefully Samarah wasn't around because he didn't really want to ambush her with his body like this.

He could hear the shower running and he said a prayer of thanks for small mercies.

He went into his bedroom and started digging for dry clothes. They needed to get back to the palace. Back to civilization and back to sanity.

There, he would be reminded to keep his distance. He would be reminded of all the indignity she'd already suffered without him adding to it.

His weakness had caused her suffering.

He paused at that thought. She deserved to know. Because if there was one thing Samarah truly cared about it was honor. It was doing right.

Though, there was a limit to what he could say without adding to her pain. Without uncovering himself completely.

One thing was certain. Before he tied her to him for the rest of her life, before he jailed her in a whole different way than she'd originally threatened, she had to know at least in part, what sort of man it was she was tying herself to.

CHAPTER TEN

THEY ARRIVED AT the palace late that evening. The ride back had been torturous. Samarah had spent so much of her life without human interaction, she'd never fully understood just how awkward it could be to sit in an enclosed space with another person when you had nothing to say.

And when you had something obvious and tense hanging between you.

That morning seemed like a lifetime ago, and yet it had only been about fifteen hours since Ferran had held her in his arms. Since he'd pulled her against him and kissed her. Since he'd brought her to the peak of pleasure on the ground outside in the rain.

She could hardly believe that had been her. And that it had been him.

In the cold of the night, she could not understand what had possessed her to go outside in a rainstorm. What had possessed her to fall into his arms and kiss him as if he was the only source of water in the desert.

She moved through her chambers and stopped cold when she saw Ferran in the doorway. "What are you doing here?" she asked.

"I came to speak to you about tomorrow. We're to have lunch with the palace event planner. To speak to her about the upcoming engagement party and the wedding."

"Oh," she said. "I had forgotten about the party."

"As had I. Since I'm not particularly interested in parties, it was easy to let it slip my mind."

"I can't say I'm a real party animal, either," she said, her tone dry.

"I imagine not. I have brought you something."

"Oh?" She really had to try and find something more intelligent to say than that.

"I feel we got off track today."

"Oh." Well, dammit. That was not more intelligent.

"I should not have touched you like that. Not knowing how innocent you are. And I regret that I frightened you."

It was on the tip of her tongue to say he hadn't frightened her at all. She'd frightened herself. But honestly, his assumption was so much less revealing that she felt like letting him have it.

Coward.

Yes. But so what? He was about to apologize and since he owed her many, in reality, she would take one for this. Even though he didn't owe her one for that incident in particular. She bore the full weight of the consequences for the foolishness of her body.

"I lost sight of what it is we are doing. This marriage is to benefit our nations. And to heal the past. What I did accomplished neither of those things."

"Well...no I suppose not."

"This is to remind you, to remind me, of what this is about." He reached into his pocket and pulled out a small black box. "I spoke to the palace jeweler, and he managed to come up with something very quickly. It is not my mother's ring. All things considered I felt no monuments needed to be built to that marriage." He opened the lid of the box and revealed an ornate, sparkling piece of art. Gold with diamonds set into an intricately carved band. "But this is from the crown jewels, as it were. And it has been in my family for many generations. It's lasted longer than a marriage. Than the rule of any one sheikh or sheikha. And I hope what we build forges a bond between our countries that is the same. I hope that what we build transcends a simple marriage, and becomes something lasting that benefits both of our people."

"Oh that's…that's perfect," she said, banishing images of them kissing, of the heat she'd felt in his arms, and bringing to the front pictures of their country. Of their people. Of all that could be built between the nations if they followed through with this union.

"I am prepared to ask you to wear it."

"Of course," she said.

She waited for him to do something. To get on one knee or put the ring on her finger. She wasn't sure if she wanted him to do that.

He did neither. He simply stood there with the box held out in front of him until she reached inside and took the ring, putting it on her own finger.

"You may not want to do that just yet, princess," he said.

"Why not?"

"I am prepared to ask you to wear it. But only after this. I want to talk to you about what happened at the oasis."

"Oh," she said, looking down, heat bleeding into her face. "You know what? I'd rather not."

He took her chin between his thumb and forefinger and tilted her face up so that she met his gaze. "Did I hurt you?"

"What? No." She shook her head and took a step back. "No, you didn't hurt me."

"Did I frighten you?"

"I…I…no." It wasn't him that scared her. It was herself. The way he'd made her feel. The fact that he'd commanded a response from her, with such ease that she hadn't even realized she was capable of feeling.

"Then why did you run?"

"I didn't…run. I was cold and I went back in the house."

"You were right to be afraid," he said.

"I wasn't afraid."

"Then you should have been."

"I'm sorry—I should be afraid of you? I beat you in hand-to-hand combat, lest we forget."

"I believe I beat you," he said. "Both times."

She scowled. "You cheated. You bit me."

"It was not cheating. But that's beside the point. I have something to tell you about that day. And you won't like it. But I have to tell you before you concede to marrying me. Because it will change things. I owe you this explanation. Though I'm certain I will regret giving it."

"Then why give it?" she asked. She suddenly felt afraid. Because she was starting to feel at ease with this man. With this situation. With the fact that she was to be his wife.

More than finding ease…she was starting to want things. From him. From life. And she was afraid that whatever he said next might take it all away.

"Because you have to know. Because if you aren't afraid, then you need to understand that you should be. You need to understand why I can never be allowed to lose control. Why I have spent sixteen years doing nothing more than ruling my country. Why I despise passion so very much."

"The same reason we both have to distrust it," she said. "Because it led our parents to a horrible end. The only innocent party involved was your mother, and yet, she suffered just as badly for having been there as any of them."

"It is true," he said. "She was the only innocent party. She was true to her marriage vows. She didn't attack anyone. She was simply there when your father and his band of men decided to make my father pay for what he'd done."

"It was wrong, Ferran. All of it. And I'm willing to put it behind us." And she meant it. This time, she meant it for real. "Because…it has to be. It can't keep being my present and my future. I can't allow it. Not anymore. I want something different. For the first time I just want to move on from it and please…please don't take that from me."

"It is not my intent to take anything from you. But to inform you of the manner of man you're to marry."

"Does it matter what manner of man?" she asked. "If I have to marry you either way, does it matter?"

"You spoke to me of honor when we first met, Samarah. You were willing to die for it, so yes, I think it matters. I feel I have to tell you. For my honor at least. What little there is."

"And I have no choice?"

"This is giving you a choice. So that you know who you let into your body at night once you're my wife. I owe you that. Or I at least owe it to my sense of honor."

Her face heated. "That was unnecessary."

"It hardly was. I nearly took you this morning at the oasis. I nearly took your virginity on the ground. Do you understand that? Do you understand that I am capable of letting things go much too far when…when I am not in control."

"You didn't."

"You stand there and blush when I talk about being inside of you. It would have been a crime for me to do that there. In that manner."

It wouldn't have been. And part of her wanted to tell him. That she was blushing because she was inexperienced. Because she was embarrassed by her response to him. Confused by the fact that she felt desire when she'd expected to endure his touch. Not because she found the idea of being with him in that way appalling.

"I don't…I don't think I would have stopped you. And if you say I couldn't have, I'm going to do my best to remind you that I, in fact, could have. Don't ever forget what I can do, Ferran. Who I am. I am not delicate. I am not a wilting flower that you've brought out to the desert. I survived that day. I survived every day after. You don't need to protect me, and I refuse to fear you."

"I killed your father," he said, his dark eyes boring into hers.

"I know," she said.

"No, Samarah, you don't. I did not have your father arrested. I did not send him to trial. I was hiding. In a closet. I heard everything happening out in the corridor and I hid. That is when your father burst into the family quarters. And he attacked my father with a knife. I stayed hidden. I did nothing. I was afraid. I watched through the partly open door as he ended my father's life. My mother was in the corner. A woman, unarmed, uninvolved in any of it. And then he went for her and...I didn't hide anymore. She begged, Samarah. For her life. She begged him to spare her. For me. For my sake and the sake of our people. For the sake of his soul. But he didn't. I opened the closet door and I took a vase off of one of the sideboards and I hit him in the back of the head with it. I was too late to save my mother. She was already gone. And I...disarmed him."

"Like you did me," she said, feeling dizzy. Feeling sick.

"Yes. Exactly like I did you. But unlike you...he ran. And I went after him."

She tried not to picture it, but it was far too easy. Because she'd been there that day. Because she'd heard the screams. Because she knew just how violent and horrible a day it had been. It was so easy to add visual to the sounds that already echoed in her head.

"Ferran..."

"I was faster than he was. Because of age or adrenaline, I'm not sure. But I want you to know that I didn't even give him the chance to beg for his life. Because he never knew I had caught him. I ended him the moment I overtook him. I stabbed him in the back."

Samarah took a step back from him, her eyes filling

with tears before she could even process what he was saying. She shook her head. "No...Ferran don't...don't..." She didn't know what she wanted to say. Don't say it. Don't let it be true. *Don't tell me.*

"It is the truth, Samarah. You should know what kind of man you're going to marry. You should know that I am capable of acting with no honor. There was no trial. He was not given a chance. I acted out of emotion. Out of rage. And it is one thing I refuse to regret. You need to know that before you agree to bind yourself to me. I killed your father and I will not regret it."

She growled and ran forward, shoving his chest with both hands. "Why must you do this now?" she asked, her voice breaking. "Why did you make me care and then try and rip it away?"

"I'm being honest," he said, gripping her arms and holding her so that she couldn't hit him again. "You have to know. Am I the man you want in your bed? Then you must know the man I am."

She fought against him, not to break free, but just because it felt good to fight against something. Because it was easier than standing there passively while all these emotions coursed through her. Grief, rage, anguish, panic. All of it was boiling in her, threatening to overflow. And she didn't know how to handle it. She didn't know how to feel all of this.

This wasn't simply breathe in, breathe out. This wasn't a calculated plan for revenge and satisfaction of honor. This wasn't even the low hum of sixteen years of anger. This was all new, and shocking and fresh.

And horrible.

Because she hurt. For what she'd lost. For her father. For the man he truly was. A man who killed an innocent woman because he was scorned. A man who was not the one she'd loved so much as a child.

And she hurt for Ferran. As horrible as it was to imagine him being involved as he had been, she hurt for him. The boy whose mother had died before his eyes. The boy who had avenged her.

As she would have done.

Oh, as she would have done to him if he'd allowed it. And then what? Would she be the one standing there with nothing but a scorched soul? With haunted eyes and the feeling that she had no honor left because in her rage she'd allowed herself to justify taking the life of someone else?

"You see now," he said, "who I am. And why I cannot permit myself to be led by my emotions? I am no better than they are, Samarah. I am no better. I am not stronger."

And neither was she. Not really. Because she'd been prepared to act as he had, but not in the heat of rage. Not in the midst of the fight. With years to gain perspective, she'd been ready to behave as her father had done.

As she looked at Ferran, at the blank, emotionless void behind his eyes, she felt she could see the scars that he'd been left with that day. It had been so easy for her to imagine him as the one who'd come out of it whole. He'd had his country. He'd had his palace. Hadn't that meant in some way, that he had won? That she had lost and therefore was owed something?

But when she looked at him now, she didn't just understand, she felt, deep down in her soul, that he'd lost, too. That there had been nothing gained for him that day. Yes, he'd ascended the throne, a boy forced to become a man. Yes, he had a palace, and he had power. But he had lost all of himself.

That was why he looked so different than the boy she'd known. It wasn't simply age.

She struggled against him, and he held her tight, his eyes burning into hers. "How dare you make me understand you?" she asked, the words coming out a choked sob.

"How dare you make me feel sorry for you?" Tears rolled down her cheeks, anger and pain warring for equal place in her chest. And with it, desire. Darker now, more desperate than what she'd felt at the oasis.

And she knew it now. There was no question. It was what she'd felt that first moment, in his bedchamber when their eyes had met. What she'd felt watching him shirtless in the gym, fighting him, getting bitten by him.

It was what she'd felt every time she'd looked at him since returning to the palace. It had just been so expertly mixed with a cocktail of anger and shame that it had been impossible to identify.

But now that she'd tasted him, she knew. Now that she'd gone to heaven and back in his arms, she knew.

Now that she understood how you could long for a man's teeth to dig into your flesh, she knew.

"How dare you?" she asked again, the words broken. "How dare you make me want you? I should hate you. I should kill you."

She leaned in and claimed his lips with hers, even as he tried to hold her back. He released one arm and reached around to cup the back of her head, digging his fingers deep into her hair, squeezing tight and tugging back, wrenching her mouth from his.

"Why are you doing this, Samarah?" he growled.

"Because I don't know what else to do," she said. "What else am I supposed to do?"

"You're supposed to run from me, little girl," he said, his expression fierce. He was not disconnected now—that was certain. He wasn't hollow. Her kiss had changed that. It had called up something else in him.

Passion.

Passion that he thought she should fear, and yet she didn't. She found she didn't fear him at all.

"I don't run," she said, her eyes steady on his. "I stand

and meet every challenge I face. I thought you knew that about me."

"You should run from this challenge," he said. "You should protect yourself from me."

She pushed against him, and he pushed in return, propelling her backward until she butted up against the wall. "You don't scare me, Ferran Bashar," she said.

"As far as your family is concerned," he said, "I am death himself. If you had any sense at all, you would run from this room. From this palace. And you would not wear my ring."

Her heart was raging, each beat tearing off a piece and leaving searing pain in its place. And she couldn't turn from him. It would be easy to get out of his hold if she really wanted to. A well-placed blow would have him at her feet. But she didn't want to break free of him. Even now.

"You need me to run, coward?" she asked. "Because you fear me so? Because I am such a temptation?"

That was the moment she crossed the line.

His lips crashed down on hers, his hold on her wrists and hair tightening. It wasn't a nice kiss. It was a kiss that was meant to frighten her. A show of his dangerous passion, and yet, she found it didn't frighten her at all.

She kissed him back. Fueled by all of the emotions that were rioting through her, fueled by the desire that had been building in her from the first moment she'd seen him again. From the moment she'd walked into the palace, with vengeance on her mind.

She had wanted him then, but she'd been too innocent to know it. And desire had been too deeply tangled in other things. But she knew now. The veil had been ripped from her eyes. And all the protection that surrounded her heart seemed to have crumbled.

Because she couldn't hate him now. Not even with the newest revelation. All she could see was what they'd both lost. All she could do was feel the pain of losing her father over again. The man who'd been a god in her mind transforming into a monster who would kill an unarmed woman. And all she could do was let it all come out in a storm of emotion that seemed to manifest itself in this.

At least a kiss was action. At least a kiss wouldn't end with one of them dead.

Though now, with all of the need, all of the deep, painful desire that had possessed her like a living thing, like a beast set on devouring her insides if she didn't feed it with what it wanted, she wondered if either of them would survive.

He pulled his mouth from hers, his hands bracing her wrists against the wall behind her head, dark eyes glaring, assessing her. "Why do you not run from me?"

"Because I am owed a debt," she said, her breath coming in short, sharp bursts. "You stole my life from me. You stole this," she said, speaking of the need she felt now. "I had never even kissed a man because I could afford to feel nothing for men but distrust and fear. I had to guard my own safety above all else because I had no one to protect me. I could never want, not things beyond food and drink. So you owe me this, Sheikh. I will collect it. I will have you, because I want you," she said. "It is your debt. And you will pay it with your body."

"So you want my passion, Samarah? After all I have told you?"

"Is it not my right to have it? If it has been used so badly against me? Should I not be able to take it now, when I want it, and use it as it would satisfy me?" Anger, desire, anguish curled around her heart like grasping vines. Tangled together into a knot that choked out everything except a dark, intense need.

"You want satisfaction?" he asked, his voice a low growl, his hips rolling against hers, his erection thick and hard against her stomach.

"I demand it," she said.

He leaned in, his breath hot on her neck, his lips brushing against her ear. "Do you know what you ask for, little viper?"

"You," she said. "Inside my body. As discussed. You seem to think I don't know what I want, but I will not have you disrespect me so."

"No, Samarah, I am of the opinion that you likely always know what you want, at the moment you want it." That was not entirely true, because she hadn't realized how badly she wanted him until today, when she knew it had gone on much longer than that. "But what I am also sure of, is that sometimes you don't always want what is good for you."

"Who does?" she asked.

"No one, I suppose."

"We all want things that will harm us in the end. Cake, for example. Revenge for another."

"Sex," he said.

"Yes," she said. "Sex."

"That's what you want? You want sixteen years of my unspent desire unleashed on you?"

"That's what I demand," she said.

He tugged her away from the wall and scooped her into his arms in one fluid movement, carrying her across the room. She put her hand on his chest, his heart pounding so hard she could feel it pressing into her palm.

"Then you shall have what you demand," he said, depositing her onto the mattress before tugging his shirt over his head and revealing his body to her. So perfect. So beautiful. Not a refined, graceful beauty. His was raw, masculine and terrifying. So incredible she ached when she looked at him. "But know this, my darling, your command stops here. For now you are mine." He let his finger trail over her cheek, his dark eyes boring into hers. "If you want this, I will give it you. But the terms will be mine."

"This is my repayment," she said. "I agreed to nothing else."

"And that is where you miscalculated, my little warrior. For in this, I am nothing short of a conquerer."

"And I no less a warrior."

"I would expect nothing else. But in the end, I will stake my claim. Run from me now, if you do not want that."

She could hardly breathe. Could hardly think. But she didn't want to think. She wanted to focus on what he made her body feel. Because this, this release that she was chasing with him, overpowered the feelings in her chest.

This desire won out above all else, and she so desperately needed for it to continue to do so. And she did not want to run.

His hands went to the waistband of his pants and he pushed them down his legs. She did gasp, virginal shock coursing through her, when she saw him naked and erect.

This was different than when she'd seen him in the lake, but she hadn't been prepared for just how different. Just how much larger he would be.

Neither had she been prepared for her body's response. She might not know exactly what she wanted, but her body did. Her internal muscles pulsed, the ache between her legs intensifying.

"Let me see you," he said. "I am at a disadvantage, for you have seen me twice, and I have only ever been teased by promises of your body."

She just sat there, staring at him, feeling too dazed to follow instruction.

He approached the bed, his hands going to the front of her dress, where it was fastened together with hooks and eyes. "Consider this *my* payment," he said. "For all that was stolen from me. For I have not touched a woman since that day. And it is fitting that you are the one who has returned desire to me."

"A fair exchange then," she said. "And in the end, perhaps neither will owe the other anything?"

"Perhaps," he said, his tone raw.

He pushed the little metal clasps apart at the front of her dress and started to part the silken fabric, slowly and deliberately. Her breasts were bare beneath the heavy material. She wasn't generously endowed there, so unless she was engaging in physical combat, there was little need for her to wear undergarments.

She wished for one now. For one additional buffer between her skin, the cool air of the room, and Ferran's hot gaze.

He pushed the dress from her shoulders, leaving her in the light pants she'd been wearing beneath them, and nothing more. He looked at her breasts, his admiration open. "You are truly beautiful. Let your hair down for me."

She pulled her braid from behind her and took the band from around the bottom, sifting her fingers through the black silk and letting it loose to fall around her shoulders, all the way down to her waist. She let the loose strands cover her breasts.

"That's a tease," he said. "Giving me only one thing that I want at a time. I want it all. I have waited long enough. Stand."

She obeyed the command, because she was more than willing to follow orders now. She was not the expert here. She had nothing but a deep, primal instinct pushing her forward, and if she stopped to think too hard, nerves were waiting in the background to take hold. They had no place here. They were not allowed to overshadow her desire.

He remained sitting at her feet on the mattress, and he reached up and tugged her pants down, along with her underwear, leaving her completely bare before him, with him on his knees, right at eye level with the most secret part of her.

"Ferran…"

He leaned forward and pressed a kiss to her thigh, then to her hip bone, his lips perilously close to…to…her. To places on her she didn't know men might want to kiss.

"You want my passion used for your pleasure, Samarah? You demand it? Then you must submit to it."

"I…I will," she said.

"Do not fight me."

"I won't."

He tightened his hold on her. "Do not fight what we both want. I feel that you're about to flee from me."

"I'm not," she said, her throat tightening, her heart fluttering.

"Liar," he said, his lips skimming the sensitive skin on her inner thigh. "Spread your legs for me," he said.

She obeyed. Because he would know the best way to do this. That she did trust. And he was right, if she wanted his passion, demanded it, then she had to accept it. Not try to control it.

He leaned in again, his tongue sliding through her inner folds, across the sensitive bud there before delving in deep.

"Ferran." She grabbed hold of his shoulders to keep herself from falling, her legs shaking, the mattress wobbling beneath her feet. He anchored her with his hands, holding tightly to her hips as he pressed in deeper, increasing the pressure and speed of his strokes over her wet flesh.

Her stomach tightened, pleasure a deep, unceasing pressure building deep inside of her until she thought she might not be able to catch her breath. Everything in her tightened so much she feared she was turning to glass, so fragile and brittle she would shatter if he pushed against her too hard.

He kept going, adding his hands, pushing a finger deep inside of her, the sensation completely new and entirely different to anything that had come before.

He established a steady rhythm, pushing in and out of

her, the friction so beautiful, so perfect, she very nearly did break. She held back, rooted herself to earth by biting her tongue, by gritting her teeth so hard she feared they'd crack.

Because she was afraid to let herself go over the edge again. Afraid of what her release would bring this time.

"Give it to me, Samarah," he said. "Give me your pleasure."

"I can't…I can't."

"You can," he said, adding a second finger as he continue to lick and suck her. He stretched her, a slight pain hitting as he did, and she used that to help pull her back again.

"I'm afraid," she said.

"Don't be. I will catch you."

He leaned in again, the hot swipe of his tongue hitting just the right timing with his fingers, and then, she couldn't fight it anymore. She let go. Her hands moved away from his shoulders as her orgasm crashed over her. Only Ferran kept her on her feet. Only Ferran kept her there. And she trusted him to do it.

She didn't try to keep herself standing, because she knew he would. Because he'd promised her.

He laid her down on the mattress afterward, rising up to kiss her lips, deep and long. She could taste her own desire there, mingled with his. His shaft was hard and hot against her hip, evidence of the fact that he'd given, again, while taking nothing for himself.

Evidence also, of the fact that he'd enjoyed what he'd done for her. A sweep of heat, of pride, pure feminine power, rolled through her. He had enjoyed doing that to her. Had relished the taste of her. He wanted her, even as he told her to run.

She didn't know why it made her feel the way it did. Didn't know why it made her feel so powerful. Only that it did. Only that it spurred her on. And this time, she didn't want to run after her climax. She wanted to stay. She wanted more. Because she couldn't be embarrassed by what he'd made her feel.

Not when he was feeling it, too.

She shifted their position and parted her thighs, the blunt head of his erection coming up against the slick entrance to her body.

"I tried to prepare you," he said, his voice strangled. 'But it will still hurt.'

"I am not afraid of pain, Ferran," she said, sliding her hands down his back, feeling his muscles shift and tense beneath her fingertips. "I am not afraid of you."

"I do not wish to hurt you."

"But in order for us to join, you have to. So don't worry. Please, Ferran, I want you. I want this."

He started to push inside of her, slowly, gently. He stretched her, filled her. It did hurt, but not as much as she'd expected. It was only foreign, and new. But wonderful. Like every other pain he'd caused her physically, it was good.

He started to pull back and she locked her ankles over his, their eyes meeting. "Ferran, don't stop."

"I won't," he said, thrusting back inside of her, deep and hard, filling her completely.

She held on to him, getting adjusted to having him inside of her. She tilted her head and looked at him. His eyes were closed, the veins in his neck standing out, his jaw clenched tight. He looked as if he was in terrible pain. She kissed his cheek and a rough sound rumbled in his chest.

"Don't hold back now," she said.

"I am trying not to hurt you," he said, kissing her hard and deep.

When he separated from her lips, she was breathless. "You aren't."

He seemed to take that as permission. He started to move inside of her, slowly at first. Achingly so. Building all of that lovely, orgasmic tension in her again. Starting from the beginning, and this time, he brought her even higher. Further. Faster.

His rhythm grew fractured, his breath shortening. She shifted her legs, wrapped them higher around his waist and moved with him. He braced one hand on the mattress, by her head, and wrapped the other around her, pulling her against him, his movements hard and fast.

His eyes met hers, and she slowly watched his control break. She could see it, in the dark depths. Could see as he started to lose his grip. Sweat beaded on his forehead, his teeth ground together.

Watching him, seeing him like this, so handsome, so on edge, pushed her closer, too. Then he thrust inside her, hard, his body hitting against the part of her that cried out for release. As it washed over her in waves, she leaned in and bit him on the neck.

A harsh, feral sound escaped his lips, and he stiffened above her, his shaft pulsing deep inside of her. And she relished it. Reveled in his utter loss of control.

He moved away from her as if he'd been shocked, his chest heaving, his muscles shaking. He got off the bed and started collecting his clothes.

"Ferran…"

"That should not have happened."

"But it did," she said, the words sounding thick and stupid. She sat up and pushed her hair out of her face. "It did." A strange surge of panic took hold as Samarah tried to process what had happened. As she tried to deal with the fact that he was regretting what had passed between them.

She had given him, the man who had been her enemy all her life, her body, and now he was telling her what a mistake it had been. Shame lashed at her as she remembered the first night she'd met him.

I would sooner die.

And I would sooner kill you.

Oh, how she had fallen.

You did not fall. You jumped.

"You don't know what you want," he said. "You're an innocent." He tugged his pants on and turned away from her.

Even as she battled with the shame inside of her, his words ignited her anger. "Hardly. I was a virgin, but that does not equate to innocence."

"Well, I am a murderer." He pulled his shirt over his head, concealing his body from her view. "Compared to me, everyone is an innocent. Good night, Samarah. In the morning, if you are still here, and if I am still here, we will speak."

"Are you afraid I'll kill you?"

He lifted a shoulder. "I trust you to act in an honorable manner."

He walked out of her bedroom and closed the door behind him. Leaving her naked. And very, very confused.

She had slept with her father's murderer. She had wanted him.

She had laid herself bare to her enemy and joined herself to him. The man she had sworn to kill. The man she had agreed to marry. The man who heated her blood and showed her desire she'd never known possible.

Why could things never be simple? This future he had offered had seemed such a miraculous thing in many ways, but the strings attached were different, unexpected. The war, the one she had sought to wage in a physical manner, had moved inside of her body.

What she wanted, right now, was to forget everything. To process what it meant to be intimate with another person for the first time. But her lover was gone. And even if he were here, it wouldn't be that simple.

He would still be Ferran. She would still be Samarah. She had never felt more alone than she did in that moment. She had spent years in near isolation, with no friends and no family, and here, with the imprint of his fingertips still burning on her skin, she felt completely abandoned.

She rolled over onto her stomach and curled up into a ball.

She felt utterly changed. By Ferran. By his confession. By his touch. And she would have to figure out what to do about both.

One thing she knew for certain, she would not allow his touch to transform her into a quivering mass. She had survived all manner of things; she would not allow herself to implode now.

She repeated the words she'd said to Ferran, just before he had touched her. Before he'd altered her entirely.

"I am still a warrior."

CHAPTER ELEVEN

FERRAN SUPPOSED HE shouldn't be too surprised by Samarah storming into the dining room early the next morning in her workout gear, her long dark hair restrained in a braid.

He also supposed he shouldn't be too surprised by the feral, tearing lust that gripped him the moment he saw her. Sixteen years of celibacy, burned away by this fearsome, beautiful creature.

"You're not exactly dressed for our meeting with the event planner," he said, gritting his teeth, trying to get a handle on himself.

"And you're not exactly dead, so perhaps you should just be grateful."

"It's true," he said, lifting his mug to his lips, "I suppose after last night, I should be happy that you allowed that."

"Again, I find myself merciful."

"I have no doubt. And are you here to tell me you're leaving, Sheikha? Though, I must warn you, I will not allow it."

"A change in tune from last night."

"After what happened, there is no way you can go."

She held up her hand and showed him the ring on her finger. "As it is, I've decided to stay."

"How is this possible?"

"I have nowhere else to go. I get thrown in your dungeon, I get sent back to the streets of Jahar, and neither option is entirely palatable to me. So I'm staying here. I find sheikha-hood much preferred to street urchinhood. Imagine that."

"I would ensure you were cared for."

"And I would live on your terms. This way I have my own source of power and visibility in the public eye. I have my rightful position. It is the only way."

"Why are you not angry with me?"

"Perhaps I am," she said, her expression cool, impassive. "Perhaps this is simply me lying in wait."

There was something about the way she said it that sent a slug of heat through him, hitting him hard in the gut. Because it made him think of last night. Of her soft hair sifting through his fingers, of her softer skin beneath his palms.

It made him think of what it had been like to be inside her. A storm of rage and fire, of all the passion she'd asked for.

And in that passion, he had dishonored her. At least, he had not done what his mother would have expected from him with the daughter of their neighboring country. A virgin princess. He would have been expected to honor her. To never touch her until marriage vows had been spoken, until she was protected.

Now, he could not send her away. It was impossible. A bigger sin than the one he'd already committed.

More weakness. How he despised it. How he despised himself. A jailer now, by necessity, because he had ensured now that they must marry.

"If so, then I suppose it's no less than I deserve," he said. "Although, marriage is a life sentence, and some might argue a life sentence is more of a punishment."

"Glad to be your punishment," she said. "I always knew I would be your reckoning. Why did you leave me alone last night?"

"What?"

"You heard me. Why did you leave me alone last night?"

"Because, it was a shameless loss of control on my part."

"You made me feel ashamed," she said.

"That was not my intention."

"Regardless," she said, her voice trembling. "You did. We have a history thick with death and hatred. But in that moment, I was just a woman. And seeing your disgust—"

"At myself. One moment I confessed to stabbing your father in the back, the next you begged me to have sex with you. It was, without a doubt, the strangest encounter I've ever had with a woman."

She frowned, her cheeks turning a dark rose. "I'm not sure how I feel about my only experience with a man being called strange."

"Do you think it's common to go from death threats to making love?"

"Does it matter what's common?"

"I handled you too roughly."

"You handled me in exactly the right way," she said. "During sex. Not after. After…I find you in much fault on the way you behaved after."

"How would you know I treated you in the right way?"

"Because. I know what feels good to me. I know what creates…release."

"Orgasms," he said, not feeling in the mood to be considerate of her inexperience. If she thought she could handle it, then she'd have to be able to handle the discussion of it in frank terms.

"Yes," she said, the color in her cheeks deepening. "Obviously I know what gives me orgasms, and clearly, it is something you know how to accomplish. So you handled me correctly. I think we can both agree on that."

"Do you know what virgins deserve?"

"Do you even remember being one? How would you know?"

"This isn't about me," he said.

"Like hell it's not," she grumbled.

"Virgins deserve candles, and lovemaking and marriage vows."

"Do they? Did your first time come complete with those things? If so, I feel I should tell you, I've no interest in sharing you with another wife. And I find candlelight overrated."

"I'm a man. It's different."

"Oh? Really? Because I'm a woman and therefore must be coddled? Because for some reason my body is your responsibility and not mine?" Her face wasn't smooth now, not unreadable. She was angry. Finally. "If that's the case, where were you when I shivered in the cold? Where were you when I was alone and starving? Where the hell were you when men approached me and offered me shelter for sex? Or just demanded that I lie down and submit to them? Or perhaps, I should have taken them up on it? Since I clearly don't know what I need, perhaps they did?"

"That is not what I'm saying, Samarah," he said. "Hell. I didn't know.... I didn't..."

"Because in so many ways, you are the innocent here, Ferran. I have lived in the dark. You only played in it for the afternoon."

"The thing about something like that is that it never leaves you," he said. "On that you can trust me. You know, even if you've cleaned blood it shows beneath fluorescent lights. That's how I feel. That no matter how many years pass, no matter how clean I think I am, how far removed... it doesn't ever really go away. The evidence is there. And all I can do is make sure I never become the man I was in that moment ever again."

"This is one of the many things about my association with you that troubles me, Ferran," she said, grabbing her braid and twisting it over her shoulder.

"Only one? Do you have a list?"

She lifted her brows. "It's quite long. I made it last night. About what I want. About what all this means for me. And about what I find problematic about you."

"Is it a physical list?"

She nodded. "But this is just one of the things. Before you, everything was black-and-white to me. I hated you for what you did. I didn't have to know your side. I didn't have to see multiple angles. I just had to know you were responsible for the death of my father. But now I know you. Now I've heard your side. I should hate you more, knowing you ended my father's life, and yet I find it only makes me feel worse for you. Because coupled with it, comes the revelation that my father killed your mother. That you saw it. That…in your position, I would have acted the same, and that in many ways, had you not made him pay for what he'd done, I would have judged you a coward."

"I should have had him go to trial, Samarah. That would have been the right thing to do in the black-and-white world. In the one I aspire to live in."

"I think of that day like being in the middle of a war zone. It's how I remember it. I was just a child, and I saw very little. I was so lucky to be protected. My mother ensured that I was protected though…have you ever considered my father would have come for us next? For her? Would he have come for me too, Ferran, ultimate vengeance on my mother, if you hadn't acted as you did?

"Samarah…you're assigning heroism to me, and that is one thing you should never do. It's conjecture. Who knows what would have happened?"

"Yes, who knows? I only know what did. But now I know it from more angles. I miss my blinding conviction. The less I knew, the easier it all was. I could just…focus on one thing in particular."

"Your rage for me."

"Yes. And I could move forward, using that as my target. And now? Now everything has expanded and there are so many more possibilities. For what my life could be. For what I could do with myself and my purpose. But it's scarier, too."

"Scarier than gaining access to my palace? Being thrown in a dungeon? Facing possible trial?"

"Yes. Because when I was in that state I didn't want anything. I had accepted that I would probably die carrying out my mission, and that meant an end to... Life has been so hard. I've had no great love for it. But you came in and you offered me more, and the moment you did...things started to change. Now...now I don't want to turn away. I don't want to go back to how it was. And yet...and yet in some ways I do. It makes no sense to me, either."

He laughed. It was an absurd thing to do under the circumstances. Neither he nor Samarah had anything to laugh about. And yet, he couldn't help it. It was as if she was discovering emotions for the first time. Discovering how contrary it could be to be human.

"Is this your first experience with such confusion?" he asked.

"Yes," she said. "Emotions are wobbly. Conviction isn't."

"I'm very sorry to have caused you...feelings."

"Thank you," she said. "I'm...sorry in many ways to be experiencing them. Though not in others. Really, is it always like this?"

"Not for me," he said. "I'm not overly given to emotion."

"I suppose you aren't. Though, passion seems to be a strong suit of yours."

"No, it's a weakness."

She let out a long breath. "You're getting off topic. I have my list." She reached into the pocket of her athletic shorts and pulled out a folded piece of paper. "Now that I'm not merely surviving, there are some things I would like. I would like to be comfortable," she said, unfolding the paper and looking at it. "I would like to be part of something. Something constructive. Something that isn't all about breaking a legacy, but building a new one."

"Lofty," he said, standing, his stomach tightening as he looked at her, his beautiful, brave fiancée, who didn't seem to be afraid of anything, least of all him. She should be. She should have run. He'd given her the chance and she had not.

Why had she not run? Any normal woman would have turned away from him. From the blood on his hands.

She should be afraid.

He moved nearer to her, fire burning through his blood. A flame to alcohol, impossibly hot and bright. She should be afraid. He wanted to make her afraid. Almost as badly as he wanted her to turn to him and lean in, press her lush body against his chest.

"Is that your entire list?" he asked.

"No," she said, her voice steady. "I want to feel like I have a life. Like I have…"

"Sex," he said, leaning in, running his thumb over the ridge of her high cheekbone. "Is sex on your list?"

He let his hand drift down the elegant line of her neck, resting his palm at the base of her throat. He knew that she wouldn't fear his wrath. She would fight him to the death if need be. Here was where he had the undisputed upper hand. Here was where his experience trumped hers.

He felt her pulse quicken beneath his thumb. "I don't know."

"If you stay, there is no option, do you understand?" He slid his thumb along her tender skin. "You are my prisoner in many ways."

And it was true. A hard truth that settled poorly.

"It is better than the streets," she said, arching a brow.

"A high compliment," he said.

"It is," she said. "For in the beginning, I would have said death was better than this."

"Oh, my little viper." He moved his hand upward and cupped her jaw. "You are so honest."

"I am not," she said.

"Your eyes. They tell me too much." Liquid, beautiful and dark as night, they shone with emotion. Deep. Unfathomable. But the presence of that emotion twisted at his gut. Convicted him.

"Do not trust me, Samarah," he said, his voice rough. "I don't trust me."

"I don't trust anyone."

"See that you don't. You may be a warrior. You may be a strong fighter. You may not hesitate to cut my throat… now. But in the bedroom, I have the experience."

"Sixteen years celibate," she said.

He wrapped one arm around her waist and drew her to him, holding her chin tight, pressing her breasts tight to his chest. "And yet," he said. "I had the power over your body. Do you deny it?"

Dark eyes shimmered, her cheeks turning pink. She caught her breath, pressing her breasts more firmly against him. "No," she said, her voice choked.

Oh, Samarah. She revealed too much to him.

He wanted to press her back against the wall, wanted to take her. To show her that he was not a man to toy with. To prove he wasn't a man to trust.

He released her, moved away from her. The distance easing his breath. "Now, unless you're planning on wearing workout clothes to meet with the event coordinator, you may want to go change."

"Yes, I may. Thank you. How thoughtful." She turned away from him, head down, and walked out of the room.

The twisting sensation in his gut intensified. He was her jailer. Not her fiancé. Being with her…it was akin to force.

He gritted his teeth as pain lashed through his chest. No. He would not force her. He had not. What had happened last night could not be changed, but the future could. At the very least, he would begin showing her the respect a sheikha was due.

CHAPTER TWELVE

SAMARAH HUNG OUT in the corridor, listening to the sounds of people inside the grand ballroom of the palace. She was still a little bit nervous in large gatherings like this. More so now that she was a focal point for attention. And she felt as if there was nowhere to hide.

As palace staff, no one had noticed her. As the sheikh's fiancée? Yes, she was certainly going to be noticed. Especially in the green-and-gold gown that had been sent for her. It had yards of fabric, the skirt all layered, billowing folds. The sleeves went to her elbows, sheer and beaded, with matching details on the bodice, disappearing beneath the wide, gold belt that made her waist look impossibly small. It also kept her posture unreasonably straight, since it was metal.

A matching chain had been sent for her hair, an emerald in the centerpiece that rested on her forehead. She *did* like the clothes, but less now when she felt so conspicuous. And without Ferran.

She relied on his presence much more than she'd realized until this moment. Of course, after she'd gone and read him her list she felt more than a little embarrassed to see him again.

Though, really, she'd been naked with him, so nothing should embarrass her with him now. It did, though, because he'd run afterward. Because, when they'd spoken earlier, his intensity had unsettled her.

He was right. In this, this need, he was the master. And he could easily use it against her.

How sobering to realize that if the sheikh of Khadra were to defeat her, it wouldn't end in screams of terror, but in pleasure.

Just then, she saw him. Striding down the hall. He was wearing white linen pants and a tunic, his concession to traditional dress. She'd noticed that he never seemed to bother with robes.

She didn't feel so conspicuous now. Because surely everyone's eyes would be on Ferran. He was taller than most men, so he always stood out for that reason. But he was also arrestingly handsome. She'd kissed his lips, touched his face, his body. And she was still struck to the point of speechlessness by his beauty.

Or maybe it was even more intense now. Because she'd been with him. Because she knew what wicked pleasure his perfect lips could provide. Because she knew what a heaven it was to be in his strong arms, to be held against his muscular chest.

"You're late," she said, clasping her hands in front of her.

He paused, his dark eyes assessing. "You're beautiful."

She blinked hard. He'd said that to her before. But for some reason it hit her now, how rarely she'd heard that in her life. Not when it was said in a nonthreatening tone. Men on the streets had called out to her, but they had frightened her. Her father and mother had called her beautiful, but when she was a child.

Ferran said it to her just because. Because he believed it. Because it was what he saw when he looked at her. And for some reason, just then, it meant the world to her.

"Thank you," she said. "I think you're beautiful, too."

"I'm not often called beautiful," he said, one corner of his mouth lifting.

"Well, neither am I."

"That will change."

"Have you accepted than I'm not leaving you?" she asked.

"I'm not sure," he said, holding his arm out to her.

She took a step forward and curled her fingers around his forearm. "You have my word," she said. "My word is good. I want you to know that, at first, I didn't intend to marry you."

"Is that so?"

"I intended to bide my time. And carry out my plan."

He tightened his hold on her, his other hand crossing his body and settling over hers. "I had a feeling that might be the case."

"But it's not the case now. I will marry you," she said. "I will be your wife. And I will not leave you. So don't try to scare me away. You'll only be disappointed."

"Is that so?"

"Yes. Because I do not scare. And just because I don't intend to kill you doesn't mean I won't punch you in the face."

"I'll endeavor to avoid that," he said. "Are you ready to go in?"

"What are we supposed to do?"

He lifted a shoulder. "Wave. Eat some canapés. Dance."

"I have never danced with anyone."

"I'll lead," he said. "You have nothing to worry about. You are strong, Samarah, I do know that. But there's no shame in letting someone else take control sometimes. It can even be helpful."

"All right. In the bedroom and on the dance floor, you may lead," she said, testing him. He had tried to prove his power over her earlier, and while he had done so, while he had left her quivering, aching and needing in a way she hadn't thought possible, she rebelled against it. She wanted to push back.

Because if there was one thing in life Samarah didn't understand, it was defeat. She had spent her life in a win or die battle, and as she was here, breathing, living, it was clear she had always won.

And that meant, in this moment, she was determined to keep fighting.

"We'll discuss the bedroom later," he said. "After our wedding."

"What?" It was such a stark contrast to what he'd said earlier. To the implied promise in his words.

"We have to go in now."

"Wait just a second. You said…"

"Did you think you were going to seize control back?" he said, dark eyes glittering. "You, and my body, no matter how it might ache for you, do not control me."

His words, the intensity in his eyes, stopped her voice, stole her breath.

"You do not want me out of control," he said, his face hard. "I remind you. Now, come with me."

He led her into the ballroom, and as they drew farther in, nearer to the crowd of people, panic clawed at her. How was she supposed to smile now? How was she supposed to deal with all those eyes on her after what Ferran had just said?

They were formally announced, and Ferran lifted their joined hands, then bowed. She followed suit and dipped into a curtsy, shocked she remembered how, everything in her on an autopilot setting she hadn't known she'd possessed. Her muscle memory seemed to be intact. Princess training obviously lurked in the back of her mind.

"Who are all these people?" she asked, still reeling from the change. From his uncivilized words in the hall to this venue that was all things tame and beautiful.

"Dignitaries, diplomats. From here and abroad. Anyone who feels they may have a political stake in our union."

"Including the Jaharan rulers, I imagine?"

"Yes," he said. "This is the first time they've been at a political event in Khadra since..."

"Yes. Obviously."

"Already, we have done some good."

"I guess that remains to be seen," she said. "Just because they're here doesn't mean... Well, I guess I'm pessimistic when it comes to politics."

"I can see how you would be."

"But I can see that people are happy to be here. I feel like...I feel like this is good."

They spent the next hour wandering through the party, making light conversation with everyone they came across. This wasn't the time for any heavy-hitting, political negotiation, but everyone seemed very aware that it was the time to get on Ferran's radar.

And people seemed to want to talk to her, as well. As if she carried influence. As if she mattered. It was so very different to the life she'd had before she'd come here. So very different to the life she'd ever imagined she might have.

"Now," Ferran said, "I think it's time for you to dance with me."

"I think I could skip the dancing," she said, looking out across the expanse of marble floor, to where gorgeous, graceful couples twirled in circles, in eddies of silk and color. She doubted very much she would be that graceful. Martial arts was one thing. She kept time to the beat of the fight. Of her body.

She wasn't sure if she could follow music.

"I will lead you," he said. "As I think I've established."

"So you have," she said, but in this instance she was grateful.

Sex and dancing were Ferran's domain, it seemed.

He led her through the crowd, and to the center of the floor. The other dancers cleared extra space for them, as if in deference to Ferran's royal personage.

He grasped her hand, his arm curling around her back as he tugged her against his chest. She lost her breath then, captivated wholly by the look in his eyes. So dark and intense. Simmering passion. The kind he'd unleashed last night. The sort she craved again.

And he was telling her now that they would wait. That he could control himself.

She didn't like it. It made her feel powerless. It...hurt her. And she would not have it.

She'd waited all of her life. She'd spent countless nights cold and alone, and she'd be damned if she'd spend any more that way, not now that she'd been with him.

"I think we need to discuss what you said in the hall," she said.

"Which thing?"

"About abstaining until the wedding," she said.

He looked around them. "Are we having this conversation now?"

"I take your point. However, you just said some very explicit things in the hall and then we were cut off. And I'm not done. I just thought I should tell you that I'm not doing that."

"Excuse me?"

"It might interest you to know that I have obtained some very brief underthings."

"Samarah..."

"They're intended to arouse you, and I have it on good authority they will."

He looked torn between anger, amusement and, yes, arousal. "Whose authority?"

"Lydia's. She provided them for me when I asked."

"And they are meant to..."

"Arouse you," she said, her face heating. "I had thought, seeing as I was to be your wife, I should set out to…behave like a wife. And then you told me…you told me no."

"Tell me about them," he said, his voice lowering, taking on that hard, feral tone he'd had in the hall, as he leaned nearer to her.

"The uh…the bra is…made of gems. Strung together. It shows…a lot of skin."

"Does it?"

"Yes," she said, swallowing hard, her face burning.

"And the rest?"

"I don't feel like you deserve to know," she said, lifting her head so she was looking in his eyes, so their noses nearly touched. "If you want abstinence, you don't want to know about my underwear."

"That isn't the case. And I never said I *wanted* to abstain. Only that it's the right thing."

"For who?"

"For you."

She growled. "Stop doing that. Stop trying to protect me. I don't want you to protect me I want you to…to…"
Love me.

Where had that come from? She did not need that thought. No, she didn't. And now she would forget she'd ever had it. And she would never have it again.

"I just need you to be with me," she said, which was much more acceptable. "I'm tired of being alone. Now that I don't have to sleep by myself anymore I would just… rather not."

He pulled her closer, his lips pressed against her ear. "Yes, *habibti*, but do you want me? Do you want my body? Do you want me to touch you, taste you. Be inside you. If all you want is companionship, I would just as soon buy you a puppy."

"I want your body," she said, leaning in and pressing a

kiss to his neck. "I want you. I don't want a puppy. I'm a woman, not a child. I know the difference between simple loneliness and desire."

"And you desire me?" he asked, his eyes growing darker.

"Yes."

"Tell me what you desire."

"Here?" she asked, looking around them.

"Yes. Here. Tell me what you want from me. What you want me to do to you. You said you wanted my passion. You said you weren't afraid. Now tell me. Remember, I have much more practice than you at abstaining when temptation is present. So if you intend to break my resolve, you'd better damn well shatter it. If you want to take my control, you prepare for what you will unleash."

"I…" She felt her cheeks get hotter, and she wanted to shrink away. To tell him nothing. To tell him something quick, and unexplicit. Something dishonest that had nothing to do with what she'd actually been thinking about doing with him.

But then she remembered her own words.

I do not run.

She tilted her head up and leaned in so that her lips were near his ear, her heart hammering hard.

"I want to take this dress off for you," she said. "While you sit and watch. I want to watch your face as your need for me takes you over." She swallowed hard. "Then…then I want to…I want to get onto the bed, on your lap, and kiss your lips."

"You want to do all of that?" he asked.

"I'm not finished."

"I may need to be," he said. "This doesn't sound very much like you're planning to let me lead."

"You were the one who said I should let you lead in the bedroom. I never agreed to it."

"We were not taking a vote," he said, his tone hard.

"I deserve to get what I want from this marriage, too."

"You aren't talking about marriage. You're talking about now."

She lifted a shoulder. "Don't I deserve to be certain of the manner of man I'm binding myself to? You said that yourself."

"And you think seducing me will reveal me to you more than my confessions already have?"

"It's the one thing you've held back for the past sixteen years. That makes me feel like it's important."

Ferran wanted to turn away from her, and yet, he found it impossible. She was too beautiful. Too powerful. It wasn't simply beauty. It never had been. She was a glittering flash of temptation that could easily be his undoing.

But she was also to be his wife. And that meant he had to get a handle on himself with her, didn't it? That meant that he had to be able to sleep with her, to make love with her, without losing himself.

Here before him was the challenge. If he turned her away now, then he proved that she held the power to take him back to where he'd been before.

She didn't. No matter how strongly she called to him. No matter how much he wanted her, he could control it. He could have her tonight, and feel nothing beyond release.

It didn't matter what she wore, what she did. He would prove to himself he had the control.

"All right, Samarah. You want me? You want my body? Tonight?"

"Yes."

"Now?" he asked.

"Now…we're…Ferran, not now."

He pulled her closer, staring down into her wide, dark eyes. "If you want me, *habibti*, you will have me on my terms."

He released her from the close hold they were in, then

laced his fingers through hers, drawing her through the crowd of people, out into the gardens. The night was cool, the grounds insulated from view by palm trees and flowering plants.

And no doubt his security detail had seen him exit with Samarah. If for no other reason, no one would be following them out here.

He tugged her to him and kissed her, hard and deep. If this was what she wanted, it was what she would have. But he wouldn't be at her mercy. He wouldn't be taking orders from her. If she wanted him, she could have him.

And he would make her understand what that meant.

He cupped her chin, his thumb drifting along the line of her jaw as he continued to kiss her. To taste her. He could drown in it. He very nearly had before. Both when they'd kissed in the rain, and last night.

There were things about kissing a woman he hadn't remembered. How soft feminine lips were, the sounds they made. How it felt to be so close to someone living. To feel their heartbeat against your own.

Or maybe he hadn't forgotten. Maybe he'd just never noticed before.

But he did now. It was like slowly having feeling return to frozen limbs. To places that had been numb for years. So much so, he'd forgotten they were even there.

In his quest to be the best sheikh, to choke out all of his weaknesses, he'd forgotten he was a man. And the touch of Samarah's lips in his brought it all back with blinding clarity.

And with the clarity came a host of other things he'd spent years trying to deny. Fear. Anger.

He backed her against one of the walls that enclosed the garden from the rest of the world, taking her mouth with all the ferocity he possessed.

"You want this?" he asked again, kissing her cheek, her

neck, moving his hand to her breast. His whole body was shaking. He could hardly breathe. He could barely stand. Touching her like this...

It had nothing to do with how long it had been since he'd touched a woman. If he was honest, he had to confess that.

It was more. She was more.

He slid his palm over her curves, to the indent of her waist, over the rounded flare of her hip. He gathered up the material of her dress, curling his fingers around the heavy, beaded fabric.

"Ferran..."

"Scared, *habibti*?"

"No," she said. "But we're in the garden and..."

"And you said you wanted me. You do not get to dictate all the terms. If you want me, you will have me now."

He moved his hand between her thighs, felt the thin silk that separated the heart of her from his touch. He pushed it aside and growled when his fingertips made contact with slick flesh. "You do want me," he said, moving his thumb over the source of her pleasure.

She arched against him, her breathing coming in short, sharp bursts. More evidence of her need for him. He suddenly felt that he might require her more than air.

"Samarah," he said, sliding his fingers through her folds.

She pushed her knees together, forcing his hand more tightly against her body, her head falling back against the wall, her lips parted, an expression of ecstasy.

If he took her now, it would be over quickly. It would be so easy to undo his pants and thrust deep inside her, take them both to release.

But then he couldn't see her body. He couldn't touch her as he wanted, taste her as he wanted.

"I want to take you to bed," he said.

"I thought you wanted me here?"

"I do," he said. "Here and now, but I also want to be able

to see you." He moved his hand from between her thighs. "I want to touch you. I want to take my time."

He tugged her dress back into place.

"You can't expect me to walk back through there. We look...well, we must look like we've been doing exactly what we've been doing."

"I am certain we do. But I have no issue with it."

"I cannot figure you out."

"I've made the decision," he said, looking at her eyes, which were glittering in the dim lighting. And he could feel the desperation within himself. Could sense his own biting need to justify his actions.

But he'd decided he would do this. So surely that made it okay. Surely that meant he had reasoned it out. She was to be his wife. He repeated that fact in his mind. She was to be his wife, and that meant that he could be with her. That meant he had to be. It was duty and honor, and it had nothing to do with the heat in his blood.

And making sure he took his time and enjoyed it was for her. For his wife.

"Come with me," he said, holding out his hand.

She took it, delicate fingers curling around his. He flashed back to the moment in his bedroom, when those hands had struck at him. When she'd looked at him with fear and loathing. It was gone now. All of it. Replaced by a desire he wasn't certain he deserved from her.

But he needed it. Because they were getting married.

That was the only reason. For his people.

Not for himself.

But either way, he needed it.

He led her back through the garden, and into the brightly lit, glittering ballroom. She was flushed, her eyes bright. She looked very much like a woman who was on the brink of release, and suddenly, he was afraid that everyone in the room would know.

Not for himself, but for her. He didn't want to humiliate Samarah. He didn't want to expose her or hurt her. And yet he feared that was what he'd done. All he would ever do.

Not tonight. Tonight she would be his, and he would worry about the rest later.

He gritted his teeth and battled with himself. With his reasoning, his justifications.

Spare me. Spare us.

No. There was no place for that memory. Not in this. This wasn't the same. He could keep control, and have this.

He could keep her.

He led her out into the hall, then down the corridor, toward his chambers. Halfway through, he swept her up in his arms. "I have no patience," he said, striding onward.

"I doubt this is faster," she said, her arms looped around his neck.

"But you are near me," he said.

Why had he said that? Why was he feeling this. Why was he feeling anything? Why did it matter?

He kicked the door to his bedchamber open and Samarah jumped in his arms. "I found that arousing," she said, her eyes locked with his.

"Did you?" he asked.

"I like your intensity," she said. "I like that you want me. No one has wanted me in so long."

He set her down and she leaned into him, curling her fingers into the lapels of his shirt. "No one has wanted me in longer than I can remember. Until you. You want me. And that matters, Ferran..."

He bent and kissed her, slamming the bedroom door as he did, the sound echoing in the cavernous space. "My wanting you is not necessarily something to rejoice in," he said, dragging the edge of his thumb along her cheek. "I am broken, Samarah, in every way that counts."

And there was more honesty than he'd ever given even to himself.

"I don't care," she said. "I don't care."

"Samarah..."

She took a step away from him and reached behind her back before unclasping her belt and letting it fall to the ground. The top layer of her gown fell open and she shrugged it off, letting it slither to the floor, revealing the simple shift beneath.

The heavy silk conformed to her slender figure. It revealed very little skin, and yet he found the sight erotic. So sexy he could hardly breathe.

She started on the little buttons on the front of her garment. She let it fall away, revealing another layer beneath. A skirt with a heavy, beaded waistband that sat low on her hips, strips of gauzy, nearly translucent fabric covering her legs. Every movement parted the fabric, showed hints of tanned, shapely thighs.

The top was exactly as advertised, and yet, nothing she'd said had prepared him for the deep, visceral reaction he had to it. Glittering strings of beads strung across her golden skin, conformed to the curve of her breasts, hints of skin showing through.

It wasn't the gems that held him captive, not the sparkling. No, he was trying to look past that, beyond that, to her. Because she was more beautiful than any gem.

"Sit on the bed," she said.

"I told you this would be on my terms."

"And I did not agree. I have a fantasy that I wish to fulfill."

"You have a fantasy?" he asked, his heart rate ticking up.

"Yes. You know, Master Ahn rented out the studio several nights a week to a dance teacher. I never took lessons, but I did watch. Sit on the bed."

He obeyed, his eyes on her, a ferocious tug in his gut.

"Take your shirt off," she said.

He tugged at his tie, then worked the buttons on his shirt before shrugging it, and his jacket off onto the bed.

She shifted her hips to the side, slowly, then back the other way, the motion fluid, controlled. "I used to practice in my room sometimes," she said. "But there was no practical use for dancing in my life. Still, I know what my body can do. I know how to move it. How to control my muscles. Dancing came naturally in many ways."

She shifted her shoulders, then reached behind her head and released her hair, letting it fall in loose, glossy waves. She kept her hips moving in time with a rhythm that was all in her head. But he could feel it. He could feel it moving through her body and on into his.

She rolled her shoulders, down her arms, to her wrists, her fingertips curling upward, her head falling back. He shifted in his seat, desire rushing through his veins, beginning to push at the restraint that he prized so much.

That he depended on.

She met his eyes, then tipped her head back, her shoulders following, bending back until he was sure she would break herself if she went farther. She held the pose steady, no strain in her muscles, then she lifted herself back up slowly.

Such a fierce, wild creature she was.

A tiger pacing the bars...

"You did pay attention during the lessons."

"Yes," she said. "But I've never had anyone to dance for. I've never had any real reason to dance. But I did it anyway. Alone. Now...now I can do it for you. I don't understand this...how you've become the most essential person to me. But you have. I almost robbed myself of you."

"You almost robbed *myself* of me," he said, gritting his teeth, trying to keep from telling her to stop talking. Trying to keep himself from accepting what she was offering. From begging her for more.

"I did," she said, walking toward the bed, each movement a temptation. Another hit against the barricade. She put her hand on his cheek, her fingertips dragging across his skin, sending a sensual spark down into his gut that ignited, desire burning hot and hard, threatening to rage out of control.

She reached behind herself and released the hold on her top, the jewels sliding down to her waist before she managed to free herself of it entirely. She put one knee on the bed beside his thigh, her breasts so close one movement would allow him to suck a caramel nipple deep into his mouth.

But if he moved, he wouldn't be able to find out what she had planned next.

The temptation was torture. Sweet, perfect torture. He'd held himself back for years, but it had never felt like this. It had never been physical pain. To have so much beauty in front of him and to refuse to allow himself to touch it, to test himself in this way…it was intoxicating. A rush he couldn't define or deny.

She leaned in, putting her hand on his belt, her beasts so near his lips his mouth watered. She worked at his belt, her fingers deft, confident, like all of her movements.

She freed him from his slacks, her palm hot on his erection. He couldn't hold back the tortured sound that climbed his throat and escaped his lips.

"Do you like me touching you?" she asked. "No other woman has done this in a long time…" She squeezed him gently and he swore. "Did I hurt you?"

"No," he said. "And yes. You're right…it's been a long time. It makes it… No, I don't think it's the time. It's you. Because nothing ever felt like this before."

She smiled, her dark eyes glistening. She looked at him

as if he was a god. As if he was her hero, not her enemy. And he felt like the worst sort of bastard for stealing that moment. One he didn't deserve. One he could never hope to earn.

And for what? Because he had given her shelter when she had none? Because he had offered her prison or marriage? He should stop her. But he didn't. Instead he watched her face and soaked in the adoration. The need. He didn't deserve it. Dammit, he didn't deserve a moment of it and he was going to take it anyway.

Such was his weakness.

"I want to…could…" She slid down, her movements graceful, her knees on the floor, her body between his thighs. "I want to taste you."

"Samarah…" He should not allow this.

"Please." She looked up at him, and he knew he couldn't deny her. What man could deny a woman begging to allow her to take him in her mouth? Certainly not him. He had established that he was weak.

Maybe for the moment he would let his guard down fully. Maybe he would let her see it all. He forked his fingers through her silky hair, curling them inward, making a fist. Holding her steady.

She lowered her head and he allowed it, holding her back only slightly so he could catch his breath. So he could anticipate the moment she would touch him.

But when she did, it was nearly the end of it. Because there was no bracing himself for this. For the sheer, blinding pleasure of her hot, wet tongue on his skin. For the unpracticed movements she made, so sincere. Only for him.

She dipped her head and took him in deep. His hold tightened on her hair, his other hand holding tight to the bedspread. Trying to anchor himself to earth. To something.

"Samarah…" He said her name like a warning. A curse. A prayer. He needed her to stop. He needed her to keep going. He needed this because it made the past feel like less. Made it feel like maybe this need wasn't so wrong. Like maybe he wasn't so wrong.

Pleasure rushed up inside of him. Hot. Dangerous. Out of control.

He tugged her head upward and tried to catch his breath, tried to get a handle on the need that was coursing through his veins like fire.

"Not like that," he said, his words harsh in the stillness of the room. "I want to be inside you. Just like you said. You said you wanted that. Wanted me."

"I do."

"Show me, *habibti*. Show me."

She rose up slowly, her hands on the beaded band of her skirt. She pushed it down her hips slowly, then stepped out of the fabric, leaving her bare to him.

"You are water in the desert," he said, pulling her close, his face pressed against her stomach. He kissed her tender skin, tracing her belly button with the tip of his tongue. "You are perfection."

She put her arms around his neck, one knee pressed onto the mattress beside his thigh. Then she shifted and brought the other one up, too. "I want you, Ferran Bashar. You are not my enemy."

Words he didn't deserve. Words he would never deserve. And yet, he did not have the strength to turn her away.

She lowered herself onto his length, slowly, so slowly he thought his head might explode. And other parts of him. But if that happened, he wouldn't get to see this through to the end. And he desperately needed to. If only to watch her face while it happened. When she reached her peak. If he could see that again…maybe he would put up the walls after. And carry that with him.

He watched, transfixed as she took him in fully, her lips rounded, her eyes closed. The pleasure there was humbling.

More than he deserved. But he was of a mind to take it all, whether he deserved it or not.

He curved his arm around her waist, his palm resting on her hip. And he put his other hand on her chest bracing her as he thrust up inside her. She gasped, her eyes opening, locking with his.

"Yes," he said. "Look at me, Samarah. Look at me."

He shifted his hold, tightened the arm around her waist, cupped the back of her head with his other hand, his thumb drifting to her mouth. She turned her head and bit him. Lightly, just enough to send a short burst of pain through him, the sensation setting off a chain of sparks.

She moved over him, with him, and he held her tight, held her against him, tried to brace them both for what was coming.

He thrust up hard as he pulled her down against him and she cried out, his thumb braced against her lips as she shuddered out her release, her internal muscles tightening around him.

He moved his thumb and claimed her mouth in a searing kiss as he thrust inside her one last time and gave in to the need that was battering him, breaking him down. And he gave in to his own need. His own desire washing over him like a blinding wall of cleansing fire. Strong enough to burn away the past. Strong enough to burn away blood.

And when they were done, he pulled her onto the bed with him and held her close, their hearts beating together.

"Don't make me go," she said, burying her face in his chest.

"I doubt I could make you do anything you didn't want to do."

"I don't know about that," she said, moving against him, her breasts against his bare chest sending a fresh shock of desire through him. He couldn't blame the celibacy. This was all Samarah.

"Maybe someday we can go back to the palace by the ocean, Ferran," she said. He stiffened, dark memory pouring through him. Like black ink on white, it stained. It couldn't be stopped. "Maybe together we can make new memories there. Memories that aren't so sad. I remember loving it. I remember…almost loving you."

Her words choked him. Made his vision blur. He didn't deserve this. A man like him. She knew he'd killed her father but she didn't know how he'd felt. The rage. The decisive, brilliant rage that had made sinking his knife into the other man's back feel like a glorious triumph…

"I don't know that we should go back, Samarah."

"We won't let the past win, Ferran. You were the one who taught me that. You were the one who made me want more."

"I should not be the one who inspires you, little viper." He was her captor, nothing more. A man who went through life ruling with an iron fist and—he envisioned the past washed in a haze of red—when he had to, blood.

And that was the man who held her.

He had enslaved her, and she was thanking him. He had robbed her of her choice, and she gave him her body. He should go. He should leave her.

He started to roll away, but she held tight to him. He felt the hot press of her lips on his back. "Don't do that," she said. "Please don't."

He put his hand over hers, pinned it to his chest. Then he turned sharply, pulling her naked body against his as he kissed her, hard and deep. He didn't deserve this. He shouldn't take it. He had no right.

But he was going to take it anyway. He lowered her back down to the bed and settled between her thighs, kissing her neck, her shoulder, the curve of her breast. "I won't do it then," he said. "Why? When we can do this instead."

"Ferran, we should talk."

"I don't want to talk," he said, his voice rough. "I don't want to talk."

"Why not?"

"Because…" He kissed her again. "Because words are dangerous, and until I'm not feeling quite so dangerous… I don't think I should speak."

"Then we won't speak," she said.

And they didn't for the rest of the night.

CHAPTER THIRTEEN

THEIR WEDDING DAY was fast approaching and Samarah felt as if she was sleeping with a brick wall.

Ferran Bashar was nothing if not opaque. He didn't want to talk. He didn't want her to talk. He wanted to make love. Frequently. Constantly, some might say, and she was okay with that. But she wanted something else. Something more.

She wanted him to feel what she did, and she had no earthly way of knowing if he did. Because she felt as if she was butting up against a brick wall whenever she tried to find out.

She thought of the woman she'd been only a month ago, and she could scarcely remember her. Angry. Hopeless.

Now her whole life stretched before her, a life with Ferran. But she was afraid it would always be like this. He talked to her more before they'd started sleeping together. At least then they'd tried. Now it felt like he only wanted to see her at night.

It could not stand. Because when she'd chosen him, she'd done so with the intent of having a life. A real life. Everything she wanted. So she would damn well have it. She was tired of feeling nothing but hunger, cold and exhaustion. Tired of only seeing to the basics.

She wanted more. Whatever *more* might be. And she wanted it with him. If she could walk away now and do anything, *be* anything. Be with anyone, she wouldn't.

She would stay here. Because her home was with him. She felt as if her heart might even be with him. And that meant it was worth pushing for what she wanted, didn't it?

Yes, it did. She would not question herself. She adjusted the tape on her fists and strode into the gym, where she knew Ferran would be. He was probably hoping for a quiet workout. But she wasn't going to allow it.

Because she wasn't simply going to accept what he gave. She was going to break through the brick wall.

"Hello, *hayati*," she said. *My life.* Because that was what he was. He'd changed her life, given her new purpose. New hope. And she would do her best to give him the same.

Ferran turned, his broad chest glistening with sweat. Samarah licked her lips. She loved him like this. It made her think of pleasure. Of being in bed with him, because he often looked like this there. Out of breath, physically exhausted.

They were an athletic couple, and they were not only athletic in the gym. The thought made her face hot, even now.

"What are you doing here, Samarah?" he asked.

"I'm sorry, were you looking for an exclusive workout time?" she asked, approaching the punching bag and treating it to a crescent kick, sending it swinging.

Ferran caught it, holding it steady, a dark brow arched. "And if I were."

"Too bad. I'm not leaving." She crossed her arms beneath her breasts and cocked her head to the side. "I want to spar."

"Do you?" he asked.

"Yes. I feel like we're both getting complacent. But when I win, I expect something in return."

"Do you?"

"Yes. I'm going to ask a question, and you will answer truthfully."

He tilted his head back, his nostrils flaring. "You think so?"

"Are you afraid I'll win, Ferran? You know my moves. I have no size advantage. But I will make a rule about biting."

"What are we playing to?"

"First to five?" she asked.

"And what do I get if I win?" he asked. "You have not offered me incentive."

"What do you want?"

"If I win, you ask me no more questions."

His expression was hard, uncompromising.

"That is imbalanced," she said. "I'm only asking for one question, and you're asking for none, ever?"

"It is not my fault if you set your sights too low."

"I do not…"

"I do not have to answer any," he said. "So I suggest you fight if you have a hope of getting even one answer. I do not live on anyone else's terms."

"All right," she said, moving into position. "We have a deal."

He took his stance, his dark eyes meeting hers. "Ready?"

Yes. She was ready to fight for her life. For this new life she wanted, with this man.

"Ready," she said. And then without waiting, she advanced on him, landing a kick that was a more of a tap, to the side of his neck. "One!" she shouted.

He narrowed his eyes and sidestepped her next move, then grabbed her arm and pulled her toward him, tapping her cheek with his fist. "One," he said.

"Bastard," she hissed, rolling out of his hold and stepping away, backhanding him gently before turning and landing an uppercut to his chin. "Two, three."

He reached for her arm again and she hopped back, side-stepping and moving to his side, flicking a snap kick into his side. "Four," she said.

He turned and countered, but she blocked. He grabbed her around the waist and tugged her against him, her feet off the ground. She wiggled, pushing herself up higher into his arms and over his shoulder. Then she shouted and felt his arms loosen, the jolt from the noise offering her just enough give to use her weight to flip herself over his shoulder, land on her feet and plant her foot between his shoulder blades "Five," she said.

He turned, his chest heaving with the effort of breathing. She knew she looked the same, sweat running down her neck, her back. But she was fighting for her relationship with him. She was fighting for a break in his facade.

She bowed, a sign of respect for him, even in his defeat. He squared up to her and did the same.

"You owe me," she said. "One question. We're getting married in two days and I require this."

He said nothing, he just faced her, his dark eyes blank. "You have earned your question. Ask."

He looked more like a man facing the justice she'd promised just a month ago.

"What are you afraid of?"

"You think I am afraid, Samarah?"

"I know you are."

"Not of anything outside myself."

"What does that mean?"

"That is two questions," he said. "But I will indulge you. Here is your prize. I have to keep control. At all costs. Because that day taught me not just what manner of man your father was. But what manner of man I was. Do you know why I keep the tiger pacing the bars?" he asked, moving to her, resting his hand on her throat. "Because if I ever let him free, he will destroy everything in his path."

"Ferran you won't..."

"You can't say that, Samarah."

"Yes," she said, feeling desperate to combat the bleakness in his eyes.

"No, because it happened before. And you can never guarantee if won't again. Unless I keep control."

He lowered his hand and turned, leaving her there, bleeding inside, bleeding for him. For wounds that hadn't healed. For wounds in both of them she wasn't sure would ever heal.

Maybe that was the problem. Maybe when she'd looked ahead and saw a life she'd never thought possible she'd only been dreaming. Maybe a life like that could never really belong to her and Ferran.

Maybe they were simply too broken to be fixed.

The day of the wedding was bright and clear, like most other days in this part of the country. Ferran didn't believe in abstracts and signs, so he considered it neither a particularly good or bad omen.

He had kept himself from Samarah's bed as a necessity ever since they'd spoken in the gym. Ever since she'd forced him to confess the one thing he wanted most to erase from his past.

The wedding was to be small out of concession for Samarah's issues with crowds. And frankly, it suited him, as well. There would be dignitaries and approved members of the press.

It suited him because he still felt far too exposed, as if his defenses had been torn down. He'd confessed his deepest sin to her, his biggest weakness. And now he felt desperate to build everything back up so no one else could see.

So that he was strong again.

So that nothing could touch him.

He strode out of his room and walked down the corridor, toward the room where the marriage would take place. It

was far too hot to marry outside. They could have done so
if they were by the oasis, or the ocean, but he hadn't seen
the point in taking the trip out to the oasis.

He walked inside the room and looked at the guests,
seated and ready. He strode down the aisle, completely
deaf to the music, the faces of everyone present blurring.
He had no family, so there was no one of real importance.

He took his position, his hands clasped in front of his
body and waited. Only a few moments later, Samarah appeared in the doorway. She had an ornate gold band over
her head, a veil of white and embroidered gold covering
her head. Her gown was white, a mix of Western and Eastern traditions.

She looked like a bride. She looked like a woman who
deserved to have a man waiting for her who wasn't so terribly broken.

But she did not have that. She had him. And he wondered if he'd truly spared her anything when he'd offered
her marriage to him instead of prison.

She approached the raised platform and took his hand,
dark eyes never wavering. He was shaking to pieces inside,
and she looked as smooth and steady as ever.

The ceremony passed in a blur. He had no memory of
what he said. Of what she said. Only that they were married in the end. Only that Samarah was his wife, till death
ended it, and he could feel nothing but guilt.

He could give her nothing. He wouldn't. Opening himself up like that could only end in destruction.

They walked through the crowd of guests together, and
he didn't know if people clapped for them or not.

"I need to talk to you," Samarah said, as soon as they
were in the hall.

And he knew there was no denying her when she'd set
her mind to something. Not really. She was far too determined.

"We have a wedding feast to get to."

"It can wait."

"People are hungry," he said.

"It can start without us. I have a question for you."

"I didn't agree to more questions."

Samarah tugged him down the corridor and into a private sitting room, closing the doors behind them. "I don't care if you've agreed. Here is my question. Do you know why I married you?"

"To avoid prison. To secretly plot my death? To gain your position back as sheikha."

"The first moment I agreed, yes, it was to avoid prison. And after that? To plot your doom. Then when I let that go, to become a sheikha and have a future that wasn't so bleak. But that was all why I was planning on marrying you weeks ago. Do you know why I married you today?" she asked.

"I'm damn certain I don't," he said.

"I didn't, either. I thought…well, I used all of those reasons. Until this morning. I was getting ready and I realized how much I missed you. Not just the pleasure, and you do give me that, but you. You're…grumpy, and you're hard to talk to. But you also tried to make me smile. No one else ever has. I dance for you. For you and no one else, because you make me feel like I want to dance. You've given my life layers, a richness it never had before. And I figured out, as I was going to make vows to you, what that richness is."

"What is it?" he asked, his throat tight, his body tense.

"I love you," she said. "I do. I am…in love with you."

"Samarah, no."

"Yes. I am. And you can't tell me no because it doesn't make it less true."

"You don't know what you're saying," he said.

"I do. I married you today because you're the man I want to be with. Because if you opened the palace doors and told me I could go anywhere, I would stay with you."

"And I married you not knowing you were going to say such a ridiculous thing. Did you not hear what I told you? I could end you, Samarah. What if I did? What if I lose control…"

"My father is responsible for it. I'm not listening to this nonsense."

"You're wrong, Samarah."

"Why are you so desperate to believe this?"

"Because it is truth," he said. "And I will never…I will never take the chance on failing like that again."

"Well, what does that have to do with me loving you?"

"I don't want your love. I can't have it—do you understand?"

"Too late."

"This was a mistake," he said.

"And it is also too late for you to have those concerns. We are married. And you know there is every possibility I could have a child. We've never taken precautions in all of our time together."

"I'm not divorcing you. Don't be so dramatic."

"You're rejecting my love and I haven't threatened to kill you. Considering our past history I'm not being over-dramatic. I'm not even being…dramatic."

He gritted his teeth, pain burning in his chest, a low, painful smolder. "I don't want your love. I don't love you, Samarah, and I won't."

"What?"

"I'm not loving anyone. Never again."

"But everything that we've… You wanted to see me smile."

"That's not love, *habibti*. That's a guilty conscience. I don't have love, but I do have guilt in spades."

"What about our children?"

Pain lanced at him, the smoldering ember catching fire and bursting into flame in his chest. "I don't have it in me.

What could I offer them? A father whose hands have stolen a life? A father who loses all humanity with his rage."

"Coward," she said. "You're right. You are weak, but
not for the reasons you mean. You're just hiding. You're
still just hiding."

"I stopped hiding. I took revenge, remember?"

She shook her head. "No. Part of you stayed back there.
Hidden. You've been out here fighting ever since, but you
left your soul behind."

"For good reason. It's too late for me. I'm sorry you
want more than I can give." He stepped forward, cupping
her cheek. He swept his thumb over her silken skin, pain
shooting through him. He had a feeling this would be the
last time he touched her for a very long time. "This is never
going to be a real marriage."

Samarah stumbled back. "Say it again," she said.

"I don't love you."

A sob worked through her body, her hands shaking.
"No. Of course not. No one ever has… Why should you
be the first?"

"Samarah…you do not love me. You're a prisoner.
You've had no one in your life, so you think you love me,
but you've been fooled. I did put you in jail today. A life
sentence. And because of the nature of things, going back
now would be foolish."

"Do not tell me what I feel!"

"You need to be told. If you think you can love a man
like me? If you think this is what love is, offering you a
life of captivity behind bars or captivity in my bed, then
you need to be told!"

"That isn't what you've done. You're just afraid. You're
afraid of—"

"I do not fear you. I would have to care first."

She reeled back, her hands shaking. "I'm going to go,"
she said.

"We have a feast to get to."

"I don't care. I'm going to…I need to go."

She needed some space. She needed to catch her breath. She'd been right the other day. She and Ferran could never have normal. They could never have happy.

The blinding flash of joy she'd felt today when she'd realized she loved him was gone now. In that moment she'd believed that loving him would be enough. That if she loved him, regardless of what he thought about himself, it could work.

But she'd been naive. She'd never loved anyone before, and she'd felt so powerful in the moment that she'd been convinced it could conquer everything. But it hadn't. It wouldn't.

Looking back into Ferran's blank, flat black eyes she knew it.

He had chosen to hold on to the past. He had chosen to stay behind his walls. And as long as that was what he wanted, there would be no reaching him.

"I can't go to the wedding feast alone," he said, his voice raw.

"And I can't sit next to a man who's just rejected my love. I won't. Don't worry—I'm not going to kill you," she said, turning away from him and heading to the door. "I'll just leave you to wallow in your misery. And I do believe that eventually you'll feel misery, even if it's not now. We could have had something. We could have had a life. As it is, I'm going to try and have one. I'm not sure what you're going to do."

She turned away from him, not wanting him to see her break. Loving always involved loss, and right now was no exception.

She'd just spoken vows to stay with Ferran forever, and in almost the same moment, she'd lost any hope she had of forging a real bond with him.

She was a married woman now, in a palace. With servants and beautiful gowns and a man who would share her bed. And she felt more alone than she ever had in her life.

Ferran hadn't realized she'd meant she was leaving. Samarah wasn't anywhere in the palace. She wasn't in his chamber, she wasn't in hers.

Panic raged through him. Had she gone? She was his wife. She had nowhere else to go. He tore at the collar on his tunic, hardly able to breathe.

He'd gone to the feast and made excuses for her being sick, and when everyone had gone, he'd discovered this.

If she had gone, he should be pleased. He should not hold her to him. To a man who might destroy her. Not knowing she was here because of coercion, whatever she said now.

And yet the thought of losing her...

"Lydia!" He entered the servants' quarters, shouting.

Lydia appeared from the dining area, her eyes wide. "Yes, Your Highness?"

"Where is my wife?"

"You do not know?"

"I don't know or I would not have asked, obviously. Do not insult me," he growled. He was being cruel, and he knew it. But he was desperate. Panicked. For a woman he did not love.

Because of course he didn't love her. He couldn't love her.

He didn't deserve her.

It was his life. No matter what he thought, no matter how controlled he was, he hurt the people in it. He saw that now. With blinding clarity.

With all his prized control, he had held a woman captive. He had forced her into marriage.

"Where is my wife?" he repeated.

"She went to your oasis. I helped her pack. She said she

needed some time away." Lydia's eyes were serious and slightly judging.

He gritted his teeth. Damn that woman. "Thank you," he bit out, turning and walking away.

He paused in the doorway, his hand on his chest. He thought he might be dying. Or maybe that was just what it felt like when your heart tried to beat against a brick wall.

He wasn't sure what scared him more. That the wall would hold...or that it might finally break for good.

After two days away, Samarah's head didn't feel any clearer. She was just wandering through the tent, such as it was, thinking about Ferran. All he'd been through. The way her father had twisted his caring. The way he'd been made to feel responsible for an insane man's secrets.

She paused at the doorway of the bedroom, her fingers tracing the woodgrain on the door as she stared out the window at the water beyond.

Had she ever offered to make Ferran smile?

She didn't think she had. He'd given her so much, and in the end, he'd been too afraid to give it all, but she could understand why. She turned into the doorway and rested her face in her hand, stifling the sob that rose in her throat.

She hadn't cried in so long before Ferran. But he made her want more. The wanting was complicated. It wasn't all blind determination and a will to live. It was a deep, emotional need that she was sure at this point was overrated.

She wanted him so much.

She wanted him to love her.

She wanted to make him smile.

Samarah lifted her head. She shouldn't be here, hiding from him. Seeking refuge from reality. From him.

And she'd accused him of being a coward.

She'd held on to her anger toward him for years. With no contribution from him. With no action from him. No confirmation that he even deserved it, and yet she'd been willing to commit the ultimate sin for that anger.

Shouldn't she love him just as much? Shouldn't she love him no matter what he gave back? No matter if he loved her? Wasn't that real love?

Pain lanced her chest. Yes, she wanted him to love her back. But if she truly loved him—and she did—it didn't matter what he said. She was no prisoner. He was behaving as though she was weak, and she was not weak.

She had to tell him that.

She had to go back.

She pushed away from the door and turned around, immediately falling into a fighting stance when she saw the man in white standing there.

She relaxed when she was able to focus on his face. "Ferran?"

He took a step closer to her, the look on his face unsettled. "I came for you," he said, his voice unsteady.

"I'm sorry. I was about to come home."

"No. Do not apologize. I had to release the past's hold on me before I could come to you. I think...I think that this was the best place for me to do this."

"To do what?" she asked.

"I am afraid," he said. "I told myself it was because I had held you captive. Because I am a monster and if I do not keep control I could easily make the same mistakes I had made before."

"I don't believe it."

"I know," he said. "And...I do not deserve your confidence."

"You do."

"You can leave," he said. "I will release you from this marriage. From me. I will give you whatever you need to start a new life. All of your decisions are your own. You have options. Live life. Live it apart from me."

She stepped nearer to him, her heart pounding hard. "Don't you understand? You're the life I've chosen. You're the one I've chosen."

"I can't believe that," he said, his dark eyes haunted. "At my core, I am a murderer."

"No," she said, putting her hand on his face. "You're a survivor. I recognize it. Because it is what I am, too. We have survived the unimaginable. And you know what? It would have broken other people. We aren't broken."

"I am," he said.

"Only because you're too afraid to put yourself back together."

"I am," he said. "Because there is every chance it would reveal a monster."

"There are no monsters here," she said, looking around the room. "Not anymore. And we don't have to let them rule our life anymore. I am not my father. I am not my mother. I am Sheikha Samarah Bashar. My allegiance is to you."

"I don't feel I can accept your allegiance," he said.

"Do not insult me by rejecting it. Not when you already insulted me by rejecting my love."

"I don't seek to insult you. It is…this is the only way I know to love you," he said. "And I find that I do. But I want to be sure that you want to be with me. That you have chosen it. Not because you are a captive. I want… If you choose to stay, I want to be able to trust I can give you passion. That I can give you everything. And you will want it. Not just feel trapped into it."

"Oh, Ferran." She wrapped her arms around his neck and pulled him close, kissing him, deep and long. "I love you, too."

"I do not deserve it," he said, his voice rough.

"I tried to kill you. I don't exactly deserve your love, either."

"Samarah…I don't trust myself."

She stepped back, then reached down and took his hand in hers, lifting it to her throat. "I do," she said. "I have witnessed your character. The way you treated your would-be assassin. I have heard the story of how you avenged your mother. How much you must have loved her to be so enraged. You are a man of great and beautiful passion."

"I have never seen passion as beautiful."

"Neither did I. Before you." She pressed his hand more firmly against her neck. "Would you ever harm me?"

"Never," he said, his voice rough, his touch gentle. "Our children…"

"I know you wouldn't. And you will never harm our children. I know your hands have had blood on them. Blood from the avenging of those you love. Ferran, you would never harm your family. But you would kill for them if it ever came down to it. You would die for them. And there is no shame in that."

"I…I never saw it that way."

"I see it. Because I see you. You are a warrior. As am I. Together we can face whatever terrible things come."

"I've always been afraid that *I* was a terrible thing."

"There was a time when I thought you were, and I very nearly became terrible, too. But you saved me."

"We saved each other."

"There will always be ugliness in the world, Ferran, but loving you is the most beautiful thing that's ever happened in my life. We have something beautiful for the first time." A tear rolled down her cheek and splashed onto his hand. "Don't fear your passion. I want it. I crave it."

"You make me treasure it," he said. "Something I never imagined possible. You told me once that you found a passion for breathing when breathing was all you had. That your desire for revenge was a passion that kept you going. That's what it felt like when you left. I breathed for you. For the one thing that mattered. And then I knew. That this was love. That it was worth anything to claim. That you were worth anything. That I would have to give you the choice to leave even though I wanted you to stay. That I would have to expose myself even though I feared what was inside me. Every wall inside me is broken down, for you. I would rather stand here with you, exposed and vulnerable, than spend the rest of my life protected without you."

"Oh, Ferran…I'm so glad I chose you instead of prison."

He laughed and her heart lifted. "I'm glad, too. It's nice to be preferable to a dungeon."

"You smiled," she said.

"So did you," he said.

"You give me so many reasons to smile."

"And I promise to continue to, every day."

EPILOGUE

THERE WAS SOMETHING incredible about the fact that he and Samarah had created a life together. After so much loss, so much pain, they had brought something new into the world.

Ferran looked down at his son, cradled in his mother's arms, and he felt his heart expand. He reached down, running his fingers along Samarah's flushed cheek. "I will never take for granted that I have you here," he said. "Because I remember a moment when I thought I was touching you for the last time."

She looked up at him and smiled. "You have a lot of years of touching ahead of you," she said.

"And thank God for it. I would like to hold my son," he said, his throat tightening as he looked at the baby in her arms.

"Of course."

He bent down and took the swaddled bundle from her. He was so tiny, so fragile. And she was trusting him with him. Just as she trusted herself to him, and had done for the past year. "He is perfect," Ferran said.

"I know," she said, smiling.

"Who would have thought your revenge would end this way?" he asked. "The creation of a life, instead of the end of one."

"Two lives," she said, smiling. "I feel like my life became so much more that day. It became life instead of survival."

"Three then," he said, running his finger over his son's cheek. "Because I was frozen in time until you came back to me. And now…now my life has truly begun."

* * * * *